D1452918

Down
AND
DIRTY

RHYANNON BYRD

MARDI BALLOU

VONNA HARPER

ELLORA'S CAVE
ROMANTICA PUBLISHING

What the critics are saying...

80

"This is an anthology that the reader will not be able to put down till the last page is read." ~ *Love Romances*

"...stories that will keep you reading until all hours of the night. The suspense builds in each of the stories so the book is impossible to put down. You have to keep reading to see what happens. The sex is hot and you may need ice water to cool off after reading this book." ~ *Coffee Time Romances*

"Each story in Down and Dirty is steamy and hot to trot. The book is a great read, although the stories are erotic the language isn't too graphic, it's just right. ... The book doesn't disappoint! I recommend that readers pick it up today!" ~ *Euro Reviews*

"Down and Dirty is truly a sparkling anthology of wit, love, thrills, and sensuality. These three authors have done a wonderful job with their stories and you won't be disappointed if you give this anthology a shot" ~ *The Romance Studio*

An Ellora's Cave Romantica Publication

www.ellorascave.com

Down and Dirty

Content Advisory:

S – ENSUOUS
E – ROTIC
X – TREME

Ellora's Cave Publishing offers three levels of Romantica™ reading entertainment: S (S-ensuous), E (E-rotic), and X (X-treme).

The following material contains graphic sexual content meant for mature readers. This story has been rated E–rotic.

S-*ensuous* love scenes are explicit and leave nothing to the imagination.

E-*rotic* love scenes are explicit, leave nothing to the imagination, and are high in volume per the overall word count. E-rated titles might contain material that some readers find objectionable—in other words, almost anything goes, sexually. E-rated titles are the most graphic titles we carry in terms of both sexual language and descriptiveness in these works of literature.

X-*treme* titles differ from E-rated titles only in plot premise and storyline execution. Stories designated with the letter X tend to contain difficult or controversial subject matter not for the faint of heart.

DOWN AND DIRTY

ഔ

SECOND TO NONE
Rhyannon Byrd

~11~

LOVE FOR HIRE
Mardi Ballou

~115~

TRACKED DOWN
Vonna Harper

~215~

SECOND TO NONE

by Rhyannon Byrd

છ

Trademarks Acknowledgement

Chapter One

❧

In a flash of feminine scent, skin and long, scarlet hair, Remy Frost crashed through the open doors of Finnegan's Pub...and straight into the strong, hard, possessive arms of Jason Hawkes.

"Oomph!" she grunted, silently cursing the uncompromising breadth of his mouthwatering bod.

Lord, it was like running headfirst into a brick wall. Everything about the man was impossibly hard. Her lungs and sides ached from her panicked run through the shadow-filled night and now she felt dazed from the force of impact into what had felt like a solid barrier of pure, ripped muscle. Not to mention the way her spine cracked when the backpack she had slung over one shoulder slammed into her side with a dull thud. Her pulse skyrocketed with what she strongly suspected was a heavy dose of arousal on top of the heady rush of adrenaline she had going—and Remy didn't even want to think about what was suddenly happening between her legs.

Damn traitorous body always reacted like this to the gorgeous goliath holding her shuddering form against his strong, beautiful length of corded sinew, long bones and starkly defined muscles. She knew he didn't work out with weights, but a man like Jason Hawkes didn't need to. The grueling years he'd spent in the military had kept him in prime physical condition. Now his work as a PI ensured that his sexy-as-sin physique didn't go to flab. Her throat went dry and she swallowed an embarrassing moan of bliss-filled pleasure. It seemed as if she'd been snuggled there for hours, dragging in gulping lungfuls of his warm, testosterone-based scent, instead of the measly second it had actually been.

11

"Damn, Remy. Slow down, honey, and just take a deep breath," the sexy brute murmured above her head as her lungs continued to work hard and fast, his deliciously solid, intensely ripped arms pulling her tighter into his shirt-covered chest. Then, with one big fist planted beneath her chin, he tilted her face up to his and, as always, the dreamy, molten whiskey-brown of his eyes seemed to drill straight through her, right down to her core, creating a flood of lust and need and hunger that she couldn't ignore. Her sex swelled, readying itself to be fucked as hard and rough as she could possibly take it, just like it did every time she so much as thought about this man. She watched with heavy-lidded, worried eyes as his nostrils flared, the heat burning hot and strong in that golden gaze, wondering for the thousandth time if his senses were as acute as her brother had always claimed.

Could Connor's best friend smell the way she went slick with desire every time he was near? Did he know an empty hollow ached in her womb, desperate to be filled by no one but him?

As if he had all the time in the world, he sent a cocky look over her head toward Connor, his deep voice rumbling up from his chest in a slow, lazy drawl that vibrated against her breasts, making her damn nipples go spike-hard from the sexy sensation. "When I demanded my prize from that last game of pool, buddy, I never expected you to pay up so soon." He looked back down, instantly snagging her gaze, and Remy could only blink at the warm, smoldering heat of physical interest flaming there, stoking a fire of her own deep within. "And I sure as hell wasn't expecting anything this *sweet*. Not often that little Remy blesses us with her presence anymore, now is it? And damn but if she doesn't get more gorgeous every time I set eyes on her."

Oh hell, she thought with a frown that had him chuckling knowingly beneath his breath. He may have been talking to her brother, but she knew the words were meant for her. He was on to her. On to the fact that she'd been avoiding him ever since he and Connor had left the Special Forces and come back home for good, ready to settle themselves back into the real world by going into business together and starting up their own investigations company.

"Stop trying to get a rise out of me, you ass," Connor rumbled as he moved off to the side of the front door. Jason nudged her forward, so that they too moved out of the path of any incoming customers, but he didn't release his hold on her. She worried her bottom lip with her front teeth, wondering just what the sexy stud was up to, but figured she had to deal with the dragon breathing at her back first. Turning her head, she watched her older brother cross his arms over his brawny chest as he pinned her with his "you're gonna explain yourself right now, young lady" look. Gaack, she hated that one…and he was a master at it.

Connor Frost—the most overprotective sibling in the world. Not to mention one of the baddest badasses around and mean-looking as hell. And his best friend, going back to the beginning of their days in the service together, was no different. Well, no different except to Remy.

Connor was the brother whom she loved like no other—the only family she had left that she could depend on…the only one left who cared. And Jason Hawkes? Well, Jason had become the bane of her existence for the last eight years of her life. God, had it been that long? Nearly a decade that she'd wasted lusting after her bro's best friend, dreaming about him nearly every night?

Man, girl, you are such an idiot. As if you could allow yourself to become just another notch on the stud's belt.

Jason Hawkes could have any woman he wanted, probably with as little effort as crooking his finger at her, and Remy knew that getting involved with him would rank right up there at the top of idiotic things she could do with her life. He'd probably breeze through a relationship with her, treating her like something fragile that needed protecting, then, when he realized how bored he was with her, end up hitting the road so fast there'd be a dust cloud left in his wake. He'd hightail it away without ever looking back, leaving her broken and wrecked, and Remy refused to let that happen.

But that didn't mean she had any control over her pathetically hungry body.

She searched for a valiant means of ignoring him, of turning a blind eye to the head-spinning effect he'd always had on her, but damn if it was possible. No matter how fiercely her sensible, logical intellect screamed *Caution*, her underfed, seriously pissed-off libido chanted the same age old refrain of *Mmm...baby*. Sad, yes...but what could she do about it? She'd spent years trying to purge him from her system and not a single goddamn thing had worked. It didn't matter how sexy or funny or attentive a man was, because in her heart, they just couldn't compare. Jason Hawkes was, quite simply, second to none. There just wasn't anyone else like him.

With one smooth movement, he took her backpack from her shoulder and slipped it over his own, then tightened his arms around her, pulling her even closer into the heat of his powerful body, making the growing bulge of his immense erection an impossible fact to miss—despite the warning growl coming from the giant standing at her back.

"Do you have to hold her so goddamn close, you perv?" Connor muttered, then turned the full blast of his ice-blue stare straight back onto her as she sent him another impatient look over her shoulder. "And aren't you supposed to be out on some date with the coffeehouse runt, Remy?"

With her Irish temper burning fiercely, she looked up at her brother, a fine tremble of angry irritation shimmying through her limbs that she knew Jason couldn't miss. Not with him pressed so snugly against her. Her hands, which had somehow found their way to his bulging biceps, tightened into fists. "Not that it's any of your business, considering I'm nearly twenty-seven and no longer in need of your brotherly supervision, but I'm not dating Roger."

A scowl pulled the otherwise handsome features of his face into a fierce expression that would have quelled most people. "I thought his name was Carson. Who the hell is Roger?"

Remy rolled her eyes and groaned at his tone. "Roger is my *friend* from Delia's Coffee House and Carson is my *neighbor*. And no, I'm not dating him either. I'm helping Carson with his thesis. And they are hardly runts, Connor. But please enlighten me," she drawled with a sweet, saccharine smile that she knew would annoy him. "Just who are you late for tonight? Is it Miss Double Ds this time or Miss Daddy Long Legs?"

Jason snickered under his breath, causing his chest to rasp against hers again, but he still wasn't letting her go. In fact, Remy didn't think it felt like he was planning on letting her go anytime soon, considering he'd clasped his hands at the small of her back, holding their lower bodies pressed together, while a subtle rocking of his hips nudged his monstrous hard-on into her stomach in a seductive pattern that was quickly tripping up her heart rate.

Connor grunted his frustration at what he always considered her "attitude", narrowing his cool stare on her the same way she imagined he did when eyeing down a potential criminal. She tried to stay just as cool and keep her cards close to her chest, surprisingly pleased that she must have succeeded when he jerked his chin at her and muttered, "Well, downtown is no place for a girl to be out by herself, even if it is the restoration area. I expect you to have more sense than that. You should have called me if you wanted to come and I'd have picked you up."

"Damn it, Connor, I am not a *girl*," she gritted through her teeth, promising herself that hell would freeze over before she 'fessed up to him about anything. If she wasn't careful, he'd have her under twenty-four-hour surveillance with his little goons on her ass night and day and she refused to be suffocated like that. And more importantly, she refused to be controlled. It might be naïve, but she liked to think that she was handling this irritating little situation pretty damn well on her own. Well, up until tonight at least. Tonight she'd ridiculously panicked and now she was paying for it big time.

"Really? Not a girl?" Jason teased as she looked back to him, his eyes wide with mock surprise, while a boyish grin played at the corners of his sexy mouth. "If that's true, then you're the prettiest damn guy I've ever set eyes on, Frosty."

A snarl of frustration started to rumble in her throat at the irritating nickname and the embarrassing memory it brought to mind of the only other night she'd ever been in his arms. But her breath stumbled in her lungs at the feel of him suddenly stroking one wide palm up the sensitive line of her spine, then slowly exploring the contours of her back on its way down again. The action should have been soothing, an offer of comfort, but Remy knew better. She wasn't sure if he was holding onto her to get a reaction out of her, or if he was trying to hide the fact that he had an outrageous erection from her brother, but it hardly mattered. The effect was still devastating. Every second spent in his arms only led her that little bit closer to a place she knew she couldn't go. Not with him. Not today. Not tomorrow. Not ever.

Lord, this entire night was turning out to be one never-ending nightmare. Granted, there were worse forms of torture, she supposed, than being held in the arms of the sexiest damn man she'd ever known. If her brother wasn't giving her his *I'm trying to read your mind* stare, drilling it into the back of her skull, she might have even allowed herself a breathless moment of enjoyment.

Just a moment. Anything more would mean the kind of personal trouble she was dead set on avoiding.

With a casual arrogance that made her want to stomp her foot, preferably on top of his big boot-covered toes—as if he wasn't turning her entire world upside down with the press of his big, hard, beautiful body and stroking palm—she watched as Jason turned his attention back to her brother. "Look, you go on and grab your date, man," he rumbled in that sexy rasp of a voice that sounded like he was drawling words into a woman's ear while he fucked her into a sexual oblivion that would ruin her for other men. Remy wondered just how many women he'd "ruined" in just that way and distinctly disliked the thought. "I'll take it from here."

She took a deep breath as she struggled for some sort of calm, but frustration renewed its roiling burn through her blood at his words. *He'd take it from here!* As if she were an "it" — a pet to be taken and controlled at his will. As if it wasn't her decision to make. And her brother was no better. As if she wasn't even there, Connor ignored her threatening growl as she turned her head to glare at him, his cold eyes intently studying the man who held her. Jason just stared right back, a silent communication taking place above her head that she found as asinine as it was ridiculous. *How dare they*, she silently fumed, no longer willing to waste her breath on the deaf, blind, arrogant Neanderthals. What freaking century did they think they were living in anyway?

Twisting in Jason's hold with a determined jerk of her hips, she poked her muscle-headed brother in his thick chest with her finger, ready to stomp on his damn foot too if he didn't look down at her, which he thankfully did.

"This overgrown ape won't be taking anything from here. You got it? I'm tired of wasting my breath explaining the facts of life to you, Con, but I can damn well take care of myself. That means I don't need rides to Finnegan's just because the sun has gone down. It means I'm capable of making my own decisions about where I go and who I see. And it sure as hell means I don't need a chaperone to see that I get home okay."

Jason's palms flattened against her stomach, pulling her back into his body, and his thick cock was suddenly nestling itself against her lower back, making itself at home. Her breath sucked in on a sharp wave of arousal and her eyes nearly crossed at the delicious sensation. Oh hell, how was she supposed to be strong when he was tempting her with something so outrageously seductive? The one blasted "thing" she wanted most in the world, other than a fairy-tale romance with the man, which she knew was never going to happen. The sheer audacity of his actions had her grinding her jaw, ready to bite, and her dumbass brother wasn't helping.

"Jason's just gonna make sure you get home safe for me, Remy," Connor explained in that grating tone that always seemed to be saying *the world would be so much easier for you if you'd just listen to me*. It never failed to set her on edge and the fact that he was leaving her to be "handled" by Jason was just the icing on the cake. "I don't know what you were thinking, coming out to this part of town by yourself."

"Oh, trust me, Connor. You really don't want to know what I'm thinking right now. And no, Jason's not going to make sure I get anywhere," she grunted, her small hands trying to pry the big, unmoving fingers from her stomach. "I hate to break it to you, Con, but I'm done being handled and managed by you. That was the reason I moved and got my own place, remember? My own life." The cold look she sent her brother promised murder if he left her in Jason's "care". How freaking humiliating could it get? And when were these two he-men going to realize that she was a fully grown, fully independent, fully capable woman?

Huh, probably when hell froze over. Maybe not even then.

Connor looked between her and the giant at her back, their expressions equally determined. Then he cast a quick glance down at the thick silver watch on his wrist and cursed beneath his breath. Running one big hand through his short, black scrub of hair, he sent her a hard, *you-better-mind-yourself* kind of stare, before giving his attention back to Jason. "Do me a favor and don't let her out of your sight until you've gotten her home and worked your way to the bottom of this."

Oh hell. He did not just say that. This? Now she was a freaking this?

She went numb with outrage, her entire body stiffening in indignation, but Jason only held her tighter. "Don't worry, Connor," he drawled, his voice as lazy as ever, as if he didn't have a care in the world, while one big palm stroked dangerously low on her tummy, his pinky finger nearly grazing the button fly on her Levi's. "I've got it under control."

Oh, like hell he does.

Remy turned to look over her shoulder at him, watching the slow smile spread over his rugged face like a smooth sin, all sexy arrogance and carnal intent, and wondered if her brother had lost his mind by leaving her with this man. Couldn't Connor see that something volatile and dangerous was brewing between them? Something threatening to rage beyond her control. And she'd worked too damn hard to gain control of her life. With a slow, deep breath, Remy glared harder, determined not to let her feelings, where he was concerned, show.

Rule number one in their legendary rules of combat—never let the enemy see your weakness.

And in this case, Jason Hawkes was both.

* * * * *

Jason watched as Remy looked back over her graceful shoulder, meeting his gaze, her clear green eyes big and wide, while one slim auburn brow arched in irritation. He bided his time, wanting this woman to himself more than he wanted his next breath. She'd been avoiding him ever since he'd come back home, for good this time, and he was tired as hell of it. Shit, it was driving him outta his fucking mind. And now that he had her in his arms, that lush little body pressed so close he could feel the rapid expansion of her lungs as she breathed, he sure as fuck wasn't letting her go.

Looking over her shoulder, he noticed the way the top button on her white cotton shirt had finally given way beneath the laboring of her panting breath, allowing the fabric to part.

From his vantage point, it revealed an eye-boggling amount of delectable cleavage that he just wanted to dive into, pressing his face and lips to all that tender, succulent flesh, sucking and licking and nipping with his teeth until he made her come from nothing but the play of his mouth at her gorgeous tits. For such a petite thing, she had an abundance of curves in all the right places, creating a sensual package that was hard as hell on a guy. The ache in his cock kicked up another notch, pressing into his zipper until he wondered if the teeth would hold.

Fuck. What was his problem? It wasn't like he wasn't capable of thinking with anything but his damn dick. If that were the case, his ass would have been dead years ago. But Remy Frost just fried his brain.

Her brother wanted him getting to the bottom of this — and there wasn't anything on earth he'd rather be doing than getting to the bottom of this fiery-haired woman. Just digging down deep, sinking into her sweet-as-sin body and staying there forever. And now he had her in his arms, right where he wanted her, and he sure as hell wasn't letting her get away. But it wasn't until Connor said "Later" and turned to leave that Jason let his slow smile of anticipation show. His arms loosened as Connor walked out the front entrance of Finnegan's, just enough to allow Remy to twist back around and glare up at him. But one look at his pained expression and her brow furrowed, some of the angry heat dimming for an instant in her big green eyes. "Are you okay?"

Jason tried to clear the lump of lust in his throat, brought on by the sight of one full, round lace-covered breast exposed when she'd turned, the top of her shirt suddenly gaping, and croaked, "Yeah, why?"

Her slim shoulders lifted in a graceful shrug. "You just look kinda…warm. You don't have a fever, do you?" Her hand lifted, as if she'd test his forehead, then dropped back down before actually touching him, as if she'd checked the impulsive action, judging it unwise.

No, but I'm burning up. Hot and hard and horny as hell, dying to sink inside of you every fucking way there is, any way you'll let me.

He just kept staring and Remy just kept fidgeting in his arms. Then she laughed, shaking her head at some inside joke she apparently wasn't going to share, and the husky sound made his dick rise up another notch. Jesus, he'd never in his life gotten as hard as he did whenever Remy Frost was around. And he'd waited too many miserable years to make her his.

God only knew he couldn't wait anymore.

They needed some privacy and quickly…which meant he was going to have to get her buttoned back up before they found it. No way in hell was he marching her lush ass through Mike's place, letting every jackass there get an eyeful of her gorgeous, lace-covered breasts. His hands lifted, reaching for the now-gaping top of her shirt, and she gasped, lurching away from him.

"What the hell are you doing?"

He jerked his chin at her revealing shirtfront. "Your button came undone, baby. Thought I'd put you back together before every guy in here gets an eyeful."

She looked down and muttered under her breath, cutting him another glaring look from beneath the delicate arches of her russet-colored brows while quickly refastening her shirt. "Gee, thanks for telling me," she sneered.

"Hey, sweetheart, I was the one trying to button you back up, remember?"

"Yeah," she muttered with a soft, feminine snort that made him laugh, "but not before you had an eyeful yourself."

"Well damn, Remy," he drawled, winking at her, "I'm not stupid."

Her cutting look said he shouldn't hold out for her agreement on that one and he couldn't help but laugh at her fire. God, he liked her. Everything about her, from her fiery

21

personality to her gutsy temper and those sultry, sexy-as-all-get-out looks, just called to him. He'd spent years trying to ignore the way he felt about her, knowing the timing was all wrong, but things were different now. He was back home, settling himself back into a world that didn't consist of enemies who wanted to cut his throat or stab him in the back, and she wasn't a freckle-faced little starry-eyed eighteen-year-old anymore. Finally, the goddamn timing was right and he wasn't letting her run from him a second more.

"Come on," Jason drawled, casting a quick look around the noisy pub—a look that Remy knew had taken in everything. He and Connor were just alike. Too much training, she assumed, to the point that she wondered if they even had the ability to kick back and relax. Heck, they probably had sex with one eye on the door and the other on their bed partner, wondering if they could trust the woman beneath them. It was sad, but then Remy knew they had chosen their paths and wouldn't have wanted to live any other way. Pulling her behind him, he set off toward the back of the pub, saying, "We can't talk in here."

It was on the tip of her tongue to inform him they weren't talking *anywhere*, because there was nothing to say, but she got distracted. They hadn't taken two steps before a woman walked by, her almond-shaped, kohl-colored eyes all but devouring Jason from the toes of his scuffed boots up to his tousled head of honey-blond hair. He sent the woman a sexy little half smile, the kind Remy had seen the Irish actor Sean Bean use in one of his movies, and despite her anger, it was devastating on her senses. Judging from the drowsy, bedroom look in the other woman's eyes as she strolled past, it was pretty damn effective on her too. Yeah, he definitely had that bad boy Sean thing going on, though Jason was a bit more muscular because of all of his physical training.

And she didn't like to think of the churning, kinda achy feeling in her stomach that had come to life when he'd smiled at the gorgeous brunette. It had Remy grating her back teeth and seriously struggling with the urge to kick him in the back of his leg. In a fit of temper, she tried to pry her fingers out of his grip, but his hold wouldn't budge.

"Where the hell are you taking me?" she huffed, knowing she sounded like a spoiled child who hadn't gotten her way, but was too irritated to care.

The look he sent her over his broad shoulder was filled with arrogant humor and intent, the smile curling across that sexy-as-sin mouth reminding her of the wolf with Little Red. Too damn bad the idea of being eaten by Jason Hawkes was one of her favorite bedtime fantasies.

Her breath caught at the wicked thought and she knew he sensed it. *Shit.*

"You're not afraid of me, Remy," he rumbled, "so why are you worried about where I'm taking you?"

"I'm not worried," she muttered as he pulled her toward a door that led into a short hallway beside the long wooden bar packed with an eclectic assortment of customers, from suits to cops to good ol' everyday Joes. Michael Finnegan was busy behind the gleaming countertop, filling orders for a group of female thirty-somethings who looked like they were right at home, flirting outrageously with the Irish hunk as they sipped their wine spritzers and batted their lashes at him. Always the consummate flirt, he had them all in his thrall. Remy couldn't help the smile that curled her lips at Mike's ability to twist females around his little finger. Then Jason tightened his hold on her hand, demanding her attention, and she glared at the broad, long line of his back, still wondering where in the hell he was taking her...and just what he planned on doing to her once he got her there.

As if he could read her thoughts, Jason laughed and murmured, "Stop glaring holes through my back, Frosty. You know you can trust me, honey."

They entered the first door on the left and Jason pushed her gently into the room, then flipped the light switch as he closed the door behind his back. "See," he laughed, watching her as she tried to surreptitiously move away from him. "It's just Mike's office. No hidden dungeons with chains hanging from the ceiling and whips on the walls."

She twisted her hands in front of her, but snickered softly under her breath at his teasing and held her shoulders back, her head high. With a funny little spike in his pulse, his heart turned over at her actions, the same way it always did with this woman. She was such a little fireball. It'd come as a shocking surprise the day he'd realized he admired her as much as he wanted her. After the things he'd seen in this world, there weren't many people who earned his admiration, but Remy Frost was one of them. Her fiery spirit and pride and loyalty were rare treasures in Jason's world and he absolutely adored the way she tried to appear so tough. Like now, moving away from him because she was scared shitless of their attraction, he knew, but unwilling to make it obvious. No, her pride demanded that she give as good as she got and he couldn't wait to see if she could hold her own against him when he finally got her sweet little ass beneath him. Hell, who was he kidding? He'd probably be the one struggling to keep up with her!

He wanted to get there *now*, just pull her into his arms and find out if she tasted as amazing as he remembered from that long-ago experience that had been far too brief—but first things first.

"Out with it, Remy."

"Out with what?" She smiled, arching her brow at him, knowing it would irritate the hell out of him.

"Connor's got a lot on his mind and he's not thinking too straight right now." *And he's sure as hell not thinking about you the way I am — twenty-four fucking hours a day.* "It's not our usual night at Finnegan's and you weren't thinking you were gonna catch us for a chat or some games of pool. So what the hell were you doing running in here like you had the devil on your ass, sweetheart?"

Remy shrugged her shoulders. "My car broke down a block up the street, over at the corner of Fletcher and Park, and the streetlights were out. It's still not the best part of town over there and I just got spooked."

"Jesus," he swore with a dark scowl. "So you go running off down a city street by yourself? Why the hell didn't you use your cell to call one of us?"

She sent him an impatient look. "The stupid battery wasn't charged. You know how Connor is always griping at me about that."

Remy watched him give a slow nod, a silky, honey-colored lock of hair falling over his brow that made her fingers itch to reach out and stroke it back into place. The tiffany-style lamp sitting on the corner of Michael's desk cast the room in a warm, sensual glow, painting the golden sheen of Jason's hair with warm streaks of vibrant color that made her want to sift her fingers through the thick, warm mass, just to watch how those mesmerizing colors would play through the shaggy, unkempt length. The guy needed to get to a barber, big time, but she couldn't deny that she loved this new rough-and-tumble look he'd been sporting since leaving the service, like he'd just rolled out of bed…after spending the night riding her through the mattress.

Damn…she had to stop thinking like that. *Now.*

He jerked his golden-stubbled chin at her left hand, where the crumpled piece of paper she'd ripped off her windshield still remained clutched in her damp fingertips. Hell, how had she forgotten about it?

"And what's that, honey?" he asked in his silky rasp, the same one that never failed to make her melt, as if warm honey had been poured onto her body, all rich and sticky sweet.

"What's what?" she asked, her voice breathless, trying to slyly slip the paper into her front pocket as she shoved her hands into her jeans. Why hadn't she gotten rid of the damn thing when she'd had the chance?

He took three steps toward her, narrowing the distance between them until she felt cornered, knowing there was no way to reach the door without him catching her first. It should have pissed her off, but she wanted to howl with frustration when the idea of being caught by him only made her hot. Hotter than she already was, as if she was the one with the freaking fever.

And to think people actually thought she was made of ice. Hah! Jason Hawkes was all it'd ever taken to set her on fire.

"You've got two choices, Remy. Either you pull out that little scrap of paper you've been twisting to pieces in your tight little grip and hand it over to me…"

"Or what?"

The corner of his mouth kicked up in a smile that was devastating in its sensuality and purely devilish in its intent. "Or, honey…I'm going in after it."

Chapter Two

ॐ

"Like hell," Remy said in a low, throaty voice. "You are *not* sticking your hands into my pants, Jason Hawkes."

"Don't tempt me, Remy. I've wanted to get my hands in your pants since I first set eyes on you...among other things," he muttered.

"Look, I told you what happened with the car," she huffed. "It's not some great conspiracy, Jason. What more do you want from me?"

"That story still doesn't explain what you were doing driving around down here at night," he pointed out in a reasonable tone, while he tossed her backpack into one of the black leather chairs situated against the wall at his right.

The gentle slopes of her eyebrows raised high on her forehead. "And maybe that's because it's really not any of your business."

Jason crossed his arms and leaned his hip against the edge of Mike's dark oak desk, arching a brow at her sarcastic tone. "Now that attitude's just not nice, Remy. Especially when I'm saving you the irritation of involving your brother in this."

Twin bright spots of color flared on her high cheekbones. "I'm not afraid of Connor, Jason."

"No, but you *are* tired of him cramping your style. Hell, you've been tired of it since you turned eighteen and moved in with him." That had been the year he'd finally met his best friend's little sister. The beginning of it all—eight long years of heaven, hell and every fucking emotion in between. "We can do this any way you like, honey. I'm in no rush to be anywhere."

"Are you blackmailing me?" she gasped, the delicate features of her face shifting between genuine shock, laughter and blatant frustration. "With my own brother?"

"Now would I do that, sweetheart?" He laughed, shrugging the wide line of his shoulders. "I'm just pointing out how much simpler this whole situation will be if we settle it ourselves, without having to draw Connor into the middle of it."

"Unbelievable. How freaking unbelievable," she repeated, shaking her head. "You're as bad as he is."

Jason narrowed his eyes, hating the way she kept trying to lump him into the same brotherly category as Connor, knowing she did so on purpose. But he wasn't going to let her get away with it. "No, angel, I'm worse," he warned in a voice so low that it would have been whisper-soft were it not for the rough edge to his words. "Trust me, Remy. When it comes to you, I'll sink my teeth in and never let you go."

A momentary flash of panic burned through her dark green eyes at such a clear declaration of intention. Then she shook it off and squared her shoulders like a soldier facing the firing squad. "Fine, whatever. If you're going to be a jerk about it, I was on my way home from a new night class I'm taking," she muttered, obviously pissed at having to explain herself to him, but choosing what she considered the lesser of two evils.

"Class?" he murmured, lifting his brow in surprise. "As in school?"

"Yes, class," she hissed, crossing her arms over her chest in a perfect imitation of his own stance. "Something *you* so apparently lack, dragging me in here like a bullheaded brute."

"Sweetheart," he drawled with a slow smile, "if you're trying to insult me, you're going to have to do better than that."

Her gaze narrowed, the thick fringe of her russet-colored lashes throwing shadows over the gentle curve of her cheeks.

"Don't tempt me, Jason," she muttered, throwing his earlier words back in his face.

He cocked his head to the side as he studied her, thinking she was about the sexiest thing he'd ever seen. Everything about her made him hard and aching to fuck. The woman was hot, no two ways about it, with her soft skin and those luscious tits that she always tried to hide. Then there was that long red hair, those damn green eyes and that heart-shaped ass. Silky lips, siren smile, throaty laugh. She'd been driving him outta his goddamn mind for years. "Do I tempt you, beautiful Remy?"

Her tiny pink tongue flicked out to swipe erotically against the lush pad of her lower lip, but she refused to answer him, simply staring him down with those piercing green eyes, giving him the coolest go-to-hell look he'd ever seen. It'd have worried him if he hadn't seen the roiling fire of need burning deeply within that crisp, verdant gaze.

The seconds ticked by, the tension winding tighter and tighter, until Remy finally said, "Is there anything actually *important* you'd like to ask me, or am I free to go, soldier boy?"

"So eager to escape me, honey?" His smile was hard, his deep voice nothing more than a low, gruff drawl.

God but she loved that voice. For as long as Remy could remember, Jason Hawkes had been under her skin, stealing into her dreams, making her life a living hell, no matter how hard she tried to fight the attraction. And the fight was only getting more difficult. Her lust-fed emotions were a vital, brilliant thing gaining possession of her will—like a spreading disease that she couldn't find a cure for. Despite her mental efforts, his words brought back memories of that long-ago night and she tried not to flinch. "I'm sorry to disappoint you, Jason, but I'm not that starry-eyed little teen anymore. And I'm not the girl who everyone thought was made of ice."

"Yeah," he rumbled, the word rolling off his tongue like a sweet temptation that she couldn't wait to taste. "I noticed. And you of all people should know that I never thought there was anything cold about you."

Remy shook her head in denial, wanting to pull the thick mass of her long hair in front of her and use it like a shield, to cover the betraying signs of desire in her body. Her damn nipples were hard and stiff and swollen, pressing against the thin fabric of her shirt, and she couldn't claim that cold was the culprit. Lord, it was ninety degrees in Michael's office. What the hell was the matter with his freaking air-conditioning?

Swallowing the thick, exciting lump of lust in her throat, she said the only thing that she knew with any certainty. "This isn't going to work."

"Why?" One word. Hard. Bitten out from between his tight lips.

Her gaze shifted to a point on the wall behind his right shoulder, refusing to meet his fierce stare. "You're like chocolate."

From the edge of her vision, she watched him shake his head in confusion, shaggy blond hair tumbling over his brow before he pushed it back with a frustrating swipe of one big hand. "Huh?"

"You're like chocolate," she repeated, stealing a quick look at his face and scowling when she caught his smiling expression.

He snorted softly. "Is that supposed to make sense?"

"Look," she sighed, "I don't eat chocolate, but it isn't because I don't want it. Of course I want it. Chocolate's my favorite food in the entire world. I'd eat it morning, noon and night if I could. But I can't, because it's bad for me. It makes me break out in hives, not to mention what it does to the size of my backside. So, I just don't touch the stuff. I may be *tempted* to have it, but after a while, that temptation starts to fade. It's the same with you. My body may be screaming at me that having an…an affair with you would rock my world like a volcanic eruption, but to give into that temptation would be nothing short of stupid. I'd have tasted the chocolate…and then I'd crave it long after all the chocolate was gone and I couldn't have it anymore."

Jason's expression turned to one of hard, cool speculation, while he tried to ignore the link his cock was making between sex and chocolate. Hearing her say she loved to "eat" the stuff had his dick jumping to attention, hoping like hell it fell into the same category. Christ, he didn't think there could be anything sexier in the entire world than seeing Remy Frost sucking his cock, swallowing him into her mouth, those plump lips stretched wide for his thick width while he tunneled his shaft in and out of that tight, pink little hole. His dick jerked in his jeans and he knew the fat head was wet with pre-cum. Trying to get his mind back on track, he asked, "Why wouldn't you be able to have it anymore? You planning on ditching me?"

She looked at him as if he'd grown a second head. "Not me. *You*, Jason."

"Me what, damn it?" he demanded, feeling like he was losing the train of conversation. Shit, maybe too much blood had drained from his brain into his damn pants. It sure as hell felt like it.

"Look, you are *not* a relationship kind of guy…but I am most definitely a relationship kind of gal. We don't make any sense. It's like oil and water. They don't mix. You'd bail the minute you thought you were losing your freedom, after stripping me of mine, and then I'd be left craving you. Better not to even sample the temptation to begin with."

"You think you've just got it all figured out, don't you, Frosty? And if I'm not careful, you'll have me fooled into thinking you really are that little Ice Queen everyone used to whisper about."

Her expression tightened, telling him he'd hurt her with that one, but damn it, he was fighting for his life here. And if he had to get down and dirty to get through to her, then he'd do just that.

"I just have one question. Are you actually buying any of this bullshit, or do you just think if you say it enough times, it'll start to be true?"

Her spine went ramrod straight and the closed expression falling over her face reminded him of the lifeless visage of a doll. He hated it. "I don't have to stand around here and be insulted by you."

"Hell yes, you do. If insulting you is the only way I can get your attention, then I'll shell out as much as it takes. I'd rather be fucking you, proving just how much I want you, but we'll play things your way for starters, Remy. But one thing needs to be out in the open here and now."

"Ooh, I'm just breathless with anticipation," she purred.

"You should be, because you're finished running. I'm done sitting on my ass waiting for you to realize that I'm here and I'm sure as hell not going anywhere."

"I wouldn't want you to go anywhere, Jason. We're friends. Shoot," she drawled with a sly smile, "we're practically *family*."

It was his turn to make that growling noise of frustration in the back of his throat. "Friends, yeah, but I'm not your fucking brother, Remy. And you know it. Cut the bullshit."

"Come on, Jason. You've known me for years. Why the sudden interest?"

"Sudden?" he asked with a knowing smile.

"Yeah," she said in a hard voice, obviously unwilling to go where his look was daring her, back to that night.

"You know as well as I do that there's nothing sudden about it. But you were too young before and after that I wasn't here. Not long enough to give you what you deserved. That's changed. You're a woman and I'm not leaving. After all this time, the *timing's* finally right and I've waited too goddamn long for this shot to let you blow it because of some stupid perception you have that I'm some dickhead Casanova."

"I heard the stories when you guys came home on leave," she argued, "staying up late with your beer and pool games. Spare me the denials."

"One, don't believe everything you hear," he said, pointing his finger at her for emphasis while trying to rein in his temper. Of course, he knew she was pushing his buttons on purpose, choosing to fight with him rather than face up to this thing between them. "And two, if there's something you want to know about my life, just ask. I don't have any secrets from you, Remy. If you want to know about women, then yeah, I've had them. But you'd be surprised how few since meeting you. And as you've gotten older, I've gone longer and longer between…"

He hesitated for a second and she purred, "Fucks?"

His eyes narrowed at the attitude she put behind that word. "Fucking anyone but you no longer holds its appeal. And that's the truth. Take it or leave it, but I've no reason to lie to you, Remy."

"No, you're just a saint, aren't you, Jason?" she drawled with a heavy dose of sarcasm.

"Goddamn it, Remy," he growled, "don't tell me you don't think about it."

She squeezed her eyes shut, then slowly opened them, meeting his stare. "Think about what?"

He barely resisted the urge to laugh at her stubbornness. "What it'd be like if we fucked. What it'd feel like if you let me strip you bare, bury my face in your sweet little cunt and tongue-fuck you 'til neither one of us can remember what year it is? And that's just for starters, sweetheart."

"Jason," she groaned, covering her face with her hands, but not before he saw the warm flush of embarrassment flare beneath her skin and the sparks of hunger fire brightly in her eyes.

"Come on, Remy. Christ, I think about it all the time. Think about *you* all the time."

Jason watched her hands fall away from her face, her gaze lower to stick on the bulge of his cock, and had only one thought. *Hell.* His hands started to shake and he felt a trickle of sweat drip down into his eyes, stinging of salt and lust and desperation.

"You…you're not hard for me," Remy argued, shaking her head in denial until her long red hair was streaming around her shoulders in a wild, fiery mass. She was ready to grasp onto any kind of straw with a desperate intensity that worried her almost as much as her heart-pounding, undeniable feelings for this man. "It was…was probably that brunette back there in the spiked heels."

He was still for the span of ten seconds. Then he moved.

Uh-oh, she thought with a sick feeling burning in her tummy as she watched him stalk away from the desk and slowly advance on her. He didn't stop until he stood directly in front of her, so close that she had to tip back her head to look him in the face. So close that she could see the sexy lines crinkling at the corners of those seductive bedroom eyes, the tips of his lashes and the small, faint scar zigzagging over his left temple.

"Stop reaching for straws, Remy. I'm too old to get a hard-on just because a woman smiles at me and I wouldn't touch Alexis with a ten-foot pole—especially with my dick. She fucking eats men for breakfast. And in case it slipped your notice, I've been rock-hard and aching since you ran into my arms."

The terrifying fact that she wanted to believe him caused the panic in her belly to spiral swiftly out of control. She heard the words spill out of her mouth in a swift, breathless rush. "I want to leave. Now."

"No."

Her eyes widened and her cheeks flushed with so much warmth, she knew she must look burned. "Isn't that my line?" she panted.

He had the audacity to smile at her. "Hey, guys can say no too."

"Yeah, I'm all too familiar with the theory," she sneered, desperately searching for a way to hold on to her anger while physical hunger struggled to take over.

"Damn it, don't you dare even think about holding that over my head right now. You were too young and I was too deep into work to be what you needed. Putting an end to that was the best damn thing I ever did for you, Remy."

"Oh, spare me, Jason," she snorted, lifting her chin in a stubborn expression of disbelief.

"You know what your problem is, Frosty?" he rasped, taking a step closer to her. "You have issues."

"*I* have issues," she sputtered, feeling the roiling frustration of his words burn a scorching path of discontent through her blood. The gall of the man! "You're the Casanova Rambo and you think *I* have issues?" she seethed.

As if he didn't hear her, he said, "Do you know I'm always like this when you're around? Hell, even when you're not near me, I think about you and this is what happens. You're the sexiest thing I've ever set eyes on or smelled or heard or known and I've wanted to fuck you since the first time Connor introduced us and you said, 'Nice to meet you. My name's Remy'."

"Damn you," she gasped, wetting her lips, her tummy flipping at the way her action made him groan and curse hotly under his breath. Then he backed her into the wall until no more than a handful of inches separated them. She shrank away, willing herself to seep into the plaster at her back, hating the way her lips trembled as she stared up at him. "That is such crap, Jason."

"You want me to treat you like a woman, Frosty? Then stop running from me and I'll show you just how much of a woman I think you are," he all but snarled at her. The feral look in his molten gaze melted into her, making her limbs go liquid and soft, until she longed to touch him with every inch of her body.

"And now I'm what?" she demanded in a breathless rush. "Convenient to fuck 'til your next screw comes along?"

The gap between them was suddenly gone and Remy felt the intensity of his heat and strength and solidity from her breasts down to her toes. She'd have pressed against his chest to push him away, but there was no room for her arms between them and she knew she was no match for his strength. Oddly, her helplessness excited her as much as it infuriated her. She glared up at him as he glared down at her and their mouths almost touched, so that when he growled at her again, she could actually feel the heady warmth of his breath against the sensitive surfaces of her lips.

"There isn't a goddamn convenient thing about you! It's been months since I've been with a woman, Remy, because I got tired of screwing one woman while imagining I was with a certain little redheaded hellion. Because the *only* one I want is you…and you've been acting like you didn't even know I had a dick!"

Months! Yeah, right, she thought, finding the idea as absurd as it was unsettling. She knew his provocative appeal— had seen firsthand how easily women gravitated to him, enticed by his ruggedly sexy looks, sharp air of command and wicked edge of danger. For eight long, painful years, she'd witnessed how they all but threw themselves at him. No, men like Jason Hawkes didn't go without. Not unless they were in love and Remy knew better than to let her mind travel down that treacherous road to temptation. With her temper steaming and her pulse roaring a pounding cadence in her head, she curled her lip and sneered, "Not notice you had a *dick*, Jason? Hah! Not bloody likely! It's hard to miss that thing when it's always hard and making a bulge in your pants worthy of any oversexed satyr!"

His eyes widened and then he laughed right in her indignant face, making her wish she could just kill him or temporarily maim him. Anything that entailed pain and torture and retribution would do just fine.

"Why, Remy Frost," he rasped in a sexy drawl that rolled down her spine like the teasing press of a lover's lips, "I do believe that's your way of telling me you find my cock as fascinating as I find your sweet little pussy."

With his hands planted against the wall at either side of her head, he leaned down and nipped at her lower lip, grinding his hard-on into the warm, wet notch of her thighs, dragging a ragged whimper from her throat. Nipping carefully at her chin, her jaw, he whispered roughly, "I'll show you mine if you'll show me yours. Whaddya say, Frosty?"

Her mind screamed that she couldn't let her body win like this—giving in so easily—even as she wrapped her arms around his lower back. Her palms first found the hard, unyielding bulge of his gun, but she'd known it would be there, since he wasn't wearing his shoulder holster. Slipping her eager fingers beneath the hem of his shirt, she bypassed the cold, deadly weapon, until her palms grazed the hot details of his flesh.

Oh god. This was Jason beneath her hands, his wicked tongue suddenly tangling with her own as he slashed his sinful mouth across hers, giving her everything she'd always dreamed a kiss could be—consuming, devouring, like a desperate ache for life that could only be found in the taste of the person in your arms. His flavor was warm and honey-sweet, exquisitely delicious, his skin hot and silky in the way that only a man could feel—like the sleek, luxuriant coat of a panther, stretched taut over deadly muscles, slightly sweaty and utterly male. His scent and taste had always been her very favorite things in the world, stamped on her, ruining her for other men. Imprinted upon her system like a mark of ownership…and no other had ever been able to compare.

How in god's name was a woman supposed to resist that kind of temptation? Her pussy was swollen and aching and empty, soaking her panties until all she really wanted to do was rip off their clothes 'til they were two naked, writhing masses of flesh rolling across the floor, fucking each other's brains out. God, that would be so sweet. The operative word there being *would*.

Damn, why couldn't she just be a mindless body and go for what her sex glands were so desperately begging? Why did she have to have a brain, one that told her Jason Hawkes couldn't possibly want her for more than anything but a quick fuck to get him by until a better offer came along? Or a conscience that made sure she knew she'd hate waking up tomorrow knowing she'd simply added her name to a long list of his meaningless sexual encounters. Not to mention a heart which told her that for her, there wouldn't be a single meaningless thing about it. Fucking Jason would be the most important, significant thing to ever happen to her, which was exactly why she couldn't let it happen.

If she gave in to this thing between them, what would happen when he gave her the brush-off and wanted to go back to being casual buds? No, just thinking about it made her chest ache and she knew she couldn't risk that kind of torment, no matter how badly she wanted to.

Closing her eyes, she turned her face to the side, trying to escape the teasing, tempting, evocative brush of his lips as he tried to recapture her mouth. "Jason, stop it," she panted, sounding as if she'd run a great distance, and all of it uphill. "*Please.*"

He pulled back, but not enough to allow her escape. "Why?" he demanded, his deep voice husky with lust. "What do you want from me, Remy? I've told you how I feel and I know you want the same thing. Christ," he groaned, pushing the hardened ridge of his jeans-covered cock against her. "I can smell your juices, Remy. Your hot little pussy's already dripping and damn near all I've done is breathe on you."

The space he'd made between their upper bodies gave her just enough room to pull her arms up and shove against his chest, allowing her to sneak out to the side and get the hell away from him. "I didn't say I didn't want it…that I didn't want you, Jason." She rubbed her damp palms on the tops of her denim-covered thighs, fighting the urge to grab hold of him and wrestle him to the ground. "I just…I can't think straight about this right now."

He planted his hands on the lean line of his hips, blond head lowered between his shoulders as he stared at the floor. "Why are you so dead set on denying this thing between us, Remy, without even giving it a shot?"

"Men leave and they roam, Jason. That's a fact of life." God only knew she'd seen it enough times. First with her dad, when he was still around. Then with her mother's endless string of loser boyfriends. Even Connor and Jason, the two most important men in her life, had always left her—and though she'd always understood the invaluable importance of what they did, the honor and trust and pride their actions deserved, it had always torn her apart to watch them leave, knowing she might never see them again.

His face lifted and he nailed her with the piercing intensity of his whiskey-brown gaze, drilling the savagery of his emotions straight into her with a brutal force that was almost painful. "That's such bullshit, Remy. You don't really believe that."

"How do you know what I believe?"

"Because I know you. And what I don't know, I sure as hell can't wait to find out. You twist me up inside, killing me with the need to fuck you senseless and just hold you close all at the same time. You think this is easy, feeling like this? You think that I've ever felt like this before…or for anyone else? Fuck, Remy, I didn't even know that I *could* feel like this, but it grows every goddamn day. When we came home, I knew what I wanted. Why the hell do you think I planted my ass here, instead of going back to Indianapolis where my family is?"

"I don't care why," she said through numb lips, lying through her teeth.

"Because of you, Remy. Because you're here and all I was able to think about was coming home and getting you under me. Keeping you there for good once I got you there. And then you go and throw that bullshit in my face, and you know what, sweetheart? I'm not buying it. Those are a coward's words, and you, Remy Frost, are no goddamn coward."

She wrapped her arms around her chest until it looked as if she were holding herself together. "I'm also no fool, Jason."

"Then stop acting like one. Reaching out for help from the people who care about you doesn't make you weak, Remy. Believing in someone and having faith in them, when they care about you, makes you stronger."

"It makes you vulnerable," she argued.

With a sweeping arc of his hand, he swiped at the thick tension in the air that lay between them. "Goddamn it, woman. So you won't even give it a chance? You don't think I feel vulnerable as hell here, laying it all out on the line while you throw my words back in my face?"

"If that's true, then why are you just getting around to this little talk now, Jason? I've known you for years. You've been home for ten months!"

"And you've been running from me since I got here," he growled.

"That's ridiculous," she mumbled, hating the way it made her sound, as if she were scared of him, running away with her tail between her legs.

"Is it? Every time I show up, you bail. If you know I'm going to be somewhere, you cancel. You haven't given me two goddamn seconds since I settled my ass here, Frosty, and I'm tired of it."

It was true. She had been avoiding him and he was a hundred percent right about why. Damn it, she *was* scared. This man terrified the hell out of her. Not physically. No, it was the emotional damage she knew he could do. The scars she knew he could leave behind that she'd never recover from.

"You need a man in your life who can be there for you, Remy," he gritted out in a deep, dark voice that seemed to stroke her skin like the rough palm of his hand, eliciting breathless pleasure in its wake.

"Stop it, Jason. I don't need a daddy."

"That's good, then," he snorted, "because I sure as fuck wanna play with you, but house wasn't what I had in mind."

"I'm not a plaything, damn you."

"That all depends on what stakes we're playing for." *And I'm playing for keeps*, Jason vowed, choking back the words, because at this point, he knew they would send her running faster than anything. She wasn't ready to let herself believe them. No, she was going to fight him like a little warrior until he fought his way past those goddamn defenses she'd built around her heart.

Her eyes moved to the door, then cut back to him. "If you don't let me leave here, I'm going to scream."

"I'll have you screaming, Frosty," he murmured, knowing if he let her go now, he might never catch her again—and he couldn't let that happen. "Just as soon as you stop running from me."

"I mean it, Jason."

It was the sharp edge of panic in her voice that had him moving farther away, suddenly worried that he'd pushed her too far. Shit, he wasn't trying to be an ass, but it was hard as hell to be rational when everything you wanted was on the line.

He took a minute to find that cool, calm place he lived in when he worked, tried to bury the emotions twisting him up inside, if just for a moment, and said, "Fine. Fuck. Whatever. If you're too chickenshit to talk about us right now, then why don't you tell me about this class you're taking? You already have an MA in design. What the hell are you going to school for now?"

Suddenly the idea of discussing school was infinitely appealing compared to talking about their tenuous relationship and Remy nearly sighed with relief. Not that they had a relationship…or ever would. And she refused to think about why that statement made her feel so damn sad and empty inside.

Taking a deep breath, swallowing the tight feeling in her throat, she moved several feet away, rested her shoulder against the wall and said, "Connor doesn't know about it, because I know he'd have one of those annoying conniptions, but I've started taking a life drawing class over at Piedmont Community College."

"A what?"

"Life drawing. It's an art class, Jason."

"I know what it is," he rumbled. "Guys come in and strip down to the buff and you draw their naked hides, right?"

"Well," she replied in a sarcastic drawl, "you make it sound so lovely, but yes, there are nude models. The purpose, however, is to achieve a better understanding of the human form. I thought it would be a good way to keep my drawing skills sharp, since I do so much graphic design nowadays."

Yeah, he knew all about her work. And damn it, he was proud as hell of the thriving business she had going. While he and Connor had been in the Middle East for the last year of their service, she had started her own PR company, specializing in everything from web design to advertising to promotions for local artists and businesses. He could appreciate her reasons for taking the art class, but that didn't mean he had to like it. Before she could stop him, he turned and walked back to the chair where he'd tossed her backpack, picked it up and set it on top of Michael's desk.

"Hey, what are you doing?" she huffed as he undid the zipper and reached inside.

"I just wanna take a look at your work, honey," he replied in a smooth tone as his fingers found the thick art tablet inside. Remy rushed across the room and made a grab for the book, but he held it up high with one hand and shook his head at the snarl purring in the back of her throat. "Calm down, Frosty. I just want to admire your handiwork."

There was no missing the flare of panic firing through her green eyes and his curiosity revved up into a higher gear. Whatever was in that little black book, she didn't want him seeing it.

"Jason, give me that," she demanded, gritting the words out through the clenched line of her teeth.

"Kiss me again, like you mean it, and I'll give it back to you," he drawled with a wicked grin kicking up one corner of his wide mouth.

"No."

The smile that spread to life from the grin was slow and sinful. "Then step back, Frosty."

She muttered under her breath as she stomped away, turning her back on him to stare angrily at a painting of an Irish landscape hanging over an oak filing cabinet. Jason shook his head at her temper, then lowered the book, flipped through the pages and was instantly reminded of just how talented she was. With his thumb, he skipped through page upon page of exquisite charcoals and pencil drawings of several male and female forms. Then his gaze landed on one that snagged his attention, riveting him. His eyes went wide, his surprise clear and loud in his deep voice as he muttered, "Holy shit! You gave this guy my ass!"

She refused to turn and look at him.

"Remy, is this or is this not my ass on this guy?" he laughed, flipping through the next few pages, all drawings of the same model. And sure enough, the model's backside had a spherical scar just on the upper curve of his left cheek. The scar from the wound Remy had seen stitched up on that fateful night seven years ago, when she was only nineteen and he was too old for her. Shit, no way in hell was this just a coincidence. She'd drawn his ass on some pretty boy's body. Pretty, he knew, since the model was lying on his hip in several of the drawings, backside to the viewer, looking over his shoulder so that you could see his face.

"Jesus, this is priceless. Why did you give this guy my ass, honey?"

She shrugged the stiff line of her shoulders, still refusing to look at him. "Honestly, Jason, it's no big deal."

"Well, who the fuck is he?"

Jason watched as she turned her head to look at him over her shoulder. "His name is Jon," she muttered, "and he's *obviously* our latest model. He took the job in order to make enough money for his summer Surfari."

"Surfari?" Jason snickered, shaking his head.

"I think it's where a surfer moves from beach to beach, traveling around so he can surf all the best spots," she said with another shrug.

"Huh," he grunted, flipping through a few more drawings. "And has he asked you out yet?"

"No," Remy snorted, "though to be honest, I'm not sure I'd know if he did." She laughed softly. "Take my word for it—listening to Jon talk is like a torture session for your brain."

Not to mention the fact she wasn't interested in the guy, because he wasn't the one she wanted...the one sharing the small, intimate space of Mike's office with her. Plus, the way Jon stared at her while he modeled, to the point of freaky, was, in short, really creeping her out, no matter how cute he was. Add to that the notes...and she was ready to steer as clear of the "surfer dude" as possible.

"Why can't you understand him?" Jason asked, the jealousy in his voice apparent, even through the veil of curiosity.

"Trust me," Remy said with a smile, "if you met him, you'd understand."

"Yeah, well, I'd still like to know why you're giving the little dickhead my ass."

A low, frustrated sound of tension vibrated in her throat. "Will you just shut up about it?"

Jason snorted. "Sure I will, just as soon as you explain why you drew *my* ass on this Jon guy."

That low vibration turned into a full-fledged, feminine little growl and he couldn't stop the corners of his mouth from twitching with humor. "It won't make any sense if I try to explain it to you," she argued.

"Yeah?" he asked, still grinning. "Try me."

Her chin found that familiar stubborn lift. "I don't think so."

"Come on," he teased, flipping to another drawing that had pretty surfer boy's equipment in far too much detail for his liking. His gut went hot at the thought of her sitting there in class, staring at this prick's naked dick. Studying it. Drawing it. "Damn it, Remy. Someone like you shouldn't be seeing crap like this!"

Her eyes narrowed as she turned around to face him, hands planted threateningly on her hips. "Someone like *me*?"

she demanded, any embarrassment apparently forgotten beneath the heat of her exasperation with him.

She took a quick succession of steps toward him, closing the distance between them, the corner of her lips kicking up in a sexy smirk that made his mouth go dry.

"I'm hardly a virgin, Jason," Remy said with a far too innocent smile, blinking her lashes at him until she saw a muscle jerk in his stubble-roughened jaw.

Okay…so maybe "hardly" was pushing it, but no way in hell was she letting him get away with this. She'd only slept with a few boys back in college, when she'd been so determined to purge the dreams of this one from her mind, but at least she hadn't been sitting on her rump, waiting for him to get over himself. At least she hadn't sulked in a corner, bemoaning the sad fact that Jason Hawkes would always think of her as too young, too naïve and too inexperienced. Maybe even too *cold*.

Oh crap, hold it right there. What on earth was she going on about? She didn't care how he thought about her, because anything between them was out of the question. Lord, why couldn't she get that thought through to her miserable, misguided sex organs? If she kept this up, she was going to be committed for split personality disorder. One part of her wanted to throw him to the ground and ride him silly. The other half wanted to run far and fast in the opposite direction, until she'd reached a place where the thought of his face no longer put that funny little ache in her chest, or that warm, twisting rush of sensation in her tummy.

"Damn it, Remy. Women like you don't —"

"Don't what, Jason?"

"You know damn well what they don't do," he snarled.

"No. I know what you 'think' they don't do, but I've got news for you, Jason. They do. You can bet your gorgeous, arrogant ass that they do."

"Connor would put you over his knee if he heard you right now."

She faced him down, feeling like an enraged Amazon, breathing fury and determination in spades. "Wrong. I hate to be the one to burst your bubble, but time didn't stand still while you and Connor were off playing Captain America. I grew up, Jason. I'm not that gangly, starry-eyed little fool anymore with a reputation for being cold. And I got tired of waiting for you to notice."

For the second time that night, she muttered, "Oomph!" The force with which he slammed her back against the wall, pinning her there with his big body, knocked the air right out of her. His fist twisted into the long mass of her hair, hauling her up hard against him with an ease that left her breathless in its wake, despite her firm intention not to fall all over him like every other woman who set eyes on him. She struggled within his grasp, her body trapped in place by two hundred plus pounds of rock-hard muscle and pure male perfection.

"Like I said before," he rasped in a husky, seductive drawl, "if you don't think I've noticed, then you're not nearly as smart as I've always thought you were."

Then his hips pressed forward, forcing the massive bulk of his cock against the softness of her belly. Her body went heavy and damp. She felt momentarily dazed by the flood of need that shot through her, melting into her core. But that wasn't the worst of it. No, the worst was watching the smug satisfaction cross his face, as if he'd catalogued her every reaction, knowing exactly how he affected her. He smiled and in another wickedly sexy drawl, he said, "And if you haven't figured out by now that I'm going to be the *only* man fucking your sweet little ass from here on out, then you don't know jack shit about men, Remy. You don't know jack shit about *me*."

A challenging smile worked its way across Remy's lips—one she couldn't help, though she knew she was playing with fire. Hell, she was standing in the middle of the pyre, dancing to the howl of the heat while the flames licked at her heels. She couldn't fight it. It just felt too damn good to know she'd ruffled a man who was known in Special Ops for the ice that ran in his veins.

He stiffened, every muscle on his incredible body going tight with tension, unbearably hard, and he pulled her even closer, nearly cutting off her air. She gasped and the soft sound was swallowed by his rough growl as his mouth opened over hers again, his tongue claiming immediate possession—a hot, heady weapon that he used to devastate her in a shivering rush of aching, violent lust. And there was something more—buried beneath the need—that she couldn't put a name to. His lips moved over hers as his head moved from one angle to another, each position finding a way for him to get deeper into her, until she felt completely ravaged, drowning beneath the onslaught of sensation.

Hell, and here she thought she'd prepared herself for this. Whatever passion she'd managed to incite in other men was nothing compared to the storm of anger and need and necessity coming from Jason Hawkes' lips, and tongue, and teeth.

Oh god, what was happening to her? She could feel her ability for rational thought simply shutting down as sexual hunger and starvation took over, something dark and dangerous churning inside her, demanding she take her pleasure from the one place she'd always wanted it. *Noooo*...this wasn't supposed to happen, damn it! She was supposed to be strong and stalwart. A rock, for god's sake, not turn into a creamy puddle of need because he was kissing her. But damn, what a kiss. Maybe she was being too hard on herself. What woman in her right mind could mount a defense against such a tactical, mind-shattering attack? It was only sensible to give in and beg surrender. To allow herself this one taste of paradise. Something to hold close and sip at for the rest of her life, when this man walked away and all she was left with was the memory.

Damn it…noooo!!!

Remy thought of pushing him away, but then pulled him closer, clutching onto his bulging biceps as if they were her lifeline in a world shifting too quickly beneath her feet. Just one taste. One touch. One moment of heaven…

Somewhere through it all she began kissing him back, though she didn't know when or how, considering he'd burned every thought from her lust-dazed brain. She was giving in to him, sobbing into his mouth as her hands moved higher, clutching at his wide shoulders as if she'd pull herself right inside him.

She bit his lip, hungry for the taste of his mouth, and the growling sound rumbling up from his chest deepened. His big hand—the one not twisted in her hair—grabbed her ass to haul her even closer, so that the wickedly impressive ridge of his cock could push against the denim-covered vee of her thighs as he dipped his knees and forced her to ride the hard bulk of flesh burgeoning against his fly. He was huge, massive, and her body clenched hungrily at the thought of having this man—this ruthless warrior who haunted her every fantasy— devastating her with that mouthwatering cock. Hell, no wonder women crawled around after him like he was god's gift to womankind.

He came up for air and she gulped down a huge lungful, not realizing until that point that her lungs were burning from neglect.

"Open your eyes, Frosty."

Her treacherous body obeyed automatically, far more loyal to his dictates than they'd ever been to her own. His mouth remained against hers, lips touching, so that she felt, as well as heard his words.

"You're mine," he grated, grinding his cock against her cream-covered core, the layers of denim separating them an insubstantial barrier beneath the heat and power of his need as his gaze snagged hers, holding her captive. He made her feel every intoxicating slide of that hard, heavy shaft promising to pound her into one endless orgasm after another. "Do you understand me, Remy? Do you understand how it's going to be between us? I was going to go easy on you, sweetheart, but maybe that's not what you need after all. Maybe you need me to show you once and for all how much I can give you—how hard I can give it to you. I'm going to fuck you 'til you give me what I want, Remy. Fuck you 'til you stop being so goddamn afraid of me and finally realize what's been waiting here for you all along."

She strained in his hold, as furious with herself as she was with him, because every word he said was true. And she knew he could make every threat a reality. Her mouth opened, but before she could deliver a biting comeback, he said, "But first things first, sweetheart," and slipped his big hand into the front left pocket of her jeans, pulling out the rumpled piece of paper she'd tried to keep from him.

Chapter Three

ઝ

Well, that couldn't have gone worse, Remy thought with a sickly smile, locking her front door behind her as she walked into her cozy apartment. They'd argued for a good fifteen minutes about the meaning of the note. Argued and bitched and aggravated one another beyond belief, but had reached no resolution. She'd insisted that it was just some kind of stupid prank, trying to explain that she'd only gotten spooked after her car had died and she'd suddenly found herself on a dark street in a bad part of town. Her run to Finnegan's had simply been because it was the closest place she'd known that was safe. But Jason was ready to call in the cavalry for protection, just like she'd known he would. Which was why she'd kept the bothersome little notes a secret in the first place. They had first started appearing on her windshield around a month ago, whenever it was parked at the school. And each one had contained the same message. *Stay away from Jonathan.* It made sense that she hadn't had one before then, since "Jon" hadn't begun modeling for the class until just before that time. What didn't make sense was why.

The why of it was really starting to piss her off. It wasn't like she'd given anyone reason to think she was interested in the "surfer dude", even if he reminded her of a young Brad Pitt. But the way he stared at her during class, like he was almost afraid to take his eyes off her, gave her the creeps, and she went out of her way to avoid him. Especially during the frequent breaks scheduled to assure Jon's muscles wouldn't get stiff from holding the various poses.

Remy's only theory was that it was either someone from her class or one of Jon's old girlfriends spying on them all, taking exception to his bizarre interest in her. She'd even tried

51

watching her car a few times from the classroom windows, but on those occasions nothing had happened. Finally, she'd spoken to Miss Hutchins about it, but the attractive, somewhat shy instructor hadn't been able to offer any insight.

Still, as odd and strangely unsettling as the notes were, Remy's gut told her they were a harmless prank, albeit a weird one. They had to be, because she refused to be suffocated by fear and intimidated into hiding herself away. It was that somewhat loner part of her personality that had earned her the painful moniker of "Ice Queen" back in high school and college, and she refused to let it be true.

So, she and Jason had argued and snarled and all but growled each other's heads off, until Michael had finally come in for an employee's paycheck and broke up their verbal scuffle. With a swift change in tactics that had had her wondering if Jason was really just trying to get her the hell away from the hunky Mike and his sexy, adorable, lopsided grin, complete with dimples, she'd found herself in a taxi, headed home, while Jason stayed behind to deal with her car. And she had to admit, she didn't mind him taking control of *that* situation, since she'd had no desire to stand out in the cold, freezing her ass off, waiting for the tow truck to come and pick it up.

But their battle wasn't over, she knew. It'd just been put on hold. He'd closed the back door of the taxi, only after informing her that they'd finish their "conversation" later. Then he'd handed the driver a roll of bills and watched them drive away. That was nearly twenty minutes ago. Before she could even think about rallying for their next verbal skirmish, which she assumed would begin with a phone call from the gorgeous jerk in the morning, she dragged her exhausted body into the bathroom for a nice, steaming hot shower.

Thirty minutes later, Remy found herself lying between her crisp, cool sheets, her hair damp and her body miserably alive with the remembered sensation of being plastered up against Jason's breathtaking, muscle heavy body, while his mouth consumed hers in such a savage, ragingly passionate way that her toes were still curling from the pleasure. Damn, but the man could kiss, and that wicked thought only led her deeper into dangerous territory, wondering what else he could do with such utter, devastating skill.

And she couldn't help but compare tonight's ravaging onslaught to the sweet, tender, intensely controlled kiss she'd experienced at his hands seven years ago. That one had been tightly leashed, probably because he'd felt guilty as hell about kissing his best friend's nineteen-year-old, virgin sister—but there was nothing controlled about the way he'd kissed her in Mike's office. Lord, her lips were still feeling bruised, so that she'd looked kind of bee-stung when she'd spied her reflection in the bathroom mirror.

Unfortunately, her lips weren't the only part of her body still reeling, bearing the marks of arousal. Her nipples ached, pressing stiffly into the soft, sheer cotton of her sleep tank. On top of that, the sensitive folds of her sex throbbed with a low, urgent beat of frustration against the delicate crotch of her white cotton bikini panties. She'd only just slipped the things on and already they were damp with her fluids. Then there was the ache that churned within her womb, making her want to writhe beneath the light covers and rub her thighs together until she could find a measure of peace.

If you don't take the edge off yourself, honey, her body purred with restless discontent, *then we won't be sleeping tonight. We'll be lying here thinking about that hot, hard, hunky stud all night long. What's it gonna be?*

With a smothered growl of frustration into her pillow, Remy punched her mattress, then rolled toward her bedside table and reached for her mini iPOD. Five seconds later, she had her ear buds in and the soft, sultry tunes of Alicia Keyes filled her senses, while the deep, moonlit shadows of her room created a cozy, intimate atmosphere. A slow smile curled around the edges of her mouth as she reached for the top drawer in the table, her pulse kicking up as she began to let the fantasy take hold of her. In her mind's eye, she created a breathtaking image of Jason as he'd looked when he was pressing her against the wall, those whiskey-brown eyes burning with savage sexual heat, the long, strong lines of his body strung impossibly tight with primitive hunger that was all for her. She moaned beneath her breath and quickly selected one of her favorite "toys", kicked away the stifling covers and shimmied out of her soaked underwear. Then she closed her eyes and lay back on her pillows, thighs sprawled while she flicked the switch at the end of the long, blue jellied vibrator and placed the flared tip against the pulsing bud of her clit.

Sensation struck straight through her body at the thought of what Jason would do if he could see her now. She bit down on her bottom lip to keep from crying out, a fresh surge of moisture flowing from her sex, drenching the thick seam of her labia. Her back arched as she slipped the vibrating toy lower, playing at the tender entrance of her pussy, and a wicked smile spread across her mouth as her fantasy sucked her under a pulsing wave of pleasure—deeper...and deeper...and deeper.

* * * * *

After knocking for a good five minutes, Jason slipped the special tool out of his wallet, inserted it into the disgustingly flimsy lock on Remy's front door and slipped into the dark living room. The rich, sensually crisp scent of incense teased his senses, the low, shimmering glow of light coming from a lamp in the dining nook casting the open floor plan in a wash of warm, mellow gold.

God, he loved her crazy apartment, with its candles and walls of books and smells of incense and vanilla—but then there were so many things that he enjoyed about this woman. He loved the way she smelled of exotic coffee in the mornings and like a lover at the end of the day, all flushed and windblown with her scarlet hair wild around her shoulders.

He loved that she never took an umbrella anywhere, but would just let the rain soak her through, laughing like a child caught out in a storm. He loved *her*, damn it, and he didn't know how in the hell to tell her, or make her understand, without blowing it. Hell, she already thought he was just out for some fun with her, looking for a way to scratch an old itch or whatever the fuck was going on in that cynical mind of hers. If he started pouring out his heart, she'd probably think he was just playing the ultimate asshole by trying to use the "L" word to ease his way into her pants. Shit, she'd run like hell in the opposite direction so fast his friggin' head would spin.

Fuck.

Rolling his shoulders to relieve the stiff, hard ache of tension in his muscles, he listened to the heavy silence of her apartment, the only sound that of the distant electrical buzz of her refrigerator in the kitchen. It was so quiet, he wondered if maybe she'd dozed off and was already too deeply asleep to hear his knocking. The corners of his mouth tilted down at the thought as he made his way through her living room, thinking that she hadn't looked all that tired at Finnegan's. Pissed, yeah, but not worn out enough to warrant sleeping through the racket he'd been making.

At the entrance to the hallway leading to her bedroom and bath, he flicked the switch on the wall, setting everything to light with a soft, low-wattage bulb that softened the harsh, basic white of the standard apartment walls...and that's when he heard the first moan. Panic sent him barreling around the corner, straight through her open bedroom door—and shock stopped him so quickly that he nearly fell over from the velocity of his forward motion.

Holy fucking shit! he thought, swallowing hard on the thick knot of lust clogging his throat before he choked on it.

With wide, nearly watering eyes, Jason watched the lush, graceful form she made as she writhed atop her covers— watched as the plastic rotating cock moved in and out of the delicate flower of her labia. Warm, thick, wet cream coated its knobbed surface as it plunged steadily into the crimson perfection of her pussy and every hard, hungry inch of his body ached with the need to be right *there*. Tongue, fingers, impatient cock, all of them wanted to take the place of that driving dildo and be fucking themselves into Remy Frost's precious little piece of pussy.

Four steps took him to the end of her bed, and all he could think was *Christ, she's gorgeous*. Her sex was small, but beautifully delicate and plump, swollen with need, a deep pussy-pink at the hot, wet center that flowered into a pale, pearly, blushing rose in her outer labia. Up above, that sweet little clit that he wanted to stroke with the flat of his tongue begged for attention. Down below, the innocent little rosebud of her ass, so tight and pretty, was just waiting to be forced open by his thick cock as he fed it into her.

She was magnificent, earthy and sultry and so fucking hot he didn't know how he hadn't just melted into a puddle of steaming need. Sweat slicked the feverish surface of his body, stinging his eyes, trailing in twining rivulets down the long line of his spine, and his fingers twitched, curling into his damp palms. His hands clenched, making fierce fists, impatient to reach out and grab handfuls of her glorious female flesh and hold on for life...forever. He wanted to squeeze and stroke and claim possession of every mouthwatering little inch. Wanted to tame and tease and drive her so far over the edge that she couldn't find her way back without him.

Fuck, he'd never have thought he was capable of feeling like this, of carrying so much emotion inside his coldly trained mind and body, but Remy had shattered any self-conceptions he'd carried and ripped him open, allowing everything to twist and turn inside him until he was all but bursting with it.

With love.

Shit, there wasn't anything else it could be and it was every bit as confusing and irritating as he'd always suspected it would be. But then, it was more magnificent and awe-inspiring than he could have ever imagined. And if she'd just give him an inch, a fraction, then he strongly suspected the irritation would fade. Only damn reason it was there in the first place was because he wanted and he couldn't have.

Until now.

In the pale, golden light spilling in from the hall, he watched as she arched her back—mouth open on a soundless scream while the delicate fingers of one hand stroked the ripe little bud of her clit, the other jamming the dildo at a faster tempo that made him choke on a moan. Then she shivered and froze, the toy shoved deep between her spread thighs, and her precious cunt began fluttering around its base as the orgasm washed through her.

"Jason!" she cried, her eyes still screwed tightly shut, voice husky and raw, and he damn near came in his jeans. "*Oh god, Jason,*" she moaned, melting back against the mattress as the tension flowed from her body and she slipped the soaked dildo free from her clutching depths. Her pussy made a wet little pop of sound when the round, buzzing head finally pulled free. He smiled, thinking of how sweet it was going to be when he shoved himself into her, cramming in every inch, packing her full.

So, so, sooo fucking sweet.

"Jason," she sighed, her voice sleep-heavy and thick, eyes still closed as she twisted off the vibrator, pulled the ear buds free and snuggled deeper into the pillow beneath her head.

"Yeah, baby?" he groaned, reaching down with one hand to flick the top button on his jeans.

Her body went utterly still. "Jason?" she croaked in a whisper-soft voice, a small crease forming between her delicate brows.

"Remy, baby, open your eyes," he muttered, beginning to carefully work his zipper down. "I'm right here, honey."

One lid cracked open, her mouth forming a perfect O before she screamed at the top of her lungs, flinging the soaked dildo to the end of the bed as if it were a poisonous snake, before lurching up against her wrought iron antique headboard. "Jason!" she screeched. "What in the hell are you doing here?"

He frowned, his hands pausing in the act of trying to work the zipper past the bulging, massive ache of his cock. "Remy, calm down, honey," he murmured, making his voice as soothing as possible in the face of her obvious panic.

"Calm down!" she gasped, green eyes as round as saucers as she looked him up and down, gaze catching on the undone button at the top of his fly. "Calm down! When you said we'd talk later, I thought you meant on the damn phone, not my apartment! Get the hell out of here!" she gritted through her clenched teeth. "This is *mine*, Jason. You can't just come barging in because you damn well please! Haven't you ever heard of fucking privacy?"

"Jesus, Remy," he snorted, "it's not like I was trying to break in on you. I knocked for five minutes. You didn't answer and I was fucking worried! You expect me to just stroll away and assume everything's okay?"

"Yes," she hissed, untangling one arm from the cord of the ear buds and setting them down beside the iPOD on top of the table. The silence of the night was thick and piercing as it closed in around them, filled only by the soughing cadence of their harsh, heavy breaths.

Oh god, how am I ever going to live this one down? Remy silently moaned, wanting to simply disappear. Anything to get her away from the searing sensual knowledge in his eyes—the flame of possession that was about to burn her alive. And she'd been moaning his friggin' name the entire time she was coming. *Crap.*

"Come on, Frosty. You know me better than that. And I *did* knock. I've probably woken up the entire damn complex."

"I can't hear anything when I have those damn things in," she muttered, glaring at the ear buds. "I didn't hear you at the door."

She could tell he was having a hell of a time trying to hold in his smile. Instead, he managed to croak out a tight, "Yeah, I don't imagine you did. I came barreling in here like a bull and you didn't even bat a lash."

Her gaze narrowed and she hoped the threat in them looked as menacing as she felt. "Shut up, Jason."

His own eyes twinkled with humor, those sexy, silk-rough lips rolling inward as he struggled not to grin. "I didn't say anything, darlin'."

"You don't need to. I can see you laughing at me in those damn shining eyes."

"I'm not laughing, honey. Except maybe at myself. It's been a long time since I've shot my load in my pants, but I'm feeling pretty fucking close to it right about now." He looked down at his bulging crotch with a bemused expression on his sexy face. "Too fucking close for comfort."

"You were going to call me," she growled.

"I never said that. I said we'd talk later and it *is* later."

"Later," she scoffed, still choking on embarrassment. His reasonable tone made her want to grab the glistening dildo and chuck it at his golden head. "What in the hell are you doing here, Jason?"

His eyes, when he looked up and snagged her gaze, shone like mesmerizing pools of fiery gold, his thick golden lashes creating a shimmering rim that any woman would have killed to possess as her own. "I'm tired of not sleeping at night. This is bullshit. I need you."

The stark emotion in his deep voice washed away the angry words hovering on the tip of her tongue, leaving her breathless and on edge, drowning in everything she felt for this man.

"And you need me too, Remy. I know you do, honey. Can't you at least give me that much?"

Ignoring his question, or at least trying to, she asked, "Just how did you get in here anyway?"

"I picked your lock." He grinned, then scowled, adding, "And you need a new one. That fucking thing is pathetic. I can't believe Connor hasn't changed it."

"Picked it with what?"

He held up the tiny length of metal, then shoved it in his back pocket. "Tools of the trade, angel."

"Isn't that illegal?"

"Well, I don't go around using it to break in on innocent people, Remy," he laughed. "And the bad guys very rarely complain about a little B and E to the cops. We *are* on the same side as the law, you know."

"Yeah, I know. But it seems you don't mind twisting it a bit to get what you want."

"If it means catching some shithead sleazebag, you bet your ass I don't."

"Well, next time, why don't you just try knocking harder, or throwing rocks at my window?" she mumbled, realizing she was beginning to feel more aroused than embarrassed. It was difficult to remember why she was fighting this thing so damn hard. With him standing there, watching her, her body alive with sensation and half naked, her reasons for denying herself what she wanted were suddenly paling in comparison to the heavy, demanding weight of need twisting inside her.

"We could make this easy and you could just give me a key," he drawled, smiling when she snorted under her breath. Remy watched his gaze search, then darken when he found the wicked sight of the blue dildo lying atop the folded comforter at the foot of her bed. A slow, wolfish grin spread across the rugged line of his mouth, dark eyes narrowing with such a powerful wave of lust, she could have sworn she felt it crash against her. "Why's it so small?"

Remy blinked in infuriated fascination. "What?"

"That little plastic cock, Frosty. Why the hell's it so small?"

Despite the emotional roller coaster she was riding, it was difficult not to laugh. "Five inches is *not* small! Now can you please turn around so I can get dressed?"

His eyes snagged on the damp curls between her legs, her tank too short to reach past her navel, panties lying somewhere in the covers. "You sure you want to do that, beautiful?"

Before she'd even known she was going to say them, the words were simply spilling past Remy's lips—soft and unstoppable. "Honestly, no, but then I'm not sure what I want right now, Jason." She wet her mouth, blinking slowly against the soft shaft of golden light washing into the room. "This whole night has been…confusing, to say the least."

"So you weren't thinking about me while you were driving that scrawny dick into your pretty little pussy?" he rumbled, stepping closer to the end of the bed. "I could've sworn that was my name you were shouting when you started coming."

"Jason," she groaned, ready to hide under her pillow.

"Don't get embarrassed, Remy. I think it's sexy as hell. And god knows I've jerked myself off enough times thinking about you. More than I'll admit to, I'll tell ya that."

"You masturbate thinking about me?" she asked, wondering when her voice had gone so low and husky…and thinking that his admission was just about the sexiest damn thing she'd ever heard.

"You bet your sweet ass I do. For years, honey. And you know what really blows my mind. You're even prettier in the flesh than in my fantasies. I can't get my fucking head around it."

"*Jason.*"

He dragged his eyes up from the tempting sight of her swollen nipples to her luminous green eyes. "Yeah?"

"What's happening to us?" For once there was no anger or suspicion in her soft voice—only need.

"Something that's been brewing for a hell of a long time. You can either run from me, or meet me halfway, but either way, it's here. It's here and I want it more than anything. *Anything*, Remy."

"Is it really me you want, Jason? Or are you just trying to keep close to me, because you don't believe me about those stupid notes?" she asked, worrying her bottom lip with her teeth.

"Look," he grunted, the long, sleekly muscled line of his body giving off that same sharp, raw-edged energy that she'd always sensed in his presence. "Forget the fucking notes. Forget that you're pissed at me. Forget *everything*. If there's one thing in this world you can believe, it's that I want you more than any other woman I've ever known. That's the fucking truth, Remy. Why don't we try to go from there?"

"Jason…"

"Please, Remy," he rasped, the sexy, utterly male line of his lips twisting with emotion. "I'm fucking begging here, honey. Whatever you want. Just tell me and it's yours."

And it was that stark emotion that broke her. That intimate glimpse into his soul that she'd never thought a dominant, purely aggressive man like Jason Hawkes would reveal, because it showed his weakness. The kind of emotion that she'd always, in that secret part of her heart that held nothing but her dreams, hoped he could feel for her.

Jason swore he could feel the heavy pulse of his heart as the seconds ticked by in a slow, painful rhythm—and then his breath caught at the fey, shy smile that teased over the bruised pink silk of her mouth, her red hair wild around her pale, sleek shoulders. She was so beautiful, it made him tremble. And the haunting perfection of her taste, like peaches and woman and Remy, burned through his blood, making the knot of lust in his damn dick nearly explode. He wanted to press his mouth to hers and taste her again, losing himself in the liquid soft perfection of her. Christ, he wanted to fucking devour her, everywhere, from the top of her head down to those cute little toes with their two silver rings.

"I guess this is one of those soul-searching moments, huh?" she said in a whisper-soft voice that spoke of intimacy and secrets. "Where you know one path will take your life in one direction and the other in a completely different one."

"Yeah," he rumbled, giving her a slow nod, wondering where she was going with this and hoping like hell that it was going to lead her into his arms…his life.

"I know which one I want, Jason."

"Yeah?" he croaked, unable to drag his gaze away from where it had caught on her pretty, pink little pussy, just visible beneath the tiny little puff of wet, glistening curls. Fuck, but it was beautiful.

In a siren-smooth move, he watched as Remy raised herself to her knees and crawled to the end of her bed. She placed her hands on the bunched muscles of his shoulders and her bright, deep green eyes burned into him, so hot he felt the heat of her stare fire across his skin. Then, with a trembling breath, she pressed the gentle cushion of her mouth against his own and he felt the sweet pull of her hands as they fisted into the shaggy strands of his hair.

"Oh damn," he growled, and was on her before he'd even realized he was moving. He came over her, pressed her into the giving softness of her down-filled comforter, held her there with the steady weight of his big, hard, heavy body, and simply soaked in the pleasure of feeling her soft, lush length trapped beneath him. Then he caught her around the waist and moved her up the bed, straddled her hips and caged her within the solid, immovable frame of his thighs. She stared up at him, those big green eyes smoky and watchful in the pale golden light, and a smile of pure, unadulterated pleasure played over his mouth, his blood pumping like a son-of-a-bitch as he rasped, "God, I love your tits."

"Excuse me?" she laughed, her cheeks going crimson, while he ran his rough hands up and down her sides, his calluses snagging at the soft material of her shirt.

"Your tits. I love them." He stared, transfixed, unable to tear his eyes away from the puffy, pointed tips beneath the thin cotton of her tank top. It was old, nearly threadbare, revealing their dark pink coloring through the hazy thread of cotton. "Always have," he moaned, stroking one peak with the tip of his finger. "And I can't get enough of these sexy little nipples."

"Oh," she gasped, arching her back as he pinched the bud between two knuckles, his gaze hot with hunger and lust.

"Love them so much I wanna fucking play with 'em and lick 'em—just fucking suck on 'em until you come."

"Oh…I, um, *wow*—"

His eyes cut up at her beneath his brows and he knew they were filled with more life, more feeling, more emotion than he'd ever shown before. "You gonna let me have 'em?"

She gave him her answer as she struggled out of the flimsy tank and it cleared her head, her magnificent breasts lying soft and proud before him, making his friggin' mouth water. At least he hoped this was her answer. If she was just fucking with him, teasing him with the breathtaking sight, Jason knew he was gonna die. Smack her sweet little ass raw and die from the burn of lust boiling through his blood. It was hot and thick, his heart pumping hard and heavy to push it in a slow burn through his veins.

His hands slammed into the giving cushion of her soft bedding beside her shoulders, palms flat, biceps bulging, trapping her beneath him. And his eyes trapped her, too, holding her in place, without even touching her. "You know where this is going, Remy," he suddenly growled, melting her with the heady sound of primitive power and aggression. "Once I get my hands on you, you won't be shaking me off again. I'm going to be rammed up your cunt, buried up to my balls, packing your hot sweet little body so fucking full, and not just the countless times I'll take you tonight. Your creamy little pussy is gonna be mine whenever I want—however I want it—for as long as I'm able to breathe."

"Don't you mean for as long as you're able to fuck?" she teased, a part of her wondering just how far she could push him.

"Remy, when the time comes that I can't get it up to fuck you, darlin', I'll be ready to die. You gettin' the picture?" he grunted, his dark voice a sexy scratch against her already weakening defenses.

Arching one brow, she smiled. "Yeah…you've painted it pretty clearly."

"You got anything to say about it?" he drawled with that crooked, boyish grin that always stole her breath.

"Yeah, actually, I do."

"What's that?" he asked as he lifted up, his attention snagging on the quivering of her belly as he stripped his shirt off and reached back for his gun. The stark black metal gleamed eerily in the low light as he leaned forward to set it on her bedside table. Then his big hands went back to the partly opened fly of his jeans.

Knocking him off balance as she rolled to her side and scrambled out from under him, Remy quickly jumped to her feet, then smiled at the look of stunned surprise on those rugged, sexy-as-hell features. Laying the gauntlet at his feet, she lifted her chin and purred, "You're going to have to catch me first."

* * * * *

Remy had known what she was doing, taking the tiger by the tail and giving a hard, teasing tug, and she loved it. Suddenly she just wanted to break free—from all of it—everything. She wanted to let go of the worry and frustration and regret, to stop living in the "what ifs" and "maybes", before she lost any chance at the "right now". Before life passed her by and she was growing old with nothing but her work and her battery-operated boyfriends.

She wanted to let go of the past.

And there was no denying that a secret part of her heart beat out one strong, steady refrain that she was finally willing to believe in...to listen to.

Trust him, Remy. This time won't be like the last.

A freeing, exhilarating wave of happiness broke over her and she laughed out loud, delighting in his rumbling growl at her back. She dodged around the corner, feeling the aggressive heat of his body closing in on her, and then she was caught, trapped in the vising, possessive hold of those wonderful arms and he was pinning her down on the smooth, polished surface of her small dining room table.

He stared down at her, the look in his dark, thick-lashed gaze making her feel like the most beautiful woman in the world, when she knew damn well it wasn't true. "Remy," he groaned, her name rolling off his tongue like a rich, sweet spill of molasses. "God, Remy, do you have any idea how many nights I've dreamed of getting you right here? Just like this."

She ran her hands over the bunched muscles of his shoulders, down to the powerful bulge of his biceps, loving the way he felt against her, all hard muscle and man, his musky, outdoors scent filling her head until she felt dizzy from the force of desire pulsing through her. "Me too, Jason."

"Yeah?"

"Oh yeah." She smiled, cupping the side of his hot face in her hand. The golden stubble on his cheeks and strong, square chin was sensually scratchy. She moved her thumb over the sexy rough-silk texture of his lower lip, laughing and then gasping when he moved his head and caught the tip between the straight white edges of his teeth.

"Tell me what you want," he rasped against her skin, nipping the sensitive pad, then laving it with a slow, sensual stroke of his tongue.

"Everything, Jason. All of you." *For as long as I can have it.*

Her breath caught at the intense, raw-edged flame of possession that blazed in his whiskey gaze—at the stark, utterly male lines of lust that tightened his expression. Remy wanted to spend days, years…lifetimes just looking at him. Investigating all that dark, golden skin across the hard width of his chest. The tiny scars scattered like stories, as if he wore his past upon the golden beauty of his flesh. He was dark and rugged and dangerous—so insanely sexy she was ready to come just from looking at him.

Leaning forward, Remy licked a hungry trail across his firm abs, then nipped teasingly at the dark disc of a brown nipple. "You're so beautiful," she moaned.

"Not hardly," he scoffed, sounding endearingly embarrassed at her words.

"You are." The words came thickly from her throat, heavy with meaning. "You take my breath away, Hawkes."

"Then I'll give it back," he promised in a husky, rasping voice that sounded like sin, rubbing his lips into hers. "Damn, woman, you make me tremble," he groaned, breathing the words into her mouth as her lips parted in keen expectation. "Nothing and no one else has ever been able to do that to me. I don't mean it to sound arrogant or like I'm full of myself. I just want you to understand…to know how it is. You're…different, Remy. Every single thing about you."

His hips nudged her thighs wider apart, settling himself within their cradle, and one hand moved between her legs, his calloused palm cupping her pussy in a possessive hold, as if it belonged right there, in the palm of his hand. Remy sobbed out some kind of strangled, broken cry under her breath and a low, purely animal sound vibrated from his chest, sending goose bumps racing over her skin. "You're still so wet, honey. But I want you wetter. I want you soaking in your cum, Remy. Want it dripping down these soft little thighs, slicking over my skin when I fuck you, all sweet and slippery."

"*Yes*," she gasped, her neck arching, and he sank his teeth gently into the exposed column of her throat.

"But right now, I'm starving, Remy. Bet you'll never guess what I want to eat?" he drawled with a slow, feral smile that had a fresh surge of cream washing through her sex. She'd never been so wet, or turned on in her life, as she was by the idea of Jason going down on her.

Before she could even respond, he was moving down the shivering, soft line of her body, pressing a tender kiss to her collarbone, before opening his mouth over the more delicate tip of one nipple. He smiled around her flesh, the teasing scratch of his cheeks only adding to the delicious, pulling sensation as he suckled the swollen nub relentlessly, until she was writhing and cursing softly under her breath, her hips lifting to rub the wet pad of her pussy against his muscle-hard belly.

"You're so fuckin' hot," he grunted, taking a quick taste of the other nipple, leaving it shiny and wet while his head moved lower, teeth grazing her navel, breath teasing the tiny patch of curls she'd kept at the top, then lower, until he was suddenly licking a long, wickedly intimate line through the heavy seam of her smoothly waxed labia. Remy arched her back, arms flung wide, and shouted out a raw, keening cry of sound that echoed through the silent apartment, while the heat in her womb twisted with such a vicious, drumming force of hunger that she struggled not to scream.

And then his wicked mouth closed over the sensitive, pulsing nub of her clit and she *did* scream—a sharp, husky sound that ripped straight up from her chest—as he licked and suckled, the heavy growl breaking out of his mouth vibrating against her tender flesh.

"So fucking sweet," Jason snarled, twisting his head for a better angle, while his big hands caught her trembling legs and forced them out high and wide, leaving the plump, pink folds of her cunt open and at his mercy. He pulled back to savor the breathtaking sight, cock feeling as if it would simply bust through his zipper, and knew that he'd never get enough of this precious little piece of woman, craving it more every day of his life. "Perfect," he growled, burying his face back into the damp, silken heat. "Goddamn fucking perfect."

Her skin was like wet, pink silk, juices creamy and honey-thick, and his tongue eagerly stroked out to lick and explore, seeking the tender, puffy edge of her vulva and shoving deep, wanting to get as far inside her as he could. He fucked her with long, strong shafts of his tongue, swallowing her sweet juices down with a greedy, savage, carnal abandon that he'd never experienced with any other woman.

But then they'd never been his Remy—the one woman that he wanted for his very own. The only one who set him on fire and twisted him with need. The only one who could break his heart with little more than a smile.

The instant he felt her hands sift through his hair, holding onto him, he stroked deeper, his thumb lifting to rasp and tease over the thrumming pulse in her clit. Her thighs were shivering around his shoulders, her warm, sweet cunt spilling down his throat, and he knew it was time to push her over the edge…and then fuck her beautiful little brains out. God knew he couldn't wait much longer to get inside her or he'd end up blowing his first load in his jeans. And he didn't want to waste it. He wanted to spend the whole night filling her up with his cum, marking her as his own.

"Oh shit, Jason," she panted, twisting and quivering with the building wave of release, her body primed and ready to break. "I'm going to come."

"That's what I want," he growled against her lush, damp folds. "I want to taste it. Feel it on my tongue. Do it, Remy. Come in my mouth, angel."

"No," she moaned, writhing beneath him, instinctively struggling against the intensity of it. "I can't."

"Hell yes, you can. Right here." He tweaked her clit with his fingers, making her shudder and gasp. "I'm going to suck right here. And you won't be able to help yourself. You're gonna spill all over my face, sweetheart."

His head dipped back down, his strong tongue licking a sinful path from the pucker of her tiny asshole up to her swollen clit, and she broke, going rigid while a low, primitive cry broke free from her throat. Jason pressed his face deep, tongue digging deeper, eager to have the sweet wash of her cum in his mouth, needing it more than he needed his next breath. She came in a beautiful, sensual dance of rippling pleasure, her tender pussy milking his tongue, hot and wet with that delicious cream that he loved...and he lost it.

One moment he was pressing his lips to her clit again, her hip, her navel, tasting the pulse of desire on every inch of her damp skin, and then he was ripping at his jeans, damn near breaking the zipper in his desperation to get his cock free. She was still rippling with the fading tremors of her release when he pressed the fat, wet head of his dick to her tiny, creamy hole and shoved hard, his jaw grinding in bliss-filled ecstasy at the incredible feel of her squeezing down on him, her pussy sucking on him tighter than a hot little mouth.

He watched through narrowed eyes at the way her hole stretched wide to take him, wider and wider as the thick bulk of his cock pushed through the resisting flesh. She was pussy-pink and so damn pretty, her delicate skin a tender, provocative contrast against the long, vein-ridged, dark reddish-purple of his bulging rod as it just kept ruthlessly pushing in—slowly, so slowly, wanting to savor every second of this first penetration.

With a rumbling, animal growl, he pulled back out a little, loving the way the top of his cock was coated in her rich cream, wanting more of that sweet tasting juice in his mouth. But that could come later. First he had to get inside that fist-tight clench of her stunningly narrow passage and claim it as his own—forever. All the way inside. Balls-deep and saturated in heaven.

"Jesus, Jason. There's too much," she panted, gasping, blinking up at him in the soft glow of the lamp, her hair damp at her temples, shockingly red against the pearly creaminess of her skin.

"You can take it," he whispered in a low, scratchy drawl, voice husky with lust, thick with need. "You'll take my cock, sweetheart. No matter how tiny this sweet little pussy is, it was made for me, Remy. Made for me to fuck. To make it feel good. I just wanna make you feel good, honey. I wanna blow your fucking mind," he added in a deep, hard tone that evidenced the strain he was under from trying to go easy on her. "You just gotta let me in first. Just relax and let me in, Remy."

Dragging his eyes off the intoxicating sight of his hardened flesh drilling slowly into her primed little cunt, Jason looked back up at her beneath his brows, knowing he was on the verge of losing complete control.

He'd enjoyed sexual encounters with more women than he could remember—knew a woman's body inside and out—knew everything there was to know about sex and fucking and then some. But this was unlike anything he'd ever known before—anything he'd ever experienced. It was as if a thousand extrasensory sensors had been planted on his cock, drowning him in sensation, and a line connected the thick purple head of his dick straight to his heart, flooding him in a riot of raging emotions. Every shafting stroke that worked him into her brought a reciprocal tug, until he was grinding his jaw, his skin soaked in heat and sweat, afraid of where this was taking him — and what he'd do when he gave himself over to it.

Her eyes were wild with need — his own savage gaze reflected back at him in the clear black pools of her wide pupils. Jason placed one hand at the back of her neck, pulling her forward, forcing her head down at an angle that he knew would put her in the perfect position to watch and witness.

"Look at us, Remy. You're so sweet and pretty, and I'm about to fucking rip you apart."

A rough groan broke from her lips and he smiled above her at the evidence of hot, thick cream gushing against his cock as he worked the wide head in and out of the suctioning wetness of her tight, clenching slit. The lush, lusty responses of her body told him that she loved it as much as he did — needed it as much — craved it.

"Do you see what you do to me, Frosty?" he asked, his smile shifting to a wicked grin. "See how hard you've got me, honey, like a fucking I-beam?"

His hips jerked forward, shoving in more inches than he had before, and a strangled gasp broke from her chest, followed by a low moan as her cunt squeezed down on him so hard it was a delicious, bruising pain. "Yeah, you feel it, don't you, Remy?"

He moved the hand clutching at her hip to stroke the strained, drenched rim of her vulva, where she was so beautifully stretched from his brutal penetration, and rasped the rough tip of his finger across the delicate tissues. "So pretty, Remy. So sweet and soft and pink. I love looking at you. Love watching the way your pussy stretches open for me. The way it fights to be able to take my cock. The way it creams and trembles when I shove into you. You're the sexiest fucking thing I've ever seen. So goddamn beautiful you make my knees shake."

His hand moved up into her wild tumble of hair, twisting long strands into his fist as he pulled her face up to his. When she looked him in the eye, her breath panting against his face, he growled, "Before we're done here, you're gonna understand, Remy. I'm gonna give you every inch, more than you've ever had, harder than you've ever had it, and fuck your sweet little brains out 'til the only man you know is me. 'Til the only cock this hot little cunt remembers is mine. 'Til I'm the only one it craves."

Her lips parted, but whatever she would have said was swallowed by the eating kiss he forced into her mouth, as if he could draw her heart out from between her lips. "Hold on," he warned. "Take a deep breath, Remy, and don't let go of me."

Remy gulped a huge lungful of air that tasted like Jason, ridiculously aroused, her entire body turned into one throbbing, beating pulse of need and lust for this man who had stolen her heart so long ago. He released his hold on her hair, gripping her knees to pull them out wider, higher, and she fell back against the table on to her elbows.

Biting her lower lip, she looked down the length of her damp body, down to the open, drenched pink seam of her sex, and there was Jason Hawkes' savage cock, only half buried inside her, and already she was fuller than she could bear. Fuller than she'd ever been, but she loved it. Loved the press of his hot, sweat-slick skin. Loved the deeply tanned expanse of his muscle-defined chest, with its small, dark nipples, and the tawny line of hair arrowing down from his navel, until it pooled into a rich, dense patch at the base of his impossibly thick erection. To Remy, his cock was as beautiful as a perfect sin, with its fat tip that gleamed dark like a bruise and the ridged, heavy network of veins. She wanted to hold it in her hand, test its weight, feel it pulsing against her palm, so vital and strong. Wanted to lower her head and map its texture with her tongue, claim its taste and its dark sensual scent of musk and man for her own. Wanted to dip her tongue into that glimmering slit on the broad head and taste the pearly fluid glistening there. It was animal beautiful, savage and raw in its power, and she craved it with a hunger that nearly undid her.

"Jason," she groaned, feeling desperate and on edge, her body hurting with its need, until the only thing she knew was that she had to have more. Had to have everything. "Please," she panted, her voice throaty and low. "I need you—all of you. God, Jason, *please*," she cried out, her hips lifting for more—her body screaming for it. She looked up at him, unable to find the precise words for what she needed and he smiled, his fingers biting tightly into her skin, holding her in place for his short, teasing strokes that were driving her mad. "Damn it," she growled, as he began pulling back again, having only given her the top portion of his cock, "don't you dare leave me!"

Jason groaned a deep, vicious sound of emotion, his words choppy and raw as he rumbled, "I'm right here, Remy. Trust me, honey, not even the devil himself could drag me away." Then he hammered his hips forward, shoving the brutal length of his shaft deeper into her sweet, clenching depths, feeling the hot cream coat him, the strong muscles rippling around him as she tried to suck him even deeper. It was perfect and Jason didn't know how long he was going to be able to hold it, but he didn't want it to fucking end.

"Do you have any idea what I would've done to have you these past seven years?" he grated out of a dry throat. "Do you know what hell it's been trying to stay away, let you have the life you deserved? Trying to keep my hands off of you, instead of claiming you as my own, when I *knew* you fucking belonged to me."

She shook her head and he took a deep, shuddering breath, then crammed every inch straight into her tiny hole with a thick, hot, scraping thrust that plunged him in to the broad root, his balls crammed up tight against her ass. She stiffened from the brutal, savage invasion and he knew everything he felt was right there in his wild, primitive stare, burning through for her to see…and she shut her eyes, shutting him out.

"No, goddamn it!" he roared, any semblance of his cool, calm, legendary control so far gone he didn't know if he'd ever get it back. All he knew was that he was fighting for his life here and they'd have to kill him before he gave in and let her walk away. From him and their future. From his love. "Don't you dare fucking shut me out. You asked for all of it and that means everything, Remy. Not just my goddamn body. Open your eyes."

She shook her head again and he leaned close, nuzzling the side of her neck, his tongue flicking out to taste the need on her skin. "I won't let you hide from me," he promised in a husky rumble, his voice as dark as sin. His mouth moved higher, teeth biting gently into the tender flesh of her lobe, her sweet cunt tremoring around his cock, killing him with the jaw-grinding pleasure. "And I sure as hell won't let you hide from what's happening here between us."

His head lifted, one hand moving to her face, and his thumb caressed the soft skin of her cheek, trailing to the tender vulnerability of her throat, seeking and finding her drumming pulse. His hips pulled slowly back, then thrust forward again with a thick, driving stroke that fed the massive bulk of his cock into the tight clench of her pussy, forcing it in, and he said, "Open your eyes and look at me, Remy. *Now.*"

Remy felt the rough pad of his thumb press against her pulse as it danced out a frantic cadence of suspense, of need…and followed his command, helpless to deny him. He stared down at her, gaze heavy with passion and lust, the whiskey-rich brown of his eyes smoldering with something so overpowering, she felt lost in it.

"Your mind doesn't fear me, Remy, because you know I'd rather die than hurt you. It's that prickly little heart you keep hidden from me that's scared shitless."

"Don't," she moaned, her voice thick with both pleasure and fear, body jolting to his strong, plunging strokes.

"I won't let you run away from me, sweetheart," he said in a low, black magic voice.

His hot lips rubbed across her cheek, his scratchy jaw rasping her chin, and then his mouth was eating into hers, his wickedly talented tongue teaching her things she'd never realized could be found in a man's mouth.

He wrapped her into the hot, protective hold of his arms and pressed deep, thrusting into her, cramming her full of all those incredibly long, deliciously thick inches until he was pressing against the mouth of her womb. The long, hard, sinewy length of his arms—roped with muscle, scarred, glowing a deep, dark golden brown in the lamplight—held her close, holding her beneath him as he drew out then pressed deep, surrounding her, filling her, steeping her in his male heat and the hungry, searing reality of his possession. She felt vibrantly alive, as if her body were being charged from within, her cells energized with the jolting force of electricity, something inside her unfurling to life that was brilliant and bright and blinding.

"Remy," he cried out, sobbing into her mouth with a masculine, utterly male, entirely primitive shout of demand as his mouth took hers in a savage, blistering kiss. His body pounded her against the table until it went driving into the wall with a roaring groan of wood against plaster and still he didn't relent. He slammed into her harder, faster, their skin going hot and slick, and Remy went crashing over the edge, arching and screaming, sobbing into his kiss.

Jason swallowed the sounds of her release down with a growling cry of victory, then threw back his head as a triumphant, snarling shout of ultimate satisfaction rumbled up from his chest, and he followed her over. It was the most intense, shattering, incredible climax that he'd ever experienced, rolling in a thick, voluptuous wave of ecstasy through his rigid shaft—hot, pulsing spurts of cum jerking deep into the hot, wet clench of her body, while his dick nearly turned him inside out.

His head fell into the hollow of her shoulder, mouth open as he breathed a ragged tempo against her hot skin, and Remy clutched at him with desperate, needy hands, never wanting to let him go, wondering with a wry shake of her head how she could have ever thought to resist him. God, she must have been mad. He was like water, air, food—something she had been starved for since the moment she'd met him. A necessity for life that without which she would go mad.

Had she thought this night was hell? No, now she knew better. This was as close to heaven as she'd ever been and, if she were honest with herself, she'd admit that the man holding her so securely in his strong, protective arms irrevocably owned her heart.

It had been his all along.

Chapter Four

Two days later, Jason found himself pulling into the crowded parking lot of Piedmont Community College, while Remy sat cool and calm in the passenger's seat. Though many things still remained unresolved between them, one thing was for damn certain—the last two days had been the best forty-eight hours of his life.

Staying at her apartment, they'd made love so many times his dick felt raw and basically tuned the rest of the world out. Since she worked from home and had just finished her latest project for a new client, Remy had simply let her phone ring until her automatic voicemail picked up. And knowing work could make do without him for a few days, he'd left a message at the office, letting Connor know he was taking some long overdue personal time. Then he'd turned his pager and cell phone off.

They'd explored each other's bodies from bottom to top, laughed and shouted out their pleasure until their throats were sore and talked about everything, except the two most important things on his mind—their past and their future. He wanted that talk more with every second that ticked by, but at the moment, he was more concerned about the *now*.

Remy directed him to the Art complex at the back of the school and he pulled into a space toward the far side of the crowded lot, on the opposite side of the building from where she normally parked.

"Your hands are freezing," he rumbled in a low voice as he reached over the center console and wrapped her slender fingers in his big grip.

"Ice Queen strikes again, huh?" She smiled, trying for a laugh that fell sadly flat as he released her hand to flick on the heat.

"Honey, there isn't a goddamn thing cold about you."

"Thanks," she whispered, watching a group of students, backpacks slung over their shoulders, scuffle their way to class.

"I don't want you getting out of this car until we know exactly what's going on here, but you're not going to change your mind, are you?"

She shook her head, the long, thick scarlet silk of her hair tumbling about her shoulders, making him just want to bury his face in the fragrant mass. "Ah hell, then I guess we're going. I can't say no to you. It's pathetic."

Remy felt her shoulders shake with silent laughter, loving him even more than she already did for the understanding she could see there in his beautiful gaze as she turned her head to look at him. The dark, masculine beauty of his face took her breath away, so ruggedly handsome in the pale glow streaming down from the parking lot lights as the sun made its final dip into the distant horizon. "I don't think it's pathetic. I think it's sweet."

"You would," he snorted, shaking his head, then shoving the still shower-damp blond streaks off his forehead. "You're not the one who's become a poor pitiful wreck of a man," he muttered, sounding adorably disgusted with himself.

"Ohhh, poor baby," she crooned, reaching behind her seat for her backpack.

"Yeah, well, I plan on doing everything in my power to redeem my manly image when we get home and I get your sweet little ass back in bed."

Her backpack landed on top of her jeans-covered thighs with a dull thud, brow arching as she reached for the door. "I do so hope you'll be *up* for the challenge."

"Sweetheart, I already am," he said with a hard smile, but beneath the smile Remy could see his concern evidenced in the warm depths of that narrow golden-brown stare, the corners of his eyes crinkling, revealing the character lines that she loved.

"Jason, you really shouldn't worry. I told you, it's just a prank. Nothing's going to happen."

"I can't help it," he muttered, reaching over to recapture her hand. His fingers opened, and with a sharp little pain in his heart, he gazed at her slender hand lying within his palm. So fragile…delicate. "I'm in love with you," he rasped out of a dry throat. His gaze lifted, catching at the bright, wide-eyed look of surprise on her face. "Asking me not to worry about you is like asking me not to breathe, Remy."

"What?" she gasped, pressing her hands to her chest. Her voice was so small that he would have missed it if he hadn't been looking at her mouth.

"You heard me," he laughed in a low rumble, the deep sound filling the musky-scented leather interior of the SUV.

Leaning over the console, he pressed a soft kiss against the sweet heat of her mouth, then forced himself back to his side of the car before he got carried away and she blamed him for being late. "We'll talk about it tonight, honey, but if you don't get going, you're gonna miss the start."

Her eyes flashed to the blinking digits of the digital clock on the wide dash. "Shit, I gotta go," she muttered, still looking stunned, and turned to reach for her door handle, then turned back and threw herself over the console. She plastered her mouth against his with a tender, eager yearning that damn near broke his heart while it made his dick go thick and his mind go fuzzy. He was just reaching for her waist, ready to pull her into his lap, the fucking class be damned, when she pulled away, gifting another tempting kiss to his stubble-covered chin. Then she flashed that precious smile that always made his belly do that funny little free fall, his heart skip a beat, and climbed out of the Jeep, rushing off through the diagonal lines of parked cars.

Jason rubbed at his chest for a moment, almost afraid to look too closely at how damn good he felt, then reached back for his denim jacket, since he was wearing his shoulder holster, turned off the engine and climbed out.

Though he'd wanted to go to class with her and keep his eyes on her the entire time, they'd finally agreed on the current plan. Remy would go by herself and he'd watch from the other lot, hoping to catch sight of someone looking for her car. And the car would be there, since they'd called the garage that morning and given Billy instructions to drop it off in that particular lot, new alternator and all. It wasn't much of a plan, but then they didn't have a whole hell of a lot to go on. All they had were the stupid notes, and because Remy still believed there was going to be some kind of harmless explanation, she'd argued against doing anything more. She didn't want him following her, scaring off whoever it was before they caught them, and she didn't want him snooping into everyone's privacy, or running checks on them either. Stubborn woman had his hands tied, and so here he was, snooping around in the dark like fucking Sherlock Holmes.

Shit, if Connor could see him, he'd laugh his know-it-all ass off.

Watching her make her way through the long lot, his eyes sharp, unwilling to take his attention away until he'd seen her make it safely into the classroom, Jason leaned his ass against the hood of the Cherokee and reached for the crumpled packet of cigarettes in his jacket's front pocket. He didn't smoke often, just if the occasion called for it, and god knew this one did.

He'd told her he loved her—first damn time in his life he'd ever said those three little words to a woman who wasn't his mother—and she hadn't given him the same words in return.

Fuck.

He lost himself in thought for a moment, until his ass went cold against the Jeep's hood, the cigarette pinched between his thumb and forefinger about to singe his numb fingers, and all he wanted was to go running after the headstrong little fireball and demand she tell him how she felt.

Fuck. Fuck. Fuck.

With another low, foul curse on his lips, Jason set off on foot, his steps silent and smooth as he stuck to the edges of the lot, a thick, towering grove of pines on his left and the dimly lit parking area to his right. His sneaker-covered feet—courtesy of the packed duffel he always kept in his Jeep for emergency assignments—silenced his footsteps against the grainy asphalt, so that no one could hear his approach. The night was cool and brisk, the ruffling wind carrying the distant sounds of the countryside to the modern landscape of the college. As he made his way around the wide, rectangular Art complex— situated at the back of the campus, with three sides surrounded by parking lots and one facing a grassy quad that also held the auditorium, cafeteria and library—his eyes remained alert. Watchful. Focused.

But his mind kept drifting back to that morning.

He'd awakened in a sweet, tangled twist with Remy atop the wrecked bedding that smelled intimately of their loving, knowing he'd dreamed again. The same damn dream of that first kiss that had been haunting him for the past seven years. The memory, as it hovered on the edges of his consciousness, was bittersweet and filled with regret.

If you'd told him seven years ago that he'd ever be waking up one day with Remy wrapped around him, he never would have believed it. Not because he wouldn't have wanted it, but because she'd been so angry and hurt when he'd turned her away that night.

He remembered all of it in vivid, wrenching detail. The pain on her delicate face when he'd pulled away from her. The ache that had followed him through the years as he'd struggled against the need to make her his, even though he knew she deserved better than he could give her. His life had been dangerous, hell, it still was, but at least now he had stability. A base. He could come home to her every night, do everything in his power to make her happy. And that's what he wanted more than anything — to make Remy happy.

He'd turned to look at her that morning, the soft, hazy shafts of sunlight falling over her sleep-soft features, and vowed that he would. Come hell or high water, this thing wasn't going to end like it had before, because god only knew he'd handled it all wrong.

He'd been in a bar fight that night, of all things, and ended up with a beer bottle stabbed in his ass, which was where the jagged wound had come from. Connor had stitched it up himself, while he was bent over the dining room table in the condo Connor shared with Remy while she was going to school. She'd refused to leave while Connor fixed him up, helping with what she could, her eyes wide and watchful at the sight of his naked backside. It'd have been impossible not to get a boner from the way she'd stared at him over her brother's shoulder, if he hadn't been in so much fucking pain.

He'd been staying with them during the short leave that he and Connor had taken and it was the pain that had brought him down to the kitchen for more Tylenol later that night, after everyone had headed to bed. And there she'd been, standing at the back door in a thin nightshirt that barely reached her knees, her soft breasts pressed against the delicate fabric, watching the moon with a faraway, dreamy expression on her young face that had captivated him. He'd wanted her for a long time. Hell, he'd had feelings for her that went far beyond friendship or lust, but she was his best friend's little sister and his life had hardly been the kind to offer to a young woman. And still, he'd been unable to turn around and take his ass back to the spare bedroom.

Instead, he'd walked to her and she'd turned to look at him, a thousand different emotions swimming through the liquid green of her eyes. He'd known in that moment that this woman belonged to him. Felt it with every fiber of his being.

"One of us needs to go back upstairs," he'd rumbled, his rough voice a rasping sound slashing across the heavy silence of the night.

"Why?" she'd asked in a breathless rush, her nipples teasing against her nightgown, making his mouth water and his dick ache.

"Because if we don't," he'd softly growled, "one of us is going to end up doing something that you'll regret—that gets my ass killed."

"You mean Connor? I'm not a child," she'd argued, wetting her mouth. "I'm nineteen."

"Don't remind me," he'd muttered and she'd jerked as if he'd slapped her.

Then she'd swallowed and asked, "Why did you get into a fight with those jerks at that bar? Connor told me what happened after you went upstairs. One of them was Brett Harper's uncle, wasn't he?"

"Just forget about it, Remy." He'd shrugged, trying like hell not to stare at the swollen tips of her breasts as they'd pressed harder against the thin cloth in a blatant sign of arousal. "It isn't important," he'd all but croaked, sounding like he'd swallowed a fucking frog.

Her back had gone straight, head high as she'd faced him down like a regal queen. "It is to me. Brett Harper is a conceited pig and so are all his buddies. I want to know what his uncle said to make you mad enough to get into a fight with him."

"Just some things I didn't like, okay? End of story." And for years after that little episode, he'd taken a shitload from Connor and the rest of the guys. He'd been trained to take down a roomful of men in hand-to-hand combat, and yet, he'd had his ass cut by some drunken beer-bellied asshole in a brawl because he'd let his goddamn temper get the better of him.

"Oh, let me guess," she'd laughed in a low, bitter tone. "Something about me being a cold fish? The Ice Queen of Cardell College?"

"Forget about it," he'd growled, hating to hear her say those things. "Harper and his tagalongs are just jealous little shits. Probably pissed that you don't put out for all of them. And you don't, do you?"

He hadn't known where in the hell the question had come from, but there it was, and there'd been no taking it back.

"No." Then she'd taken a step closer to him and his cock had jerked in his pants just from the scent of her skin and her hair...the dark, heavy look of want in her eyes. "I don't. They don't tempt me."

"And do I tempt you, beautiful Remy?" He'd laughed, trying to be an ass, hoping like hell he'd have the strength to leave her alone or she'd tell him to fuck off. "Come on, Frosty, you can trust me. I won't tell Connor your dirty little secret."

"Why are trying to be a jerk?" she'd said in a low, hurt voice, turning to leave, but he'd reached out and grabbed hold of her arm.

"So eager to escape me, honey?" He should have let her go, but instead, he'd taken a step closer to her and growled out a demanding, "I want an answer, Remy. Do I tempt you?"

Her whispered "Yes" had sliced into his desire-thick system like a sword, breaking him down, and the next thing he'd known he was kissing her. He'd made a choked sound of frustration, grabbed her around her slim waist, pulling her into the hard, hunger-crazed length of his body, and captured her mouth.

It'd been the hardest thing he'd ever done in his life—clawing to maintain his control—as she'd surrendered the lush, sweet promise of her mouth to his. She'd been so perfectly untutored, so obviously innocent that he'd been terrified of scaring the hell out of her. And so he'd choked on his own hunger, drinking in the addictive taste of hers. Shy passes of her lips, her sudden jolt when he'd slipped his tongue gently into her mouth, tasting her with slow, torturous strokes that had somehow been painfully erotic. A slow, meaningful, tender tasting, where he'd been able to take in every detail, every flavor and texture and breath, and it had scarred him for life. Ruined him for other women. And stolen his heart. Her smiles and her laughter, those shimmering green eyes and that faunlike beauty that he'd known was going to mature into the kind of sensuality that would be hell on a man, had dented his defenses until they'd crumbled one by one.

"God help us," he'd grated into the sleek, delicious well of her mouth. She'd moaned a sound of pure carnal abandon, pressed her lithe, young body against him, and the knot in his cock had thickened into a primal, painful ache. She'd tasted as if she'd belonged to him—tasted like *his*. Fresh and pure, and yet, like something forbidden—something meant to be worshipped from afar—and he'd known it was wrong. Lust had surged hard and savagely through his blood. He'd used every ounce of his training to keep from losing control and pulling her to the kitchen floor, eating at her mouth like an animal while he fucked her precious little pussy into one screaming orgasm after another.

He'd fought it, but then he'd touched her tummy, just with the stroking backs of his knuckles, and she'd sobbed out a raw, hungry kind of sound into his mouth that had nearly shattered him. The next thing he'd known, he'd had one hand on her ass and the other pressing between her legs, the thin barriers of her nightshirt and panties between them, and even then he had still felt the slick, sweet heat of her cunt. She'd been soaking, hot and ready, and he'd wanted to fuck her so damn badly that he hadn't trusted himself to keep touching her…kissing her. If he hadn't pulled back when he did, he'd have had her over that table, his dick buried up inside her sweet depths, and there wouldn't have been a force in hell that could have stopped him.

And her life would have been ruined. Hell, what had he had to offer her? Months spent alone, worrying about him, while he risked his life on the other side of the world, so deep into work that he wouldn't have even been able to contact her for weeks at a time. No, he hadn't been able to do that to her.

He'd panicked, knowing he wouldn't be able to control himself if he touched her a single moment longer, so he'd pushed her back with his hands at her shoulders and stepped away. "No, damn it," he'd grunted. "This isn't going to happen."

She'd looked at him with big, bruised eyes, rolling her lips inward as a fat tear had caught and hung suspended from the tips of her thick lashes. "Why? Is it…is it because I really am cold?"

"Cold?" he'd grunted, pushing his hands through his short hair in furious frustration. "Not fucking hardly. But this isn't right. Get out of here, Remy, now, before we both regret it."

And so she'd left him, choking on tears as she'd run from the room.

* * * * *

With a frustrated snarl, Jason tossed the butt of his cigarette on the ground, stamping it out in the same way he wished he could do to that goddamn memory, and reached for another. He'd just lit the slender column, drawing a long, satisfying drag in from the side of his mouth, exhaling a spiraling plume of smoke through his nostrils when the door to her classroom opened. Taking another long drag, he waited while students filed out for one of the quick breaks Remy had told him they would take. It was easy to spot her as she walked with a small group to the cafeteria, her red hair catching his gaze like a beacon in the dark of night. The corners of his mouth twitched with a grin when she looked over her shoulder toward the lot three times, trying but failing to see him. Then a lone, familiar-looking figure dressed in loose sweats walked out of the class, his sun-bleached hair hanging long and loose around his shoulders, and Jason knew instantly who it was. He watched through narrowed eyes as the blond headed around the corner, in the same direction that Remy had just taken.

Jason slipped silently out of the shadows, finding himself reacting on pure, jealous instinct at the thought of the guy prowling after her. All it took was five seconds and he had the pretty-faced beach boy plastered against the side of the building, one arm twisted up behind his back, before the guy even had the time to blink. Squeezing his fist around the model's wrist, he leaned down and muttered in his ear, "Just where the fuck do you think you're going, Jon?"

"Shibby! How the hell do you know my name, dude?" Jon gasped, yelping when Jason twisted his arm higher, his thick fingers biting into the sensory centers that he knew would cause the most pain.

"Uh-uh. I ask the questions here, got it? What the fuck are you doing sneaking off after Remy Frost?"

"Remy?" the guy grunted as Jason added a bit more pressure.

"Yeah. You know, that gorgeous little redhead you stare at during class, until it's enough to make her skin crawl, you sniveling little shit."

"You better chill, brah! No reason to go aggro on me. I only stare at her because she's the most bangin' Emma in there—after that boglius little Betty with the bodacious ta— Ouch, man!" he muttered, panting, while Jason increased the pressure on his wrist. "I swear, dude…I just didn't want everyone in there knowing how hard I've nose-dived for Miss Hut—"

"Bangin' Emma?" Jason snarled, shaking his head as if to clear it. Ah hell, he was starting to comprehend just what Remy meant about understanding the guy. It sounded like English…but his brain was having trouble making head or tails of it. "Boglius little Betty? What the fuck are you talking about?"

"My sunshine girl with the killer baby blues," Jon gritted through his teeth. "She's like a —"

The pain-garbled words were suddenly cut off as two gangly young men, both looking to be in their early twenties, one with shocking pink hair and the other with curly, soft brown locks that gave him the appearance of a cherub, came running over. "Hey, did we hear someone say Remy?" Pinky gasped, out of breath, while Cherub wheezed, "Yeah? We've been looking all over the school for her. Do you know where we can find her?"

Jason turned a sharp, narrow stare on them and suddenly they both went wide-eyed, backing a slow step away, as if only just realizing what they were seeing.

"What the hell do you two want with Remy?" he asked in a low, hard voice that demanded an answer, while Jon shouted, "Make this asshole let me go. Get help! He's totally flailing on me and I've got no barnie with the dude!"

Pinky mumbled "Uhh…" while Cherub stared down at his Converse-covered feet, then at the dark sky, then at Pinky, his soft green eyes looking anywhere but at Jason and the struggling model, while he swallowed so hard you could see his throat working.

When it became obvious that they'd both been stunned into silence, Jason muttered, "Hell, don't move," then turned his attention back to Jon.

"You've got two seconds to explain to me what those fucking freaky ass little notes are about, or you're not going to like what I do to that pretty face of yours. And let's try it in English this time."

"Notes?" Jon grunted. "Kiff, man? What the hell are you talking about?"

"Don't play stupid with me, you little shit."

"As if," Jon groaned, his voice tight with strain. "Listen, man, I don't know anything about any notes. This is all some kinda killabrenda! I'm telling you the truth! The only reason I stare at Remy is so that no one will realize how badly I've tubed for Miss Hutchins!"

"Who?"

"The instructor," Jon muttered, trying to look at Jason over his shoulder. "The school had some kind of whacked harassment case last year between a model and one of the professors. So now they've become majorly paranoid. I didn't want to get that pretty little Betty into any trouble just because the sight of her makes me feel like I'm pulling a three-sixty on the face of a killer wave. You know what I mean, brah. Like I'm executing some major tunnel love."

"Oh shit, I don't fucking believe this," Jason growled, and yet, his gut was buying it. With a disgusted growl at the whole goddamn situation, he shoved Jon away and crossed his arms over his chest before he gave in to the urge to punch someone. "So you mean to tell me that you don't know anything about the notes warning her to stay away from you? And you don't have a crush on Remy?"

"Hell no, dude! We've got no beef, man. This is bogus. I don't even know what notes you're talking about," Jon argued, rubbing his sore arm as he took three stumbling steps away. "No way would I thrash the bitchin', totally boss feeling of transcendental connection, like we're one with Mother Ocean, I feel for my wickedly sweet little crippler chick. Just the sight of that blonde hair and those sweet blue eyes messes with my head...makes me feel totally amped. Like I'm totally carving, man. Without a doubt, it's da kine, but it makes me feel like I'm gonna pull a total kali, too. Like I'm on a major cruncher. She's got killer class and I'm out of my element, brah, feeling like I've just been totally launched. Like I've maytagged big time. Caught up in a spin cycle. Like I'm in orbitzville. Like I've—"

"Oh Christ," Jason grunted, cutting off the seemingly endless spiral of nonsense, while Pinky and Cherub both choked on sudden mouthfuls of laughter. "Where in the hell did you learn to talk like that?"

"Like what?" Jon asked, blinking his long, sun-bleached lashes.

"Like a bad surf movie on acid," Jason muttered.

"I can't help it," the young man gritted through his immaculately white teeth, nearly blinding the three sets of eyes watching him. "I embrace the waves, man, and this love thing is wickedly doke. She makes my head spin, man, and it's epically danza. Supremely nar nar. Inspiring, dude. You should try it sometime."

Oh, Jason was feeling inspired alright. Inspired enough to thump Jon the Dude on his pretty boy backside. Turning to Pinky and Cherub, he demanded, "And just what the hell do you two want with Remy?"

"What do *you* want with Remy?" Pinky surprisingly demanded right back, obviously finding a little backbone.

Jason took an intimidating step forward, wondering how this whole situation had become so friggin' bizarre. "*I'm* her boyfriend."

"Remy doesn't have a boyfriend," Cherub argued, feeling brave now and trying to stare him down.

Jason let his meanest smile spread slowly across his mouth. "She does now."

"Yeah?" Pinky asked, standing a little straighter as his gaze flicked over Jason's right shoulder, back toward the parking lot. "Then why don't we ask her?"

Jason swung around, and sure enough, there was Remy walking toward him, dragging a protesting, middle-aged woman behind her. He narrowed his eyes as he tried to see her better. Then a pale beam from an overhead parking light illuminated her face, aided by the soft glow spilling down from the silvery moon, and his heart nearly stopped.

"Why the fuck are you bleeding?" he roared, ready to take someone apart with his bare hands, nearly losing it at the sight of her bloody lip.

"She refused to come with me," Remy said calmly, though a bit out of breath as she reached his side. Then with a smug smile, she added, "So I insisted."

"Who the hell is she?" he demanded, shooting a quick look at the frowning woman who had the makings of a fierce black eye coming on.

"Miss Hutchins," Remy replied, while her green eyes shone with laughter. "And I snuck out of the cafeteria and into the parking lot just in time to catch her trying to slip a note on my car, while you were busy terrorizing these three."

"It was *her*?" Jason shook his head, feeling as he'd been poleaxed between the eyes, unable to keep the shock out of his voice. Miss Hutchins appeared to be somewhere in her forties, with light gold hair and big round eyes the color of cornflowers. Overall, she was quite a looker, though a bit too buttoned-up. She had the schoolmarm image down to a T, but Jon was all starry-eyed the moment Remy came walking up, dragging the reluctant, red-faced instructor behind her.

"I told you it wasn't me," Jon grumbled as he stared intently at Miss Hutchins. "So you can stop giving me the stink eye, man. And just so ya know, I think this is totally bogus. No way could it have been this fine little Betty. She's too nectar...too—"

"Oh, for the love of god, put a sock in it," Cherub mumbled, while Miss Hutchins flushed a deep crimson at Jon's words, her mouth forming a small O of stunned surprise.

Jon cut a glowering look at the snickering duo of Pinky and Cherub. "Why don't you two go get bent? This is so waxed. I'm tellin' you, someone so hella soft and dank could never—"

"Honestly, Jon, listen to the guy and put a sock in it or I'm going to shoot you just to shut you up!" Jason grunted. The instructor at Remy's side gasped, trying to twist out of her hold, but Remy wasn't letting go.

"And you had better explain yourself right now, young lady," he demanded in his deepest, I-want-answers-this-very-second voice.

"Explain myself?" Remy gasped, looking like he'd just slapped her with a fish. "Young lady?" she snarled, shooting daggers at him.

"Yeah, you were supposed to be hanging out with your classmates, not snooping around out here."

"Well, it's a good thing I was," she huffed, raising her chin to that stubborn angle that he loved, "or you'd have missed her while you were busy beating up on Jon!"

"I'm not gonna hurt him, honey. I'm just gonna rough him up a bit," he delivered in a slow, sweet drawl, as if he were looking forward to it…even though he was only teasing.

Of course, his words sent Miss Hutchins into a flying panic.

"*Noooo!*" she cried, tearing out of Remy's grip to throw herself in front of the pretty-faced model, her bountiful chest still swinging well after her body had stopped, looking as if her bosom would sway away from her, never to return. "Don't you dare lay a hand on him, you…you…macho-headed bully!" she screeched.

"It's hard to believe," Remy laughed, giving a wry shake of her head, "but she wants him. Um, his interesting vernacular and all."

"Jon?" he muttered, unable to keep the disbelief out of his voice. "Are you telling me that all of this was really just because she has a thing for the ass guy?"

"You're the ass guy," Remy snickered, which had the small crowd looking at him with expressions that ranged from shock to intrigue, to suppressed laughter. "But yeah, it was all about Jon. Miss Hutchins just 'fessed up to leaving the notes when I'd go into the cafeteria to get a soda during break. Said she didn't think she could ever have him for her own, but it still worried her that he had some kind of crush on me and that I'd decide to make a go for him. She just wanted me to stay away from the guy."

"And you already got all of this out of her?"

Remy lifted her shoulder in the same cocky movement he'd seen her brother use a million times and he felt a slow grin spreading across his face.

"And you gave her the black eye, too?"

"Yeah, but only after she bloodied my lip trying to run away. I think I scared the hell out of her when I snuck up behind her and caught her red-handed slipping another one of those notes under my windshield wiper."

"Damn, honey, you really are a little badass, aren't you?" he laughed, voice full of pride.

Remy winked at him. "I tried to tell you I could take care of myself."

"Yeah, I guess you did," he rumbled, wanting to pull her into his arms and kiss her silly. He would have, too, if Jon hadn't started spouting out enough transcendental surf slang to fill the Pacific Ocean, apparently trying to convince the older Miss Hutchins that he didn't have a crush on Remy and didn't care about their stupid age difference, swearing that he'd always think she was a major Betty.

"There was no need to leave any notes, Miss H," Jon said, shaking his head, his sun-bleached locks falling softly around the perfect features of his face. "You should have just talked to me. I'm not sweet on Remy. I only stared at her because looking at you makes me feel like I'm on a major railer and I didn't want to land you in a gnarly barnie with the school. Plus," he added with a sheepish grin, "I was worried those killer baby blues of yours might have me sporting a harpoon in front of the whole class if I wasn't care—"

"Jon, shut up," Jason muttered, pinching the bridge of his nose, a headache pounding behind his eyeballs that made him want to snarl...only he was *already* snarling again. Shit.

Looking over at the blinking, owl-eyed instructor, he tried to find a measure of calm and grated out, "Miss Hutch—"

"Betty," she said in a soft, lyrical voice as she turned to look at him.

"What?" Jason grunted, half-afraid she was going to start drowning him in that nonsensical surfer slang too. Damn, his freaking head was going to explode!

"My name is Betty," Miss Hutchins murmured, shooting quick, hunger-filled looks at Jon, where he stood right at her side.

"See," Jon smiled. "She's Betty...and she's *a Betty*. It's so hella cool. It's—"

"Not. Another. Word," Jason bit out through his teeth, staring the surfer dude down until the guy held up his hands in surrender.

"Kiff?" Jon said with a wide grin, his hungry gaze catching again and again on Miss Hutchins' flushed face. "Whatever, brah. Like I said, no barnie, man."

Taking a deep breath, Jason tried not to lose his grip on that scant amount of patience he'd managed to claw onto. "Look, Betty, I'm trying to make sense out of this and god knows that's more difficult tonight than it should be. Now—"

"I'm sorry," the shy blonde cut in, her voice a low, breathless rush of anxiety as her big blue eyes flickered between him and Remy. "I didn't mean to worry Remy," she mumbled, gnawing on the corner of her bottom lip as she wrung her hands together. "I just wanted her to stay away from him and I couldn't think of any other way to handle it, without giving away how I feel. I know the notes were childish, but they were all I could think of."

"If you…er, are interested," and he tried not to choke on the idea, "in Jon here, then why didn't you just talk to him? Let him know."

"I wanted to tell him," she said in a low, miserable tone, turning a dull shade of red. "I couldn't care less what the school thought, but I just didn't think…" she stammered, her turbulent gaze casting quick, hungry looks at Jon, as if she couldn't keep her eyes off him. "I mean he's so beautiful, and I'm so much older than he is, and it's not like he would have…at least I didn't think, but—"

"Sweet Mother Ocean," Jon said with a dazzling smile, wrapping his arms around her and pulling her flush against his long, lean body, while a startled, pleasure-filled gasp escaped her lips. "You should have just told me you're sweet on me, Betty. I think it's da kine. Da mamie. Majorly dunza, my bangin' little Emma."

"Why *does* he talk like that?" Pinky asked, staring at the cooing couple as if they'd grown second heads.

Remy shook with silent laughter and smiled as Jon called the blushing woman the totally wooka, tropical summer breeze of his heart. "Sounds like he's been watching too much *Bill and Ted's Excellent Adventure*," she snickered. "Or maybe *Point Break*."

"You've actually watched those movies?" Jason snorted, shooting her a disbelieving look.

"*Hello*," Remy laughed, "they have Keanu Reeves in them. You bet your 'bodacious' backside I've watched them."

Jason scowled at the way she all but purred Keanu's name, then jerked his chin at Pinky and Cherub. "And just who in the hell are these two?"

"This is Roger and Carson," Remy said with a smile, then, as if suddenly realizing they weren't supposed to be there, she scrunched her nose at them and said, "What are you guys doing here, anyway?"

"We were worried about you," Carson muttered, "and we knew you had class tonight."

"Yeah, I've been leaving messages and you never called me back," Roger grumbled, flipping his hot pink hair back from his forehead with an angry toss of his head as he cut a glaring look at him that made Jason want to smile. He made two of the guy, but Remy's friend was more than ready to take him on if she needed the help, and damn but if it didn't make him like the runt. "Like Carson said, we were worried."

"Yeah, and I knocked on your front door for thirty minutes yesterday morning," Carson muttered, not wanting to be left out, "but no one came to the door."

Jason tried to remember if they'd heard knocking and ignored it, then decided that they'd probably been fucking in the shower when the kid came by and just didn't hear. With a slow, feral smile spreading across his mouth at the memory, he said, "We were —"

"Probably out," Remy cut in, shooting him a glaring warning, while she used her sleeve to dab at her bleeding lip.

Jason shook his head and let his smile widen, deciding to tease her a bit for not trusting him. He'd only been going to say "Busy". It's not like he was going to announce to the world that they'd spent the entire time fucking like bunnies. "I don't know that I'd say out, honey. I think in would be better. Yeah, definitely deep in —"

"Jason, another word out of you," she warned, narrowing her eyes to mere slits, "and you won't be *in* anywhere, you get it?"

He opened his mouth, but both Roger and Carson started in again, and suddenly his fucking head was spinning with the nonstop chatter as her friends talked over one another and Remy tried unsuccessfully to get a word in edgewise. Then Jon started spouting out more of his confusing surf babble and suddenly all Jason wanted to do was walk over to the wall and start banging his damn head against it. For a brief moment he considered shooting his gun into the air, then thought better of it. What went up had to come back down, and with the way this bizarre night was going, he'd end up shooting himself in the goddamn foot.

Then the pretty-faced surfer went down on his knees, professing his "righteous" feelings for Miss Hutchins, while the flushed blonde teetered between smiling beatifically at the young man's attentions and sheepishly apologizing to Remy for her embarrassing jealousy, while Carson bugged her about going to the exhibit with him and Roger whined about her missing their lunch date the day before. Finally, when he couldn't take it a second longer, Jason shouted, "Enough!"

Everyone went silent, staring at him with wide, worried eyes.

"Look," he barked, pointing one finger at Roger, "she'll call you tomorrow. And you," he added, turning toward a red-faced Carson, "we'll *both* take you to the damn exhibit, got it?" A quick look at Remy showed her wearing a grinning, bemused expression at his words. Then he turned to Jon, whose sun-kissed face was all but glazed with passion as he gazed at Miss Hutchins. "And you, stop spouting that beach bum mumbo-jumbo, forget about the goddamn class, and take her ass home, where you can show her how you feel, for god's sake!"

Then, before anyone could mutter another word, he turned to Remy and swept her up into his arms, cradling her against the hot, vivid heat of his body, and carried her off into the night.

* * * * *

When they found a quiet, deserted nook created by the outside wall of the auditorium and a maintenance shed, he let her slide down the long length of his body, pressed her against the wall at her back, and in a voice heavy with insult, muttered, "How could you give that pretty-faced 'surfer dude' my ass?"

"Because," she murmured, "when everything started going weird, drawing your hunky backside just made me feel better. And, as painful as that night was when you got that scar, it was still the most romantic thing anyone's ever done for me."

Connor had given her brief details of the fight after he'd stitched Jason's backside up, cleaning out the glass and then sewing the torn flesh back together with tiny, neat sutures that she knew he'd been trained to perform, in case one of their men was injured in the field. It had sickened her to see Jason's body hurt, bleeding, and yet, there'd been that undeniable part of her that had been breathless at the sight of his taut, golden buttocks, firm with muscles and so surprisingly sexy. She'd never have guessed she'd be turned on by a guy's butt—until she'd gotten an eyeful of Jason Hawkes'.

"That scar is still one of the sweetest memories I've ever had. Up until two nights ago," he rumbled, pressing a searing kiss into the slender hollow of her throat, tilting her head back. "Do you know how hard it was for me, that night, not to toss you over that table and cram you full of my dick?"

"Mmm…knowing that only makes the memory sweeter," she laughed, arching against him.

"And do you know how much I regret not grabbing hold of you then? I was so wrapped up in coming to terms with how I felt about you. Shit, you were so young when we met. So innocent it made me feel dirty just to think about the things I wanted from you."

Her mouth opened, the argument right there on the tip of her tongue, but he held up his hand and held her off, determined to get it said. "Despite this vast experience you claim, you're still innocent. It'll take a hell of a lot more than those boys you've known to destroy that. And you're Connor's baby sister. It was a lot to take in."

"And what about now?" she asked in a quiet voice. "I told you my gut was right about this—that there was no great danger. It turned out to be no big deal, just some silly misunderstanding…or whatever you want to call it, and now this whole 'Remy needs protecting' thing is over."

"That's one way of looking at it." His expression shifted, that pure, mischief-made grin of his that she loved curling across the wide line of his ruggedly sculpted lips. "Or…"

"Or?" she asked, looking up at him while a thin flame of hope began to burn in her heart, spiraling out through her body in a breathtaking wash of suspense.

"Or," he rumbled, a deep breath expanding his lungs, "you could say it's just beginning."

That thin flame flared, burning fierce and bright…and she struggled not to bubble over with it.

"The way I see it, we've about said everything that could be said except for the two most important things, Remy."

She swallowed hard at the emotion in her throat, wanting to smile and laugh at the same time, and he hadn't even told her what they were yet. But she could tell she was going to love them, just from the burning heat of emotion smoldering in those whiskey-brown eyes, so beautiful they were already melting her heart.

"I fell in love with you that night, seven years ago, and I've been in love with you ever since."

"Seven years ago!" she screeched and he shook with laughter.

"Yeah, though how in the hell you didn't figure it out before now is beyond me. Everyone else knows. Even your brother. Shit, he probably had it figured out before *I* did."

Remy watched that sinful, bad boy grin kick up the corners of his wide, beautiful mouth, wondering if her heart would shatter from the thundering of her pulse. "Oh god," she gasped, blinking at the salty wash of tears suddenly blurring her gaze, "you loved me? Then? But you left me, Jason. You pushed me away, walked away, and I didn't see you for an entire year after that. *A year!*"

"Yeah, I know. And staying away from you was the hardest damn thing I've ever had to do. But I did it because I *did* love you, baby. If I hadn't, I'd have carried your sweet little ass off with me and your life would have been a living hell. I couldn't do that to you, Remy. Not with the way I felt about you."

"Jason," she groaned, pressing her palms against the solid slabs of his chest, feeling the heavy beat of his heart through the soft cotton of his shirt. "My life *was* a living hell."

He leaned his forehead against hers. "Mine too, but I thought I was doing the right thing, Remy. I didn't want to fuck your life up. And it didn't seem like it was right, until I came home and settled in, but you didn't want to have anything to do with me by then," he muttered, his voice betraying the strain of the last ten months she'd spent running from him.

"Only," she growled, "because I thought you hadn't wanted me. I thought this new interest was just some kind of need to grab a taste of something you'd passed up. I didn't know… I had hoped…but I was too afraid to hope for too much."

He looked down at her, that rich, molten brown gaze squinting against the feelings she could see swirling through their golden depths. "And now?" he asked, the sexy line of his mouth tight with tension.

"Now I'm ready to grab hold of everything. Of you."

"Thank god," he said in a strong, gusting rush of air, "because honey, once I stick, there's no shaking me loose."

"What?" she laughed. "You stick like glue?"

Jason smiled, letting the happiness sink sweetly into his system. "You bet your sweet ass I do." He lifted his hand to her face and cupped the gentle curve of her cheek. His hungry gaze caught on the erotic sight of his big thumb as he rubbed the lush pad of her lower lip, wiping away the last smear of blood, while a tumble of erotic images and desires took shape in his mind, catching at the beat of his heart. It could be theirs. All of it. It was all right there, just waiting for them to grab hold of it.

"I fall deeper in love with you every day and I'll just keep falling, baby, until the day I die. You, Remy Frost, just push me over the edge," he rumbled, his rough voice thick with the powerful combination of lust and tenderness. "You make me go fucking wild with the need to love you, to take care of you, and to fuck you so hard that you can't even think about walking for the next twenty-four hours. The only thing I want you thinking about is how far you can spread them, how deep you can take it, and how loud you can scream."

"Why, Jason Hawkes," she hiccuped, clutching onto his shoulders, her eyes shining while her lips spread in a slow, sweet smile, "who would've ever guessed there was a poet buried beneath all these wicked muscles and badass scars?"

"You love my muscles and my scars," he growled, pressing the bulge of his erection into her soft tummy as he bit at the tender skin beneath her ear. Then he pulled his hips back, his big hands already going to work on the fly of her jeans, tugging them down to her knees. Remy gasped, but before she could protest, he had two long fingers digging beneath the edge of her satin panties, two fingers digging deep into the flesh that was already going juicy for him.

"You know what else you love?" he rasped, working a third in alongside the other two, filling the tiny hole of her cunt to bursting with three thick fingers, loving the way she creamed all over him, so sweet and clean and fresh. He wondered how bad she'd kill him if he just went to his knees and buried his face in her damp folds right then and there, and treated himself to some of that sweet, delicious, addictive little pussy to hold him over until he got her ass home. "Me," he rumbled, growling the words into her mouth as her strong, tender channel clenched around him, sucking on his fingers in a lusty, provocative rhythm that was quickly unmanning him. "You love me, don't you?"

"Yeah," she sighed, kissing the hammering pulse in the base of his throat. "I love you, Jason. I always have. I always will."

"Oh, hell," he groaned, knowing he wasn't going to be able to wait, not when she'd just given him the one thing he wanted above all others. The only thing that had ever really mattered.

The warm, smoldering look in his gaze told her exactly where his train of thought had taken him. "Do you *ever* think about anything other than sex?" she laughed.

"Of course I do," he drawled, sipping from her lips as if he were starved for the taste of her. "I think about you. I'll admit a lot of the time I'm thinking about fucking you, but there's more there."

"Yeah, like what?" she sniffed.

"Like the way you smile. I think about making you happy. I think about us spending the rest of our lives together, which is the second thing we needed to talk about. Having kids, dogs, a whole goddamn menagerie. Creating a family so that our house is loud and full of life and laughter and we have to sneak off every chance we get for hot, satisfying quickies, until they all go to bed at night and I finally get your sexy little ass right where I want it. I think about creating a life with you, Remy. One that matters. One that lasts.

"I know what I want, Remy, and I've known it for a long time. I know that what I feel is real. More real than anything I've ever known, and more important, I know it's going to last forever. That it's the most important thing to ever happen to me and always will be. I know I'd die before I ruined it or hurt it and I know that I want to spend the rest of my life making you understand just how fucking much I love you."

She shivered as he pulled his fingers free of the tight hold of her body, tilting his face down so that he could hold her stare, unwilling to release that glistening look of warm, melting emotion swirling there in that luminous green gaze that drilled straight through him. "You want to know what now?" he smiled, lifting his damp fingers to paint her lips with that delectable, dewy pussy-juice that he couldn't get enough of, loving the way her eyes went heavy with a carnal hunger that perfectly matched his own as he stroked the plump, slippery surface of her mouth. "Now I get to spend the rest of eternity so madly in love with you, it makes every other woman green with envy."

Her shoulders shook at his words. "You're such an arrogant shit, you know that?"

"Yeah," he grinned, "but I'm *your* arrogant shit."

A single tear tracked down the side of her hot face, leaving an iridescent river of moisture across the silky perfection of her skin, but he knew it was okay. Knew they were tears of emotion, because his eyes felt hot too. Then the edge of that siren-sexy mouth tilted up in the most endearing smile he'd ever seen and she blinked a look of love and need up at him that damn near stopped his heart. Her palm lifted to brush his hair back from his brow and she sniffled an adorable little sound as she said, "I love you, Jason Hawkes. With all my heart, I love you and I want you forever. For always."

"I won't ever get tired of hearing it," he groaned. His mouth found hers before he could think about skill or seduction or blowing her mind. He was driven by need and hunger and the possessive necessity of stamping his claim all over her. His lips ate at the silken perfection of her plump mouth, tongue driving past her soft lips to seek and enter and claim the sweet, warm well. He tasted her tongue, her teeth, the hollows of her cheeks, desperate for all of it, every intoxicating inch. Emotion trembled through his body, setting him to a fine, uncontrollable shiver, and he could feel any last vestiges of control being swept away on a wave of something so overwhelming, he knew was being carried away with the tide...and loving every minute of it. "Hell, I love you so much, woman. Always, Frosty. I'll never be able to get close enough, in deep enough, have you enough. More," he growled, knowing he sounded desperate, but too damn in love to care. "I'll always want more, Remy."

In the next instant he'd lifted her, carrying her deeper into the shadows, until suddenly they were submerged in darkness, the shimmering dampness of her love-filled eyes illuminated by nothing more than a pale shaft of iridescent moonlight as it painted the beauty of her expression with an ethereal glow.

Remy felt the cold, hard stone of the auditorium at her back, her front covered by hot, hard, trembling male animal as he seemed to be everywhere at once. There was no practiced seduction in his touch. No, he was nothing but primal need and hunger and she loved it. Reveled in her power over this magnificent beast and gloried in her own surrender to the wonder of everything he made her feel.

Strong, hard, callused hands grasped the soft denim of her faded jeans and shoved them all the way to her ankles. Then one long-fingered hand ripped at the delicate scrap of her panties so quickly, her head spun from the rush of pleasure pumping through her.

"Have to fuck you...be inside you...now. Sorry, baby, but I can't wait," he muttered, ripping at his jeans, his actions revealing his desperation. Her breath caught at the hot, searing heat of his thick cock as it pushed between her thighs, nudging at the sensitive folds of her sex. "Fuck, I can't wait."

And he meant every word.

Jason came the instant he shoved the brutal width of his shaft inside her, instantly filling her with a powerful surge of cum that eased his way, so that he was able to press even deeper, shoving the fat head against the mouth of her womb and holding it there. He pressed her hard to the wall as the vicious, teeth-grinding pleasure pulsed through him, jerking through the core of his cock like a hot, blistering wave of lava, and muffled his raw shout in the fragrant silk of her hair.

He didn't know if he'd passed out or what, but suddenly she was shifting in his arms, her tender sheath rippling around him in urgent, hungry little pleas for more. "Ah hell, I don't believe I just did that," he muttered, his husky voice tight with embarrassment at his appalling lack of control.

"Shh," Remy whispered, "it's okay. I loved it. It was so sexy. I love feeling you come inside of me."

"Thank god," he grunted, loving the feel of her hands on him as she stroked the hot skin of his throat, his ears, sifting her fingers through his hair, "because I love doing it."

Remy made a purring sound of contentment and arousal in the back of her throat, shifting in his arms, and he groaned, "No. Don't move. Not done. Nowhere near fucking done," he gritted through the savage bite of his teeth, his breath hot and moist against the sensitive side of her throat.

He was still rock-hard, packing her so full it felt as if he took up all her space, stretching her to that point that he always took her to, where the pain blended so erotically with the pleasure that she craved that stinging bite, that stretch, loving that she was woman enough to take everything he had to give. She reveled in her power to take him, to take her pleasure from a man who was so much...*everything*. Her sex grew heavy and wet and he moved thickly through the hot slickness of his own cum as it coated her narrow inner walls.

"Ah damn," he grunted, his voice scraping and hard in the dark, silent night. "I love fucking you. Can't get enough of the way you take me, squeeze me, suck me in like you're trying to swallow me whole. There isn't anything like it in the world, Remy. You were made for me."

"Always for you, Jason."

He shoved back into her creamy heat, the slick, warm rush of her juices covering him, and Remy reveled in the intimate, wickedly sweet sensation of his naked dick as he fed it into her, forcing his way inside. "Only for you," he rasped.

She watched as he smiled down at her, his whiskey-colored eyes burning with love, bright and intense and mesmerizing in their beauty. "Your cock, woman. Every inch, all for you, Remy. And I'm going to give it to you every fucking chance I get. You getting the point?"

"Yeah," she gasped, jolting to the pounding rhythm of his strong, thick strokes as he worked the hard, vein-ridged length of his shaft into her, forcing his way through the tight clench of her sex. "I'm getting your point, Jason. And enjoying every second of it."

"Ah hell," came a deep, familiar voice from the dense shadows off to their side, maybe fifteen feet away. "I really, really don't want to be hearing this shit."

Remy shrieked, trying to pull him into her body as she clutched at his shoulders, and Jason groaned long and low, dropping his forehead against the crown of her smooth, silky hair. "Oh fuck, you've got really shitty timing, you ass."

"Well, when I came looking for my sister," Connor snorted, "I didn't know I was going to find *this*."

"What the fuck are you doing here?" Jason snarled, while Remy kept trying to curl into a tighter space between him and the wall. He could hear her muttering something softly under her breath, then smiled when he realized she was chanting *"No, no, no, this is sooo not happening"* over and over again.

"I went by Billy's to check on her damn car and he told me you'd had him bring it here," Connor drawled, thankfully not sounding any closer.

"And so you just had to come and investigate, huh?"

"Hey, she's my sister. Then I ran into Carson and Roger in the parking lot and they pointed me in this direction." There was no mistaking the wry edge of humor in Connor's deep voice. Jason figured he should be happy his best friend wasn't trying to pound his ass into the ground, considering he had his baby sister nailed to the wall with a monstrous hard-on.

"Well, I'm sure Remy appreciates your concern. Now get lost before this gets any weirder. We'll call you later."

"With pleasure," Connor snickered, "just as soon as she tells me she's okay."

"Yeah, she's fine. More than fine," Jason drawled in a husky rasp that left no doubt to anyone that he was no longer talking about her health and safety.

"Christ, you couldn't have waited until you got her home at least?" Connor grunted.

"It was…uh, kinda urgent," Jason choked, trying not to laugh.

"Hawkes," Connor growled in a menacing snarl.

Remy sank her teeth into Jason's shoulder, making him say, "Ouch." Then, in a blush-filled voice, she muttered, "I am fine, Connor. Now go home."

"Love you too, Remy," her snickering brother laughed, turning to leave.

"Hey," Jason called out, "just so you know, she's decided she loves me."

Connor muttered a few choice phrases beneath his breath, then said, "That right, Remy?"

Jason could see her slow smile in the pale moonlight as it played softly over her mouth. "Yep, I'm afraid so," she mumbled. "Though I probably wouldn't mind killing him right about now."

Connor's soft laughter carried huskily on the wind. "Yeah, and knowing Hawkes, honey, I reckon you're gonna feel like that again."

"True," she sighed, "which means he's damn lucky that I *do* love him."

"Here that, *bro*?" Jason snorted. "We're gonna be family now, man."

"Oh hell, you two are gonna make me sick," Connor muttered with disgust, though they could both hear the smile in his voice as he muttered the words.

Jason waited thirty seconds as they listened to Connor's boots ringing clearly now against the hard concrete of the walkway as he moved away. Then he licked his tongue over her still damp, sweet pussy-flavored bottom lip, smiling when she moaned and shivered from the wicked action.

"Now where were we?" he rumbled, smiling as he slowly pulled his hips back, so that she felt the brutal rasp of his thick-rimmed cock head dragging against her tender, sensitive walls, before pumping back in with a hard, possessive thrust.

"You mean before the humiliating moment when my brother caught me getting nailed to the wall?" She laughed, nuzzling the base of his throat with her mouth, then flicked her tongue against the slick heat of his skin once, then again…and again.

He felt the growl work its way up from the soles of his feet, vibrate through the core of his cock, and gave in to the grinding need to fuck her deep and hard and raw. "Connor aside, you like being nailed to the wall with my cock, gorgeous."

"Yes," she gasped, holding onto his shoulders for dear life. "Yes I do."

"And you're going to get it again and again. I'm so fucking crazy about you, Remy. I'll never be able to get enough. Never. You're going to be getting fucked like this for the rest of our lives."

"Then I guess that makes me a lucky girl."

"It makes you mine, Frosty. All mine."

"Makes you mine too. And you, Jason Hawkes, are second to none."

"Yeah?" he smiled, "I like the sound of that, darlin'. But as long as I'm yours, I'll be happy. From the moment I met you, that's all I've ever wanted to be. I'll try not to smother you and I'll do everything I can to make you the happiest woman in the world. But, just to warn ya, honey, I'm never getting over this need to protect you. You mean too goddamn much to me."

"I'm fine with that, Jason," she moaned, breathless and shivering on the verge of a climax so powerful, it threatened to blow both their minds. "Really, I am. There's just one problem."

"What's that?" he groaned, wondering if she was going to lay into his ass again for being a bullheaded brute.

Remy pulled him down for another soul-scorching kiss that left them both breathless, then nipped his bottom lip, making him jerk deep inside her. "I'm just wondering who's gonna protect you from me?" She smiled, her soft voice full of sensual challenge that made them both chuckle.

And they were both still smiling when they fell over the edge.

Also by Rhyannon Byrd

∽

A Little Less Conversation
Against the Wall
Alpha Romeos (*anthology*)
Horn of the Unicorn
Magick Men I: A Shot of Magick
Magick Men II: A Bite of Magick
Triple Play
Waiting For It

About the Author

∽

Rhyannon Byrd is the wife of a Brit, mother of two amazing children, and maid to a precocious beagle named Misha. A longtime fan of romance, she finally felt at home when she read her first Romantica novel. Her love of this spicy, ever-changing genre has become an unquenchable passion — the hotter they are, the better she enjoys them!

Writing for Ellora's Cave is a dream come true for Rhyannon. Now her days (and let's face it, most nights) are spent giving life to the stories and characters running wild in her head. Whether she's writing contemporaries, paranormals…or even futuristics, there's always sure to be a strong Alpha hero featured as well as a fascinating woman to capture his heart, keeping all that wicked wildness for her own!

Rhyannon welcomes comments from readers. You can find her website and email address on her author bio page at www.ellorascave.com.

LOVE FOR HIRE

By Mardi Ballou

ഔ

Chapter One

ଛ

Foolproof. His whole operation had been foolproof. So why was he sitting in his least favorite place in the world—an FBI office—listening to his high-priced lawyer mortgage his future?

"The prosecutor's office has incontrovertible proof," one of the officers droned.

Nick forced himself to focus.

"If that's the case, why are we sitting here, bargaining?" argued Carlton Hughes, the top criminal defense lawyer in Princeton.

Good. Maybe he's finally going to earn his ten-thousand-dollar retainer.

"Because we can offer Mr. Love a unique way to use his talents for the public good," Agent Ford said quietly, taking a sidelong look at Nick. It was the first time he'd opened his mouth in the long day's proceedings.

Nick started to say something, but Hughes very subtly shook his head. "My client is not admitting to anything. Including the possession of any dubious creative talents."

Ford pursed his lips. "Let's cut the crap here." He looked at his watch. "We deal or we turn your *client* over for prosecution."

Hughes started to rise and motioned for Nick to do the same. Nick could tell the guy was bluffing, and he expected Ford could too. Though he tended to find little to admire in cops, even of the Fed variety, Nick grudgingly granted this agent a small measure of respect.

"We'll take our chances." Hughes began to pack up his papers. Nick felt less sanguine, but he had to figure the lawyer knew what he was doing. Both men stood up.

Ford rose also. He waved his hands dismissively. "Grand juries here in Jersey have been hard-nosed the past few months. Sounds like a trend to me."

Hughes lay his attaché case down on the table. "What exactly are you offering?"

"You ready to play ball?" Ford asked.

Hughes shrugged. "My client is a curious guy. Wants to hear what you have to say."

Ford turned to look at Nick, who kept his face devoid of expression. "Let's all sit back down," the agent said.

Hughes nodded. "We're not committing to anything. Just want to hear your plan."

Ford shuffled some papers. "We know that Nick Love has been operating a lucrative business providing false documents to a particular type of customer. Namely scum. Numerous fugitives have escaped from justice using his papers."

"Though he admires your imagination, if not your vocabulary, my client does not admit to any such activity." Hughes looked almost bored.

Ford's eyebrows shifted fractionally upward. "Save it for the jury. We, on the other hand, propose that Mr. Love use his talents to help us stop an operation dealing with identity theft." He turned to Nick and glared. "You with us? Or you want to spend some quality time with the team of prosecutors salivating to get you?"

Nick opened his mouth to answer, but Hughes beat him to it. "I advise my client not to respond."

Ford slammed his hands on the table in disgust. "For Pete's sake, man, you're not in the courtroom now, so can the dramatics. Choice time, Love."

"Without admitting anything," Nick said to placate his lawyer, "I want to hear more." Nick had a particular allergy to prosecutors. And he liked Ford's style. Maybe, just maybe, Nick would be able to get out of the mess that selling documents to Raoul Gelure had landed him in.

Waving off his lawyer's objections, Nick listened.

* * * * *

"Happy birthday!" Stephanie's friends and family called out the moment she stepped into her parents' living room.

Her face grew red with embarrassment and frustration. She hated surprise parties. And, most of all, she hated being reminded that today was her birthday. Memories of last year, when she first realized how badly Raoul Gelure had screwed up her life, had left permanent scars on the day. All she wanted was to be alone to wallow in her misery. But her friends and family wouldn't indulge her that way.

"Guys, you shouldn't have," she said, hoping to sound modest instead of pissed.

Stephanie saw her mom exchange I-told-you-so glances with her best friend in the world, Gretchen Hanley.

Gretchen came over and put an arm around Stephanie. "Enough with the 'Bah, humbug'. It's your birthday, girlfriend. Time to reclaim the day and resume living."

Stephanie felt her lip curl with contempt. The last thing she needed today was any more of the do-gooder, rah-rah, get-your-life-back-on-track advice that Gretchen and everybody else seemed intent on doling out. She looked around at all the decorations and food everyone had gone to a lot of trouble to provide. Though she hated to sound like an ungrateful grump, she'd have preferred to be alone to lick her wounds.

"What if saying 'Bah, humbug' is my first choice?"

Gretchen waved off the objection. "Just think of us as a birthday version of Scrooge's ghosts. We won't let you persist in your bad attitude any more than they would."

With a rejoinder on her lips, Stephanie watched her friends, their faces shiny with happiness and caring, surge around her. She didn't want to mess up the party. So she'd go along with their plans for a bit. Maybe if she smiled and played nice, ate a little cake and drank some bubbly, they'd all pack up their gear and go home soon.

Though she'd struggled for the past year—reimbursing every client Raoul had cheated, trying to rebuild her shattered reputation and career—acting sociable tonight took far more effort. Once she'd put on a happy face and chatted with all her guests, Stephanie figured she could plead exhaustion. She'd retreat to the room in her parents' house that being broke had forced her to move back into. How pathetic was that?

She'd manage to smile for about three and a half more minutes. After which time she should be up in her room, where she could retire the smile. "I don't know how to thank you all for coming..." she said to get the goodbye ritual going.

"But the party's not over yet," Gretchen protested. "Not by a long shot. You haven't opened your gifts."

Stephanie repeated "Gifts?" as if Gretchen had proposed she volunteer for exposure to a rare strain of avian flu. Though she could remember a time in her life when she adored getting birthday gifts, now it seemed like one more onerous chore.

"Where are they?" she asked, cringing at the whine in her voice.

"Voilà!" Gretchen pointed to a table in the corner of the room. She walked over and lifted a green velvet throw to reveal a pile of gorgeously wrapped packages of all different shapes and sizes.

Yeah, it was all breathtaking. But Stephanie knew no one could give her the one thing she wanted—her old life back.

She oohed and ahhed her way through the ritual. Her friends and family had fabulous taste, gifting her with clothes, books, toiletries, cosmetics and tickets to shows and concerts she had no appetite for. But she said her thanks and would write the appropriate notes.

"Wait, there's one more." Gretchen handed her what looked like an oversized card. "Open it."

Stephanie followed the directive. When she saw what the envelope contained, her face flamed several shades of red. "Gretchen, thanks but no thanks."

Her friend's face looked mock-harsh. "I had to pull all sorts of strings to get you priority consideration. Now take advantage of it. Or we'll be forced to do a kidnap-intervention to get your life back on track."

The last thing on earth she needed or wanted was the "golden opportunity" in her hand—the chance to date three hand-picked bachelors chosen by the Elite to Meet Online Dating Service.

"Promise me you'll call them and go out with the three guys," Gretchen said. "After all, you never know where it might lead."

Stephanie wanted to reevaluate her need for a best friend. But Gretchen and everyone else were watching with an intentness usually reserved for Oscar night. Stephanie knew it would be futile to protest. "Yeah, okay. I'll go."

"Great!" Gretchen hugged her.

Thank goodness the party broke up soon after. Though Stephanie had no intention of actually following through and calling the Elite to Meet Online Dating Service, she suspected Gretchen would bug her 'til she did. So she decided to get through the three quickest, nastiest dates known to woman. Then she'd be able to tell Gretchen to back off and leave her to her misery. Forever.

But before she had a chance to contact the service, the "top bachelors" began to contact her. And she quickly crossed two off her list. Just one to go…

* * * * *

"Sooo…Stephanie, I really like the sound of your voice."

She made a face at the phone. "I told you, I'm not interested in going out with you." Or anyone else. Though she had to admit he sounded good. But not as good as keeping her head and heart safe.

"Meet me for coffee. How much of a commitment is that? You don't like what you see, you pick up your marbles and go home."

She gritted her teeth. Darn Gretchen with her stupid birthday gift. "Just coffee," she snapped into the receiver.

"Right. Five o'clock at Bradley's Brew on Nassau Street. If we both agree, we can go on for dinner."

"Don't count on it," she said after she'd put the receiver down. She should have said no when he told her his name. Nick Love. Right. Like that could be anybody's real name. You'd think the joker would have the subtlety to come up with a better alias.

Well, at least this so-called Nick Love would be the last guy she'd have to go out with before Gretchen got off her back. After this one went bust, Gretchen or some other misguided gift giver would have to throw more money at that danged service for additional names. And no more gift-giving excuses loomed on the horizon 'til Christmas, more than six months away. So Gretchen had no such pretext for meddling in her life.

Now more than a year had passed since she lost her art gallery and her Tribeca condo in the wake of Raoul's massive scam. Finally, Stephanie was beginning to pull her life together. Given her incredible misjudgment of character and bad luck with men, she intended to get involved with another one right after fish began riding bicycles.

She looked at the clock. Another two hours 'til she met the current bozo and crossed her name off his to-date list. Then she'd come home, report the failure to Gretchen, and spend the night working on her plans to rebuild her shattered reputation and bank account.

* * * * *

Nick Love looked out his office window at Kingston's main street a few miles north of central Princeton. "Office" was a bit grandiose to describe the small room he operated out of, but the compact space suited him. After all, he didn't spend much time here.

He went back to his desk, opened a computer file and typed in a few notes about his meeting, make that his *date*, with Stephanie Wilson in an hour. She'd sounded classy on the phone, her accent labeling her as old Princeton money. Which made her perfect.

He told her he'd be wearing black leather. She refused to give him a description and sounded cool, disinterested. Made him wonder why she'd signed up for the dating service in the first place. Maybe she'd been burned badly, which made her careful. Anyway, her voice conjured up an image he liked — the classic Princeton princess. Probably tall, slim, with legs up to her chin. Since he was a leg man, his cock twitched. Blonde hair that didn't come from a bottle. Late twenties according to the dating service. Yeah, he was going to enjoy meeting Stephanie Wilson.

Too bad he'd have to keep his mind on business. But no one had said he couldn't have some fun.

* * * * *

Stephanie dressed with the idea of putting Nick Love off from the get-go. Considering that anyone with a name like Nick Love would probably prefer women to wear low-rider jeans and halter tops, she put on her conservative, asking-the-bank-for-a-loan navy blue suit. Two-inch heels would probably make her tower over the guy, which was enough to intimidate some. She pulled her wheat-blonde hair into a tight bun and put on the black-framed glasses she occasionally used to read fine print.

Satisfied with her look, Stephanie walked the half mile to Bradley's Brew. Spring had finally come to Princeton, and she let herself savor the smells and sounds of the new season. Students milled in the streets of the campus, spilling over into the shops lining Nassau Street. They all looked impossibly young, the way she'd once been. Though she was only a few years older than the undergrads, she felt ancient. The last year had aged her more than a decade.

She figured in half an hour, tops, she'd get rid of Nick Love and walk back home. After finally getting a local gallery owner to agree to meet with her, she was pulling together a résumé that might get her back to work. Maybe, just maybe, one day she'd have her own place again.

As she walked to the coffeehouse, Stephanie thought over the year that had passed since Raoul disappeared. According to Interpol, he and an unidentified female accomplice were currently enjoying the high life in Brazil, where there was no extradition. They probably were still laughing at her. She shook her head. She had never suspected, 'til it was far too late, that Raoul had systematically substituted forgeries for much of the original fine art her clients paid top dollar for.

It had taken all the proceeds from the sale of her gallery and her condo to reimburse her clients. Unfortunately, this restitution had not sufficed to clear her name completely. Luckily, she'd been able to move back to Princeton, where her loving parents offered to support her in any way she wanted. They'd be willing to stake her to open another gallery, even enable her to get a new condo. But she was determined to pay for both on her own. So, for now, she was living back at home with them. Though she adored them for their kindness and generosity, she couldn't wait to be independent again.

Stephanie looked in the window of Bradley's before she entered. No guys in black leather. Wouldn't it be something if

Nick Love stood her up? That would certainly save her having to brush him off.

Rather than appearing to wait for him, Stephanie decided to walk around the very long block before she either entered Bradley's or went home. She turned on her heel and started to walk away, crashing into a guy in a black leather jacket.

"Stephanie?" he asked, his mouth in a lopsided grin that did funny things to her insides.

"Nick?" The surprise of running into him startled her into being less cool than she'd planned. Why would a guy like him have to resort to an online dating service? To call him gorgeous vastly understated his appeal. Tall, broad-shouldered and narrow-hipped, wearing tight jeans, Nick Love looked about thirty. He also looked like he needed a shave, which made all the clean-shaven men passing them seem insipid.

His black hair fell neatly over the back collar of his jacket. He had dark eyes that looked nearly as black as his hair, a full sensuous mouth over even white teeth, a straight nose. Definitely eye candy. Stephanie stiffened. Raoul had been amazing to look at too. Though not as much as this guy.

"You up for some coffee, or would you rather go some place where we can get a drink?"

She could sure use a drink. Which was exactly why she said, "Coffee sounds great." He put his hand at the small of her back and she felt an unwelcome jolt of warmth. Though she fully intended to drink her coffee and head home pronto, something about Nick Love set off a warning bell in her head. This guy was not going to be as easy to walk away from as the other two had been.

* * * * *

She looked just as he'd expected, but so much hotter in the flesh. Stephanie Wilson looked like a class act. Her hair was a shade darker than he'd imagined—even better. But where the heck did she get the old-lady duds and the glasses? With any luck, he'd get her to shed both before too long. Yeah, he was definitely going to like this. And it fit in with his assignment... For the first time since the FBI had dragged his ass in, Nick regarded his personal glass as half full.

At this hour the coffee shop was fairly empty. Nick and Stephanie found a table, where she sat while he went to get their drinks. In moments he returned with two coffees. "You want anything else?" he asked.

"This is fine."

He grinned at her and sprawled in the chair opposite her. "So what's a great-looking girl like you doing signed up with a dating service? Not that I'm complaining. Glad I have this chance to meet you."

She bristled at his question, and he could tell he'd hit a sensitive note. "I didn't contact the service."

"Really? So how come—?"

"My best friend Gretchen, make that my *former* best friend, paid for the basic package for my birthday. For some reason she thought it was a good idea."

"And you don't?"

She rolled her eyes. "Right now, I have neither the time nor the interest to date. Not that it's any of your business."

"Being your date for the evening, I'd say I have a right to be curious."

"You are *not* my date for the evening." Her voice could have set off a blizzard but the look in her eyes promised heat. "I'm meeting you for coffee." She broke eye contact, though he'd have sworn she didn't want to, looked at her wristwatch and said, "I expect to be going home soon."

He held up his hand. "Let's backtrack here. I'd really like to get to know you, and it looks like I just asked the wrong question. What's the right question, Stephanie?"

Her eyelids fluttered and she didn't answer right away. For just a moment, she looked vulnerable, something he never expected to see in a Princeton princess. As amazing as she was in her usual pose, seeing the flash of her inner self melted something inside him.

In a moment her face went back to slight disdain. "There is no right question. I really have to go."

This was not going well, and he definitely needed to see her again. Both for himself and to get the FBI off his case. She was totally perfect all around. Which meant he'd better get his shit together and figure out a way to convince her to want to see him for more than a cup of coffee. "There's got to be a right question."

* * * * *

His voice caressed her and made the word "question" an invitation she was scared to accept, only she couldn't back off. Those eyes. She could drown in his dark eyes. Stephanie fought against an image of letting herself get lost with him. For just a little time she could forget the hell the last year had been and just let someone hold her for a bit.

No, she couldn't let herself go there. Were the goose bumps racing up and down her spine from the way he aroused her—or was that her inner warning system telling her to get out before her life went down the tubes again?

"There is no right question."

"You sure?"

His mouth quirked, and she could easily imagine herself kissing him. The feel of his lips on hers, on her neck, on her breasts. She squirmed in her seat. She had to pull herself together.

"I'm totally sure." Time for a change of subject. "So what do you do for a living, Nick Love?"

He drummed his long fingers on the creamy white coffee mug. "Is that really what you want to know?"

"Yes." Her voice came out as a whisper.

He reached across the table and lifted her hand to his lips. Heat coursed through Stephanie and arrowed straight to her clit. Barely able to breathe, she crossed her legs hard. He grinned, and she felt he knew exactly what was happening in the most intimate part of her. He traced the lines of the palm of her hand with his index finger, and she shivered. "Words are overrated." His voice sounded hoarse, raising vibrations deep in her. "There are so many more effective ways to communicate."

She pulled her hand out of his and swallowed hard. "Nick Love. Is that your real name?"

He raised a dark eyebrow. "You don't think it sounds like a real name?"

"That's not an answer." Okay. She felt more in control of herself now, and she relaxed.

"Nicholas Benjamin Love. The name on my birth certificate. Though the family pronunciation is *Lo-vay*, with the stress on the second syllable."

"And where was that birth certificate issued?"

"Right here in Princeton. I'm a local boy. Now, see how much you know about me? More than I know about you."

"Stephanie Carrington Wilson. Also born in Princeton. Now we're even." Another glance at her watch. "Thanks for the coffee. But I really have to go." She said the words. She should have stood up and left, but she felt rooted to the spot.

"I know a great place for pasta, and it's dinner time. We can walk from here. Come with me. I promise you'll find out lots more about me. I'll even answer any five of your questions to your complete satisfaction."

"Five out of how many?"

He laughed, and she was a goner. "Good one." Then his mouth quirked again. "Come with me."

She shouldn't. Damn how much she shouldn't. But she wanted to…and she couldn't have given a rational reason why. For once, she knew she was going to ignore the warning bells. Okay. So she'd get to know him a little more, get over whatever was intriguing her about him. But she'd be on guard constantly, making sure he didn't get past the defenses she'd needed to survive the past year. Whenever she wanted to, she'd leave. "All right."

He put his hand on her elbow as they exited the coffeehouse. The simple gesture made her feel safe.

"You said we can walk?" Stephanie asked. "Where are we going?"

He grinned. "My place."

* * * * *

Before Nick could blink, Stephanie had bolted. Just turned around and started walking away from him. Nick caught up with her in about two seconds.

"Uh, Stephanie, you're going in the wrong direction." He took her arm in his.

She glared at him, and her eyes went from warm blue to icy. People of all ages filled the sidewalk, moving with springtime exuberance. The crowd separated, walking around them. She pulled away from him.

"I am *not* going to your place."

"Why not? I make great pasta. And I figure we can have a chance to really talk there, with some privacy. Which we won't get in any of the restaurants around here."

She actually blushed. He couldn't remember the last time he'd seen anyone blush, and the candor and freshness touched him more than he wanted to admit.

"I'll go out for dinner with you because I'm curious. An early dinner since I have a ton of work to do tonight. But at a restaurant. As in totally out in public."

127

He seized on that. "What kind of work do you do?"

She shook her head. "Long story. I don't feel like going into it right now."

"Suit yourself. But I meant what I said. Come to my place for the reasons I gave you." He paused and looked hard at her. "What are you afraid of?"

She tilted her chin up. "I'm not afraid of anything. I just choose not to go to your place." She looked him up and down. "I'll pay for my own dinner."

He shook his head. "No way. I invited you. Okay, compromise. We go out for dinner, and if we still like each other, you come to my place for dessert." He wanted to be alone with her so they could really talk. Yeah, okay, for other reasons too. His cock twitched to remind him, as if he'd forgotten.

* * * * *

Stephanie couldn't have given a good, intelligent reason why, but despite her good sense, she felt herself falling enough under Nick Love's spell to agree to spend more time with him. She let herself listen to him, all the while picturing him touching her in places where she hadn't been touched in far too long. Places that Raoul Gelure had been the last one to touch.

Which made her wary.

It didn't keep her wary enough. By the time they'd been served salad and pasta and drunk some wine, she found herself wanting to go to Nick's place. For a quick dessert, she told herself.

The possibility that she might *be* dessert crossed her mind, and a delicious warm shiver of anticipation snaked up her spine. Something in his aura announced challenge, almost daring her to see if she was woman enough to be with this man.

"Where exactly do you live, Nick?"

"Just a few blocks away. You can ride on the back of my Harley. It's parked right out there." He pointed to a shiny black motorcycle easily visible through the window they sat in front of.

The image of her hugging him, holding on as he sped through the streets of Princeton, flashed before her. She wanted that sensual contact, wanted to bury her face against his leather-clad back. Nothing turned her on like the smell of leather mingled with a man's musky scent. Okay—time for a reality check. She'd have to pull her pencil skirt up around her hips to climb onto his bike. "I don't think so."

"You could ride sidesaddle. It's not far." She shivered—was this guy reading her mind? Another red flag flew up. Or had he been around so many women that he knew the way they thought?

"I have work to do at home tonight." She definitely needed to pull back from the places her mind was taking her.

"We can walk. It's really not far. My car's parked at my place, so I can drive you home whenever you want." He sounded relaxed, like it really wasn't a big deal to him one way or the other. The ball was in her court. She picked up a last forkful of pasta and chewed.

"I don't think so," she repeated. Her voice sounded wavery to her, not strong or definite.

He shook his head. "Sorry, I couldn't hear."

As he'd warned, it had gotten noisy in the restaurant. "I said no." This time she spoke loudly and clearly.

He drained his wine and looked her deep in the eyes. "The noise level here is only going to get worse. I want to hear everything you have to say the first time you say it. Come home with me. I promise. Great dessert, we'll get a chance to hear each other. I'll take you home whenever you say."

First she told herself the noise was getting to her. Then she grudgingly admitted to herself that she felt curious about Nick Love. Where did he live? What was his place like? He looked like the poster boy for trouble, but he'd acted like a gentleman so far. And the dating service did check out the people who signed up with them. "What kind of great dessert?"

If he'd smirked at her surrender, she'd have taken off. But his smile signaled only pleasant agreement. "Let that be a surprise."

"I don't like surprises," she said sharply. Not after the one Raoul Gelure had sprung on her.

He shrugged. "I don't remember what I have in the freezer."

His candor disarmed her. She stood up. "It had better be good."

He threw some bills down on the table and nodded to the server. Then he stood close to her and promised, "It will be."

Chapter Two

ဢ

The bright colors of a gorgeous sunset lit up the sky. Too bad about her not wanting to ride sidesaddle. Nick wanted to feel her arms around him as they rode. Well, there would be other times. He led Stephanie on foot through the few short blocks to his apartment in a large old house.

"Just dessert and that's it," Stephanie reminded him after he unlocked the door and motioned her in.

He saluted her smartly. "I'll take you home whenever you want." He pointed to the stairs and, gazing at her tantalizing ass, followed her up.

The apartment consisted of a kitchen, living room, bedroom and bath. Not much furniture, though what he had fit well in the old-fashioned high-ceilinged rooms. The rental agent had labeled the place "charming". He viewed it as convenient.

"Kitchen's here." He turned on the overhead light and motioned for her to sit at the wooden table. "You want some wine?"

She paused in her perusal of his living space. "That's what you're offering me for dessert?"

He raised an eyebrow. "You're making me sound uncouth. Like I'd invite a lady for dessert and neglect to have one to give her."

She rolled her eyes. "No offense intended." She sat down at his table.

He opened the freezer door. "I can offer *madame* a selection of ice cream to her taste. Two, count them, *two* amazing flavors to choose from. Pistachio Ripple or Chocolate!

131

Chocolate! Chocolate! Or any combination of the two. Also strawberry pie. Just a matter of minutes in my trusty microwave and you'd swear it came right from the bakery."

"Sounds irresistible," she said in a flat tone that told him she wouldn't have any problem resisting.

"You can have all three. Together. With whipped topping. With coffee, wine, beer. You name it, it's yours."

She laughed. "Coffee, pie, and the Chocolate! Chocolate! Chocolate! A lot of coffee, small portions of everything else."

He brewed the coffee and served up the pie and ice cream.

"This is good," Stephanie said, taking a taste of the coffee.

"You sound surprised."

She looked hard at him. "You're a surprising guy, Nick Love."

He caught another glimpse of that vulnerability, and he wanted more. But he had to move slower than he wanted with her, let her get more comfortable with him before he moved them to a more intimate place. He poured himself a glass of wine, offered her some, which she refused, and toasted her.

"So tell me about Stephanie Carrington Wilson, beautiful lady residing here in Princeton. I want to know everything. What do you spend your days doing? And your nights?"

Stephanie took a sip of her coffee and looked at the man across from her. Now that she'd had some time to study his face, she realized whom he reminded her of. Frank Langella in the old Dracula movie. Somehow answering his questions made her feel like she was opening herself up to the vampire. Silly fantasy. He'd only be as dangerous to her as she let him be. After all, she was in control. The thought of Nick sprouting fangs and running their sharp points along the tender flesh of her neck raised her pulse and got her hot. She banished the image with a frisson of regret. "Right now I'm spending tonight talking to you. Putting off the work I need to get done. Most nights I'm working."

His eyes burned with intensity. "Really? Is this how you want to spend your nights?" His voice caressed her, and the air filled with tension.

Major alarm bells went off as she thought of many different ways she could be spending those nights—with him, their bodies entwined in hot and sweaty sex. Where did that come from? She shouldn't be listening to him. Hell, she shouldn't look into his hypnotic eyes. Not that she didn't want him. She did. Lord knew she did. But she'd just met him two hours before. She'd let him convince her to come to his apartment. He scared her as much as he turned her on. No, he scared her more. Her rational self rose up and screamed. Stephanie put down her coffee. "Delightful as dessert has been, I really should go. Now. Please take me home." She got up from the table and walked to the living room.

He followed right behind and turned her around to face him. "What are you afraid of, Stephanie Wilson?"

She laughed cheerlessly. "You want the list in alphabetical order?"

He put both hands on her arms. Stephanie gritted her teeth in her struggle to ignore the electric spark that jolted her. "As bad as all that?" he murmured. "What terrible things have happened to you?"

Something broke inside her. She wanted to nestle in his arms and confide in him, let him comfort her and reassure her that all her problems would be resolved, soon and brilliantly. To her self-disgust, a tear welled up in her eye and fell to her cheek.

With his thumb, he tenderly wiped the tear away, and she wanted him to keep touching her there forever. But he lowered his thumb to her lips and gently parted them. A sigh formed in her throat, only to disappear into a kiss that shook her world.

* * * * *

God, she overwhelmed his senses. But he had to keep his head on straight. After all, he was with her for a reason, not just fun and games. Which was really hard to remember when she set his blood to boiling, lifting him up like he'd just landed in the midst of a tornado and had no idea where or even if he'd come back to earth.

She shuddered in his arms, giving silent witness to the storms she'd passed through. He couldn't keep from kissing her. Her lips parted for him, and she ran her hands through his hair, holding him to her like she'd never let him go. She tasted like perfection. Spring strawberries, sunshine, the freshness of a meadow coming back to life.

"Oh, baby, don't hold back. Let me be with you." Nick held her to him, stroking her face, the hair that had come loose from her tight little bun.

Hard as a rock, he pressed his erection to her. She groaned, a sound fraught with desire and pain. She was so hurt, so fuckin' damaged. Who'd hurt her like that?

Later he'd have to hear her story. Right now, all he could know and sense was how much he ached to be with her. In every sense of the word. He would make it up to her, whatever had brought her down in the past. He stopped himself. What would happen when she found out…

She touched his erection through his jeans, and Nick nearly went through the roof. Her hand on his cock made him forget why he'd contacted her in the first place. The fact that he'd have to "set her up" to untangle his mess with the law. Maybe it wasn't too late, maybe he could stop what he'd already put in motion. The last thing she needed was to be hurt anymore.

* * * * *

It was all going too fast for Stephanie, but she wanted it never to stop. The feeling of magic and the haven she found in Nick's arms. The delicious thrill of his mouth on hers, his hands taking possession of her body. She felt like she'd forgotten all the cautions and safeguards she'd surrounded her heart with over the past year. All the barriers she'd put up were falling down, and instead of trying to stay safely within them, she found she was only too glad to bid them a not-so-fond farewell.

Nick wanted her. When she touched the bulge in his jeans and felt his cock react, her pussy creamed so hard she nearly cried out.

"Oh, God, baby, tell me what you want. Let me pleasure you now," he whispered.

She wanted him.

She wanted to lie spread-eagle on his bed and feel him penetrate her.

She wanted to ride up and down on his huge cock.

But all she could bring herself to do was mutely nod. Once again, her eyes filled with tears, which slowly streamed down her face. He cupped her chin with his hand and raised up her face. Then he slowly kissed and licked her face, gathering her tears to him as if they were precious gems.

She wanted him to touch her everywhere, to know every inch of her intimately. But all she could do was sob.

And then he feverishly unbuttoned her suit jacket and ran his fingers over the white silk shell she wore underneath. Stephanie's nipples pebbled into tight, hard nubs as he circled the delicate areolas. She wanted his mouth on her there, and she pushed his head down to the spot.

"Let me take this off," he murmured, putting his hands on the hem of the shell.

"Yes," she whispered, the word torn from her core. He pulled off her top, flung it aside, and laid her down on the blue cotton-upholstered couch. In moments, he was licking and kissing her breasts, tonguing down one and up the other before he took her areola in his mouth and sucked.

She held his head to her, savoring the tingles and chills that took hold of her with each of his moves.

Just as she'd feared earlier when she thought about riding on the back of Nick's Harley, her skirt was now fully up around her hips. But now that fear feathered into anticipation. She loved knowing he was looking at her, taking in every inch of her body with the barrier of the skirt gone. Her nylons, the black garter belt holding them up, and her black silk thong were completely exposed to his hungry gaze. Or would be if she let him lift his head from her breasts.

His cock pressed ever harder against her thigh. She wanted him in her pussy, and she shifted to get him up against her mound. She reached down to open his zipper and free his cock, but though it was obvious that he wanted her, Nick put his hand on hers to stop her. "Not yet," he said. "First your turn."

With Raoul, she'd never come first. In anything. She reluctantly moved her hand away from his cock, where she wanted to linger, and let herself follow his lead for now.

His lips still playing with her nipples, Nick at last reached down and touched her pussy. Stephanie gasped at the sheer pleasure of his touch there. Reaching under her thong, he began to massage her steamy-hot slit. She moaned and pushed herself against his fingers. God, she must be saturating them with her wetness.

He drew his hand away from her pussy, and she moaned. He licked a finger that had been touching her and smiled seductively before kissing her. She savored the taste of herself on his tongue. Thank goodness he had another hand, which quickly got busy exactly where she wanted it. He played with her clit, stimulating her to the bursting point.

With his thumb on her clit, Nick put a finger inside Stephanie and began to explore. Soon he added a second and a third. Lost in pleasure, Stephanie rode Nick's fingers with complete abandon. All she knew was how amazing it felt, how much she wanted the sensations to go on and on. As her pleasure rose, she trembled with a new awareness of how much warmth and desire she could feel. She felt herself riding on a crest too fragile to last. Soon her sensations would spill over, taking her with them.

Nick murmured encouraging words, telling her how beautiful she was, how much he was getting off on all the pleasure she was getting.

For the first time in over a year, Stephanie was going to come with a lover that didn't rely on batteries. She began to pant, thrashing from side to side as her orgasm began to build. All she wanted in the world was to let go in an enormous release and to let Nick know exactly how amazing he was for her to be with.

"How is this for you, baby," he murmured.

"Nick," she breathed in response. "Oh, god. Nick. *Oh, god. Nick.*" Her voice got louder as the intensity of her closing and opening to him raised her to a new pinnacle of sensation.

And then she landed back on earth. Her eyes feasted on Nick's cock, which looked set to explode out of the fly of his jeans. She wanted it all.

Nick kissed her, murmuring how beautiful she was, how precious her climax. And then, to her total delight and amazement, he slid his face down to her pussy, where he proceeded to begin kissing her again. So soon after her mind-blowing orgasm, she never would have imagined that she could so quickly be aroused again. With his tongue, teeth, and lips, Nick succeeded at getting her attention quite thoroughly.

Only this time, she wanted to take him with her. She wanted that cock in her.

Then the phone rang.

* * * * *

Nick ignored the phone's insistent ring. Disruptive as the sound was, he knew the damn thing wouldn't continue for long. He had his machine set to pick up after three rings. Which was exactly what it did.

Nick was noisily slurping Stephanie's abundant and delicious juices when he heard the worst possible voice to intrude on them at that moment. Fuck. He must have left the speaker on.

It was his ex-girlfriend, Natalie. "So, Nick baby, how's the date with the hoity-toity Princeton dame? The one you said would be perfect for your plans? Pick up if you're there. Shit. Come on, Nick, I really want to know what's going on."

Thank God she finally shut up. Nick hoped Stephanie was too distracted to listen to the phone message. No such luck.

With a yelp of pain, Stephanie jolted upright, slamming him off her. "What the hell was that? Who was that calling?"

Of all the rotten timing. He could wring Natalie's neck.

Still hard as a rock and evidently doomed to stay that way, Nick scrambled to figure out what to say. How much had Stephanie heard? Judging from the look on her face, evidently too much.

"Would you believe me if I said it was nothing?"

Gathering her clothes around her, she gave him a don't-be-ridiculous glare. "Don't treat me like an idiot. And for God's sake, don't try to tell me that whoever's on the phone is talking about a different hoity-toity Princeton dame."

He held his hands out to her, but she slapped them away. "I'm going home now, like I should have done before..."

She bit her lip and Nick could tell she was about to cry again. Great. Despite his best intentions, he was already hurting her.

In moments, she had her clothes on. Not as tidy as before, but decent. She put her hair up in another bun, though not nearly as tight as the first one. When she'd put on her shoes, she announced, "If you're taking me home, let's go. On second thought, maybe I should just walk or get a cab." She sniffled, and his heart wrenched.

"I'll drive you," he said softly. He picked up his keys.

"At least have the decency to tell me who was on the phone." Stephanie picked up her purse and looked around, probably to see if she'd forgotten anything.

He shook his head. "Just an old girlfriend, very much an ex. I don't really know exactly what she was referring to, but it has nothing to do with you."

She snorted. "And I'm supposed to believe that because…?"

He shrugged. Good question. Why should she believe anything he had to say? Though his saying Natalie was an ex was the total truth. Not even really an ex, more like a never-had-been. Natalie didn't view it that way, but Nick couldn't fix that. He looked hard at Stephanie. "It really wasn't anything important. Look, I know it may be hard for you to believe, but what she said wasn't about you. Natalie was, in her own stupid manner, referring to something else." He paused, seeming to gather his thoughts. "I'm not lying about this."

She rolled her eyes. "Been there and done that. Listened to lies and ignored the truth 'til it knocked me over the head." Without a look backward, she flew down the stairs.

He flew down after her.

"Please, Stephanie. Just give me one more minute. I don't want the night to end like this, especially not because of a stupid phone call."

Though she knew she should keep on walking, Stephanie paused. "One more minute."

The two of them were out on the street now, in front of Nick's house. Thank goodness the street was quiet, with no one to witness their conversation or intrude on it. Nick took her arm and they walked. Stephanie idly wondered about the state of his erection, then pulled her mind back. Yeah, he turned her on big time. But she couldn't give in to that.

"Natalie was referring to a client I was working with," Nick said. "Before we broke up, I made the mistake of telling her about my client. We stopped seeing each other while I was still working with her. Natalie, for some reason that eludes me, became fascinated with her. She thought the client and I were having an affair and blamed her for the breakup. Only we didn't have enough of a relationship to even call the end of it a breakup. But she just doesn't let go."

From not enough information, Stephanie had gotten too much. She formed about ten questions based on what Nick had just said and wanted to get each one answered. "You referred to a client of yours. What kind of work is it that you do?"

"Come back upstairs and I'll tell you."

He shouldn't have been important enough to her already to be able to bribe her like that, but he was. Well, she'd shown she could and would walk out. The option remained open. "Why do I feel like a fly stepping voluntarily into the spider's web?" she asked warily.

"Look. Two arms, two legs. I'm definitely not a spider," he said, steering her back up to his place.

Once they were again seated on the couch where he'd just pleasured her, Stephanie repeated her question. "The nature of your work, please."

"I'm a private investigator," he said tersely. "With expertise in documents."

"That's fascinating," she said. A million more questions arose, and she wanted answers to every one of them. But before she could ask, he kissed her again, and her mind went blank.

Chapter Three

૭

This time they didn't stop. Faster than she'd have believed it possible, both Stephanie and Nick had their clothes off and strewn around them on the floor. When Stephanie looked at Nick, she remembered a sculpture she couldn't bear to sell. A man of perfect proportions—cold perfection. But Nick was warm and pulsing and held her in his arms. His erection pressed strongly against her, making demands on her, tantalizing her with promise.

Wordlessly, the two raced for his bedroom and dove into his bed. "I want you, Stephanie," Nick murmured.

"I'm here."

She lay back against his pillows and he caressed her with kisses and touches. Fingers trembling, she encircled his cock and began to stroke him. He gasped.

She wanted to play with him, but not now. Later she'd explore his cock by touch, watch as he grew in response to her stimulation. She'd touch his balls, the sensitive skin. But foreplay was over now. With a grateful groan, she opened her legs and drew her to him.

Nick's cock was thick and long. "Oh, baby," he whispered as he slowly slid into her feminine core.

He filled her in a way she'd never before known. "Nick." His name grew into one long exhalation.

He lowered his face and began to nibble her neck. Her vampire fantasy returned, turning her on. She pressed her neck against his mouth, wanting to feel the sting of his teeth, the slight pain that would, in contrast, raise her pleasure.

As he nibbled and licked, she thrust her hips upward, wanting to take more and more of him into her as her arousal flared. She hadn't thought he could get any harder and bigger than he'd been when he entered her, but now he stretched her, opening her up to him as he plunged deeper into her. "I want all of you," he whispered so close to her neck that she shivered.

Now they were both moving faster, harder, their rhythm completely in tune. There was no new-lover exploration here — it was more like they'd known each other forever.

Stephanie wanted to clutch him to her, to hold on to him and to what they had together at this moment. She felt her nails dig into the taut skin of his back, the muscles that rippled at her touch. Nick's scent was as familiar to her as her the fragrance of her own breath, yet new.

"You are so beautiful, so hot," he whispered.

She kissed him in response, tasting wine and the chocolate of their dessert, the spice that was Nick.

He raked her sides with his fingers, kissed her, and all the time he thrust in and out of her, pleasuring her as she caressed his cock.

Despite her earlier climax, Stephanie felt herself begin to gather to an even more explosive release. Only this time, she wouldn't be alone. She loved that Nick would also come, that they would have the intimate bond of being together in this.

Even though she'd climaxed with him earlier, she wasn't prepared for the force of the release that was shaking her. She wanted to laugh, to cry, to shout from rooftops. Probably the sound that came out of her resembled all three. And then Nick outdid her, holding her to him as he came deep inside her.

Intimate as they'd just been, Stephanie felt even closer to Nick as they lay together afterwards. Usually she wanted to talk afterward. Raoul used to laugh at her for that. Ugh. Why had she let him creep into her thoughts at a time like this?

Even if all she and Nick would ever have were these moments, Stephanie wanted to cherish them, live them fully.

Nick stroked her face. In the back of her mind, Stephanie knew she could leave and go home. But she wanted this night. She wanted to drift off to sleep in Nick's arms. And she did.

Later, she woke from a deep, restful sleep with a smile on her face. For just a moment, all the pain and disappointment of the previous year melted into the warm coziness of her comforting nest. And then reality struck when she caught sight of Nick Love, asleep in the shadows. And then the details of the whole previous night came back to haunt her. She rose as quickly and quietly as she could to dress in the dark. She had to get out of this place, leave before she got in any deeper.

As she struggled into the underwear she'd blithely tossed on the floor, Stephanie chided herself. She couldn't believe she'd let herself succumb to Nick's seduction. Even if it was the hottest, best sex she'd had since Raoul. Actually, the only sex since Raoul, not counting her vibrator. She buttoned up her blouse and stepped into her skirt. She wouldn't bother with her hose, though going barefoot in her heels would be uncomfortable.

As long as she was being brutally honest with herself, the sex had been way hotter and better than anything she'd experienced with Raoul—or anyone else.

Not that it would ever happen again with Nick.

She checked her watch. Three a.m. Shit. Would she be able to get a cab at this hour? She did not relish the prospect of the walk home.

Heels in hand, she tiptoed to the door. "Where are you going?" Nick's voice was just above a whisper.

Stephanie stiffened, her first reflex being to offer an explanation. Then she forcibly reminded herself that she didn't owe Nick Love anything. And she wasn't about to trap herself into acting as if she did. "Didn't mean to disturb you. Figured I'd call a cab."

Half-dressed and barefoot, he seemed more in a condition to head out to the street than she was. And totally sexy. She bit back a desire to trace the muscles of his chest, to finger the dark, small nipples.

"Why are you leaving now? Stay the night."

Stephanie tilted her chin out with determination. "I need to go home, where I should have gone hours ago. Before I let you talk me into…"

His teeth gleamed as his mouth turned up in a wolfish grin. "I didn't hear any complaints."

Stephanie hated that she'd allowed herself to be so vulnerable with him. Talk about letting down her guard. "No complaints. No anything else. I'm going home."

"Stay. Please stay."

Yeah, she wanted to. Especially when he raised his hand to stroke her face. His fingers made promises she couldn't let herself begin to believe. She shook off his hand. "The only thing I want now is to go home. End of discussion. Where's your phone?"

"If you're serious, I'll drive you." The look in his eyes said he didn't believe she meant what she said.

"I'm totally serious. I want to go now." She stopped. If she let him drive her home, he'd know where she lived. She didn't want to admit that she didn't want him to know her address, didn't trust him.

Right. After Raoul, she'd vowed never again to trust any man. And not to care whom she offended with her distrust. "I'd prefer to take a cab."

"Suit yourself." He turned on a light, walked to a small desk, and handed her a headset. "Call."

Both relieved and vaguely disappointed that Nick had backed down without more of an argument, Stephanie dialed the number she'd memorized years before, when she'd first started dating.

A polite voice informed her that all cabs currently in service were out on calls and she'd have at least an hour's wait.

An hour. She could try another company. Or, of course, she could phone home or one of her friends. But she'd hate to disturb anyone this late. When calls to two other cab companies resulted in her having to settle for similar delays, Stephanie hung up the phone.

She didn't relish hanging around Nick Love for another hour. Resolved as she was that nothing more would ever happen between them, she saw no reason to test the strength of her resistance. Not when the sight of Nick standing before her was enough to make her pussy cream. Reluctantly, she decided the least of all evils would be to have him drive her home. In the short trip back to her house, she'd tell him exactly how things would be. As in, tonight would never be repeated. And she didn't want him ever to contact her again.

* * * * *

Nick wanted to be back in bed with Stephanie. Never one to spend an entire night with a lover, his usual practice was to go to her place and be the one who left.

He didn't want to look too hard at why he wanted to spend the whole night with this woman. Not now when he needed to keep his senses sharp. Later he'd contemplate what was going on inside him. Now he needed to make sure he'd be with Stephanie again. And not just because of his deal with the FBI.

Nick pulled himself away from Stephanie to throw on a shirt and shoes. "Where do you live?"

She hesitated. Nick sensed her unease. Clearly, someone had done a major number on this woman. Hurt her on some very fundamental level.

The legal system classified what Nick had done as a crime. But he'd never hurt any person. That was where he drew the line.

"I live on Upper Great Bear Road," Stephanie said, looking him straight in the eye.

Nick mentally whistled. She called the most expensive stretch of real estate in Princeton home. He bowed and handed her his arm. "My chariot awaits. Unless you've changed your mind. The invitation stands."

Stephanie shook her head and led the way out. With a last regretful look at his bed, Nick followed.

* * * * *

The drive through the quiet streets passed quickly. As they distanced themselves from Nick's house, Stephanie allowed herself to relax. "You can just drop me on the corner," she said as they approached her house.

"I'll walk you to the door. Make sure you get in safely."

"That's totally not necessary." She opened her purse and put her hand around her house key.

He turned to her. "Not sure whether to kiss me good night or not?"

Thank goodness it was too dark in the car for Nick to see the blush that heated her face. As if a good-night kiss could be an issue after the way they'd made love…

Stephanie struggled to find a response that would suffice to keep him at bay yet allow her to hide her misgivings. After floundering for several moments, she gave up. No point in prolonging the agony. "Look, Nick. Tonight was a mistake. It's not going to happen again. I'd prefer it if we could both forget what…what passed between us. To be honest, if not seeing exactly where I live would help you to block your memory, I'm all for it."

He pulled over to the curb and shut his engine. She reached for the door handle, but he was faster.

"My memory's too sharp for that, and I expect yours is too." Nick wasn't about to let her cut them short just like that. He wouldn't allow the deer-in-the-headlights look in her eyes to weaken his resolve.

"Nick," she said, her voice pitched low, "I can't do this."

That was the one thing she could have said that would get to him. Not that she didn't want to be with him, but that she couldn't. "Why not?"

She sighed and shook her head. "It's a long and very sad story. Not one I particularly want to share with you now. I've messed up my life, big time. And the only way to get back on track is to keep my life simple. Meaning no entanglements."

He cupped her chin in his hand so that they were looking deep into each other's eyes. "From where I'm standing, your life looks pretty damned good. And you're a very special lady. That's not what I'd call 'messing up'."

She pulled away from him but didn't try to escape from the car again. "I'm twenty-eight and living back home with my parents. Pretty pathetic."

He shrugged. "Why do you have such a low opinion of your life?"

She appeared to consider for several moments. "All right. You asked for it. I'm going to give you the condensed version. And then you'll see why I really am better off alone."

He opened his arms. "I'm all ears. But lean against me. Not as cozy as my bed, but it'll keep us warm while we talk."

After another short hesitation, she moved into his arms and snuggled into the perfect spot. He grew hard when he felt her settle against him, and he squirmed to keep his erection away from her for now. He nuzzled her softly, inhaling her warmth.

"If you do that, I can't think," she whispered in protest. Good. He wanted his touch to affect her. But he also wanted to hear what she had to say, so he eased off.

"I used to own an art gallery in New York."

"Impressive. Are you an artist?"

She shook her head. "I'm more a wannabe. I dabble. But when it comes to knowing art, having a great eye, that's where my talent lies. Which was why I opened my gallery. And I was very successful."

"What happened to change that?"

She sighed and shook her head, seeming to find it difficult to reply. At last she spoke. "The wrong guy. My boyfriend." She spat out the last word. "My partner in the gallery. He ripped off my clients by foisting forgeries on them. He also stole everything from my condo before he and his girlfriend hotfooted it off to Brazil. I had to sell the condo and what was left of the business to reimburse my clients. Which is why I had to move back home."

A shiver of misgiving snaked its way down Nick's spine. "Sounds like a total asshole creep. Uh, when did this all happen?"

"A year ago. A very long year ago." She shook her head again. "Don't you see, Nick? I'm just starting to crawl out from under. I can't let anything in my life distract me from that."

"What was your boyfriend's name?" It couldn't possibly be...

"I don't even like to say it. Why do you want to know?"

Why? Because he had to know. He hoped it wasn't what he suspected. "It'll give me a more complete picture."

"I don't see how or why."

"I know people. Maybe there's something I can do to help you get back at this guy."

"I doubt that. He appeared to have a very foolproof plan. Brazil has no extradition, lots of beaches. He and the bimbo can live high on the hog for a long time."

Yeah, what she was talking about sounded very familiar. He knew about a guy and his girlfriend who had to escape to Brazil, but he'd understood it was to get away from her insanely jealous, powerful ex. "The guy's name?" he asked hoarsely.

She screwed up her beautiful lips, looking as if she'd just taken in a mouthful of brackish water. "Raoul. I don't want to say his last name now or ever again."

Shit. It had to be Raoul Gelure. How many Raouls could there have been running around needing papers last year? Providing Gelure and his girlfriend with the false documents that got them to Brazil had led to his current situation vis-à-vis the FBI. And now to find out that Gelure had screwed up Stephanie's life… And Gelure couldn't have gotten away without Nick's documents.

Shit, shit, shit. Nick wanted to confess it all to Stephanie, and, most of all, to tell her that it wasn't her fault. Gelure was an accomplished con, which Nick didn't learn until he found out that the creep had given Interpol his name. From a mutual acquaintance, Nick had learned that Gelure wanted to make sure any link to him would be destroyed.

Nick bit his lip. He couldn't imagine there'd be any way Stephanie would agree to see him again if she found out the connection between him and Gelure. And Nick knew, better than he knew his own name, that he wanted to see this woman again. To be with her. Both for himself as a man and because he needed her to get the Feds off his back.

He needed to think, a challenge with her so near. "I want to see you again, Stephanie. Maybe I can help. But most important, I want to be with you. Nothing you said convinces me we couldn't be better together than apart."

"Were you even listening?" She sounded exasperated.

"More than you can imagine."

"I give up. You can walk me to my door. And you can call me again."

That was probably as much as he could expect her to agree to tonight.

"Right. I'll call you tomorrow. Or do you just want to save time and set up to meet tomorrow night?"

"Call me. Don't make any assumptions about tomorrow night." She reached for the door handle. This time he got out of the car and went around to her side. When she got out of the car, he put his hand at the small of her back. "Which house is yours?"

She pointed to a large-columned house halfway down the block. Huge, gorgeously landscaped. It looked exactly like the kind of house he'd have expected her to come from. The kind he wanted for his future because it sure hadn't been part of his past.

The night air felt quite cool. Stephanie shivered, and Nick put his arm around her. They walked up the long drive to her door in companionable silence. And then she drew out her key to unlock the large wooden door.

No debate. He drew her to him, and his lips found hers. Starting softly, he felt himself invited into her warmth. She responded to his every nuance, the subtlest touch of his mouth and teeth on hers. And then he felt her tear trickle down from her eye to his cheek.

* * * * *

Stephanie felt Nick's erection burrow into her. She wanted nothing more than to grind herself against him, to feel again the pleasure of his cock in her. But she could never allow herself such abandon again. Though she hated to believe it, this kiss would be their very last contact. Tomorrow, she'd instruct the housekeeper and anyone else who might ever answer the family phone that she didn't want ever to talk to Nick Love.

Chapter Four

80

Determined to avoid thinking about Nick, Stephanie kept herself very busy the next day. To her surprise, she managed to accomplish more in one day than she had the whole week before. Which was almost enough to distract her from the fact that Nick never called. Not even once was she able to have whatever small thrill she might have derived from knowing that someone told him she wasn't available.

At moments, she found her mind drifting back to the night before. She could close her eyes and reexperience the feel of Nick's touch, his breath warm on her. Her pussy contracted pleasurably at the sensual memory of being with him. Stephanie promptly squelched the frisson of pleasure that threatened to light her up. She couldn't let herself go there, needed to keep her emotions on a tight leash.

After all they'd experienced together, he still didn't call. Just like every other creep her girlfriends complained about. Why did men say they'd call and then didn't? One of the eternal mysteries of the universe.

Stephanie printed off a letter, firmly affixed her signature to the bottom of the page and frowned. She'd imagined Nick would be different. Ha! Her magnificent lack of judgment about the character — or lack of character — of a man struck again.

She'd been so sure Nick would be more trustworthy than Raoul. But so far he was showing himself to be in the same league. She snorted. He'd made such a big deal about seeing her tonight. If she'd been fool enough to say yes, he'd probably have stood her up.

What was it with men anyway?

* * * * *

"When do you expect to have access to Wilson's credit card information?" Jackson Pelletier, Nick's contact at Elite, asked. The largest diamond Nick had ever seen glittered on a thick yellow gold ring whenever Pelletier moved his hand.

Nick squirmed. These days, he was role-playing on so many levels that he needed a score card to keep his own identity straight. He was Nick Love, who'd told Stephanie he was a private investigator — a necessary lie he winced at. His real work, former creator of documents to help people over the complications in their lives, had made him good money — and led directly to where he was now — working undercover for the FBI. As such, he was supposedly an independent contractor of the Elite to Meet Online Dating Service, assigned to act the part of one of their clients. The deal was for him to use his role as an eligible bachelor to help Elite with their flourishing identity theft business.

It killed him to know he was going to have to act like he was setting Stephanie up for the identity theft scam. Especially in light of what had gone down with her and Gelure.

The upside of the whole affair, if there was one, was that he wasn't going to call her. Which meant he wouldn't be using her as a mark. The downside was she'd probably hate his guts, seeing him as another lying creep. But if he broke off contact with Stephanie, Elite would have to find some other victim for the plot, keeping her out of it. Even though he knew the mark wouldn't really be harmed this time, he wanted Stephanie clear of the temporary pain that being Elite's target would cause.

The real downside was how miserable he felt without her. Which he had no intention of letting Pelletier suspect. "Wilson won't go on a second date with me. I must have bombed."

Pelletier looked skeptical. "That's hard to believe. A smooth operator like you? I'm sure you can find a way to get her to change her mind and date you."

Nick raised a brow. "You know these rich women. They don't answer their own phones. I've left her a dozen messages, called at times I was sure she'd be home. Nada. Zip. Maybe you'd better give me another name to try."

Pelletier's mouth curled in disgust. "Candidates of Wilson's caliber do not come along every day. She's currently our top priority—a prime target." He looked Nick over. "I didn't think you'd need advice for handling the clients."

Nick bit back an angry response. Despite his personal disappointment at realizing he shouldn't contact Stephanie, he'd ultimately felt some relief at keeping her out of the inevitable legal crap that would come up when the case cracked. He figured that once he cleared his name and saw Elite put out of business, he'd be able to return to Stephanie with a clean slate. Well, an almost-clean slate. He'd have to rethink how he made his living—he'd have to have a lot more to offer than a hot time with the document maker who'd helped the crook who ruined her life. "I struck out. It happens. Not often, but it happens."

Pelletier scowled. "It isn't going to happen this time. You get Wilson to go out with you again and you get her to trust you with her data. Make her fall in love, that sorta shit. Or you're out of here. You've got three days."

Nick knew the FBI wasn't going to give him any second chances either. But three days didn't give him much room to maneuver.

* * * * *

Stephanie had an appointment with the owner of a small gallery in Princeton, the first time she'd actually been able to get anyone from the art community to meet with her. Her first reaction to getting the appointment had been to want to share the news with Nick. Amazing, and sad, how much he'd gotten to her in just a short time.

Lois Hudson, the gallery owner, showed Stephanie around the small showroom. The Hudson Gallery primarily showcased the work of one artist, a painter who specialized in scenes from France and Italy. Stephanie admired the work, but, most of all, she savored being back in a gallery atmosphere. Even if it wasn't her gallery, even if the jolt of envy at being in someone else's gallery wrenched her gut. Some day — soon, she hoped — but some day, she'd have her own gallery again. Only this time, she wouldn't let anyone take it away from her.

"As you can see, I really have only a small operation here," Lois Hudson said after the tour as she poured a cup of coffee for Stephanie.

"I love the way the artist uses light and shadow," Stephanie said.

Lois sat back in her chair and smiled. "Yes. That's the exact reason why I chose to sell his art. And marry him."

Stephanie had to swallow back the tide of jealousy that threatened to engulf her and spew forth in flames. Also the flood of misgivings. A marriage license was no guarantee of anything. Maybe Lois Hudson would be ripped off as badly as she'd been. "You opened the gallery just to represent the artist?"

The other woman appeared to ponder the question. "I wouldn't put it quite like that. Vittorio actually put up the funds to start the business. He also devoted a great deal of energy to persuading me to cast my lot with an artist." She smiled with evident contentment. "It's been ten years. Our lives together just keep getting better and better."

Okay. Jealousy, real and massive, was entirely justified. Unfortunately, she'd have to keep that thought bottled up inside. "But doesn't your husband have to travel a lot for his painting?"

"Vittorio's semi-retired now, so he doesn't travel as much as he used to. We're starting to bring in other artists' work for when he decides that he will no longer paint." She grew quiet for a moment. "His eyesight isn't what it used to be."

"I'm sorry," Stephanie said, surprising herself as she realized how genuine her emotion was.

"He's philosophical about it. Regards his art as a gift that's transitory. Once he stops painting, he'll take a greater hand in the day-to-day operation of the gallery. Probably teach, help to bring along young artists."

"He sounds remarkable."

"He is." Lois appeared to enjoy a memory for a moment. "So now that you've seen the gallery, do you feel you want to take it on for the next month?"

Here it was. Her first solid chance to rebuild her life. "I would be honored to have the opportunity."

Lois put down her coffee cup. "And we'd be thrilled to have someone of your caliber taking charge in our absence. You see, Vittorio wants me along this time when he returns to Europe for what will probably be his last painting expedition."

Stephanie blinked back the tears that sprang to her eyes. Geesh, the past few days, she'd been on an emotional roller coaster. Ready to cry at the drop of a hat. No reason for her to be sad. Not when it sounded like both Lois and Vittorio easily accepted what was going on in their lives.

After Stephanie and Lois concluded their arrangements— Stephanie would spend a week at the gallery while Lois was still there, and after Lois left, she'd be in charge—Stephanie decided celebration was in order. She stifled the impulse to call Nick. She could have called Gretchen or one of her other buddies but, after all, it was the middle of a work day for most. Even, probably, for Nick.

Instead, she'd have lunch out then head home to begin getting ready for her upcoming work.

She couldn't have explained why she chose to eat at the same restaurant where she and Nick had eaten. It didn't have anything to do with wanting to have a piece of him involved with her good fortune, right?

She'd just lifted her wineglass to toast her change of fortune when she looked up— and her eyes locked with those of Nick Love.

* * * * *

He couldn't avoid her. Not now. Not when he'd caught the look of naked hunger in her eyes, and she'd surely seen the same in his.

"Champagne brunch?" he asked, sitting down uninvited opposite her.

She put down her flute and appeared to debate several possible responses before she answered. "You said you'd call." Her voice sounded wounded.

Trust a woman to come up with the standard opening salvo. "And would I have gotten through to you if I had?" He was going on pure intuition here, but her wince told him he'd guessed right about her layers of protection.

"Maybe." After a nonchalant shrug, she nodded to an approaching server. "Another flute, please."

Nick relaxed. Obviously, she was going to invite him to join her. Now if only he could be here as himself instead of as part of the Elite scam—and FBI undercover. "So why the champagne?"

She smiled, and the places in his heart still intact melted. "Good news, Nick Love. I have a gallery job for the next few months."

The server brought the flute for Nick, removed the bottle from the cooler, and poured a generous helping of the bubbly. Nick toasted Stephanie, and they both sipped. "Talk to me. Where, when, what, how?"

Stephanie cheerfully shared her news. Along the way, they ordered a dish of strawberries, which tasted amazing with the champagne. "So you'll be staying here in Princeton for the next few months?"

She nodded. "I could get my own place, but that would take time and energy away from maximizing my gallery experience."

"You're always welcome to crash with me."

She made a face. "Aside from the fact of our meeting by accident today, I have no intention of continuing to see you."

"There are no accidents." He reached out to take her hand and closed his eyes at the rush of pleasure that coursed through him at the merest contact with her. He traced the lines of her palm and treasured the slight moan of longing she allowed to escape from between her tightly closed lips.

He wanted to taste her, to lick the champagne that lingered on her mouth. "You know you want to be with me again. Don't say things you don't mean."

She snatched her hand from his and looked at him with pain in her eyes. "Is that particular privilege reserved for men only?"

Now it was his turn to wince. How could she ever understand the complexity of what was going on in his life? The last thing he wanted was to hurt her, to lie to her. But if he had any shot at ever being with her, he'd have to lie to get there. After all, Stephanie Wilson was not the sort of woman who'd be waiting around for years 'til he got free of his legal hassles. Which meant he had to get it all resolved before he could really tell her everything he wanted to.

None of which stopped him from wanting to be with her. Especially now, when she deserved and needed someone to share her good news. "I'm not responsible for the bad behavior of other men."

"True. Which brings us right back to the fact that you didn't call." A glint of sadness returned to her eyes.

"Give me a break on that, okay?" Later on, he'd have to ask her for a lot more than that. If there was going to be a later on for them.

"And I should do that why?" she challenged him.

"Trust me on this."

She shook her head. "Don't even go there, Nick."

He held his hands up in a hear-me-out gesture. "I won't use the T word. But I will tell you there's stuff going on, stuff I can't tell you about now. I promise I'll tell you everything as soon as I can." He could imagine she wasn't any happier about the word "promise" than she was about "trust". Too bad he couldn't avoid using either.

Instead of responding with words, Stephanie threw some money on the table, rose, turned on her heel, and left.

Nick jumped up and flew out the door after Stephanie. He wasn't about to let her get away from him, not this time.

"Stephanie, stop. Please." He grabbed hold of her and wouldn't let go. The two of them excited only mild notice on the Princeton street.

"Thank you for ruining my first happy moment in a year!" she hissed, shaking him off.

"I don't want to ruin your happy time, I want to expand on it. Look, I know we've got some issues. But how about we take today as a time-out. So we can really celebrate in a magical way before you have to throw yourself into your hard work."

She regarded him warily, but she didn't run away. "A time-out?"

He grinned. "Yeah. Just you, me, and the ocean. Let's go down the shore and shout your news out loud enough so they hear you in Europe."

* * * * *

It was like he keyed in to her favorite fantasy. She loved the ocean, loved living near enough to head for the shore whenever the hurt got too unbearable. "You like the shore?"

"Love it. Started building castles when I still had to crawl to collect the sand."

"Everything's closed down now. It's out of season."

"Like the shore can ever be out of season," he scoffed. "I look at it like there won't be crowds of people getting in our face. We'll have the sea and the sand to ourselves."

Suddenly nothing she could think of sounded like a more delightful way to celebrate than being at the shore with him. She imagined him in skin-tight trunks, taking her by the hand and pulling her out into the cold water. And then she pictured him out of those trunks, the water lapping their skin and washing away traces of sand.

Stephanie shook her head and attempted to push away the fear of going to her favorite place with Nick Love. What better way to celebrate the upturn in her life. But she wasn't going to hand him an easy win. "I can go for a short time. As in we'll have to turn around and head for home soon after we get there."

He mock-saluted. "Today's your party, my lady. You call the shots. I'll just fire up my bike, and we're off."

A shiver of pleasure caressed her spine and rode the back of her neck at the thought of making the trip nestled behind Nick. "Which shore do you go to?"

"Seaside."

Nick handed her a helmet. "Ever ridden a bike before?"

Even if she hadn't, she'd have faked it. Luckily, she had. "Of course." Luckily also, she'd worn slacks to her interview. Having to deal with a skirt would have been a major deal breaker. The sun shone down warmly, and every tree seemed to have chosen just that time to go into full bloom. The promise of the coming summer lay heavy on the air. Ready as Stephanie felt to rejoin the world of people who worked regularly, a hint of spring fever threaded its way into her consciousness. Indolence, the long, lazy days of summer tempted her—though not nearly as much as Nick Love did. Wedged behind him on his bike, she leaned her cheek against his leather-jacketed back and clasped her hands around his waist.

* * * * *

The feel of Stephanie's arms around him hit Nick with a jolt of sexual adrenaline. His erection tented his jeans and he squirmed on the bike's hard leather seat. Great! He did not particularly look forward to the drive down the shore with a hard-on, but he couldn't seem to lose it while this beautiful lady held him. He'd live up to his own words and take the day as a reprieve, a time when he didn't have to think about his legal situation. Today would be a gift for both of them, something they could look back at once the shit hit the fan.

The wind whipped them as they sped to the shore. The tang of salt air soon surrounded them. "We're here," he murmured, maneuvering his bike through the maze of streets that would take them out to the boardwalk. Nick parked his bike, the sole vehicle in a long stretch. His erection, feeling like a permanent fixture whenever he was near Stephanie, cried out for relief.

* * * * *

Stephanie had gone into a dream state during the ride down to the shore. Now the roar of the waves and the bite of the cool salty air stirred her to wakefulness. Feeling more energetic than she had in months, Stephanie wanted to embrace the whole scene and make her mark on the beach.

The moment Nick parked the bike, she grabbed his hand. "Race you to the water." She pulled him just a short way, then dropped his hand and ran out ahead. For just a moment, she ran alone, experiencing the joy of the wind and the ocean spray caressing her face. And then Nick caught her in his arms and lifted her high in the air.

* * * * *

He couldn't wait, not a moment longer. Now that he had her in his arms, he thought he'd explode if he didn't have her — here, now, totally his.

With her hair whipping loose around them, Nick whispered hoarsely in her ear. "I need you so."

Was it his imagination or did she nod her assent? He didn't pause to ask. With a groan of pent-up desire, he captured her mouth with his lips and drank deeply of her essence. The salt of the sea blended with her sweetness, bringing the world of sensation to their cozy corner. As he tasted her, probed her with his tongue, he hugged her to him. And then she slowly slipped from his arms, standing upright next to him. Her arms went around him, and, with a sigh of relief, he pressed his erection against her taut belly. His balls contracted, and he couldn't keep from deepening their embrace even more.

He wanted to kiss her more, but he also wanted to taste her everywhere, to experience the convergence of his lips and her body so that she was totally his.

"Ah, Nick," she sighed.

"I'm here." He ran his hands firmly down her sides, thrilling at the beauty of her curves. He buried his head in her breasts and grasped her so tightly that their clothing molded to every aroused millimeter of skin.

Stephanie stiffened. Using every ounce of willpower, Nick pulled away from her for just a moment. "I can't do this," she whispered, but her eyes gave him a different message. He slid down along her body and held her to him, his face in her belly. He could feel her quiver, and he heard her moan softly. "Yes, you can," he whispered, forming the words against her belly. Her gentle tremor answered him.

His face pressed into her, Nick ran a hand up Stephanie's leg, lingering on her upper thigh. Stephanie thrust her hips forward, and Nick knew she wanted him. He helped her ease down her slacks as he made soft sounds of invitation, telling her how much he wanted to please her, to bring her to ecstasy. He palmed her pussy, and Stephanie sighed her agreement.

With infinite slowness, he began to caress her lovely mound, warm and wet with her desire for him, through the thin silk of her panties. Something crumbled in his heart at the realization, again, that this beautiful woman was opening herself up to him. The subtle rhythmic rocking of her hips matched the deliberation of how he stroked her. And then they both began to move with more urgency.

Stephanie groaned, and the sound flew upward to join the faraway call of a gull. Nick slipped one finger inside her panties and felt her wet warmth engulf him.

Stephanie nuzzled his neck with her cheek and made small incoherent sounds that he understood as her way to ask for more. With his thumb he circled her sensitive clit, feeling her shudder from the sensation. Soon he slipped a finger inside to touch her there. His cock, straining hard against the fly of his jeans, throbbed to be where his finger was. Nick gritted his teeth. He'd never been one for patience. But for now, all that mattered was her pleasure.

* * * * *

The world began and ended with the two of them on this beach, with Nick's fingers touching her most intimate spots as the sun shone and the waves lapped against the shore. She'd lost all sense of modesty, of caution, letting him see this side of her that craved only gratification at his hands, nothing more.

Stephanie wanted the ecstasy to continue forever, the intense buildup that raised her ever higher. But, as much as she longed to climax, she knew that once she did, this pleasure would come to an end. Still, she couldn't hold back. When she felt Nick raise her up, bringing her to the dizzying heights of her orgasm, she could no better keep herself from coming than she could stop the waves from spraying the shore. "Oh, Nick," she cried when her moment was upon her. "Now, like that. *Now.*"

"Oh, baby, it's all here for you," he whispered. The sound of his voice got lost in the swirl of pleasure taking her over and in her own cries of relief.

When the last shock wave of her orgasm passed, Stephanie collapsed against Nick. He gently nuzzled her. She'd never felt as close to anyone as she did at this moment. Her face now stained with tears she couldn't explain, she brought her lips to his for a long, deep kiss.

In that kiss, she told him everything she didn't have the words to say. How much she wanted him, wanted to be able to open herself to him and trust him. How afraid she was and yet how being with him made her want to be unafraid.

From the way he answered her with his lips and teeth and tongue, she understood that his feelings ran as deep as hers. He'd also been hurt in the past, also had his trust betrayed. Maybe, just maybe, they could find a very special place together. A place where they both could begin to believe again.

Then, through the haze of her sensation, Stephanie felt Nick's hard cock pressed against her. It wasn't like her to be selfish. Here this marvelous man had just pleasured her nearly out of her mind. Now it was his turn. She ran her hand down his burgeoning length. His gasp delighted her. She loved having the power to make him react, just as he'd done to her. In moments, her fingers trembling, she'd undone his zipper and freed his magnificent cock. Then, with her hands running down his sides, she sank to her knees.

* * * * *

So excited, Nick had to grit his teeth not to come the moment she touched him. He hadn't felt this out of control since high school. And then when Stephanie sank down to her knees, he almost lost it. She stroked him once, twice, and then she opened her beautiful mouth and took him into her. Lost in the sheer sensation of having her tongue and teeth surround him, Nick felt like he'd gone out of the ordinary world to a whole new planet where he could feel a pleasure unlike any he'd ever known before.

In moments, Stephanie had his pants down and was clutching him by the ass as she licked and sucked him with gusto. He gently held her head to him, opening his eyes briefly to look down and see her gorgeous wheat-blonde hair whipping around her in the delicious wind that did little to cool him off.

Just when he believed that nothing could raise the level of pleasure he was experiencing, Stephanie tentatively began to finger the crack of his ass. He couldn't take much more.

What still remained of his mind flickered to the etiquette of the current situation. He knew he was about to come, but he didn't know how Stephanie would feel about him coming in her mouth. The question in his mind sufficed to help him last a bit longer. More than anything at this moment, he wanted to come in her mouth. He wanted that completion. Well, maybe not more than having his cock buried deep in her pussy, but that wasn't going to happen this time around.

The touch of her fingers on his crack escalated the level of sensation. All the while he thrust forward, he moved his butt to maximize her touch back there.

The meanderings of his mind did little to slow the action. "Stephanie, I'm going to come. As in right now." He figured this was her chance to take her mouth off him.

To his surprised pleasure, she began to suck even harder and held him closer to her. He lost it. With a triumphant cry he let go. And go and go.

When he at last subsided, Stephanie slowly withdrew. Then she looked up at him, her smile moist with his cum.

His heart surged, and he was a goner. He was hers—for as long as she'd let him be. And beyond.

* * * * *

Stephanie had never done anything as spontaneous as what she'd just done with Nick. For once she really just gave in to her instincts, without second-guessing herself.

After they'd both righted themselves, they walked along the beach, arms around each other, in companionable silence. She wished they could just continue as they were, right now, both warm in the glow of their spontaneous loving. But she knew they could keep real life at bay only for a limited time. In fact, she should be returning home now. Very soon. Her celebration of her new job had turned into much more than she'd imagined possible. But that, unfortunately, didn't mean that she could continue to play hooky from her real life. Now that she had the opportunity to start rebuilding her career, she couldn't let anything stand in the way. Not even her growing feelings for Nick.

"Where to now, babe?" he asked softly.

"I need to get home," she said with regret.

He turned to her and cupped her chin in his hand. "I thought you were going to take the whole day off to celebrate."

She shook her head. "Can't afford a whole day. I really need to go home and start going over all the reading material my new boss gave me."

That gleam in his eye would do her in. "Shouldn't take long. You are a speed reader, aren't you?"

"I'm pretty fast, but not that fast." She laughed. "Nick Love, you're going to ruin me with all your temptation. But I've got to say no."

He spread his arms wide, indicating the full expanse of the beach. "You're really going to say goodbye to all this magnificence?"

Saying goodbye to him would be a lot more difficult than leaving the beach, but she wasn't about to tell him that. "In a word, yes. Please take me home."

"Your wish, my command." He mock-bowed. "But how about we go out tonight for a really great dinner. More champagne to toast your new job. All the burgers you can eat. What do you say?"

"An offer I can't refuse."

He scowled. "Was that sarcasm I just heard from the magnificent lips of Stephanie Wilson?"

She rolled her eyes. Actually, burgers and champagne was beginning to sound pretty good to her. But she wanted to see how far he'd go with the joke.

"Not a big fan of champagne out of paper cups at the burger place? Even with fries?"

"Now you're hitting below the belt. How can a girl say no to fries?"

"Oh, so you'll reject me but say yes to fries?"

They continued to banter as they walked back to where he had parked his bike. She really did find it difficult to leave the shore, which had been dream-perfect today. But there would be other perfect days. After the year she'd just gone through, she knew she couldn't count on there always being other opportunities for her to rebuild her career.

"Tell you what," he said, sounding like a carnival barker. "If I can't pull you away from your work with an offer of burgers, how about dinner at Chez Clay. Champagne included. And me."

Now there were several offers she couldn't refuse. Chez Clay was a hot new restaurant her friends had been raving about. Celebrating there with Nick… A girl could only be so strong.

"What time?" she asked in capitulation.

"How about I pick you up at seven-thirty."

She nodded. "But now I really have to get home. No way I'll be able to enjoy dinner if I don't get through everything I planned to read today."

By now they'd reached his bike. He saluted. "Fair lady, I'm at your service."

With a small shiver of regret, Stephanie said goodbye to the shore and climbed on behind Nick for the ride home.

Chapter Five

✍

"So, Love, you made any progress with the Wilson dame?" Pelletier's voice blared from Nick's answering machine. Nick frowned. For just a short time today, he'd almost been able to forget about the Elite to Meet Online Dating Service and the FBI, his reality. "Get back to me as soon as you hear this message." Though Pelletier didn't add "Or else", Nick heard the implied threat.

He couldn't do this. He couldn't jeopardize what was growing between him and Stephanie. Though Pelletier had been adamant about not switching Nick to another client, Nick would try again. This time, he'd have to come up with the right argument. He practiced it in his head as he drove down to the office. Fortunately, his man was in. Nick began talking before he sat down. "Stephanie Wilson is personally broke and in debt. To be honest, now that I've gotten to know her, she's a piss-poor candidate for your deal."

Pelletier eyed Nick warily. "The Wilson family is well-known in the community and beyond for their wealth. Stephanie's living with Mom and Pop. Sounds perfect to me."

Nick made a moue of disagreement. "She's only living at home to have a roof over her head while she regroups. Seems that she lost her business and her home in New York after some scandal involving her boyfriend." Who was it who'd told him that the most effective way to lie was to include some elements of truth in your fabrication?

"What are you saying, Love?"

"That she's very independent and keeps herself separate from her parents when it comes to access to assets. As soon as she's got enough dough put together, she's going to fly the coop again to set up on her own."

Pelletier looked unconvinced. "Even with her wings clipped like they've been, Wilson is probably worth your special attentions."

Damn. Nick didn't feel like he was getting anywhere. "You really gotta trust me on this one. Her credit card limit is barely into four digits. She's not worth the effort. Set me up with another date and I'll deliver the goods. But Wilson isn't going to give enough of a return to be worth any more investment of time or money."

Pelletier stroked his chin and appeared to be considering what Nick had to say. "All right, Love. But we want you to get on this pronto. We can't have a nonproductive associate on our books for as long as you're turning out to take. I'm going to assign you to another candidate who just signed up. Billionaire family. You can call and make a date for tonight."

Nick almost reeled from the speed at which Pelletier changed course. Now the focus of Nick's problem had shifted from appearing to exploit Stephanie to appearing to dump her to date someone else.

Though at this point it was difficult for Nick to believe he and Stephanie had the possibility of any sort of a future, he wanted tonight. He'd made a date with her, and he owed her. Whatever happened—or didn't—from this day forward, at least they'd have tonight. He owed it to both of them to make it a true night to remember.

* * * * *

Stephanie couldn't help herself. Like it said in that old Broadway show tune, she felt like a "cockeyed optimist". She grinned at the word "cockeyed". In view of Nick's gorgeous cock the word seemed to take on a whole new dimension of possible meanings.

After the year from hell, it seemed like her life was finally headed in the right direction. She'd paid off all the debts Raoul had left her with, she seemed to be on a path to earning back her good name and a place in the art world, and, real caution here, Nick Love had come into her life. Despite her initial resistance, he was claiming a place in her life that she was becoming more and more eager to have him take.

Tonight, it would all come together when he took her out to celebrate her new job. And then, talking about coming together… Stephanie caught her reflection in the mirror. No surprise to see she was blushing like a neon light. At exactly what point would she finally stop blushing? Probably wouldn't happen as long as Nick Love continued to be around. For however long that might be.

She grinned to herself as she pulled out the perfect dress. With great effort, she banished all her misgivings and the usual self-torture she had a tendency to put herself through. Tonight, she'd live in the moment. Enjoy the celebration and the man and not second- or third-guess what was going on.

* * * * *

Nick took a deep breath before he rang the bell discreetly placed beside the elegant double doors of Stephanie's house. Stephanie's family's house. He didn't put on a suit and tie for just anyone, and now he resisted the urge to loosen the collar imprisoning his neck.

The collar wasn't the only thing he felt tightening around his neck. How would Stephanie feel if she knew tonight would be their last time together? Would she hold back, try to protect her feelings? Everything he knew about her told him she would. And he didn't want her to hold anything back tonight.

Nick didn't know what to expect when he heard the doorbell's chime echo through the huge house. Would some servant or a snooty butler answer the door? Direct him to the withdrawing room? Feeling like he'd just overdosed on Masterpiece Theatre, Nick shook his head. Whoever answered, he'd deal. Even if it was Stephanie's father holding a Princetonian's equivalent of a hillbilly shotgun.

To his delight and relief, Stephanie, looking totally amazing, answered the door herself. So much for his biases and prejudices. In a flowing dress splashed with big peach-colored daisies and her hair down past her shoulders, she looked like the goddess of spring. Forget dinner. He wanted to nibble on the tender skin between her neck and shoulder, bury himself in her fresh, sexy scent.

"You clean up good," she said by way of greeting, giving him the old up and down survey. She stepped out of her house, closed the door, and gave him her arm.

"You can do better than that," he growled, helping himself to the first of what he intended to be many kisses. He wanted to ask her why she'd answered the door instead of staff, but decided the question sounded too naïve.

Fortunately, Stephanie supplied the information without any prompting. "The housekeeper, cook, and driver have the night off. My parents are out of town for separate conferences."

"Anyone else live here?"

She shook her head. "My brother and sister moved out years ago. I can't believe I had to move back. Neither of them ever did."

He scanned the impressive façade. "For a place to be stuck moving back to, it ain't bad."

She rolled her eyes. "I know that. It's just, being the youngest, I always had to put up with their acting like they were superior. Now they've both proven it."

He stopped, held her tight against him and kissed her 'til they were both breathless. "I consider you superior. In all ways."

Though he'd have liked to spend more time doing just what they were, he'd nearly had to sell his soul to get the reservations at Chez Clay for tonight. He figured showing up late would not win friends or influence the right people. "Come on, Stephanie. We've got a whole lot of celebrating to do."

In moments, they arrived at his BMW and drove off.

* * * * *

A-list restaurants were nothing new for Stephanie. Her parents had made a point of starting her dining-out experiences while she was still in a highchair. But Chez Clay was something brand new. Or maybe being in the elegant bistro with Nick tipped the whole evening into something extraordinary.

She couldn't have said why. But tonight, the colors and scents of the flowers on their round table captivated her. Each bite of the food felt like a whole new sensory discovery; the wine tasted like nectar for the gods. The background music set the perfect tone for the dining and the conversations around her. All the other diners appeared especially elegant and amiable. But Nick's presence dwarfed all else in its significance. Every moment with him was a celebration. After toasting her new job and all the opportunities opening up before her, Stephanie truly did begin to feel like a whole new chapter in her life was about to begin. A chapter she felt lots happier about than the one she'd been stuck in for the previous year.

Each moment felt supercharged, almost magical. Still, the evening flew by. And then it was time for the next phase. Stephanie had no doubt that they would spend the night together. What she didn't know was how or where. Only with whom. And she was more than content to leave the details to Nick.

* * * * *

Nick almost couldn't stand it. Being with Stephanie this whole evening felt closer to perfect than anything he'd ever before experienced. No way was he going to let a single moment of this night be spent away from her. He wouldn't let the realization that this would be their last time together impinge in any way on the exquisite web of sentiment between them.

When they exited Chez Clay, darkness gently cloaked the Princeton streets. A cool spring breeze lightly refreshed people strolling on the sidewalks, gazing at shop windows, chatting companionably with other walkers. With his arm around Stephanie's waist, Nick guided her in a slow walk. "Your place or mine?" he asked, his light tone belying the seriousness of his question.

Stephanie laughed. "I expect the staff have returned home by now. They're usually in bed quite early, especially Mrs. Hutchins, the housekeeper with a thousand ears and eyes."

"Ah, no privacy in the mansion."

She tsked. "It's not really a mansion. And I'd say there's lots of privacy, despite Mrs. Hutchins' evil eye. On the other hand, she does have an uncanny ability to see and hear through thick plaster walls." Stephanie found herself enjoying the mild game they were playing, wondering when he'd make his move.

"Stephanie Wilson, I don't want tonight to end. Not yet. Come to my place. Now. There's nobody around there. I'll show you an even more special way to celebrate."

To prove his point, Nick began to nuzzle her on the sensitive spot along the side of her neck, the spot she'd come to think of as perfect for his vampire nibble. Hmm, if he knew how delicious that felt, he'd be really dangerous.

Okay. Game over. "Lead on."

* * * * *

The moment Stephanie said yes, Nick's heart slammed into overdrive. Much as he'd savored every moment of the date and the chance to celebrate Stephanie's good news, he'd been waiting all night for this chance to be alone with her. Now he'd have to make every moment count.

* * * * *

Returning to Nick's place, Stephanie had the curious sensation of coming back home to a place that she knew well and had visited far more often than once. She sensed some sort of shift in Nick, as if he were treating her with special care, as if she were someone precious, out of the ordinary. Though on the whole she liked the feeling, something about it almost scared her. As if Nick knew something vital that she remained in total ignorance about.

He offered her a drink, which she turned down. All she wanted was Nick. Standing behind her, he held her to him with his hands poised on her shoulders. Stephanie leaned back against Nick and felt something electric surge between them. His hard cock wedged against the top of her butt crack, and she found herself pressing back to increase the strangely stimulating contact. Nick lowered his face and nibbled at the soft skin just below the base of her neck. When she increased the pressure on his cock by tightening her cheeks, his moan reverberated through her body.

Though she'd never had any desire to have a man take her from behind, now she found herself longing to have Nick come into her in this way. Only she found herself suddenly shy, unable to ask for what she wanted.

* * * * *

Only moments after they'd come up to his place, Stephanie was already blowing his mind—taking him in a whole other direction than he'd been thinking about. He'd gone the whole nine yards to make tonight's celebration really special for her. After the fantastic dinner at Chez Clay where they'd toasted her triumph with champagne, he'd planned to punctuate their lovemaking with chocolate truffles and even more champagne. But Stephanie had him bypassing those goodies and going to a place he'd never expected to go to with her tonight.

Her derriere was too delicious and classy to resist. With a hard-on like his, saying no to the pressure of her pressing back against him would have gone against nature. He needed to be in her there, now. And the lady seemed to be shouting a loud emphatic yes.

Just in case he wasn't getting the message loud and clear, she reached around behind him and grabbed his ass with her hands, pushing him closer to her. His cock throbbed against her, and she murmured, "Mmmm." All his senses kicked into high gear as he tilted his hips and ran his cock slowly down her crack.

In moments, Stephanie joined in the rhythm he'd initiated, sliding her crack along his hard bulge.

"I want you," she hissed, raising goose bumps up and down his extremities, including the one where most of his energy focused right now.

"Oh, baby," he responded, articulate as all hell at this moment of supreme desire. "You've got me. Any way you want me."

"In me. Now. That's how I want you."

They needed to get naked. Only problem to that was having to move apart long enough to throw their clothes off.

He couldn't wait that long. Neither, evidently, could she. She pulled away from him for just a moment, long enough for her to bend over and lift the skirt of her beautiful dress up over her back. To his delight, he quickly registered that she wore only a garter belt and stockings. No panties to get in their way. Almost as if she'd been planning this very moment for hours… His cock twitched at the thought. With a growl he tore the zipper down and freed his cock about a moment before it would have burst out on its own. But this freedom did not suffice. He forced himself to stay away from ecstasy just long enough to drag his pants down and step out of them. Then, after lubricating Stephanie with a lick and a promise, he positioned his cock at the rosebud of her hole and willed himself to remember to be gentle.

* * * * *

When Nick kissed her on the hole between the cheeks, Stephanie felt a moment's hesitation before she allowed herself to savor the sensation of his tongue touching this intimate place. Thank goodness she'd convinced herself to wear her white lacy garter belt and stockings tonight. Oh, now she felt his cock right at her opening, poised to come into her. She'd been creaming all night, but now that Nick was about to enter her, her pussy began to tingle with anticipation. Just when the sensation of her clit throbbing made her wiggle and pull Nick into her, he began to stroke her there with his long, strong fingers. Now he was kissing her back, alternating the brushes of his lips with nibbles and licks.

His erection was so huge. She felt him fill up the space between her cheeks with his cock, moving up and down the narrow opening. "Oh, Nick," she encouraged him. For once, she couldn't find the words…and she didn't need to. He seemed to know exactly what was going on for her, exactly what she needed and wanted.

"You are so incredible," Nick whispered.

In response, she tried tightening her butt muscles around his cock. His groan told her the move had the desired effect.

Talk about desired effect. The combined pleasure of his cock in her butt and his fingers expertly stroking her pussy had Stephanie shaking with her building excitement. She'd never before experienced sensations of this intensity, and she almost didn't know how to react. First she panted, then she moaned. He manipulated her clit and nearly drove her out of her mind. Her cries of pleasure wouldn't have been considered ladylike by any of the criteria she'd lived by before.

All she knew was that she wanted more. She wanted to let herself explode like an overfilled boiling teakettle gone wild. In moments she'd be spurting off her steam and her cream and screaming to raise the roof. And there she was, coming to a climax that would leave her shuddering with release and amazement.

* * * * *

Nick couldn't believe the wonderful gift of herself that Stephanie gave him when she came. And came. And came. Through the wonderful sounds she made, Stephanie told him over and over how great she felt, how special this orgasm was for her. Which made it special for him. After her quaking orgasm subsided, he could no longer wait. With a whoosh of pent-up passion and a grunt, Nick began to spasm into a major come. And after he'd pumped all he had into her sweet ass, Nick sank to his knees and buried his face in the small of her back.

How could he ever bear to give up being with this wondrous woman?

* * * * *

After the loving, Nick and Stephanie lay together in a hazy kind of doze. And then Nick pulled away from Stephanie, and she ached to renew their contact. If she couldn't bear to be apart from him for just moments, how could she possibly deal with him leaving her life? This realization startled Stephanie with its ferocity. When and how had this man become so vital to her?

"Time for a champagne toast," Nick announced.

"I've had lots of champagne already," Stephanie murmured sleepily. What would this surprising man come up with now?

His mouth quirked up in his trademark grin, one side up higher than the other. The look that melted her. "But you've never sipped your champagne in the shower." While she considered that, he added, "With me."

That stopped her. Actually, even if she'd ever drunk champagne in the shower with any other lover, which she hadn't, the act of drinking with him would make it all unique and new.

Champagne bottle and two flutes in hand, Nick quietly urged Stephanie up from his bed.

Stephanie groaned. Suddenly "Lazy" had become her middle name. But Nick wasn't the kind of guy to settle for less than total compliance with his invitation. He popped open the champagne, poured some in a flute, drank some, and gave her a full champagne kiss. The drink tasted almost as delicious as he did. Wanting more of him, Stephanie sat up. She reached out for him, but he backed away just beyond her hand. Now she could see that her elegant host was totally nude. Her dress fanned out around her and felt like too much cloth. Groggily, Stephanie got to her feet and lurched out of the bed. Nick, teasing her with his smile and a slightly devilish laugh, continued to elude her.

Resolved now to catch him, Stephanie pulled her dress up over her head. Braless, she stood in her garter belt and stockings. That got his attention. Nick's cock pointed straight at her, and she nearly crowed with the glory of her power over him.

With a groan he turned around and raced for the bathroom. Stephanie lusted to get her hands on his gorgeous butt, which looked sculpted to perfection.

By the time she caught up with him, he had the shower turned on and was singing, amazingly off-key, an old Stevie Wonder song about calling to say he loved her.

Loved her. That stopped her in her tracks. Last time she'd let the word "love" into her life had been when Raoul bamboozled her. Though she could feel love in the air she breathed with Nick, she couldn't, just couldn't let herself go there.

Ah hell, all she wanted tonight was sensation and celebration. No more thinking, no more self-conversations. She shook her head to clear it and stepped into the shower with Nick.

* * * * *

If she hadn't come into the shower in one more minute, he'd have gone out, soaking wet, and scooped her up and carried her in. Which, all things considered, would have been delightful.

But she came in under her own power. As Nick poured them both flutes of champagne, he feasted his eyes on her glowing beauty. She was so amazingly gorgeous that he just wanted to worship her with his body again and again and again.

He couldn't lose the awareness that tonight would be the last time he'd ever be with her. How could he possibly make love to her enough in this one night to last him the lifetime that would stretch empty before him once she was gone?

The warm water poured down on them with just the right amount of pressure. Judging by the smile on her face, Stephanie really enjoyed the feel of the water sluicing down her body. They toasted each other and drank. With the champagne still tingling in his mouth, Nick began to trace the contours of his lady's face with his tongue. She shivered slightly in his arms, bringing out every protective instinct lurking within him.

"No fair that you have all the ammunition," Stephanie pouted.

He pressed his hard cock against her. "Hey, that's how things were set up. You know, I got the blue blanket, you got the pink one."

She rolled her eyes. "That's not what I meant, and you know it," she argued playfully. "I'm talking about the champagne."

"Catch-up time," he said by way of apology. He refilled Stephanie's flute and, his eyes locked with hers, gave it to her.

The minx proceeded to take one sip of the champagne and then pour the rest over his head. This meant war! The hell with the flutes and dainty behavior. He picked up the bottle and poured the rest of the champagne over her.

"What a waste!" She looked at him in shocked surprise.

"Waste not, want not," he mumbled before proceeding to suck and lick the champagne from all the delightful places on her body where it trickled down.

Stephanie planted her hands on either side of her head and began to laugh and wiggle as his tongue action led him to a thorough exploration of her body.

And then the laughter led to something more. Suddenly he needed to be in her more than he needed to continue breathing.

"Wash-up time," he murmured, covering his hands with the citrus-scented liquid soap he'd bought earlier that day.

"Mmm, I really like that," she whispered as he soaped the folds of her pussy. When she returned the favor and undertook a thorough cleansing of his cock, Nick felt like he'd died and gone to heaven.

Without words, they decided to speed up the cleansing process to move on to another phase of their celebration. Another time, he'd want this to be a slow process. Maybe even in a luxurious bathtub.

If there could ever be another time... But, for now, other needs drove them.

Chapter Six

ೞ

By the time she got back to Nick's bed, Stephanie was hotter than a Fourth of July rocket for him. As if they hadn't just made love before the amazing foreplay of the shower. The way Nick looked at her, she felt like a goddess adored in her most intimate sanctuary. It wasn't all just about his body, incredible as that was. The look in his eyes, the hunger of his parted lips...

"Stephanie." He exhaled her name like a prayer. All she knew was that she wanted to give this man everything he was asking for. Because whatever he wanted, she wanted too.

How could his merest touch raise such sparks of longing from her? She felt like she could self-combust at just the touch of his fingertips. His mouth fastened on hers, and whatever faculty of thought she still had evaporated into the mist of lust that enveloped them.

Stephanie shivered. Never before had she so reveled in loss of control.

Starting at her forehead, Nick traced a finger down her face, lingering at the bridge of her nose. She opened her mouth and her tongue darted out to taste another of Nick's fingers, which dangled tantalizingly nearby. Was that a sizzle they both heard where the tip of her tongue touched the callused skin around his nail? Nick reacted, moving back from her as if startled for just a moment.

They didn't linger on this gentle exploration for long. Nick cupped her chin, gazed into her eyes and, with a sigh, drew her to him for a total kiss.

Heavens, he tasted delicious to her. Exactly right and so much better. Spices and an undertone of something sweet. Just like the man himself.

While his tongue and teeth probed her with ever-increasing urgency, Nick stroked Stephanie's hair, gently nudging her cheek before running his fingers through the wheat-blonde mass. At that moment, Stephanie could have sworn there was a direct link between her hair and her clit. Tingles ran up and down her legs, her back, to converge at the center of her most sensitive spot. Now so wet for him and with a growing hunger, Stephanie pressed herself against him. Nick groaned, and Stephanie opened her legs around his and pressed her mound against the flesh of his hard thigh.

The desired contact set off waves of relief and aroused hunger throughout her. All that existed at this moment was her enormous appetite and the man who could bring her to resolution. Climax. Stephanie felt herself slide against Nick's leg as the force of her desire pushed her to cling ever tighter.

Now Nick was whispering words of encouragement. "You take it, baby. Take everything you want. I'm here for you. Only for you. Whatever you want, however you want me. Show me, tell me, ask me. Know how much I want only you, only what will bring you pleasure."

His words fell on her ears like a gift of joy, better than all the celebration her soul had previously luxuriated in.

Any last hesitation or inhibition crumbled in the tidal wave of sensation that engulfed Stephanie. While Nick sucked on her breasts, licking her nipples to hard peaks that his tongue then played with, she pressed her clit harder against his leg. He was doing some pressing of his own, namely the way he thrust his huge hard cock against her hip. Stephanie whimpered. Much as she wanted that cock in her, she couldn't get her legs to release their hold around his thigh. Not when the sensation of the contact sent arrows of quivering pleasure out across every nerve in her body.

Once Stephanie began to move her hips, she was committed. On the climax road, whether she wanted to be or not.

Trying to keep track of Nick's pleasure as she took her own, Stephanie began to stroke his shaft. Damn, she was nearly on sensation overload between what was happening in her pussy and the feel of his cock, which was so hard for her she thought he'd burst.

Maybe he thought the same thing because he removed her hand and said simply, "Your turn now."

With Raoul, it had never been her turn. But now she chose not to let thoughts of her former lover intrude upon the magic between her and Nick.

Her turn now. She'd remember he said that and make sure he got a turn too.

But first things first. Her climax had begun to build, and Stephanie prepared to give everything up in a release that would rock her.

As if she had a choice, with Nick faithfully moving his leg just enough to make her crazy. "It's all here for you, baby. I love it when you let me please you. You're so beautiful."

She felt beautiful. And free. And everything she'd ever longed to feel. Nick knew exactly how to contract his leg muscles to bring her maximum pleasure.

Panting, Stephanie howled out her orgasm, coming in waves that left her shattered — and whole.

When the sensation slowly began to ebb, Stephanie, who still felt suffused with the warmth of being with Nick the way they were, now clung to him as if from some deep visceral fear that he'd disappear if she let go for the merest moment.

* * * * *

When she came, Stephanie was hot and vulnerable, beautiful and adorable. Most of all, she was generous, both in how she opened up and shared her pleasure and in how she wanted him along for the same ride.

Yeah, his cock was bursting. And if he didn't get into her in the next minute or so, he might very well expire. But once he got intimate on that level, he'd be hard-pressed to hold on to any powers of observation. And he wanted it all. Including the knowledge and sensation of knowing every aspect of how his woman looked, tasted, acted, sounded, and felt when she came.

Her pussy warm and wet, she quivered and trembled in his arms where he wanted her to remain always.

This time, when she reached down to touch him, he didn't move away. Now he was going to love her with his entire body, imprint himself on her so she'd never forget him.

Nick lay down on his back and drew Stephanie toward him. After a quick lick of his cock that nearly sent Nick to the ceiling, she straddled him, now taking his entire groin between her legs just as she'd held his thigh to her.

"What do you want, baby? Name it, it's yours."

Stephanie Wilson, Miss Proper Princeton personified, giggled. Actually giggled. "I want the ride of my lifetime. And you're the man to give it to me."

Nick's inner voice reminded him that Stephanie had to need some recovery time from the ride she'd just taken. He stroked her gorgeous butt, remembering how it had been to be inside her earlier, and her pussy kissed his belly where they touched.

Which totally put him over the top. Fortunately, she was right there with him. With a flirtatious grin and a wink, she lifted up her butt and brought her pussy down on his hard cock. Just a small wiggle, and she had his cock nestled into her hot, wet opening. In a blink of an eye, she'd sucked him up deep inside her, where he'd been longing to be.

* * * * *

185

If Stephanie hadn't been so intensely focused on the sensation of having Nick in her, maybe she'd observe herself or even laugh at her wanton behavior. But she was otherwise occupied.

All she could say about how Nick felt in her was... She didn't have the words. Not a way to describe the sensations that overwhelmed her and became her whole world.

Nick kept his hands on her ass, tenderly holding her cheeks, from time to time stroking her crack, fingering the hole where he'd entered her before.

Nick in her was like a song with perfect harmony, where each succeeding note followed the previous with complete inevitability. As he slowly thrust his hips in rhythm with her movements, he touched every surface, bringing divine friction to her slickness.

The word "love" hovered in the air around them, touching down so lightly on each of her senses that she didn't dare to brush it away. She alternated between tenderness toward him and wanting to express her demands and needs loudly, clearly, so there was no possibility for questions.

Delicious as her seated position on him was, she wanted the full skin contact of their bodies touching everywhere. With her hands she slowed him down. For a moment, they lay stock-still, the sound of their breaths all that broke the electric silence. But neither of them could maintain this stillness for long. Before he could resume his movements, she stretched out full-length. His powerful legs stretched under hers, and her breasts leaned into his muscular chest. Tempted as she was to savor the feel of his body beneath hers, she couldn't linger there long. Not with the urgency of Nick's need driving him and upping her own pulse rate as she sank down on him.

* * * * *

The night stretched out like one long amazing wet dream — only it was real. She was here with him, a woman far more amazing than any fantasy had ever brought him. All he could do was to keep touching her, convincing himself she was real, she was here, with him.

Every sensitive nerve ending of his penis vibrated with the stimulation and energy of her sleek movements. Stephanie controlled their kisses, deep and rich, as they both climbed toward the release waiting for them. Her tongue probed him deep, as if she wanted to know him thoroughly, be totally sure of the man she was with. Thank God, no matter how deeply she probed, her kisses wouldn't unearth the secrets he sought to keep from her. At the thought of what lay ahead for them, Nick experienced a momentary hesitation. And then he felt like Stephanie was asking him, "Why? What's the reason for this pause, this pulling back?" For now, he wouldn't ruin what was between them by dwelling on it. He owed it to her, to both of them, to be thoroughly with her for as long as that was possible.

Now she nibbled his neck and her hair brushed across his face. He could love her just for her hair, the color of wheat in the sunshine. But there was so much else to love her for…

Dangerous terrain, that. And this woman had already gotten to him far more profoundly than he'd ever let anyone else before. Or ever would again…

Nick felt Stephanie shudder in the movement that he knew signaled she would come shortly. He'd be right there with her, reaching the climax he'd started building toward the moment they first touched.

"Oh, Nick," she moaned.

"Stephanie…"

At the height of her orgasm, Stephanie bit Nick's shoulder, sharply underlining the force of their mutual come. Instantly, she apologized. "I don't know what got into me," she panted.

"Me. I…got…into…you," he crowed as he released his juices deep inside her.

Laughing and, for some mysterious reason known only to the female mind but making her even more precious to him, weeping, Stephanie clung to Nick long after their breathing and heartbeat rates returned to normal.

Arms and legs entwined, sated for the moment, Stephanie and Nick fell asleep.

Chapter Seven

ॐ

They made love three more times that night and had to tear themselves from the bed when the sunlight refused to go backward and extend the night. Stephanie had places to go, people to see. Her whole new life was starting that morning after a night of celebration unlike any she'd ever experienced before. Nick had lived up to his promise with that.

After a morning quickie, they both bowed to the inevitable and rolled out of bed. "The celebration continues," Nick announced. "It would hardly be complete without my famous pancake breakfast. Complete with fresh-squeezed orange juice and coffee guaranteed to make you sit up and take notice."

"I don't eat breakfast," Stephanie said. After another shower—this time alone for the sake of speed—she gingerly put on her clothes of the night before and looked at her wristwatch. "My God, I've got to get home. Change my clothes. I have a gazillion appointments to make today, things to do. You know I'm supposed to spend time at the gallery, see how they do things there. I'll be on my own there soon."

"All the more reason to start the day with the right fuel. Didn't they ever teach you that food guide pyramid stuff in school?"

Stephanie snorted. "Like that stuff doesn't change every two weeks anyway."

Nick folded his arms in front of him and put on his no-nonsense face. In a mock Euro accent he said, "I vill not take no for the answer. You vant to leave here to do your day's vork, first you eat the proper breakfast. You vill thank me later."

Her heartbeat accelerated at his mention of the word "later". No matter how close they'd been during the night and the morning, she knew neither of them had expressed any commitment to there being any more to them than the time they'd already spent together. Now Nick had used that word, and she probably overreacted, reading a future relationship into one little, easily tossed-out word.

She decided to ignore her instinct and not pounce on the word. She'd pretend he didn't say it, wait to see if he said anything else that could be construed as meaning that there'd be a future for them.

He didn't. Instead, he ushered her into the kitchen where, as promised, he served her a magnificent breakfast of fluffy buttermilk pancakes, real maple syrup, fresh strawberries, orange juice thick with pulp and no pits, and a fragrant brew of French roast coffee that rivaled any she could get at her favorite coffee shop. With a breakfast like that, she could conquer the world. Heck, with a breakfast like that, she'd probably expand and take over the world.

Well, it wasn't like she was going to eat like that every morning. Or even ever again.

She tenderly kissed him goodbye without hearing a single word from him that implied they'd see each other again.

Heck, it was the twenty-first century. "Nick, I'll call you tonight." There, she hadn't said anything scary or tried to pin him down to a commitment. So why did his face get all funny, making her heart lurch in a way it hadn't since Raoul pulled his disappearing act?

"Yeah, okay." Nick waved his hand dismissively. "I'm going to be kind of busy the next few weeks. Might have to go out of town for some business."

Ooh, she didn't like the sound of that. Not quite a brush-off, but pretty darn close. Stephanie felt her heart harden in self-protectiveness, but she wouldn't question him, wouldn't put a voice to her suspicions. Her heart and post-breakfast gut considerably heavier than they'd been earlier, Stephanie left Nick's place. She declined his offer of a ride. If there was one thing Stephanie knew, it was how to get herself home.

* * * * *

Nick watched Stephanie leave 'til she disappeared from sight. Letting her go had to be one of the hardest things he'd ever done or would do in his life. Maybe there was a chance… He couldn't let himself think about that. Now he had a job to do that would require his complete focus.

Pelletier picked up as soon as Nick rang through. "Forget the broad I mentioned to you yesterday. We're setting you up with another one that just came in. This dame's not quite as rich as Wilson, but if you can get the goods on her, we can move you up to hotter prospects."

Nick listened for the details. He'd call this woman, do what he had to all around. Maybe, once he got through and redeemed himself with the FBI, he'd be able to get in touch with Stephanie. Maybe, just maybe, she'd be waiting for him. And she'd understand when he explained.

Right. And maybe ponies would fly over the rainbow.

Nick dialed the number Pelletier had supplied him. Tamra Tomassi sounded nice on the phone. Eager, but not too much so. Her voice had that certain patina that not having to work for a living gives people. Maybe she was a woman he'd have been interested in before Stephanie. But now, it wouldn't matter what Tamra had going for her. Because Nick had found the woman who moved him the way no one else ever had—and no one ever would.

Too bad. Too late.

The Elite to Meet Online Dating Service was springing for tonight's date to take place at Chez Clay. Unlike the night before, which Nick had paid for. Elite had made all the arrangements. Though Nick didn't want to return there, not with his memories of Stephanie so fresh, he couldn't figure a way to tell Pelletier it would be unacceptable. He'd have to suck it up and deal.

* * * * *

The day went smoothly for Stephanie—one of the best she'd had in a long time. Everyone she wanted to talk to was available. She loved what she learned about the way the gallery functioned. Lois Hudson, she was happy to see, organized the place the same as she would if it were hers. Slipping into the gallery's routine would be a simple matter. Furthermore, being there would greatly help to expand her network of contacts. By the time she finished this assignment, she'd be sitting pretty. Working one or two more gigs would probably suffice to restore her name. Then she could nose around, maybe get on the path to opening her own gallery again. Maybe she'd consider some place other than New York. Or not. She was far from having to think about that now. As for the money, well, she'd proudly proclaimed that she wouldn't do anything 'til she'd earned enough money to finance her gallery herself. But maybe this time it would behoove her not to be so stiff-necked. Her parents would back her in a heartbeat. Maybe she should let them, at least partially.

So she should have been feeling good. But there was the incontrovertible fact that Nick hadn't called. Not on her cell phone, not to leave a message at home. Her heart lurched. It was coming true, exactly as she'd feared. Nick had come to mean more to her than it was smart to have let him, and now he'd lost interest. Or maybe he'd never really been interested in more than a roll in the hay—a slow, sensual, unforgettable one. Maybe she'd been fooling herself all along, as she'd shown herself so capable of doing before.

After several hours of unhelpful self-talk and a phone call to Gretchen, Stephanie decided she was being an idiot. She'd bite the bullet and phone Nick. All he could say was he'd told her he would be busy. Or he could ignore her phone call. But, nothing ventured, nothing gained.

When she called his home number, Stephanie got his answering machine. With a cringe, she remembered her first night at Nick's place and the answering machine message from his ex. Guided by this unpleasant memory, Stephanie had decided ahead of time not to leave a message.

Several minutes of internal debate followed. Should she try his cell phone? For some reason that she couldn't possibly have explained in any rational way, calling his cell felt more intimate than calling his land line. She crossed her fingers and dialed. He picked up on the fourth ring, just before Stephanie decided to hang up and forget about trying to contact him tonight.

"Love here." He pronounced his name "Lo-vay" instead of like the word that described the emotion she was beginning to feel.

Though she almost hung up without saying anything, she'd have regarded doing so as cowardly, unworthy. It behooved her to show the courage of her convictions, to sign her actions with her name, just as an artist did with her work.

"Nick, it's Stephanie."

"Stephanie." He spoke softly. She heard some music in the background, a tune that seemed very familiar but she couldn't quite put her finger on what it was. Something she'd heard recently, unique because of the arrangement, the particular instruments used. "It isn't a good time right now…"

She was about to ask when it would be good when she recognized the background music as what she'd heard the night before at Chez Clay. She'd commented on it to the server, who told her the album had been commissioned by the restaurant's owner. Barring pirates, people wouldn't hear this anywhere else but Chez Clay in Princeton. Not even in the sister restaurant in San Francisco, which had its own music.

Which brought up the question, why was Nick at Chez Clay again tonight? Stephanie couldn't imagine that anyone would go to the restaurant every night, no matter how much they loved the food.

Mumbling an apology, Stephanie hung up the phone.

She also couldn't imagine that Nick had gone there alone. He could be there with a friend or relative. But then, why didn't he just say so?

Which meant what she'd been trying too hard to avoid thinking. He was there with another woman. Not even twenty-four hours after they'd made fantastic love that left them panting and weak, he'd taken another woman to the place where they'd started off their night of celebration.

She sure could pick them, couldn't she?

* * * * *

Nick apologized to his date, Tamra Tomassi, and nodded to the diners at adjoining tables. A ferret-faced middle-aged man at the next table seemed especially put out and glared at Nick, who figured a brief apology should be enough. Though he'd usually turn off his phone or ignore a silenced one during dinner, he hadn't expected any calls tonight and figured it had to be urgent. Stephanie calling was urgent—for him personally, but definitely not part of tonight's plan. Having to put her off added to his pile of regrets about tonight.

He felt bad for wasting Tamra Tomassi's time and money, for his part in the scheme to rip her off. His part in Elite's scam was, when the check came, to act like he'd forgotten his credit card. When Tamra, who didn't know that Elite was paying for the date, offered the use of hers, he would use his cell phone camera to take a picture of the card and her signature. He'd pass this all on to Pelletier, who would have sufficient data to begin to steal Tamra Tomassi's identity. Until the victim caught up with the scam and discontinued her accounts,

Pelletier and company could collect as many goodies as the card would bear.

Nick had the feeling that tonight's act was really just a way for Pelletier to test him. After all, a smooth operation could find a hundred more efficient ways to commit identity theft. But Nick was stuck having to follow Pelletier's script. He despised everything that was happening tonight. No way could he miss the hurt and disappointment in Stephanie's voice. His gut told him she knew he was with another woman. Why else wouldn't he spend a moment talking to her? She'd have to consider him as much of a lowlife as Raoul Gelure had been. Lying to her, taking someone else out after all they'd been to each other just last night.

Tamra Tomassi had everything going for her—looks, an outgoing personality, brightness. At twenty-two she was on the young side for him, but he couldn't hold that against her. Tamra's only fault was not being Stephanie—and her mistake, just like Stephanie's, was getting involved with the bunch of crooks at Elite.

Nick had to focus. All he wanted was for the night to end. He wanted the whole caper to be over, to be square with the FBI, to be able to call Stephanie and be honest. But, at best, the prospect of getting any of what he wanted was premature.

His so-called date kept trying to engage him in conversation. Bright and bubbly, she came up with one interesting topic of conversation after another. He felt like a boor, fobbing her off with monosyllabic responses. He wanted to warn her off the dating service, to tell her a great girl like her didn't need a service to meet a guy. Heck, whatever happened to hanging out at clubs and other places where people went to be social? But he had to keep his mouth shut.

Despite all Tamra's efforts and an excellent dinner, the evening limped along 'til it was time for Nick to ask for the check.

He hoped Tamra realized what a lost cause he was, hoped that she didn't start hinting about a repeat performance.

Though he figured Tamra to be resilient, he knew that too many disappointments would take their toll on the sunniest of women.

The waiter discreetly placed the check in front of Nick. He picked it up and used all his acting ability to keep a straight face while he read it and reached for his wallet. Fumble, fumble, fumble. Ferret-face from the next table once again seemed engrossed in what Nick and his date were up to. Nick shrugged off a vague feeling of unease.

Looking more attentively at Tamra than he had all evening, he said, "This is so embarrassing."

Something flashed in her eyes, a wariness that made him think for a moment that Tamra wasn't going to be such an easy pigeon after all.

But the defiance or whatever it was subsided. Tamra opened her jeweled bag and withdrew a small leather card holder. "We can put it on my card," she said nonchalantly. Clearly the money charged wouldn't matter to her.

"I'll pay you right back. I can send you a check in the morning."

"The proverbial 'the check is in the mail'?" She raised a well-shaped brow and looked hard at him with a slight smirk.

Nick winced. Yeah, he knew it was the oldest story in the book. Compared to what he was doing to Stephanie, this deal with Tamra was small potatoes. But the guilt of both roiled in his gut.

After Tamra put down her card and began rifling through her bag for something else, Nick held up his cell phone and prepared to shoot the requisite picture. Couldn't get to the right angle without being completely obvious. More to the point, he couldn't bring himself to do it. With a frown, he lowered the cell.

Yeah, both Elite and the FBI would get on his case—for very different reasons. Elite would fire him, then the FBI would haul his ass to jail, and there would go any chance of a future anything with Stephanie.

But, even so, he couldn't bring himself to take the photo that would save his hide. Every time he tried to rethink how to come up with the right goods to get Elite and the FBI off his back, Stephanie's face rose before him. This Tamra seemed like another decent woman. Just because she came from a rich and privileged background didn't automatically make her a pigeon to be plucked. No matter what it might cost him, Nick couldn't make himself snap a photo. He'd think of another way out of his mess, one that wouldn't hurt any more innocent bystanders. Otherwise, he'd never be able to face Stephanie again. The server picked up the check and the card.

Out of the corner of his eye, Nick saw ferret-face get up from his table. As he passed Nick and Tamra's table, he bumped into the server, apologized, and left. A few minutes later, the server returned to the table. Tamra signed for their meal and put away her card.

"I'll take you home now," Nick said. "Unless you want to stop off at my place for me to write you a check."

She eyed him closely. "Is this a ploy to get me up to see your etchings?"

He didn't want any misunderstandings along those lines and held up his hand as if to take an oath. "My intentions are totally aboveboard. The check and nothing but the check."

"That's what I was afraid of." Despite the tone of her words, Nick didn't think she was seriously attracted to him. Shrugging, Tamra confirmed his impression. "Just take me home. But be sure you send me the money first thing in the morning, or I'll set my big brothers on your tail."

"Big brothers, eh?" Nick raised his eyebrows. "Even without that particular threat, I promise."

She raised her hands and laughed. "A joke. I know you're good for it, even if we didn't hit it off."

At another time, they might have hit it off. Or maybe become friends. In addition to everything else she had going for her, Tamra had a dynamite sense of humor. But, for right now, he'd have to continue with the scenario he'd started. Namely to call Pelletier and tell him he'd blown tonight. So Nick would probably get fired for failing tonight's test. But maybe the FBI would find another way for him to clear his name. Or maybe they'd toss his ass in jail.

* * * * *

Nick woke up to the jangling of the phone. "The pictures from last night. Bring them to the office now." Hearing Pelletier's voice first thing in the morning ranked up there with waking up to a news story about the body count from a natural disaster. Nick focused bleary eyes on the clock radio next to his bed, registered that it was six forty-five a.m. and mentioned that fact to Pelletier.

"I don't need you to tell me what the friggin' time is," Pelletier shouted. "You're already late. Get here with the goods within an hour or you're canned." The slam of the receiver completed Nick's wake-up call.

He could have told Pelletier on the phone that he had no goods to deliver, but he figured he'd go in person. Now that he knew his employment at Elite would come to a rapid end, Nick would need something other than his part in the prospective scams to hand to the FBI. They'd given him some spy gear to use as Plan B. He figured it was time to go there.

After a quick shave and shower, Nick put a tiny voice-activated recorder into his jacket pocket. Then he wrote a check for Tamra Tomassi and got on his bike to drop it off at her apartment. Last night she'd told him how moving into the small place, barely a mile from her parents' home, had only come about after a protracted battle for independence with overprotective parents. Yet another reason he'd come to like her.

198

When he was about half a block from Tamra's apartment, he saw her come out of her building. Only in the bright light of the morning, she looked different than she had last night. Tougher, older, less "cute". She crossed her arms in front of her and jutted her chin out at a very determined, "don't-mess-with-me" angle. With her were two big bodyguard types. The older brothers Tamra had threatened him with?

Nick kept his face averted. Between the helmet and the fact that Tamra was busy talking to the men, he felt reasonably sure that she hadn't spotted him. The girl he'd dated last night had disappeared, turned into a streetwise woman not to be messed with.

What was up with that?

* * * * *

Stephanie was happy, dammit. She gritted her teeth and reminded herself repeatedly exactly how happy she was. After all, she finally had the chance to get her life the way she wanted it. So why was she so miserable, going through the motions without her heart fully in any of it?

Chance. That word reverberated in her head whenever she had to remind herself to focus, to live totally in the moment and to take advantage of all the opportunities finally coming her way. This was her chance and she wouldn't let anything or anyone ruin it for her.

She had a lunch meeting scheduled with the two assistants she'd be working with at the Hudson Gallery. Though Stephanie had been nervous that the two longtime employees might resent her coming in and taking the top job, even temporarily, Lois Hudson had assured her neither wanted that type of responsibility. Stephanie hoped not. She wanted the experience to be clean and free of hassles, emotional and otherwise.

After a morning spent examining the gallery's records, during which she'd had to remind herself several hundred times to stop daydreaming, she felt gratified to see how much she agreed with the way Ms. Hudson ran things. On a wave of positive energy, she prepared to go to lunch with the assistants, Lorraine Higbee and Madeleine LaRoche. And she vowed to keep thoughts of Nick Love from disrupting her progress.

At least this one had shown his true colors before she got deeply involved.

Right. Stephanie had a hard time convincing herself that what had passed between them didn't actually signal involvement on her part. Like she could so easily dismiss the breathtaking intimacy of their time together.

Get a grip, she told herself. Judging by the raised eyebrows of Lois Hudson, who was perched on a stool across the office from her, Stephanie must have said the words aloud. *Lovely,* she thought. *Talking to myself will make a super impression. The artists are supposed to be eccentric, not the people who sell their work.*

Ms. Hudson smiled indulgently. "I guess that's enough work for one morning. Why don't you three head off for lunch."

The morning had flown, another good sign. Determined to make the best impression possible, Stephanie walked out with Lorraine and Madeleine. And left Nick behind.

* * * * *

Pelletier truly was pacing his office like a caged panther by the time Nick, who'd opted to mail Tamra's check after all, arrived. He hadn't taken the time to check out her apartment number but he could do that later, after Pelletier fired him.

"Give me the photos. We've got something cooking and we need the data." Pelletier held out his hand.

It was now or never. "You never told me why you want the data. What exactly do you do with it?" Nick knew his recorder was operating.

Pelletier narrowed his eyes. "Cut the crap. Hand over the goods or get out and don't come back."

"I don't hand over anything without knowing exactly what it's going to be used for."

Pelletier went over to his desk and hit a buzzer. In moments a door opened and ferret-face from the restaurant walked into the office. "According to Eric here, you don't have any goods to hand over," Pelletier growled.

Still going for nonchalance, Nick shrugged. "I told you I don't hand anything over 'til I know exactly what's going to happen with it."

Now Pelletier's face twisted into a nasty grin. "Lucky for us we don't have to depend on you. Seeing as how unreliable you turned out to be." He nodded to the other man. "Eric here, he delivers. Can't use him to go out on dates, not with a mug like that."

Ferret-face shrugged. "The wife's the jealous type, even in work situations. Women." He made a what-can-a-poor-slob-do? gesture.

"Yeah, broads can be pure death. On the other hand, they can also give a man who knows how to deal with them a decent living. You, Love, are not the man for the job. Get out now."

Nick tried to extend the conversation, but Pelletier clammed up and practically threw him out. Nick hadn't gotten anything on valuable on tape. Without some solid evidence, he had nothing to offer the FBI. But he'd go and tell them what he did know. At least Pelletier had pretty much said that his company hired so-called dating candidates. Sounded like fraud to him. He figured that the FBI must have something to go on or they wouldn't have put him in this position in the first place. Then he'd never have met Stephanie, both the best and worst thing that had ever happened to him.

Chapter Eight

ജ

Thank goodness and the powers of the universe, the next two weeks went by quickly. Stephanie easily slipped into her new position at the Hudson Gallery. Determined as she was to make a huge success of the temporary assignment, she worked probably three times harder than was necessary. As a workaholic who at last had work to do, putting in the long hours came as second nature.

Not to mention that wearing herself out made it almost possible to forget how Nick had gotten to her. Even two long, silent weeks after he'd dumped her, she still had to stifle the impulse to call him, to share with him how great things were now going for her. As if he'd care. Though an inner voice that she couldn't shut up kept nagging that he really would want to hear from her. That his lack of contact didn't signify a lack of interest.

Right. She could delude herself as well as the next woman, maybe even better. The fact was, Nick Love took her out for some fun and games, got tired, and moved on. Time for her to do the same. Cut her losses. Not that she particularly wanted to go out with anyone else anyway. She really wanted to get her life together before she tried any of that again. With Nick, she'd dipped her toe into the cold water of dating and gotten burned. Her life didn't make any more sense than that mixed metaphor. Heck, she'd dipped more than her toe. More like jumped in at the deep end. Though the initial dive might have started out graceful, she'd ended up in a major belly flop.

Her parents were out again. Mrs. Hutchins had left her dinner, some chicken and pasta concoction, warming in the oven. Eating alone, she figured she could get away with reading the paper. Her mother despised newspaper-reading over meals, a pleasure Stephanie and her dad deprived themselves of to keep peace in the house.

She poured a glass of Chardonnay, took the warmed dish out of the oven, and sat down at the kitchen table. After kicking off her shoes and tiredly rubbing one foot against the other, Stephanie took a swallow of wine and a bite of the chicken.

A headline caught her eye, and she nearly dropped her fork. Online Dating Service Implicated in Massive Identity Theft Fraud. It couldn't be, could it? Surely there was more than one online dating service…

Her dinner and wine now forgotten, Stephanie quickly read the article. The FBI now had clear evidence that the Elite to Meet Online Dating Service—the one Gretchen had hooked her up with, the one that brought her and Nick together—was part of a national chain perpetrating many varieties of identity theft. Stephanie shivered. As far as she knew, no one had taken anything of hers that could be used against her that way. As far as she knew. Though her gut told her that Nick had kept her safe from any such intrusion on her well-being, she felt far from safe.

Forcing herself to concentrate, Stephanie read the rest of the article. It seemed that Elite was denying all charges, which were spearheaded in Princeton by an agent using the code name "Tamra Tomassi". Elite claimed that Ms. Tomassi's identity theft was due to the malfeasance of a former employee, Nick Love. Once they realized how Love had abused his position of trust in their organization, Elite promptly fired him. Now they were willing to cooperate in the ongoing FBI investigation, do whatever they had to do to clear their good name.

Boy, she could identify with that statement.

Stephanie felt sick. She couldn't even bear the thought of dealing with the dinner in front of her. Yeah, she really could pick them. Nick Love was as big a crook as Raoul Gelure. At least he hadn't gotten the chance to mess up her life the way

Raoul had. But this was small comfort now because, truth be told, he had gotten to her. On several million levels.

Her phone rang. In disgust, she threw down her napkin and went to answer it.

* * * * *

Nick had been working exclusively with the FBI for the past two weeks. Though they hadn't exactly let him off the hook and Agent Ford had reamed him out for getting fired from Elite, Nick thought he'd be able to maneuver out from between the rock and the hard place where he was right now. His lawyer was finally coming through, smoothing Nick's path. He figured once he got a solid hold on his future, he'd phone Stephanie and try to pick up the pieces.

And then the newspaper story broke. Much sooner and in much worse shape than he'd wanted, he had to tell her everything.

She picked up after three rings. "Stephanie, it's Nick Love." A draft of pure ice shot through the phone line to him. But at least she didn't hang up.

"Why are you calling?" she hissed after an uncomfortable silence. "Need me to come bail you out of jail?"

Despite its not being totally off-target, he bristled at her accusation. "I'm not in jail."

"No? Sounds like you will be soon. Identity theft. How could you stoop so low?"

She believed the worst about him. That realization smacked him in the gut like a sucker punch. "Not guilty as charged." Guilty of other crimes, yes. But not this one.

Her laugh sounded harsh. "Yeah, that's what they all say. Just like Raoul telling me he had absolutely no idea why my clients were calling the gallery, hysterical. 'Alleging fraud and forgery.' He accused them of being post-menopausal harridans."

"I'm not Raoul Gelure," Nick said quietly.

A silence ensued. Then, "How did you know Raoul's last name? I never mentioned it, I never tell anyone."

Great. Nothing like revealing damning information when you're trying to save your ass. "Long story. I promise, Stephanie, I will explain everything. Only give me a chance to talk to you."

"You've had your chance," she yelled. "I sincerely hope you and Raoul rot in hell together." After which pronouncement she hung up the phone.

Nice, Nick thought. *She's really ready to give me a chance, hear my side of the story. Despite appearances, she has faith in me. She believes in me.*

Not.

So much for his dream of being able to get together with Stephanie. His life would go on. And the world was filled with ladies. Lots of them. In ten or twenty years, he'd forget Stephanie and move on to one of them.

Not.

* * * * *

Stephanie threw herself into her work and took a vow of celibacy. Figuring she had terminal bad taste in men, she decided her life would be much smoother, calmer, and happier once she admitted she was doomed to keep making the same mistakes. So she'd buy another vibrator and many batteries and devote herself to her career. What she'd been through in the past year proved there were far worse options.

Running the gallery brought back how great life had been when she had her own place. The art world was her natural milieu, and she loved being able to help people find the paintings and sculptures that would grace their walls. Now that she was working in a gallery again, she could reconnect with a whole network and community that had felt closed to her for more than a year. With gratitude, she found people accepting her once again. She'd never take that for granted.

As for the hole in her life that Nick had begun to fill... Well, she kept busy. And she trained her mind not to dwell on him or on thoughts of what might have been. Now that she had her second chance, she knew that she couldn't afford to mess up again. Third chances were unheard of.

One morning a young woman came into the gallery and asked for her. "I'm Stephanie Wilson," Stephanie told her, her hand out.

The woman, who on second look was not as young as she first appeared, totally shocked Stephanie by whipping out a badge. "Tina Terranova, special agent," she said. "May I have a few words with you?"

In a haze of déjà vu, Stephanie felt the floor shake beneath her as her knees trembled. Dear Lord, it couldn't be happening again. She couldn't again be connected with any criminal behavior that would splatter her with its taint. Not when she'd just started getting her life together. "What is it, Agent Terranova?" Stephanie's voice sounded shuddery to her ears, and she was sure she'd turned pale as parchment.

The other woman smiled, and Stephanie felt her anxieties relax the slightest bit. Last year, agents weren't smiling when they talked to her. "I just have a few questions I'd like you to answer to wind down an investigation. Is there somewhere we can sit and talk?"

Stephanie perked up. Had they found Raoul and somehow managed to extradite him and the girlfriend from Brazil? She'd love to have a shot at getting back what Raoul had stolen, not to mention how much she'd enjoy having ten minutes to tell that creep exactly what she thought of him. As if he'd care.

When they were both seated at Stephanie's desk in the gallery office and drinking coffee, Agent Terranova said, "You might be aware of the investigation of the Elite to Meet Online Dating Service here in Princeton?"

From that opening, it seemed clear that Raoul's crimes were not going to be the focus of the conversation. "I've read about it in the paper and heard the radio stories."

Tina Terranova nodded. "We understand that you were a client of Elite and that you went on several dates with someone they matched you with, Nick Love."

Stephanie couldn't help it. She went beet red and stayed that way for what felt like a very long time. The agent continued, "I went out with him too, from the same source. To Chez Clay, I think the night after he went there with you."

So it was true. Nick had dumped her for an FBI agent. Though Stephanie objectively had to admit Tina was fairly attractive, it felt difficult to be kindly disposed to someone who was, in effect, a rival. Of course she wasn't really a "rival" in any true sense of the word. As Stephanie kept reminding herself, she didn't have anything real with Nick. There had been nothing real to lose.

Tina appeared to be watching Stephanie's face and reading a lot into what she saw. Her voice got low and sounded reassuring. "He didn't dig me. Not at all, not in more than a buddy sense. Since then I've been working with Nick on the Elite case, and we're buds. I think I know him well enough to realize how hung up he is on you. Didn't leave any room for anyone else to creep in."

Stephanie gasped. Tina's remark filled her with pain — and pleasure. "As an FBI agent, you of all people should understand. After what I went through with my previous boyfriend, I'm done with liars and cheats and criminals of any kind."

"Good for you. I agree with you in general. But Nick, well, he's different. Yeah, he's done some bad things in the past. But we couldn't have busted this case open the way we did without him. And part of being able to do that had to do with his not telling you how he was involved with Elite."

Stephanie felt like someone had just smacked her, hard. Breathing normally was a challenge and a half. "What are you telling me?"

"Working undercover for us, Nick got a job as an 'escort' for Elite," Tina began.

"You mean he wasn't really looking for a match?" Now why did that surprise Stephanie? She'd suspected right off the bat that he wasn't the kind of guy who'd use a dating service. She'd let her suspicions slide…

"No. You've read about the whole identity theft scam. Elite targets wealthy women, or, in some cases, wealthy men. But many more wealthy women. Let's face it, Princeton is a prime area for them to locate their prey. Nick was supposed to get information about your personal accounts and feed it to his contact at Elite. But he refused. Elite gave him a second chance, when they matched him up with one Tamra Tomassi. That was my pseudonym for this case. As Nick later confessed to me, he couldn't bring himself to steal my information because of the way being with you changed him. But one of the supposed customers at the restaurant was a plant from Elite. He copied my credit card info and I would have been on my way to becoming Elite's next victim had it actually been mine. Seems they built up quite a dossier on the false identity the bureau set up for me."

"Nick said he couldn't do what he was supposed to for Elite because of me?" Stephanie suddenly had a weird sinking feeling. Nick hadn't been able to bring himself to commit a crime, even a sham one. Here she'd judged him so harshly and so incorrectly. She could try to blame her experience with Raoul for this, but the fault really lay with her.

"Correct. Now I just want to verify that you went on several dates with Nick Love after your introduction from Elite?"

Blushing again, Stephanie nodded.

"And he did nothing to steal personal information from you?"

"That's correct," Stephanie said in a very little voice.

* * * * *

Once the truth came out and the FBI dismissed Nick, he found himself at loose ends 'til he got clarity on exactly what he needed to do. He was studying a map and planning how to proceed when he heard someone knocking. Not expecting anyone and mildly resenting the interruption, he went and opened the door.

Stephanie, the last person he expected and the one he most wanted to see, stood there. "Come in," he said when he could locate his tongue. He wanted to grab her up in his arms and show her everything seeing her made him feel. But he restrained himself and said merely, "I've missed you. What brings you here?"

She came in and sat down at the edge of his couch. "Why do you have a map out? Planning a trip?"

He waved his hand dismissively. "Something like that. How've you been?"

"Very good," she said, her voice not quite convincing him. "Busy. Nick, I know about the FBI. I just wanted to tell you how sorry I am… Sorry that I thought the worst of you."

Now that she was actually there with him, he couldn't stand it, couldn't stand to hear her apology when he was the one who had to apologize. "No need."

"But there is a need. You see, I thought you were out to cheat me and, when you didn't get the opportunity, dumped me and moved on to the next victim."

A man could take only so much. Damn it all, who had he been before he met her? "Don't you know? I couldn't even pretend to cheat her. Not after I got to know you. Now I couldn't cheat a person if my life depended on it."

A look of anguish sharpened her features. "I saw all that in you and tried to deny it. Saw that you're a really good guy underneath."

He snorted. "Based on the past, you'd need dynamite to dig far enough for that."

"Not true. Don't put yourself down like that. I won't hear of it."

"Why not?" Self-disgust mixed with his desire to have her stay with him and make love like there would be no tomorrow. But he couldn't have the lies between them. Not anymore. "I have only two words to say to you. Raoul Gelure." He spat out the name, which stung his tongue.

Now her eyes opened wide and she looked stricken. He realized she must remember now that Nick knew Raoul, which had to bother her. "How did you know him?" she asked. She looked determined to face the truth, but her voice trembled.

Nothing had ever hurt as much as the confession he was about to make. "At the time I worked for him, I didn't know you. I only knew he needed some papers for him and his 'lady' to get out of the country. You see, with my background on the so-called wrong side of the tracks, I've always sided with the underdog. But in this situation, I didn't see how much the underdog was acting like a bizarre beast. Felt like I was being my version of Robin Hood, helping the poor slobs up against the rich abusive husband. My bullheadedness made me do it. I helped him hurt you. Which is how the FBI and Interpol got their hooks into me."

She exhaled hard and sat back. "You gave Raoul the papers that made it possible for him to get away?" she parroted.

"Guilty as charged."

She looked away and tears began to form in her eyes. He took both of her hands in his. "I am so sorry, Stephanie."

She didn't say anything. He took a deep breath and decided this was the perfect time to make his announcement. "I know I can never make up to you what my helping Gelure cost you. But I want you to know how sorry I am, and how willing I am to do anything to show you. Which is why I'm headed to Brazil. Leaving in two days."

"Brazil?" From the expression on her face, Nick could see that she didn't get it.

"That's where Gelure is. I'm going to track him down and get him to make it up to you." Nick was determined to use his FBI connections and every trick—in the book or out of it—to bring the creep to justice. Though the FBI had no jurisdiction in Brazil, the agents he'd become friends with had connected him to people who did operate there.

"You can't do that," Stephanie said softly.

Not the reaction he'd expected. "Why not?"

Now a grin began to play around the edges of her mouth. "Because I'm going to Brazil to catch him and take him down as soon as my work at the Hudson Gallery ends. Now that I'm more than ready to move on in my life, I hate to leave details hanging."

Light was beginning to dawn for Nick. "What, you mean I can't go because you're going? Last I heard, Brazil is a big country." He reached out and traced the outline of her lips with his thumb. "Lots of places to explore," he added hoarsely.

She put her hand over his.

"We make a great team," she murmured.

"Unbeatable," he whispered as she scooped her up in his arms and carried her off to his bedroom for some advanced tactical planning of the horizontal variety.

Also by Mardi Ballou

ℬ

Nibbles 'n' Bits (*anthology*)
Pantasia I: Hook, Wine & Tinker
Pantasia II: For Pete's Sake
Pantasia III: Forever On the Isle of Never
Photo Finish
Reunions Dangereuses
Tingle Bells
Young Vampires in France
Young Vampires In Love

About the Author

ℬ

Exploring the erotic side of romance keeps Mardi Ballou chained to her computer—and inspires some amazing research. Mardi's a Jersey girl, now living in Northern California with her hero husband—the love of her life—who's also her tech maven and first reader. Her days and nights are filled with books to read and write, chocolate, and the pursuit of romantic dreams. A Scorpio by birth and temperament, Mardi believes in living life with Passion, Intensity, and Lots of Laughs (this last from her moon in Sagittarius). Published in different genres under different names, Mardi is thrilled to be part of the Ellora's Cave Team Romantica.

Mardi welcomes comments from readers. You can find her website and email address on her author bio page at www.ellorascave.com.

TRACKED DOWN

By Vonna Harper

ഇ

Chapter One

ဢ

Some men can flat out loosen a woman's teeth.

Watching the athletically built, dark-haired man stride toward her looking for all the world like a bull elk, Carlin Witmer amended her initial observation. This prime example of what the male beast should look like could loosen a hell of a lot more than just what was stuck in her jawbone. With not so much as a glance in her direction, he'd revved what lay between her legs to life. True, there wasn't much about the male animal she didn't like, but it made her day when one who lived beyond the top of her hunk list showed up on her property.

Wild. Yep, that's what he is. Wild.

Sighing in regret, she reminded herself that Stud Studly hadn't come here to prime her pump. Damn it, he was *simply* a client.

One hell of a client.

"Lonato Ray," she said and stuck out her hand. "And if it isn't you, I gave at the office."

Eyes straight out of the bottom of a cave bore into her as the man closed his strong, rough fingers around her own. He wasn't all that tall, probably no more than six feet, but muscles on top of tendon and bone supplemented by even more muscles had a way of adding to the impact. "What office?" he asked. Although the obligatory shake was behind them, he continued to hold her hand—not that she was complaining.

"Good point." Somehow she managed to keep eye contact going while indicating their surroundings which consisted of a dozen large dog pens, obstacle courses, her small place, and a separate garage. "Actually, I do have one in the house, and since I'm both boss and employee, I control all donations." She thought about pulling free then decided he was trying to learn something about her from the extended flesh to flesh contact. No way was she going to let him believe she felt overwhelmed since she'd barely ever experienced the emotion. "You are Lonato, aren't you? The man from Recovery."

"Yeah. This place isn't easy —"

Before he could finish, ninety-five pounds of Doberman slammed into his thigh. Rocking back on his heels, he released her. She was glad he made no move to try to defend himself against Rio. If he'd raised a hand against her baby, she would have drop-kicked him.

"Beautiful," he muttered as he spread those so alive fingers over the search and rescue dog's back. "An incredible creature."

"He is," she acknowledged. *And it takes one incredible creature to identify another*, she silently added. "He's my prize pupil, or maybe I should say I'm his because I'm not sure which of us is in charge."

"I'll be using him?"

"Not you, me."

Something that reminded her of a rain cloud slipping between sun and earth settled in his eyes. "We need to talk about that."

If you say so. I'd rather do something else, big boy.

She said nothing, and the man from the agency that had retained her and her trained dogs to search the wilderness east of the Oregon coast turned his full attention to Rio. For his part, now that he'd done his part as official greeter, Rio was content to lean against a strong male thigh and have his head rubbed. Watching the interplay, she came to the damn easy conclusion that her first impression of Lonato had been incomplete. Yes, he still put her in mind of a bull elk because of the proud, easy way he carried himself, but there was also more than a bit of junkyard dog to him, although perhaps wolf was a more apt comparison. Despite its size, an elk was, at its core, a prey animal while a wolf was a carnivore, a hunter. So was this man.

Shaken by what she now accepted as fact, she pondered what had turned him into a hunter. It could simply be a by-product of the Native American heritage borne out in his dusky flesh, solid stature, and longish dark hair and eyes, but she couldn't quite convince herself he'd been born that way. Life had infused him with a hunter's mentality. He'd even dressed for action as witnessed by his hiking boots, jeans, and ride-his-chest olive chambray shirt.

Although he continued to give Rio the attention the dog would be content to suck up indefinitely, Lonato fixed his unsettling eyes on her. At least they weren't wolf-yellow. "You agreed to Recovery's request," he said, each word no-nonsense. "If you don't understand how the agency works—"

"Oh, I understand. You may not know this, but my father is a DA. He's told me a great deal about your *agency*."

His gaze became even more intense. "As much as we choose to reveal to law enforcement, you mean. Recovery accomplishes what it does because we're selective about what we share with the outside world."

Although she hated doing so, she had to admit he was right. According to her father, Recovery was part private detective agency, part mercenary unit, part do whatever it takes at all costs. People came to the select group of operatives when they wanted things done that couldn't be accomplished within the normal parameters of law and order. Acknowledging that the male human beast in front of her lived by that code sent her a loud and clear message. Beating him at his game wasn't going to happen.

But it didn't matter that she didn't yet comprehend what his game, his mission was. She held the trump card in Rio. And from what she knew of the situation, an elite wilderness-tracking dog spelled the difference between Lonato's success and failure. "What are you saying?" she demanded. "You believe that because you don't answer to the bureaucracy you can tell me how it's going to be? Not going to happen." She snapped her fingers. "Rio, the best tracking dog in this state, answers only to me."

Even before she'd relaxed her fingers, Rio had left Lonato's side and now stood before her, every line of his body as alive as she felt. "Rio, guard."

Fangs instantly bared, Rio whirled on Lonato. The Doberman made no sound, but his body language said it all. "If I tell him to, he'll kill you," she said.

"Unless I get to him first."

Lonato hadn't done more than drop his hand to his side so how the hell had the slim and deadly knife appeared in his fingers? He didn't point his weapon at Rio, but he didn't need to. She got the message.

"Standoff," she acknowledged.

"Not really. You aren't going to sacrifice your dog."

"No, I'm not." She snapped her fingers again, and Rio went back to his *what do you want next, boss* stance. Feeling not so much defeated as understanding, in part, what made this man tick, she rubbed Rio's head. "But neither is he going to work for you. You want someone found. I'm part of the deal."

"There are guns out there."

"I figured that."

"And men who won't give a damn that you're a woman."

"I didn't figure they would."

"Then why—"

"My reasons are mine," she interrupted. "Tell me something. If I demanded you explain why you do what you do for Recovery before I agree to have anything to do with you, would you?"

He smiled. At least the gesture resembled a smile more than anything else. "No."

"So where do we go from here?"

By way of answer, he trailed his gaze from her eyes down over her body. With each passing millisecond she felt more and more naked, more in tune with her sexuality, more focused on the desire to jump his bones. Damn, but the man could heat flesh and muscles without so much as a touch. What the hell would happen if he laid his hands on her?

Unnerved by the image of her body smoking and being reduced to ash, she forced herself to stand there while he continued his survey. She'd always thought of herself as long and lean, although in truth she had enough muscle tone thanks to her physical lifestyle that lean didn't really qualify. If he wanted soft and curvy, he wasn't going to get it. She kept her reddish-brown hair cut short and seldom bothered with makeup. She owned one business suit and two dresses, all seldom used.

But if he had complaints, she sure as hell didn't. Far be it for his clothes to hide the packaging. The formfitting shirt said he had no need to hide a soft middle while the jeans—hell, the jeans said *not hard to see what's underneath, is it?* No way could he get away wearing slim-cut slacks with those muscular thighs. He had not so much as a bump of a belly and what she could see of his ass was tight with a capital T, but not only that, he was built for action, for an active life, for staying power.

Staying power? Granted, she couldn't tell much about the discreet bulge except that she hadn't, so far, given him a hard-on, but if his cock lived up to the same billing as the rest of him, any woman lucky enough to ride it would have no complaints.

Feeling her cheeks and other parts heat, she reached for what she hoped was the shutoff switch to her libido. "We're not going to get very far today," she pointed out. "I've arranged for someone to stay here with the rest of my animals and cleared my calendar for the week. I'm guessing you want to take off in the morning."

"He might not have the time."

"He?"

"The man I'm looking for."

"Who is he?"

"Sorry. I'm not giving you that."

"Why not?"

"Because I don't want you telling your dad and involving the legal system. This is private, not public."

"In other words, if I knew who Rio is being asked to find, the cops would want to do the same thing?"

"And the press."

"Hmm. And that's a bad thing?"

"Yeah, it is."

Feeling as if she was being sucked into something she should have nothing to do with, she shook off her sense of unease. Too often her and her dogs' work was complicated by the presence of law enforcement, the media, family members, the curious. Having this between her and Lonato had a certain appeal. She just hoped she wouldn't regret it. "What do *you* want to do?" she asked, throwing things back at him. "How do you hope to handle things?"

"Except for giving my backpack a final check, I'm ready." He indicated the all but new rig he'd driven up in. "My gear's in there."

It belatedly dawned on her that he no longer held the knife. What was he, a magician? "And I already keep what I need for a protracted search ready and by the door," she pointed out. "If I get a call about a lost kid, I want to be able to move fast."

"Damn it, I don't want you along."

He'd said it soft enough, but she wasn't the only one who'd caught the hard undertone. Rio looked over his shoulder at Lonato, ears perked forward.

"Doesn't matter. You're getting me."

"No."

"Look, I've had Rio since the day he was born. I put hundreds of hours into training and working with him. More than a few people owe their lives to him. I might let you have another of my dogs, but you're paying for the best. Where Rio goes, I go."

Chapter Two

ဢ

Although he hadn't been to southern Oregon for several years, Lonato knew mountains, specifically that things got cold there at night, which it now was. As a consequence, he'd pulled on a sweatshirt before getting out of his vehicle.

The determined young woman he hadn't been able to shake had done the same. Then without a word from him, she'd gone about setting up her one-person tent on a level spot near where he'd parked along the side of an old logging road. As soon as it got light, they'd strike off on foot. She hadn't asked how he'd determined that this was where they needed to start, but he saw no harm in telling her he was going by what he knew of the three men who'd supposedly taken the obscenely wealthy Robert Jacob Dowells from his Portland, Oregon office and what an observant ranger had seen two days ago. What he hadn't revealed to Carlin was the name of his quarry.

Not enough added up about the abduction of the CEO of a publicly traded auto enterprise, but his marching orders were to locate and rescue Robert for the corporation's board members before the press, police, and, most importantly, investors got wind of what appeared to have happened. Details such as any ransom demands and the motives of the maybe abductors could wait until later, if at all. He'd taken the assignment, not because he needed the money, which he didn't, but because he'd been bred to track. Like his ancestors, he loved pitting his skills against his prey. Just because he'd been born too late to go to war against enemy tribes or attack unwanted settlers and soldiers didn't mean he couldn't feel the same satisfaction, the same need for revenge his ancients had.

The only difference between him and his great-great-grandfather was that he did his human hunting under the guise of civilization. He used four-wheel-drive vehicles, not horses. He relied on cell phones, binoculars, and GPS systems, not just tracks. And at times like this, he turned to highly trained search dogs and their bullheaded handlers.

As Carlin went about starting a small warming fire on the rocky logging road, he amended bullheaded to include sexy and sensual and a no-doubt-about-it distraction. While on the scent of his target, he could go days without food or sleep, but tonight he didn't need to make either of those sacrifices. As a result, he thought like a man. Hell, he'd started thinking with his cock the moment he'd first seen her.

From the way Rio went about exploring his turf, Lonato didn't believe another human had been here for a long time. The Doberman still had his balls, and Carlin had explained that she was training several of his pups, making him think the dog would understand why he was contemplating what it would take to get inside her jeans. Getting a woman to shed her clothes had never been much of a problem.

"You smell like testosterone," a woman he'd briefly thought about marrying had told him. "Hell, male oozes out your pores."

But just because his bedpost sported a lot of notches didn't mean sex was all he wanted from a woman. Shaking his head against a mental journey he didn't want to make tonight, he turned his attention to his own tent. As he drove pegs into the hard ground, he acknowledged that they'd be sleeping deep in the forest tomorrow night. Maybe he should be content to indulge in the relative ease and rarity of a hot meal and a snug shelter, but in truth, he could hardly wait to start stalking his prey. He was like Rio and the dog's pups—he lived for the scent.

"You want to get some water from the jeep?" Carlin said. "As soon as it's boiling, we can have dinner."

Dinner would consist of the dried stew she'd brought along. In the morning they'd indulge in real eggs and potatoes, also compliments of her larder. After that they'd *dine* on the trail food he'd supplied. Although they disagreed about a number of core matters, at least they felt the same about wilderness work. Creature comfort didn't factor in.

Sitting on logs across from each other, they ate in silence. The moon was little more than a sliver, but the stars lit up the sky, putting him in touch with his surroundings. He tuned his senses to the sound of night birds and an occasional breeze punctuated by Rio's soft snoring. In his mind he saw owls and bats and sent his thoughts, his soul even, into the air. Modern men didn't rely on spirit helpers to help them survive, at least none of his fellow operatives at Recovery did, but he didn't care. Tonight felt right for communicating with *Wolf*.

I feel your presence, he told the life force that had embraced him when, as a fourteen-year-old, he'd gone into the wilderness to think, pray, fast, and commune with nature as his ancestors had done. *You knew I could be coming here so you waited for me. I ask you to guide my eyes and ears and hands during this journey. If my mission is just and right, I ask you to show me the way, and if I should not be doing this, I ask you to share your wisdom with me.*

Wolf didn't respond in a way anyone else would ever understand, but Lonato felt himself relax. The questions about whether he should be looking for Robert Jacob Dowells ended because *Wolf* had given him the truth. *Yes, find this man.*

"You do this a lot, don't you?" Carlin asked.

He focused on what he could see of her. Firelight had smoothed away her edges, allowing her to seep into her surroundings. "What? Look for people?"

"No. I rather suspected that because that's a lot of what Recovery stands for. I'm talking about being in the mountains."

"Not as much as I want to. Sometimes I work in a city."

"But you don't like it there."

"No."

"Me either."

Her admission reached deep. "The bright lights don't appeal to you?" he asked.

"Bright lights make me crazy. The wilderness gives me peace."

He'd wondered why, beyond not having to worry about neighbors complaining about barking dogs, she'd located her business in the country. "You live alone, right? You feel safe?"

She laughed, the sound touching nerve endings. "I'm surrounded by dogs. Not too likely anyone's going to sneak up without them sounding the alarm. How do you know I live alone?"

"One cup in the sink. One pair of shoes by the door. Only one of the chairs in front of the TV showing wear."

"You're observant."

"Yeah."

"What about you?" she asked. "You have to share the remote with anyone?"

The question could be casual, but he didn't think so. She wanted to know as much as possible about him. Because her life might depend on her ability to trust him, he gave her what he could. He had the TV remote all to himself, not that he watched that much TV or was home enough to get into the habit. He'd worked for Recovery for nearly three years and before that had done everything from bridge construction to guiding fishermen into remote lakes and streams throughout the west. Formal schooling had ended with the tenth grade, but he didn't tell her that although he'd gotten decent grades, the walls closing in around him had driven him outside. He was full-blooded Indian—his mother had been Apache, while the drunk who'd fathered him had been Comanche. Because she asked, he told her that both parents were dead but kept the details to himself.

When she asked where he saw himself in ten years, he deflected by turning the question on her. She gave a dismissive shrug. "I don't see much changing," she whispered.

The fire needed replenishing. As a consequence, he now could barely detect her shadow. They'd turned into disembodied voices reaching out in the dark. "I love working with dogs," she continued. "And I'm damn good at it. I've been looking into training someone both to handle what I don't have time for and to give me more time to train police dogs. Occasionally I take my dogs to elementary schools, particularly special ed. I love seeing a child come out of his shell when a dog lets him know he's loved."

"What about children of your own?"

She didn't answer. He sent out his emotional antenna and tried to gauge her mood, but she'd closed herself off.

"Wrong thing to ask?" he said at length.

"None of your damn business."

"Duly noted. What about marriage?"

"Maybe."

"Maybe as in you don't have much faith in the institution or maybe as in you haven't come across any likely candidates?"

"I'm not willing to give up who and what I am." She stood and stepped into the night. "If a man can't understand that, I'm not interested."

He waited until she'd returned and placed a few more logs on the fire. "Does that work both ways?" he asked. "You won't try to change the man?"

"Depends."

"On what?"

"On whether he picks up after himself, occasionally takes out the garbage, stokes the fire."

"Guess that means I've failed your test."

For a moment he thought she wasn't going to answer. Then, "Not necessarily. You have a lot going for you."

"Like?"

She laughed. "You have a hot bod."

* * * * *

What a damn-ass thing to say.

Watching Lonato turn away so he could warm his backside, she amended her self-critique. Telling him he had a hot bod wasn't original, but it certainly was right-on. His sweatshirt covered a lot of his upper body but thanks to what she'd done to the fire, she had a sweet view of his butt. A man with glutes like that had to know their effect on a woman. She could pretend she was immune, but in effect lying to him didn't sit well with her. Who knew whether her life might depend on him before this, whatever it was, was over with.

She wanted to be honest and expected the same from him, at least when it came to sexual attraction. She might not be willing to reveal her hopes, fears, and uncertainties about being a good mother in the wake of going through her teen years without one, and it was obvious he wasn't ready to open up about his own background, but they hadn't come here to psychoanalyze each other.

On the other hand, the night could be a long one.

He'd already told her that he had a piece of the subject's clothing and had good reason to believe the mysterious man's abductors had taken him into this section of the Siskiyou Forest, so as she saw it, they didn't need to say more on that score until Rio picked up a scent. She could tell him good night, crawl into her tent and try to sleep, but she knew herself well enough to admit trying wasn't going to get her anywhere for a long time, if ever.

Damn him for giving out the vibes he did, for being put together the way he was. And damn her for being horny.

"What are we going to do about it?" he asked.

His unexpected voice made her start, but she quickly recovered. Either that or his tone had snaked around her to flame coals just waiting for a little encouragement. "About what?"

"Damn. I told myself not to do that. I hate game playing." He walked around the fire and stopped maybe two feet away. Heat boiled off him. She didn't think all of it came from the flames he'd been standing near. "I want you and I'm pretty sure you want me, right?"

No game playing, he said. Remember, no games. "Yes."

"Then we could either sniff around each other and wind up scratching our own itches, or we could fuck."

"You don't beat around the bush, do you?"

"Life's too short."

"Are you saying that because what we're doing is dangerous?" she had to ask, although with his body sending out certain messages, she half believed she could live forever.

"Life is short. My parents taught me that."

"So did my mother," she blurted. She'd been sitting when he'd come near, but somehow she'd wound up standing. Close to him like this, she felt the impact of his size and strength, the untamed quality.

She waited for him to ask about her mother, which would have given her the opening to probe about his parents, but when he didn't, she silently thanked him. Tonight she wanted to be a woman with a man, nothing else.

"Give me your hands," he said. When she did so, he laced his fingers through hers and held the union up so the firelight and stars highlighted them. "That's what I noticed first about you. They're strong and capable."

"Not what most women want to hear."

"What about you?"

"I need strong and capable hands," she told him. After that, she couldn't think of another word. She understood feeling as if she was melting at the moment of climax, but she still had her clothes on. He hadn't touched her intimately. And yet, hell—so this was what it felt like to stand too close to the flames.

Maybe he sensed her vulnerability and maybe he was being driven by needs that echoed hers. Whatever it was, she wasn't surprised when he released her hands, took hold of the hem of her sweatshirt, and smoothly drew it over her head. Not since early teenage gropings had she felt less in control of a sexual situation. She believed in, demanded, equal billing. At least she had until tonight.

Now, standing before him with her sweatshirt dangling from his fingers and her nipples tight and hard, she felt as if she was on the receiving end of whatever he wanted and demanded.

"Are you on the Pill?" he asked.

"Yes. But that isn't enough. I insist—"

"Rubber? Always."

He'd brought along protection? Shit, was the man that sure of himself? Trying to answer her question made her slow to react to his next move. To her discomfort, he spread his fingers over her throat. True, she could have jerked back and freed herself, but what if he came after her? Despite the possibility of danger, she remained in place. His fingers transmitted not exactly an electrical current but primitive energy. He was testing her in ways she couldn't comprehend, maybe testing himself. Her fingertips buzzed. Her temples felt hot.

"You like sex, right," he said.

"Yes."

"Want it. Need it."

"Yes."

Slow, so slow, he traced the tendons at the side of her neck and then circled her ear. Despite the unbelievable tingling, she leaned into the caress. Head lifted, she sought out his eyes. Darkness protected them, but she could imagine, could pretend they held more than animal lust.

As for why she wanted to connect with this stranger…

All around them the night pulsed. It spoke with an ancient rhythm that stripped away the modern world. Despite the cell phone at her waist and the nearby vehicle, she felt connected to a world far more basic than any other she'd ever known. Working in the wilderness had always put her in touch with nature, but the connection had never felt this intense or intimate.

Wanting to thank him for providing the path, she lifted her heavy arms and closed her fingers around his forearm. He paused, then returned to mapping her. Small, hot shivers ran through her when he found the valley between her breasts. She couldn't say how he'd managed to unbutton the top buttons on her flannel shirt. Perhaps he'd somehow rendered her senseless during the necessary maneuver.

It didn't matter. She lived where his fingertips touched.

When her hands transmitted acceptance, he pushed past her bra's barrier to envelop soft, full tissue. She sucked in a breath, increasing the space between fabric and flesh. Perhaps understanding the unspoken message of her arousal, he continued his journey. Even before he touched her nipple, shivers traveled down her belly to house themselves in her core. She made no attempt to pull her awareness off the delicious sensations. She hadn't had sex in several months and had no prospects for changing the condition, at least she hadn't before this man had entered her life. Now, just like that, he was offering fulfillment.

And she, who'd just openly admitted she thrived on sex, could barely wait.

With a mental shake, she reminded herself of the value of foreplay, of the benefits of not behaving like some animal in heat, of keeping physical and emotional distance between her and this dangerous stranger.

As he worked her already taut nipples, her hands grew too heavy to continue her hold on him. Giving up, she let them fall to her sides. He abandoned her breasts long enough to finish the unbuttoning and reach behind her to unfasten her bra but didn't strip her. She supposed he was taking the cool air into account although maybe a slow disrobing turned him on.

Finally he pushed the bra over her breasts, cupped his hands along the outsides of her mounds and used his grip to draw her closer. She felt trapped, owned, possessed. In her mind she struggled against the living bonds. In reality, she leaned into him, and her fingers reached out and found him.

He was erect, hard. The solid layer of denim made it impossible for her to judge width and length, but the mound pressing against its barrier filled her hand to promise a great deal. She contented herself with rotating her palm over his sheltered flesh, but even as she explored and tested him, she knew she was being tested.

Insane! Animal insane!

I know and I don't care!

She felt him shift but was slow to realize he'd taken a step closer. The move trapped her hand between their bodies. She left it there as he bent toward her so he could run his tongue over her throat. Sounding too much like a small, wounded animal, she threw back her head and exposed her flesh to him. The difference between their heights was such that he had to bend even more and she had to rise onto her toes, but they made it work. His mouth found and then covered a breast. Heated by his breath and her reaction to the intimate contact, she became part of him.

Surrender. Acceptance. Gifting him.

He bathed her flesh, but although she came close to begging for it, he only briefly touched her aching nipple. Her cunt bathed itself. She felt fluid, flowing.

"Please," she whimpered.

He didn't ask what she wanted, thank goodness, because she wasn't sure she could tell him. When he switched his attention to her other breast, the suddenly lonely one instantly reacted to the cold air. It puckered and pulled, causing her to shiver. In contrast, the breast under his control and touch felt full and wet and warm. The heat in her cheeks reached out until even her eyes felt hot. She couldn't pull in enough air so opened her mouth and drank.

"Please," she repeated.

Perhaps he heard this time because he released her mound and straightened. For a heartbeat she feared he'd leave her, but he clamped hard on her buttocks and pulled her roughly against him. Her hands sought his neck. She clung to him, pelvis grinding against pelvis, nearly fucking through the layers. He held her with almost frightening strength, and she gripped back with a mountain climber's power. They rocked and pushed, briefly pulled away only to crash together.

Please, please, please.

Wild, she shoved him away and grabbed blindly for his waistband. He stood motionless and yet trembling while she fumbled with the button and zipper. Then he arched toward her to make her disrobing of him easier. She had to release him while he dispensed with his boots but increased her stance so he could use her body to balance himself. Finally, finally, he stood before her wearing only briefs.

And his shirt, she reminded herself.

Thinking of little except the need to run her hands over his chest, she pulled up on his shirt until it bunched at his armpits. Instead of yanking it off, she grabbed fabric and drew him to her.

"Maybe I'll keep you like this all night," she whispered.

"Maybe you won't."

Putting action to his words, he spun away from her. Instead of seeking freedom however, he shrugged off the shirt before pushing her own top down to her elbows and tethering her with it. He gripped the cloth in one hand and used the other to free her jeans from around her waist.

"Push them down," he ordered.

She started to obey but couldn't complete her mission because he hadn't released her shirt. As a result, she now stood with her jeans under her buttocks and her arms pinned to her sides.

"Maybe I'll keep you like this all night," he said.

"Maybe you will."

He chuckled before pulling her against him. Off balance, she leaned into him, trusting him to keep her from falling. Compelled by something she didn't understand, she looked up. He'd become a blur, all strength and darkness. She wondered if he'd try to kiss her and if she'd let him, or wanted that brand of intimacy. Fortunately, or perhaps unfortunately, he didn't lower his head.

"It's too cold," he pointed out. "We can't fuck out in the open and our tents are too small."

"So?"

"So we need a sleeping bag."

They wound up using his because he'd reached into his tent while she was getting out of her jeans. He unzipped the bag before making short work of his briefs and slipping on the rubber. Then he dropped to his knees. Although she couldn't see his expression, he sent out an undeniable and inescapable message.

Next to me. Now.

Although she'd never allowed a man to order her around when it came to sex, everything felt different this time. Not taking time to try to access the change, she removed her panties and dropped them in the vicinity of his briefs before stepping toward him and lowering herself. He immediately lay her down. Then he stretched beside her and threw the bag over them. She felt trapped and sheltered at the same time. On her side, she reached for and found his waist. His heat seemed to envelop her. It seeped into her flesh, settled deep in her muscle, housed itself in her bone marrow even. Mostly she felt him along her so far untouched cunt.

When he pressed her head against his chest, she briefly felt caressed and protected. Then, perhaps because she barely knew him and certainly didn't trust him, she straightened. Still, she kept her hands on him.

After positioning himself on his back, he gripped her waist and used his hold to leverage her on top of him. She now straddled his hips with his heated cock pressing against her mons. It would take so little to swallow him, to ride him.

Instead, she cupped a hand over his cock and drew it up toward her belly. His fingers dug into her hips.

Are you afraid I'll hurt you? As if you'd let me, or anyone, do that.

It occurred to her that he didn't often trust, not even in bed, but with her nerve endings screaming, and her pussy hot and wet and loose, she couldn't put her mind to the reasons. Even with Rio nearby, she had no existence beyond what was taking place and about to take place in his sleeping bag, so focused on laying claim to him for as long as he allowed. She was no shrinking violet, no naïve innocent ripe for a man's plucking. Surely her hands on his cock told him that.

Then he pushed up on her hips so he could reach between her legs and all control shifted.

Unerringly, masterfully, he dragged his fingers over her labia. Mewling, drenching his fingers, she released him and leaned back. She felt as if she was losing all definition and melting for him, heating to his flame. He kept at her in his practiced way, ruling and directing with a touch here, a nail brush there. In he dipped, then out again.

He let her know how much of her response began and ended with her clit by over and over again touching the too-sensitive bud. Like a man holding a racehorse in check before the opening bell, he brought her to the brink again and again.

Trying but not always succeeding, she fought the whimper clogging her throat by trying to grind herself against him, but he insisted that she hover above him so he could have his playground. She scratched his arms and tried to do the same to his chest.

Because the sleeping bag was unzipped, cool air often touched her. Even though it didn't go far enough, she relished the contrast with her hot flesh. When she managed to focus, she locked into the wilderness night. Everything revolved around Lonato. He played her as if he'd known her body intimately for many years, but although she found that unsettling, she also loved being handled by a master of the art.

Not once did he fall into a rhythm. Not once could she anticipate his next move, which gave her no opportunity to plan, to prepare, to anticipate even. Instead, she felt like a puppet dancing to his strings. Without him to direct them, her muscles might unravel. Her sensual reaction could be nothing more than the excitement generated by fucking a dark and dangerous stranger, but although he represented the unknown in every possible way, she felt comforted by his whisper touches and heated pressure. Comforted and directed.

Locked into the messages her core was giving out, she relished the exhilarating pressure caused by not just one but two fingers being buried deep and strong within her. This time he didn't extricate himself as he'd been doing. Instead, he remained in her so she felt skewered by him. Sure of himself and her acquiescence, he pressed his free hand over her belly until she felt suspended between the two contacts. Her pussy wept. A climax nibbled at her edges, and she clamped her cunt muscles around him.

"Not yet."

What was half whisper and half growl caught a measure of her attention. Yet she didn't fully understand until he withdrew what she'd nearly convinced herself was his cock. Before she could begin to make sense of things, he used his grip on her pelvis to lift her up and onto him.

Her folds embraced him. Her core welcomed him home. She felt him sliding deeper, fuller, until his cock seemed to be reaching for her belly. Surely it had already made its way into her womb. Crying without tears, she pressed her knees against the ground and began leveraging herself up and down. The covering fell off her back, but she barely felt the chill. As they began working together, sweat formed on her spine. Locked into her once again nibbling climax, she acknowledged the effort she was putting out.

Her world existed nowhere except her body. The greatest sensation was centered on and around her clit, but even her toes and the top of her head seemed to have ignited. She gave everything, demanded everything.

And when the hot crash came, she shuddered in waves before collapsing down, on, and around him. His climax might have come a breath before hers, she couldn't tell. The only thing she knew was that they went on and on.

Chapter Three

୫

Lonato couldn't always keep Rio in view. Occasionally the dog would disappear into the underbrush, but although minutes might pass while the Doberman searched, he always returned to Carlin's side before ranging out again. He'd watched police dogs at work so knew how far the animals traveled, but he'd never studied one in such heavy vegetation before. If Carlin had any concern about Rio's ability to remember where they were, she didn't show it. Instead, she waited patiently.

After a quick and mostly silent breakfast, they'd put on their backpacks, and she'd introduced Rio to the shirt he'd supplied. Because of what he knew of the subject and his *abductors* and what the ranger had told him, he'd been relatively sure they were on the right road, but so far Rio hadn't picked up anything. If he'd been misinformed—

Tongue hanging and panting heavily, Rio appeared again. This time instead of briefly touching Carlin's hand before taking off once more, the dog sat in front of her.

"He's found something," she said. "He wants us to follow him."

Instead of making a fool of himself by asking questions, he let her lead the way through close-growing brush, so tall he couldn't see around it. At first Rio seemed to be heading back toward the logging road, but before long, the rough terrain straightened and the vegetation thinned, allowing the Doberman to trot. When they caught up to Rio, the dog was sitting at the side of an even narrower logging road than the one they'd left his jeep on.

"Guess I was a little off," he acknowledged.

"Not bad though," she said with a small smile that threatened to distract him. "I've seen enough maps of the area to know these roads are all over. Most of them haven't been used in years, not since logging was curtailed."

"He's found human scent, right?"

"Not just human, *the* human you're looking for."

A thrill snaked through him. No matter how many times he'd gone after two-legged prey, the sense of anticipation had never grown old. Most of his fellow operatives preferred doing their hunting in urban areas and relied on gossip, loose lips, and sometimes bribes. He, however, would much rather pit himself against someone who wrongly believed the wilderness would hide his or her tracks. Those wanted men and occasionally a woman didn't know what they were up against in him, which was what gave him the advantage.

Instead of asking if she could determine how many humans Rio had located, he dropped to his haunches and studied the packed earth and rocks. Hikers could have come through here, or the boot prints could have been made by rangers or foresters, but although the signs were faint, he knew at least one human had been here since the last rain.

Rio had trembled when Carlin first presented the dog with the shirt. Now he felt the same way. *I'm coming after you, you bastard. It's just a matter of time.*

The realization that he'd thought in the singular stayed with him as he straightened. True, the vice president who'd been with him when Robert Jacob Dowells was grabbed swore that strangers had pulled off a kidnapping, but signs pointing at a simple abduction weren't adding up. Something else was happening here. He just didn't understand what.

Giving himself a mental shake, he turned his attention to Carlin. Like her dog, she stood looking at him, her body at rest and yet alert. "What is it?" she asked. "Rio isn't the only one on a scent. You feel the same way, don't you?"

"Comes with the territory."

"The hell it does." She stalked closer. "Look, I let you get away with this damn veil of secrecy because I figured you knew what you were doing, but this is dangerous. I need to know as much as possible."

Knowing he might unwittingly risk her life if he didn't give her an honest answer, he nodded. "I told you I didn't want you along," he said.

"I am. End of discussion."

For a clean and wholesome-looking woman, he'd be a fool to think of her as an innocent. Besides, she'd aptly demonstrated her earthy nature. "What do you want to know?" he asked, careful to keep his attention on her eyes and not the rest of her mesmerizing body. Even with his gaze under control, however, he had no control over the messages his own body was giving out. *Fuck the lady, now!*

"For one." She spoke in a measured tone. "What made you at least suspect this joker you're looking for and whoever took him are around here? Why'd you question Siskiyou rangers? There are tens of thousands of acres of forest all through the state, if he's even in Oregon. Who's to say he isn't stashed in some back alley?"

"It's possible," he admitted. He briefly considered taking her in his arms, but not only wouldn't she buy his attempt at distracting her, he didn't trust his reaction. "But I have reason to believe the most likely place for him and his *abductors* to stay out of sight is around here."

"What reason?"

"I can't tell you that."

"Yes, you can," she insisted. "Damn it, you aren't paying me enough for me to play dumb."

You aren't stupid. "All right. This much I can tell you. The subject and certain members of his inner circle had a cabin built in the Siskiyous. Unfortunately, none of the board members who hired me know exactly where."

"Nice to have something so remote," she muttered. Then, as he suspected, she frowned. "Wait a minute. You said this guy we're looking for had the cabin built. How would his kidnappers know about it unless..."

"Unless it isn't a real kidnapping."

She stared, mouth slightly parted and nostrils flared. He could all but see the wheels turning. "Let me guess. Money's the motive, money paid as *ransom* our so-called victim hopes finds its way into his pocket."

He didn't speak.

"But if it's a big corporation, isn't he already richer than dirt?"

"Used to be. Not anymore."

"Lousy investments?"

"Lousy gambler."

"Shit." She shook her head. "A desperate man doing desperate things—things that could get someone killed."

"You want to go back?"

He fully expected to see fear in her eyes. In truth, his own system had been on high alert ever since the pieces started falling into place. If he wasn't ruled by the hunt, he'd have called in the cops. Watching the thoughtful expression pass over her features, he wondered if he'd found someone just like him—a predator.

"No," she said.

"Why not?"

"Lonato, when I was thirteen I watched my mother die. It took the cancer two years to beat her down. In the end, she simply wanted to be free. She told me to take each day for what it was but not be afraid of the grim reaper. I try to live by that code."

He wondered how many people she'd told that. Not trying to talk himself out of it, he placed his hand over her cheek. Leaning into the touch, she blinked back the moisture in her eyes. "My parents died when I was eleven," he heard himself say. "You're right. It leaves an impact."

"At the same time?" She placed her hand over his. "Accident?"

He didn't look at her as he spoke. "My old man was drunk when he shot my mother in the head and chest. Then he took another drink and blew himself apart."

Silence punctuated only by birds and the wind working the trees went on for a long time. Finally she closed in on him, lifted herself onto her toes and kissed him. "You were there, weren't you?"

"Yeah."

* * * * *

Damn it, why hadn't she been able to think of anything to say?

Staring at Lonato's back as he walked behind Rio had done precious little to free her from the question. She'd tried to tell herself there hadn't been much she could say and after all these years, the last thing the man needed was to reopen old wounds, but from what little she knew of him she was willing to bet he hadn't spilled that story many times, if at all. Maybe he'd opened up with her because he figured she'd been down the same road. Maybe she'd been such incredible lover that there wasn't anything he wasn't now ready to admit to her.

Yeah, right!

He was the incredible lover anyway, not her. Even now, hot and sweaty, and hungry and thirsty, just thinking about last night was nearly enough to catapult her onto his back.

Wouldn't that be something! Right there in view of Mother Nature she'd rip off their clothes and do whatever it took to work him into a frenzy. At the moment he might be focused on whoever the hell he was looking for, but the right touch from her and he'd—

No you don't! Any more of that thinking and you're going wind up pulling down your pants and doing what you accused him of.

Her inner battle continued to claim her attention, making her slow to note the change in Rio. He'd been walking nose low to the ground along the excuse for a logging road ever since she'd given him the command to follow the scent. Now, however, he'd stopped and was stretched out on his belly.

"What is it?" Lonato asked.

She'd seen this message from her dog before, trained him to do it in fact, but that didn't make the reality any easier. "He's smelled death," she said softly. "Human."

"Death."

"It's close," she whispered back. "Otherwise he would have had to go looking for it."

Lonato reached out his hand, indicating he wanted her closer. Glad to oblige, she stood next to him. He spoke softly, his mouth near her ear. "I checked. My cell phone doesn't work right here. Yours doesn't either, does it?"

"I haven't checked but probably not." *No calling in the posse.*

"Rio can locate the body?"

"Of course."

"All right." He continued at the end of a long sigh. "I don't suppose there's any way of knowing how long the corpse has been there."

"Sorry."

"What if there's someone alive around?" He more mouthed than spoke the question.

For what was probably the first time in her adult life, she pressed against a human being for reassurance. But even with the potential for danger, she acknowledged her nerve endings' response to the contact. Damn, but her sexuality was on high alert. "I'm sorry," she whispered. "He's trained to track scent and as a cadaver dog. It's too much to expect him to assess everything."

"Oh, he knows what's out there. He just doesn't know how to tell us." Speaking low so their words wouldn't travel, he rubbed his thumb against her palm. "Tell him to locate or whatever he does, but I don't want you coming with me."

"I've seen bodies."

"Damn it, the killer or killers might be here."

She'd already put that particular one and one together but hearing it from this trained hunter of human beings made it even more real. She might have argued that she was SOL if something happened to him, if it hadn't occurred to her that concerning himself with her safety might distract him from his own need for caution.

"Bones, Rio," she ordered in a low tone. "Find bones."

* * * * *

The man's head had been bashed in. So much damage had been done to his face that Carlin couldn't begin to guess what he'd looked like before the deadly assault. From what she could tell, he'd been dead at least twenty-four hours.

Although Lonato didn't say anything as he slowly and carefully circled the victim, she suspected the nearby splintered limb had been the murder weapon. Because he'd been carefully trained, Rio didn't need to be reminded not to disturb the crime scene. Like her, the Doberman remained at a distance. Now that he'd found his target, Rio was content to chew on the rawhide she always rewarded him with. She, however, wasn't the least bit interested in food.

Trusting Rio and Lonato equally to alert her if someone approached, she avoided looking at the ruined head while she studied the surroundings and tried to recreate what had taken place. The man's pants were unzipped and his flaccid penis poked out, making her think he'd been taking a piss when he'd been attacked. He could be whoever Lonato was looking for, but she didn't think so as witnessed by the corpse's worn boots and inexpensive shirt. He lay mostly on his side, giving her a view of several of his pockets. Nothing resembling a wallet bulged. Neither was he carrying a weapon. Maybe identification had been deliberately taken, and of course a dead man had no need for a gun or rifle.

Thanks, Dad. See what I get for being a DA's daughter? I think like a cop.

Or maybe the truth was, she was being influenced by Lonato's behavior. She'd watched TV programs showing wolves and other meat eaters around a kill—this man put her in mind of them. At least his fangs weren't bloody, but his total focus was the same. She swore he was sniffing the body. And he'd already thoroughly covered the area around what she thought of as the killing field just as any predator would to assure himself that he was safe.

When he dropped to his haunches next to the body, she half expected him to begin tearing and clawing and was relieved when he did nothing more than push hair away from the corpse's forehead. In his unique way he was conducting a crime scene search but instead of using modern forensic equipment, he was relying on skills maybe he'd inherited from his ancestors. He seemed in no hurry to get to his feet and if his thigh and calf muscles burned from the precarious position, he gave no sign.

A man like that had staying power. *He* had staying power.

At length, Lonato got to his feet, but although she sensed his body relax, she did nothing to break his concentration. When he took off his pack and pulled out a digital camera and took pictures, she mentally applauded his thoroughness. Even Rio, who usually napped after a job well done, appeared impressed. Yesterday she'd taken the handgun strapped to Lonato's waist as nothing more than another tool of his trade. Today she acknowledged its deeper meaning.

"He didn't see it coming," Lonato said as he put the camera away. "There aren't any marks on the ground indicating he tried to get away."

"And he didn't get a chance to zip his fly."

Like her, he saw nothing funny in her observation. "Whoever killed him waited until he was occupied," he said.

"He was one of the kidnappers, wasn't he?"

"What brought you to that conclusion?"

When she told him what she'd concluded from his blue-collar clothes, he nodded. "What are you going to do?" she asked.

"Leave him, for now."

"Then it's a good thing you took those pictures because scavengers are going to find him."

"Yeah, they are." He glanced back at the body and then seemed to dismiss it. "Now you *have* to leave."

"No." She spoke quickly and decisively because she'd already anticipated him saying that. "Rio won't—"

"I've watched you work with him. I know the commands."

"He won't do anything unless I release him, and I'm not going to."

His eyes asked the question. *Why are you doing this? Do you want to risk your life?* Feeling more in tune with him than she remembered ever feeling around another human being, she debated her reply, then decided on honesty. But first she took his wrists and drew him away from the body. She had no need to go on holding him, but she did, absorbing his heat and strength.

"I've never fucked a man I just met," she told him. "Hard to believe after the way I acted, but I always believed I'd need to know someone before the hormones would take over. But you've tapped into a part of me I didn't know existed. I don't fully understand it, but I want to. I need to."

With a movement she nearly missed, he shifted so he now gripped her wrists. She had no doubt he was a master of control when necessary. "You're playing with fire."

"Aren't we both?"

The question made him frown. "Yeah, we are. And not just because there's a killer out there."

She should be focused on that, shouldn't she? Her career had taken her to murder sites before but never without cops and their weapons and authority in attendance and certainly never with the possibility that the murderer might be nearby and determined not to be caught. But if anything, that awareness only heightened her response to Lonato.

"Tell me something," she said. "How many times has your life been at risk?"

"Why? It turns you on?"

You turn me on. "Don't be a smartass." She kept her gaze locked on him and didn't try to fight the fingers running along her nerve endings. He led her further away from the body before continuing.

"I'm just trying to get to know the lady," he whispered before settling his mouth over hers. The world blinked out, leaving her locked inside the shelter and prison he'd created with his presence. She hadn't completely dismissed the possibility of danger but trusted him to know more about the reality than she possibly could.

He'd keep her safe. Safe and satisfied.

Alive with sexual hunger, she probed his mouth with her open one. The message she gave out by allowing his tongue access came across loud and clear. Whenever, however he wanted her, he'd get it.

The contact spread until arms, chests, bellies and hips came together, the pressure hard and unmistakable. She felt as if he was drinking from her and using the freely given gift to increase his own reaction. At the same time, she demanded an equal gift. Whether deliberate or a by-product of her hunger, she found herself being fed by him. She no longer felt her weary legs or empty stomach. Now everything centered around her cunt and breasts. She, who had dealt with uncounted bitches in heat, became one herself. Like them, her message of availability and desperate need was being spelled out throughout her body.

Tilting her hips forward, she brought her pelvis into greater contact with him. In turn he pressed his hard and trapped cock against her. She fought to continue the kiss. Her desperation shocked her, but she couldn't put her mind to trying to fight it. She had no fear for her own life, but he lived his on the edge. He took chances and faced down human animals. For him, death wasn't a vague notion but an everyday possibility.

And for as long as he lived, she'd take what he had to give.

Feeling as if she held quicksilver in her hands, she forced herself to ease off on the ferocity of her embrace. She needed to feel not just his power but what was soft and real and alive about him. Perhaps he understood because he began running his hands up and down her sides almost as if he was caressing her. The change did nothing to lessen her need, but in his masterful way he'd managed to bring her back from the brink of desperation. She tried to do the same for him by relaxing her death grip on his neck and running her fingers over his shoulders. She couldn't quite convince herself to pull back on the pelvis to pelvis contact. If he slid his hand between her legs, she might go off.

"Not now."

Trying to make sense of what was more of a growl than spoken words, she leaned back but kept her hands on his upper arms.

"This is insane," he said. "And I don't do insane."

* * * * *

Even as night began claiming their surroundings, Lonato continued to ask himself whether his proclamation about having his act together was a bold-faced lie. It seemed incomprehensible that he'd dismissed a violent act simply because Carlin turned him on, and yet he couldn't deny that he'd come within a rational moment of fucking her right then and there.

She hadn't said much after directing Rio to start following the subject's trail again. Her silence should have given him plenty of time to put the pieces together, but once he'd come to the not too brilliant conclusion that the body was one of those who'd supposedly kidnapped Dowells, his mind had done little more than float, although if he was being truthful, he'd spent more mental energy keeping his hands off her than anything else.

Damn it, he didn't want it like this! Awareness of and appreciation for his surroundings had more than once spelled the difference between life and death. He knew better than to allow himself to be distracted!

Only *allow* hadn't factored in.

"It's been at least a day since they were here," he said as he stood after studying another boot print.

"How do you know?"

"Someone kicked aside this branch. The ground under it has had time to dry."

"So we're safe? Time for several minutes worth of commercials before the action picks up again?"

"A man's been murdered," he shot back. "This ain't no TV show."

"You think I don't know it? Damn it. This isn't the first murder scene I've been to. And I watched my mother die."

"And I saw what bullets did to my parents, but that's not why I've got to watch both our backs."

"You, me, and Rio. Lonato, I'll never make light of death." Her voice had fallen several notches. "I mourn for the man we found earlier and everyone who cares or ever cared for him, but we're in the wilderness where eat or be eaten has been played out since the beginning of time."

She was right, righter than he wanted to admit.

"It's primal out here," she continued, coming closer. "Civilization hasn't made it all the way into the forest. I hope it never does."

"Primal," he repeated and pulled her against him. Enough daylight remained that they could have traveled a little further, but a few hundred yards more wouldn't make that much difference. Besides, the wild land and his wild heritage had made its impact. Tomorrow or next month he'd deal with bills and taxes. In the morning he'd continue hunting for a killer or killers.

Tonight was for other things.

Chapter Four

ဆာ

Carlin lay on her back on the sleeping bag Lonato had unceremoniously spread out a few minutes ago. Neither had spoken while they removed their clothes, and although she was hungry, she didn't care when or whether she ate. Once again daylight had fled, a switch suddenly turned off. Night's cold made its impact. The moon would soon arrive. In the meantime, she folded her arms under her breasts and waited for her warrior.

He wasted no time with subtle foreplay. Instead, he spread her legs and bent her knees slightly. Once he had her in position, he began by stroking her breasts followed by a quick, strong journey down her belly and over her mons. Charged, she struggled to breathe and keep her hips still. She reached for him, but he pressed her arms by her sides.

Trust me, she heard. And because she had no choice, she continued to give herself to him. After briefly running his hands over her inner thighs, he changed position so he could place his head near her apex. Even before his tongue touched her, she started shaking. The first stroke was so light that for a moment she thought maybe she'd imagined it. Then she felt her primitive reaction and knew he'd found her clit.

The next touch lasted longer, felt warmer. As she fisted her hand in his hair and he closed his fingers over her pelvis, he bathed and ignited. Assaulted, she rocked from side to side but kept her movements as slight as possible so he could remain in contact with her unbelievably sensitive clitoris. She didn't try to swallow her moans. Neither did she make any attempt to keep her rapidly building climax under control.

He worked her so quick, so expertly! Again, again, and again he stroked until she felt herself shooting over the top. If she'd ever climaxed in less time, she couldn't remember and didn't care. Waves of pleasure caught and held her. Her legs shook. Her pussy burned and wept.

She'd just begun to come down when he went after her again. This time he spread her legs wider and brought his mouth even closer so he could slide his tongue inside her. In and out he worked, in and out. Her head thrashed. She clawed at what of him she could reach.

"Stop! Please, stop. I can't take—"

"Yes, you can. And you will."

After his growled warning, he forced her to spread herself yet more. His tongue and breath caresses covered her, concentrating on one spot and then another with no sense of pattern, no way for her to anticipate or control her response.

She climaxed again, or maybe he'd simply kept the first one going until she felt as if she might come endlessly. Sweating and barely able to breathe, she cried out into the night. Maybe something about her helpless sobs reached him because he pulled back so now only his harsh breaths reached her.

The wave began to recede. She started to come back in touch with herself, to take back ownership.

But only momentarily because he propped himself up on an elbow and replaced his mouth with his fingers. As she lay there boneless and crying a little, he slid a knuckle between her nether lips and inserted as much of his finger as he could. He pressed, the pressure most intense on her clit. As he'd done before, he used random movement to keep her off balance and on fire. More times than she could count, he rubbed and stroked. The overstimulated nub responded as it had been designed to do, and the rest of her body followed suit.

With the side of his thumb resting against her cleft, she once more lost control. Shuddering waves held her, exhausting her in ways no strenuous day could. When, finally, the last wave died, she couldn't find the distinction between consciousness and unconsciousness.

"No more," she whimpered. "Please, no more."

"You like?"

"Like?"

"Multi-orgasmic." He made it sound like a compliment. If he hadn't straightened and closed her legs, she had no idea when she'd have thought to do that.

"Never *that* multi before," she admitted before ordering herself not to reveal any more. Damn him. It had been so easy for him to claim ownership of her. Even now, spent from the waist down, she knew how easily he could force or coax another explosion from her. His power scared her and yet she'd soon crave another demonstration. "Let me up."

"No."

Maybe the single word should have alarmed her. Instead, she insanely embraced it and became part of it. He'd made her his prisoner. Part of an Indian raiding party, he'd run her down and thrown ropes over her. Despite her struggles, he'd taken her back to his teepee and secured her to the center pole so he could do what he wanted with her.

Pulling the fantasy around her, she turned from strong and independent modern woman into a captured pioneer desperate to do whatever it took to remain alive. Or maybe the truth was, the pioneer she'd become in her mind desperately craved be taken by this savage.

"What do you want?" she asked.

"Arms over your head. Arch your back and lift your pelvis."

"Just like that? Damn it, I—"

"Now."

Against all reason, his command seeped into her and became part of her. Compliant, she did as her *captor* ordered.

He stretched out over her and braced his upper body with his arms positioned on either side of her chest. Although she wasn't sure her body could handle another assault so soon, she bent her knees, planted her feet, and tilted herself to receive him.

His legs were heat against hers. Despite the dark, she felt his gaze boring into her and locked onto him. He wanted. She wanted. They'd both take, both receive.

Tomorrow was soon enough for fear of his control over her.

Every move one of command and ownership, he entered her soaking cave. She felt her sensitized flesh close around him, cradling and sheltering, housing the savage.

As he began thrusting, she acknowledged that her nerve endings hadn't had time to recover from the intense stimulation they had received. But even if a climax eluded her, she could gift him as he'd *gifted* her if that's what it had been. Grateful for her physical life, she presented herself over and over again while providing the resistance his cock demanded. Even as his breathing lost all cadence and he trembled, she thought, not of a man caught in his body's most primitive and demanding needs, but a stallion, a stud who has mounted his possession. He still owned her, not the other way around. He'd melted her down and turned her compliant. In gratitude and surrender and disbelief, she became what he demanded.

And when the sweet, hot cum shot into her, she joined him in climax.

* * * * *

"I didn't use protection," he told her.

"No, we didn't," she responded. When he didn't say anything more, she blew on the small fire made from dry wood that barely smoked, and then watched for the outlines of bats and owls against the moon and stars. Anything was easier than looking at him.

He'd rested on top of her for a while after emptying his seed into her, but when she'd told him he was getting heavy, he'd gotten up and handed her her clothes. As she'd dressed, the feel of denim had erased the last of the savage-captive fantasy. And when he'd started gathering wood, she'd realized she'd gone from being hungry to starving. Last night they'd sat across from each other with the fire between them while they ate, but this time he'd positioned himself beside her. She felt both trapped and renewed, as much him as herself.

"We need to talk," he said.

Don't tell me you intend to do the right thing if I get pregnant. I don't want to hear that.

"What about?"

"I've killed before. I can do it again if I need to."

That she hadn't expected to hear. "Do you think it might be necessary?"

"It's an occupational hazard."

"Then why do you do it?" she asked even though she believed she knew. This man operated according to a code she'd once believed existed only in thriller movies and books. His world was rough and raw, survival of the fittest. Hadn't the rough and raw way he'd taken her demonstrated that?

"Someone has to."

"Who do you think you might have to kill this time?"

"Whoever tries to kill me. Or you."

He'd risk his life for her? The thought was surprisingly appealing, the protective male guarding his woman. She chewed.

"Do you understand why I don't want you to be part of this?" His voice was harsh. "Really understand? No one is playing."

"I realize that." She wasn't sure whether her comprehension of the line between life and death would ever be as deep as his.

"I hope to hell so. What you need to understand, what you have to do is do everything I tell you to. If I say hit the ground, you obey, immediately."

"You aren't kidding, are you?" *Damn it, you know he isn't!*

Fortunately he didn't throw her stupid question back at her. "I'm not going to go into all the dangerous situations I've been in because they don't matter beyond providing necessary experience and background information."

And maybe because you don't want me knowing what you're capable of. But didn't she already have an inkling as witnessed by the way he'd taken control during sex?

"All right." Her voice faltered a bit. "Ah, do you have any idea what to expect this time with this situation? You must have some sense of what we're getting into."

"Yeah, I do. There's no way I'm buying that shit about Dowells having been kidnapped. The man isn't stupid. He's not going to walk into that pathetic excuse for a trap. My guess is he paid a couple of men to help him set up the scam. He's going to come up with a ransom demand all right, but he's deliberately delaying it."

"Why?" The name of the man he'd been hired to find sounded vaguely familiar. She wondered if Lonato had deliberately finally told her. Of course he had.

"My guess, so he can first dispose of the two people who can blow the whistle on him. And so he's sure he's where no one can find him until he wants to be found."

"This Dowells planned to kill the men he hired?"

"One's already dead. Maybe the other one too. Rio just hasn't found him."

If Rio had any inkling of the role he might be playing in this, the dog gave no indication. At the moment his full attention was on his rawhide chew.

"I see," she said because something was expected of her. "Wouldn't Dowells have to kill them at the same time? Otherwise, the living one would try to do Dowells before he was offed." *Offed? Who do you think you are, a gang member?*

"Not necessarily if the *kidnapper* hoped to get all the ransom money. He might decide to play along with Dowells. Hell, maybe he did in the guy we found as a way of demonstrating his loyalty. Carlin, these people operate in ways I don't expect you to understand."

But you do because you've been in the world of people like them. "It sounds as if you haven't come to any conclusion about what we're going to encounter when we find whoever is still alive."

"*I.* I'll find them, not you."

On the brink of telling him she wasn't about to let him take all the risks, she shut her mouth. Was she crazy! She wasn't being paid to put her life on the line. Lonato got off on that, not her. He knew the risks and had faced them before. But what if it turned out to be two, or more, against one?

"Ah, so you think there is going to be a ransom demand?"

"Has to be. This is all about money, money the board has to cough up."

"But how is Dowells going to get his hands on it? He's in the forest." *With us.*

"He only needs to stay here until he's sure they've bought his story. Then he'll *escape.* The money will have been to some place where it can't be traced. It'll never be found, just like the kidnappers."

"You're sure of that?"

"It's my best guess."

"But how—"

"The details aren't important, and I don't intend to explain any more to you than I have to. My plate was full before you came on the scene. Now I have to factor in your safety."

For a moment she was tempted to tell him she'd rethought her position and agreed that he needed to remain a sole warrior as he'd originally intended. But one man had already died in this forest. She couldn't leave him, she wouldn't!

"Carlin? Are you listening?" he prompted.

"Loud and clear. But if you wanted me to ride off into the sunset, you shouldn't have fucked me."

"You wanted it."

"And you should have known our having sex would change the way I look at you." *And the way I hope you think of me.*

"Yeah," he whispered. "I should have."

* * * * *

Damn, damn, damn!

Cursing himself, Lonato turned onto his back. Although he'd set up Carlin's tent, he hadn't bothered with one for himself. Figuring she'd be too sensitive for more sex and not trusting himself around her, he'd insisted they sleep separately. She'd agreed, making him think he wasn't the only one who needed distance.

Damn, damn, damn.

As if hearing him, Rio scooted closer. Instead of pushing the Doberman away, he lightly stroked the dog. "You're going to need to earn your keep," he whispered. "Let us know everything you pick up, not just what she tells you to. Put your mistress's life first. And second."

First? Although he lived by the code that placed a client's needs ahead of his own, if he'd ever truly contemplated risking his life to save someone else before, he couldn't remember. It was one thing to live by a "protect and serve" mentality. It was quite another to feel that code in his pores, his heart.

His heart? No, damn it! He was being influenced by the setting, danger's siren call, an attractive and sensual woman. What red-blooded man wouldn't be turned on by a broad with the skills and competence she did, let alone her quick-to-excite nature and mature, enticing body? He'd been called brave and courageous—and a damn fool—more than once. No wonder he was drawn to the same in the opposite sex.

But once this assignment was over, he'd be on to the next. One last roll in the hay and he'd suit up and be on his way. It had been like that for as long as he'd been working for Recovery, even longer. He didn't want or need ties.

Just you, Wolf, he acknowledged as he tried to find the door to sleep. *You're all I ever need.*

Chapter Five

𝕤𝕠

Thunderclouds were building on the horizon as they reached the top of a rocky hill the next afternoon. Studying them, Carlin's only thought was that she didn't mind being rained on. She just didn't want to be in the woods while lightning flashed.

Then Lonato turned and looked at her, and she amended her thought. She cared about him too, specifically his undeniable impact on her nerves, skin, bones, tendons, fingernails, and other body parts. "What?" she said when he continued to stare.

"We've been walking for hours. How are you holding up?"

"I haven't given it much thought." She indicated Rio whose entire attention remained riveted on the ground. "The way he's been acting—"

"We're getting closer," Lonato finished for her. He walked the few steps back to her, dark eyes seemingly even darker than before. "Can you release him from the scent for a while?"

"Of course but why?"

"Because I don't intend for us to walk into something I'm not prepared for."

Mulling over the use of *us* and *I* in the same sentence, she nevertheless gave Rio permission to relax. The dog gave her a puzzled look that reminded her of when he'd been a puppy and she'd stopped him from tearing into her mop. Then perhaps figuring he'd done enough work for a while anyway, he sank to the ground.

"I'm going on ahead for a while," Lonato said. "We've been heading northwest and I'll continue in the same direction."

She nearly argued that she had no intention of being left behind, but this was hardly a childish game. He was the one who understood danger in all its forms and functions, not her. Bowing to a brand of expertise she never expected to equal, she nodded. But when he slipped off his pack and readjusted his pistol so it was closer to his right hand, she impulsively reached for him.

"Be careful." She didn't care how hackneyed the term sounded, only that she meant it with all her heart.

"I will." His answer was soft, his attention split between meeting her gaze and acknowledging her hand on his arm. "I'm not leaving you here alone."

He could have pointed out that he was determined to fulfill his mission, but he hadn't. Instead, he'd put her first. Not fully understanding either his words or her reaction, she slid her arms around his neck and stood on tiptoe. Sighing, he bent down to meet her upturned lips. He began by barely brushing his mouth against hers, but when she impulsively and needfully arched her pelvis forward, the kiss turned hot. He clutched her to him, his mouth savage, the embrace inescapable. In a heartbeat, she ceased to exist beyond him. She felt heat and desire but something else as well, something deeper. Frightening.

Perhaps he experienced the same intensity because he abruptly released her and stepped away. "Stay here," he ordered. "I'll be back."

"When?" Her voice shook. Her cheeks felt inflamed, and she'd dampened her panties.

"As soon as I can."

"Be careful," she repeated before turning away so she couldn't see him leave.

* * * * *

Had time stopped? Although her barely moving watch told her otherwise, the afternoon felt endless. If only she'd had something to occupy herself with, but beyond refreshing herself with what little water from her canteen she thought she could spare, Carlin simply sat and studied the miniscule insect life that shared the ground with her. She wished she could sleep the way Rio did but couldn't imagine Lonato returning to a snoring woman.

Besides, although she fought the memories, they won. In her mind she saw the discarded body of the man Rio had found yesterday. When that didn't consume her, she relived her mother's sad final days. But most of all she embraced the times she and this man she barely knew and didn't understand had fucked. She tried to tell herself that by replaying the frenzy and heat, she'd cleanse herself of his body's impact on hers, but it didn't turn out that way.

How could she expect it to be any different? She'd never met a man like Lonato, hadn't even believed that a flesh and blood one existed. Bounty hunters and mercenaries existed only in the movies, right? Real men didn't put responsibility and honor ahead of their lives. No code existed which said the target must be met regardless of danger.

But those things existed inside Lonato, at least she now believed they did. He lived with a recklessness she would call suicidal if he hadn't imprinted her with proof of how much he embraced life, or at least life's carnal elements.

Carnal. Raw. Real.

That's what he was, those things and more. In her mind he became the Lone Ranger, Batman, maybe even Indiana Jones. Adventure and danger brought him to life and fulfilled him. Without those things, he'd simply exist.

Or would he?

Exhausted from trying to figure him out, she settled her back against a tree. She was trying to find a smooth place to plant her ass when, in no more than a blink of an eye, Rio went from a prone to alert position. His hackles rose. Although he'd never been a growler, he did so now. Jumping to her feet, she strained to hear. Rio's growls turned to a whine, and he gave her a puzzled look.

"What is it?" she more mouthed than spoke. "What do you hear?"

Once again the dog resumed staring in the direction Lonato had gone. The hair along his back continued to stand up. If reading the Doberman's body language hadn't become second nature to her, she would have thought he'd caught the scent of some creature he was dying to chase. But because she knew him, she understood.

Something's happening that shouldn't, Rio said. *I don't understand the message but I need to. We both do.*

Wishing for the first time in her life that she carried a firearm, she gave Rio permission to follow his instinct. Without waiting to see if she intended to follow, he trotted off in the direction Lonato had gone. Grabbing up both backpacks, she hurried after her animal. As she concentrated on her footing and keeping Rio in view, she struggled to keep dark images at bay but couldn't.

Something had happened to Lonato. Maybe Rio had heard sounds of fighting or even worse, a gunshot. Had Lonato cried out? Was he all right? Alive?

The last thought stole the air from her lungs, leaving her weak. Feeling both numb and electrified, she managed to get her pack on so she now clutched Lonato's to her breasts. He couldn't be dead! He couldn't.

But if he was, what would she do?

Kill whoever had killed him.

The uncivilized response expanded inside her. Some part of her insisted that she couldn't take the law into her own hands, but a stronger voice, one imprinted with what Lonato had done to her body and soul, overrode it. If someone had killed Lonato, that beast's blood would saturate the ground.

Both because she was accustomed to walking in the wilderness and because she'd studied Lonato's stealthy, silent progress, she managed to trot all but soundlessly, and Rio made no noise. He seemed delighted to have a task to accomplish, and she envied his ability to simply do his job without emotion. She preferred working with search and rescue dogs to those law enforcement used. Police dogs' value came in part because they'd charge into danger. If they understood life and death, the concept didn't get in the way of what their humans commanded them to do.

"Rio," she hissed after they'd gone maybe a quarter of a mile. "Here."

The Doberman spun around and trotted back to her side. If he'd heard something, which she had no doubt of, it couldn't have been much further than they'd traveled. Besides, she had no intention of letting the beloved and valuable animal blunder into danger.

"Stay," she ordered and dropped the packs to the ground. Rio shivered and looked crestfallen but did as ordered. After removing her utility knife from her pack and putting it in her waistband near her canteen, she struck out alone. Now that she was moving at a slower pace, she noticed an unusual number of birds. At the same time, the trees ahead of her seemed less invasive as if something up there wasn't capable of sustaining their growth.

A lake.

Wouldn't someone wishing to have a remote cabin build it near a lake?

Carefully choosing each step before she took it, she bent low and crept forward. She felt for all the world like a wolf stalking prey. The only difference was she didn't know her prey's identity while a wolf would never make that mistake.

Mistake!

Something flashed to her right. She started to turn in that direction, but before she could complete the movement, a force crashed into her and sent her sprawling on the ground on her belly. *A man!*

Desperate to free herself, she struggled against the warm and living weight, but even as she fought, instinct told her not to cry out. Obviously her attacker didn't know what she was thinking because he clamped his hand over her mouth. At the same time, he straddled her waist and hips and even her legs, pinning her to the earth.

"It's me," the man whispered against her ear. "Don't speak or move."

Lonato!

Relief so intense it brought tears to her eyes rushed over her. Although his palm continued to press on her lips, she managed to touch his flesh with her tongue. She ordered herself to relax, to simply accept his larger body on and over hers.

"You understand?" he asked, his voice more of a rumble than spoken words.

She nodded and remained limp.

Taking her response as her answer, he rolled off her and helped her sit up. Ignoring the pine needles and other debris on her shirt, she snuggled against him.

"What the hell are you doing here?" he whispered. He stroked her neck.

"Rio heard something. I had to—"

"An axe," he interrupted. "They were chopping wood." He jerked his head in the direction she'd been heading. "The sound echoed."

"They?" Like him, she kept her voice low and knew not to risk being seen by standing.

"Yeah. There's two of them."

* * * * *

Although he had his arms around her and her heart beat against his chest, Lonato still struggled to accept that she was here. He wanted her just as she was. Hell, thoughts of what might happen between them once he was free to return to her had distracted him from the need to turn into a tracking machine. But he'd told himself that those mental and sensual images weren't about to become reality any time soon and he'd better get rid of them. He'd succeeded when he spotted the lake and cabin and become the wolf he patterned his actions after, focused on his goal, put his mind fully on what he needed to do to accomplish that goal.

Then something, his nerves maybe, had told him that she'd found him.

Holding her close, both so they could carry out a whispered conversation and because—hell, because he needed to, he told her what he'd learned. Robert Jacob Dowells was here all right along with a man he'd never seen before. The two had been outside when he arrived. He'd been alerted to their presence by their argument. Although he'd been too far away to hear most of what they were saying, Dowells was obviously berating someone he considered his inferior. The other man hadn't called Dowells on his attitude so much as he'd continued to insist that he was right.

"I needed to understand the dynamics between them," he told Carlin. "That way I have a better idea how to deal with them."

"There's no doubt? Dowells isn't the other man's captive?"

"Hardly. And from the description I got, I'm positive the other one is one of those who *kidnapped* Dowells."

"Why is that other man dead?" she asked. "Which of these two killed him?"

"The only way we're going to have the answer to that is by asking them."

"How are you going to do that?"

The $64,000 question. Before Carlin had shown up, he'd decided to wait until the men had separated and then disarm and disable them in turn. He hadn't worked out the details, but that hadn't worried him because he'd dealt with uneven odds before. Surprise always worked, surprise and stealth and a predator's mindset. He saw no reason to change his plans, but now he had to factor in her safety, make it his priority.

"Go back," he whispered. "I need to concentrate on what I'm doing, not you."

"I can't leave," she told him, her voice husky. "Worrying about you has already driven me half crazy."

"I'm sorry," he muttered.

"Don't be." She positioned his hand so it rested on a breast.

"What the hell are you doing?" *What the hell am I doing running my fingers under your blouse and bra so I can feel your warmth?*

"There's more than sex between us, Lonato, a lot more."

Much as her earthy words pushed buttons in him, he knew she was right. He didn't understand how it had happened or how he'd come to care, really care about her. And now wasn't the time to try to figure that out.

When he looked into her eyes, they seemed a little clouded. "Those men are murderers," she said. "At least one of them is."

"Yes."

"They *have* to be brought to justice."

"That's what I was hired for."

"And now you have an assistant."

No, he wanted to yell, but he knew how useless that would be.

"What are we going to do?"

He told her that he didn't want to risk getting trapped by going into the cabin and had been intending to wait until he'd isolated one man at a time outside before making his move. It wouldn't be dark for hours. He could afford to be patient.

"So can I," she said.

"You aren't taking them on." Although he didn't mean to hurt her, he closed down on her nipple to get her attention. She arched her back but didn't try to move away. "You aren't trained in this business," he pointed out. "You'll be more of a hindrance than help."

"I told you, I'm not leaving. I can't."

I can't. He meant that much to her?

* * * * *

One hour rolled into two and still the cabin door hadn't opened. At Lonato's insistence, she'd moved away from him, but although he'd gestured for her to increase the distance between them, she'd set up what she thought of as her own surveillance where she could still see the cabin, not that the expensive-looking structure could be considered a cabin. How Lonato had managed to fade into his surroundings puzzled her but then couldn't a wolf conceal himself until he was ready to attack?

Her mind played with a number of scenarios, each ending with Lonato having overwhelmed and overcome the two men. Refusing to allow the possibility that he might get hurt or worse to slip past her subconscious, she mentally pictured him tying the defeated men's hands behind them. Then he'd secure their ankles and check them for hidden weapons before calling the authorities.

Or maybe he'd have to kill them.

Memory of how the dead man Rio had found looked should have repulsed her, shouldn't it, but she also ran through the conditions that might force Lonato to use deadly force. If it turned into a case of two against one or he believed she was in danger, he'd fire his weapon.

And maybe he wouldn't need a reason, an excuse to kill.

She tried to bury that thought, but like her, it refused to leave. She didn't know him, not really, so how could she say what he was capable of or what code he lived by. These men were murderers—what about an eye for an eye? And if the killing took place out here, who would know more had been involved than self-defense? With the men dead, Lonato wouldn't have to concern himself with responsibility for them.

A wolf. A predator and a killer. And when he'd finished with his deadly task, he'd turn to her, his woman.

She'd begun to imagine Lonato morphing from man to beast when a sudden sound caused a chill to race down her spine. Blinking, she watched the front door open. After a few seconds, a man emerged from the shadows and stood on the stoop that led to two redwood steps. She imagined Lonato at attention, his mind racing with plans and possibilities.

"No matter what happens, you will *not* get involved," he'd ordered. "I will *not* have you hurt."

Not have your presence endangering me, she'd mentally translated. But could she live up to the curt nod she'd given as response?

The man stretched and made his way down the stairs before starting toward the lake. Going by his body language, he was bored. No wonder. He'd probably been here for at least a day with no contact with the outside world. How long did he intend to hide out here? Did he have any idea how precarious his situation was now that Lonato had found him?

I want to take them one at a time, her lover had said.

Anticipating and half sick at the same time, she strained to make out Lonato's form but couldn't. She began to sweat and for some insane reason, she felt sexual excitement.

The man was now heading purposefully for the sturdy dock that reached over the lake and held a new fishing boat she'd concluded had to have been flown in by helicopter. With every step, he was putting distance between himself and where she believed Lonato was. If he didn't act soon—

When the new sound came, her brain was slow to register its meaning. Then, chillingly, it did. Rio. Rio emerging from the trees and slinking toward the man, his every move that of a search and rescue dog who has found his target.

No!

"What the hell?"

Disbelieving, she stared as the man turned to confront Rio. For several seconds man and animal studied each other, neither moving. Then Rio again started walking toward him. Every line of his body spoke of his single-minded purpose. He looked magnificent, a large male Doberman in his prime, teeth exposed, paws silent.

The man didn't back away. Only his right hand moved. To her horror, she realized he was reaching for something tucked in his waistband. Even before he pulled out the pistol, she knew what she'd see.

"Who's out there?" the man demanded. "Listen. Whoever the hell came with this dog, you've got five seconds to show yourself or I'm going to shoot."

No! Not Rio.

Driven by love for the dog who'd become her constant companion and friend, she stood up. The man turned in her direction but kept the weapon aimed at Rio.

"Rio," she said. "Down."

Rio dropped to his belly, head high, eyes intent on the man. To the uninitiated, his body language might not mean much, but she understood. He didn't trust.

"A broad?" The man shook his head. "Get your ass over here."

Although she now heard only the wind and a solitary bird, she imagined Lonato's voice. She didn't believe he'd curse her for trying to save her dog's life, but what would he do now?

"I'm sorry," she said when maybe ten feet separated her from the man. Thinking fast, she injected as much fear and confusion into her voice as possible. "I didn't mean— He isn't vicious."

"What the hell are you doing here?"

"I-I'm hiking. That's all. Just hiking." She shrugged and then let her arms drop to her side, the picture of naïveté. "Please, don't hurt my pet."

"*Just* hiking?" He waggled his gun at her. "You expect me to believe that shit? Lift arms. Turn around."

This man was accustomed to giving orders, she decided as she complied. Although she desperately wanted to look for Lonato, she carefully kept her gaze unfocused. By the time she'd completed her circuit, she'd calmed enough that she could start thinking again. She had no doubt that her life was in danger, hers and Rio's and Lonato's. Thank goodness she didn't have more than her utility knife on her. If she'd shown up armed, it would have set off red flags. Now if only she could keep the man from realizing Rio's true purpose in life.

"I'm sorry, sir," she said, careful to stare submissively at the ground. "I knew I shouldn't be here. I didn't expect to come across a cabin. I-I was just curious, that's all."

His grunt said he wasn't about to believe her out of hand. "This is the middle of nowhere. What the hell are you doing here?"

"I told you, hiking."

"Mitch!" he yelled. "Mitch!"

A few moments later, the cabin door opened and another man stepped out. This one was at least fifteen years younger with broad shoulders and a long upper torso but short legs. His dirty-looking hair stuck to his neck, and like the man she took to be Dowells, he hadn't shaved for several days. He carried a rifle cradled in his arms.

270

"I heard you," Mitch snapped. "Been watching through the window since you yelled the first time." He came to stand near Dowells. "Pretty little piece, isn't she?"

"Stop thinking with your cock and act as if you have half a brain!" Dowells ordered. "Shit, I've never seen such a one-track mind."

Mitch glared at the older man. His clenched jaw told Carlin things she needed to know about their relationship. Despite his whiskers and less than clean clothes, Dowells had the air of a man used to spending money on himself, a man who understood what money could accomplish. She was close enough to see that his nails had been manicured, and his hair had that professionally styled appearance. She'd already noted his perfect teeth, and the skin around his forehead and eyes had a tightened quality, probably the result of plastic surgery. He looked like he was in his mid-thirties but had to be older.

"Let me get this straight," Dowells said to her. "You want me to believe that you just happened to be traipsing clear out here with just the dog to keep you company? That you just happened to stumble upon this lake? It's a two-day hike from the highway, sweetheart."

"I didn't start out alone," she replied, thinking quickly. Somewhere, somehow Lonato would do what he had to. In the meantime, she had to quiet the men's suspicions. "My boyfriend and I, we wanted some time to ourselves."

"Where is he?"

"I don't know, and I don't care." She shrugged and took a chance on lowering her arms. She didn't like the way Mitch kept staring at her breasts. "We had a fight this morning. I left. I hope he's lost."

"And the dog?"

"He's my boyfriend's," she improvised. "My *ex*-boyfriend. That's what we fought about, part of it anyway. Rio kept chasing after rodents instead of staying with us. That bastard started kicking him. I wasn't about to leave Rio with him." She worked up what she hoped passed as a smile. "Besides, Rio likes me better."

"Where are your belongings?"

Because she'd anticipated the question, she was ready with an explanation that in her rush to put distance between herself and someone who now disgusted her, she'd left her pack behind. "At least I'd already strapped on my canteen." She indicated it at her waist. "And I have this knife, for what it's worth. But I haven't eaten since last night. I thought, when I saw the cabin, I thought there might be some food in there."

"You were hoping it'd be empty so you could break in."

About to protest, she shoved her personal code aside and became who she believed she needed to become in order to survive. "It was worth a shot, but 'cause you're here, I'll come out and ask. But, please, put that gun away. It's making me nervous."

Mitch chuckled and aimed the rifle barrel at her crotch. "That's what it's supposed to do, bitch."

Dowells stared at Mitch. Something crossed over his features that might have been wariness. Unable to comprehend the complex relationship between the two, she struggled to find her way through her limited options. She had no doubt that Lonato was taking in the scene, planning his moves, whatever they might be. If only she knew how to be the most use to him.

Disarm them.

When Mitch came closer, she forced herself not to back away. Instead, she stood as tall as she could. Eyes hooded now, he shifted the rifle so it rested under his right arm. He clamped his free hand under her chin. "Coming up roses, bitch. Roses for me. You want something to put in your belly? First you let me in your pussy."

"You can't—"

"I can and I will." With that, he hooked a leg behind her ankles and shoved, causing her to lose her balance. She landed on her ass, arms behind her to catch her fall.

"Damn it, you bastard!" Dowells bellowed. "What the hell are you doing?"

"We can't let her live." Mitch didn't take his attention off her. "But she doesn't have to die yet. Not until I'm done with her."

After assuring herself that Rio had only gotten to his feet but was waiting for a signal from her, she concentrated on controlling her heart rate. This wasn't a game. They were going to kill her.

"You're right," Dowells said at length. "Get some rope."

"Get it yourself." Mitch extended a boot toward her, prompting her to slide back a few inches.

"Now!" Dowells ordered. "Don't forget who's paying you."

Cursing, Mitch turned from her. As the larger man stalked toward the cabin, she turned her attention to Dowells who positioned himself a few feet away. The pistol aimed at her didn't waver. She imagined him using the same self-assurance to take charge of board meetings. He might not be accustomed to having those he considered his inferiors, like Mitch, stand up to him, but he knew how to put them in their place. Wasn't he using his commanding presence to do just that to her?

"You should have made up with your boyfriend," he told her almost conversationally. "If you had, you wouldn't be in this fix."

"I didn't mean anything. Please, don't let him—"

"Shut up."

She did. Whether the real Carlin or the dim bulb she was trying to present herself as had obeyed she couldn't be sure. *Lonato, I don't know what I'm supposed to do. How to help you.*

"You aren't the one in control here, young lady," Dowells informed her. "You've stumbled into something you shouldn't have. Unfortunately, it's too late to do anything about it. I'd explain, but in a little while it won't matter to you." He indicated the cabin. "In the meantime, the goon in there needs to be pacified. He'll be more manageable that way. And I intend to get as good from you as he does."

"Anything. I'll do anything. Just don't hurt me." Because she hadn't been given permission to stand, she remained where she was. No need to push him.

"Oh, we'll *do* all right. As for hurting you—" He smiled, giving her a leisurely look at his perfect teeth.

Just then Mitch slammed open the door and stomped back with a goodly amount of rope coiled in the crook of his elbow. He'd exchanged the rifle for a handgun. Ignoring his *employer*, he closed in on her before shoving his boot against her chest and knocking her onto her back.

"Every man's fantasy," he proclaimed as he held her in place. "At least mine. This is going to be good. Damn good."

"Tie her," Dowells ordered. "And gag her."

No! This isn't happening. No!

"I know what I'm doing," Mitch barked. "Where I come from a man knows how to keep a bitch in her place."

"We aren't there," Dowells shot back. "And I'm calling the shots, not you. Hands behind her."

Leering in a way she'd never forget, Mitch tucked his gun in his waistband. At the same time, Dowells positioned himself so he stood over her. His weapon covered her. When Mitch lowered himself onto his knees beside her, she forced herself not to try to get away. At the same time, she glanced at Rio, briefly lifting her hand with her palm down, ordering the Doberman to remain where he was. Teeth bared, he reluctantly complied.

By the time she looked at Mitch again, the man, who reminded her of a seedy bit-player in a mobster movie, was reaching for her shirt. It took every bit of willpower she possessed not to scratch, bite, and kick as he ripped the buttons free. If she struggled, Rio and Lonato might try to come to her rescue, and it wouldn't take an instant for Dowells to fire.

Although hatred for Mitch nearly consumed her, she remained passive as he pulled her arms out of her blouse and flipped it aside. She'd never felt ropes on her, never imagined having her wrists bound could be so terrifying. *Don't lose it. Don't!*

Once he'd secured her, Mitch yanked her into a kneeling position and forced rope between her teeth. He tied off the ends in such a way that she couldn't close her mouth. She made no attempt to see whether she could still make a sound. Unshed tears burned her eyes when he reached behind her and unsnapped her bra. Looking pleased with himself, he yanked at the straps, freeing her breasts. Feeling less than human, she had no choice but to remain on her knees in the dirt, all but naked from the waist up.

Raped. I'm going to be raped.

And Lonato will see.

Fresh fear took her thoughts away from her situation. If she knew Lonato the way she thought she did, he'd lay down his life before allowing her to be violated. But did she truly know him? The distinction between his mind and body might be greater than she could comprehend, and his determination to fulfill his task might make it possible for him to remain hidden until he was sure of success.

Mitch grabbed her hair and hauled her to her feet. Then he used his hold to pull her head back so she stared at the sky. "Soon as I get her inside—" Mitch started.

"No. Are you crazy?"

"Don't you call me that, damn it!"

"Then don't be an idiot," Dowells countered. "You take her in there and she's going to leave hair and who knows what else for the cops to find."

"What we going to do with her once we're done with her?" Mitch asked. "Drown her?"

"No. They might drag the lake. I know I said no one would ever think to look for us here, but when she turns up missing, there's going to be a search. Besides, certain people know about this place. I can't leave anything. And I can't risk burning it down and alerting the Forest Service." Dowells stepped close to her and ran his knuckles almost gently along her cheek. "Once she's dead, we'll take her body deep into the forest. Animals will take care of the rest."

Any time, Lonato. Please, ride in on your white stallion.

"Just like they're taking care of Bugger," Mitch said and released his grip on her hair. "What a piece of ass! When I get lucky, I get lucky. Time to see the goodies."

The only way she could deal with her disgust and the fear she couldn't quite master was by biting down on the gag. She was still risking a broken tooth when she belatedly realized Mitch had taken hold of her jeans' waistband. As she shivered, he undid the snap and started to tug down on the zipper. She jerked free and back-peddled.

"Damn it, bitch!" Mitch yelled. He grabbed her elbow and tugged.

She was fighting him when she became aware of Dowells. He'd aimed his pistol at Rio who had once again stood up and was slinking closer. "Get the message, bitch?" Dowells asked calmly. "Fight us and the dog dies first. Play nice, and I might spare him."

Defeated, she stopped struggling. Her head sagged. Whatever it took to spare Rio's life, she'd do it. And she'd endure the rapes she saw as her fate without complaint so Rio wouldn't attack.

Mitch took his time. He began by running his gritty fingers all over her breasts, leaving them feeling not aroused but dirty. Maybe disappointed because he hadn't gotten more reaction out of her, he turned his attention back to her jeans. As he finished with the zipper, he stuck his tongue out at her. He continued to taunt her with it while he pulled her jeans down as far as her boots allowed. She thought he'd remove her shoes, but he obviously knew what he was doing by leaving the jeans tangled around her ankles. Leg irons couldn't have done a better job of keeping her in place.

"Look at those damn panties." He seemed to be talking to himself. "Belong on an eighty-year-old woman. Well, time to get rid of them." With that, he roughly forced her panties down over her hips so they joined her jeans. He rubbed the heel of his hand against her newly exposed flesh. It took all her willpower not to gag.

Although she knew what he had in mind, bile rose into her throat when he forced his hand between her tethered legs and dipped a finger into her. "Nothing. What's the matter? Need more encouragement?" He grinned his animal-like grin at her, causing her to vigorously shake her head.

"What the hell do you know? Probably never been manhandled before. That's all right. You aren't the first bitch I've worked. Bet you didn't think you'd wind up in the hands of a master today." He laughed.

She would have head-butted him if he hadn't pulled out of her. She swore she would have! But before gratitude over having his finger out of her could take hold, she watched in growing horror as he licked his fingers and came at her again.

"What are you doing?" Dowells demanded. Despite his harsh tone, Carlin spotted something hot in his eyes. He was turned on.

"Priming her. You think you know so damn much. Sit back and take notes while I show you how to handle a bitch."

With that, he again pushed his hand between her legs and forced her to spread herself as wide as the jeans allowed. Doing so put her balance in jeopardy. She felt his fingertips against her cunt, felt them searching for entrance, sobbed.

Laughing, Mitch continued his assault. He'd directed his rough fingers off-center so they pressed against bone instead of slipping into her. Pain tore through her. She cried out again.

Chapter Six

ဆာ

"Get away from her!"

Mitch jerked upright. Moving with a speed that didn't seem possible, the man snaked an arm around her waist and half pulled, half lifted her in front of him. At the same time, he yanked his pistol out of his waistband. Only then did her captor stare at Lonato.

Lonato stood in the shadows of the trees, but she could still see his two-handed grip on his weapon. He took a step and then another, the gun aimed at Mitch. But if he fired, he'd hit her.

"Looks like a standoff," Dowells said almost conversationally. Drawing from Lonato's example, he gripped his pistol with both hands. "She's the only one without a weapon."

"Let her go," Lonato ordered.

"Not going to happen," Mitch retorted. He shifted his grip so he now held her by her throat. "This your bitch? Must be. Macho man coming to save his property, only you're outnumbered."

Sick because Mitch was right, she struggled to breathe and concentrate. Damn those jeans and her bound arms!

Once she'd managed to pull a little air into her lungs, she forced her mind onto the situation. As long as Mitch used her as a shield, Lonato couldn't do anything. Her cry must have forced him out of hiding, but it was a mistake, a deadly mistake!

I'm sorry. Sorry.

"Drop your weapon," Dowells ordered Lonato. "Down slow and easy."

Instead of complying, Lonato turned the pistol on Dowells. The two men now had their weapons leveled at each other almost as if they were preparing for a duel. "I know a lot about you," Lonato said in a mild tone with deadly undercurrents. "Enough to know you've never fired a gun in your life. Thought about it but could never work it into your schedule. You might hit me, but the odds are you won't. As for your goon, he's at a disadvantage because he only has one hand he can use. Despite what you see on TV, one-handed accuracy is all but impossible to achieve."

"Shoot him!" Dowells ordered Mitch. "Damn it, blow him away!"

"Think about it." Lonato sounded for all the world like a patient father explaining a simple fact of life to a young child. "He *might* get me in his first shot, but if he doesn't, I won't miss." He lifted his pistol a couple of inches so it pointed at Dowells' throat. "And even if he hits me, I'll still have time to fire. I don't miss. I know my reaction speed. You can take that to the bank."

I'm responsible. I put you in this position. Lonato, please forgive me.

"Who the hell are you?" Dowells demanded.

"Your worst enemy."

Something in Dowells' expression told her he agreed. "What about the bitch?" he asked.

Lonato shrugged. "A man gets lonely at night. I hit on her, and she couldn't resist my charms."

"She doesn't matter to you?"

"Two days ago I didn't know she existed. It's her damn fault she tried to hang around after I told her I'd gotten what I wanted from her."

You can't mean that! You can't.

Even as she struggled with the denial, memories flashed. He'd told her about how his parents had died and had encouraged her to be open about her mother's end. What he'd just said had been to throw the men off. It had to be. And yet there was no denying he'd repeatedly ordered her not to get involved with his mission.

"Here's the deal," Lonato was saying. "What's your name?" He indicated her captor.

"Mitch. Mitch McDougal."

"Glad to meet you, Mitch McDougal. I want you to think of me as a hunter, a hired gun. My employers are particular associates of Robert Jacob Dowells." He grinned at Dowells before returning his attention to Mitch. "They're willing to pay me a great deal of money to ensure that Dowells is returned to them safe and sound. You and I can look at this one of two ways. Either I take you out because you represent a threat to someone they consider a valuable commodity, or we join forces to ensure that Dowells sees the error of his ways. I was assured that money is no object. Name your *finder's* fee and I'll make sure you get it."

"He's lying!" Dowells sputtered. "Don't believe him!"

"Shut up!" Mitch retorted. "Why else would he be here?"

The explosion of sound jerked Carlin upright. It took an instant for her to realize Dowells had fired. Her brain registered that he'd missed Lonato. At the same time, she sensed Mitch's sudden tension. Out of the corner of her eye, she saw the man's free hand stretch out, the fingers around the gun turning white at the knuckle.

"No!" she screamed into her rope gag and threw her weight against her captor. The two of them started to fall. Another shot shattered her world. *Dowells! Firing wildly. Lonato shooting back.*

She landed mostly on top of Mitch who immediately shoved her off him. Because he wasn't hampered by ropes and clothing, he reached a kneeling position before she did.

Dowells was still standing but slumping more and more. Blood coated his chest. He stared at what had been done to him, tried to straighten but couldn't. Almost gracefully he sank to his knees and then pitched forward.

"No!" Mitch bellowed.

Icy fingers touched her heart because Lonato hadn't spoken. Struggling to keep her balance, she forced herself to look over at him. Like Dowells, her lover lay unmoving on the ground.

"No!" she sobbed against her gag. "No!"

"Shit," Mitch muttered. "Shit, shit, shit." He stared at her for a moment, then turned his full attention to the scene before them. She did the same.

Dowells' body twitched. His legs seemed to be dancing against the ground of their own accord, but with each passing second, their movements quieted. His upper body already appeared stripped of life, and his pistol lay just beyond his outstretched fingers. *Dying. Maybe already dead.*

Unable to put any more thought to the man responsible for her meeting Lonato, she focused on the man she considered the embodiment of everything male. Lonato had fallen in such a way that his back was toward her. She thought he hadn't lost his grip on his weapon, but what did it matter? She couldn't see any blood but neither did he move.

"Oh shit," Mitch repeated and stood. Tightly gripping his gun, he started toward Lonato. She lived in terror of him firing. "Goddamn shit."

He has to be alive! Please, he has to be alive.

Mitch stood over Lonato for what seemed hours while she struggled to read her captor's body language. If his actions gave off the message that Lonato was dead, she'd die herself. She tried to tell herself he was waiting for Mitch to relax his guard before taking him by surprise, but he wouldn't have fallen if he hadn't been hit. He wouldn't.

Mitch muttered something she didn't understand, then planted his boot against Lonato's back and pushed, forcing Lonato facedown on the ground. Next he walked around him and kicked the gun out of Lonato's hand. Only then did he relax a little. "Damn you. Goddamn you." Mitch's stance left no doubt that he was berating Lonato. "You killed him, you bastard. Killed my meal ticket."

After cursing Lonato some more while he kicked him repeatedly in the side, Mitch left him and slowly walked over to Dowells. Despite his obvious reluctance, he crouched down and placed his hand against the side of Dowells' neck and held it there for several seconds. Looking agitated, he switched to checking to see if Dowells was breathing.

"Goddamn it. Damn, damn, damn."

She didn't care that Dowells was dead. Only one person mattered.

Mitch returned to her and picked up some unused rope. Hope flared in her as Mitch used a couple of strands to tie Lonato's hands and ankles. Because he'd had to move him in order to secure his hands behind him, she finally got a look at her lover's face. Except for the slash of blood along his right temple, he looked unnaturally pale. Despite Mitch's manhandling of him, his eyes remained closed, his body limp.

"There," Mitch said when he was done. He seemed to be talking to himself. "Gotta think. Shit, gotta think."

Returning, he planted himself in front of her so she had to look up at him. "Hell of a mess. Never thought something like this would happen." Then to her surprise, he laughed. "If your boyfriend wakes up, I'll have to tell him he did what I've been wanting to ever since that bastard hired me. Damn fucker thought he could treat us like shit because he waved money under our noses. Bossing us around, calling us stupid, thinking he knew so goddamn much. And when Bugger told him he'd taken all he was going to and threatened to blow the whistle on his scam, Dowells bashed Bugger's head in. Kept pounding long after he stopped breathing."

Mitch frowned, making her wonder if he hadn't expected to say so much. After a moment he opened his mouth but instead of continuing, he reared back. His gaze slid from her eyes to her exposed body.

"You don't know what it's like," he told her. "Wanting to get my shit together but it not happening. Doing whatever I gotta to feed my habit." After glancing back at Lonato, he continued. Despite his disjointed explanation, by the time he was done, she understood he'd been battling a drug habit since the age of sixteen. He'd dropped out of school and tried to work construction but had lost a number of jobs. His need for drugs had increased, and he'd started stealing. He took pride in having only been arrested twice. Both charges had been dropped. Then he'd made the mistake of breaking into one of Dowells' apartment complexes while high. Instead of calling the cops, the security guards had called his boss. Dowells himself had come to where he was being held.

"He gave me a choice," Mitch finished. "Work for him or learn up close and personal what happens when someone tries to cross him. That's what got me into this shit."

The whole time he'd been unburdening himself, Mitch had continued to stare at her breasts and belly and what he could see of her crotch. Her knees ached from what she was kneeling on, but she believed that learning all she could about her captor might be what kept her alive. Despite the horror clawing at her throat, she knew not to let fear for Lonato strip her of the ability to think.

Behind Mitch she spotted Rio. Although the shooting had taken place several minutes ago, the dog's scruff was still on edge, and his attention remained fixed on Mitch. For the first time since she'd begun working with Rio, she regretted training him to respond to her instead of heeding his instinct. If he had, maybe he would have attacked Mitch—and risked getting killed.

"I'm not going to get no money," Mitch told her. "Thanks to your boyfriend, my meal ticket's dead. Dowells was feeding my habit, did I tell you that? Keeping me mellow and happy. Then when he cooked up this damn scheme of his and we took off for here, he turned on me. No crack, no nothin' until the job was done. He wanted me and Bugger's heads clear and for us to be beholden to him. Withdrawal's a bitch." He pressed his hand against his belly. "But a clean system gets other things working again." He demonstrated by fondling his cock.

"Payback time, bitch," he said and pushed her onto her back.

Rio growled.

* * * * *

What felt like a branch dug into Carlin's shoulder blade. Pain from having her arms behind her with her weight on them brought tears to her eyes, but even if she'd been able to speak, she wouldn't have begged.

Even as Mitch unzipped himself, she felt herself closing down, taking her mind and body someplace he couldn't reach. He'd rape her, but in order to do so, he'd have to free her legs. When the opportunity presented itself, she'd kick him where it would do the most good. Her attack might pave the way to freedom, or it might get her killed. Either way she'd know she'd been more than a helpless victim.

Be proud of me, Lonato.

With his pants around his buttocks, Mitch knelt before her so he could remove her boots and then her jeans and panties.

"Gotta get to the goodies," he explained. "But I ain't taking no chances on getting myself kicked." He looked around. "Damn. Gotta have more rope." After moving to her side, he clamped both hands over her belly and started stroking. Out of the corner of her eye, she saw Rio's muscles tense. The dog's gaze never left Mitch. "So damn many decisions. Inside. Yeah, inside on the bed. That way I can spread-eagle you and take my time. Burn down the cabin when I'm done."

With me in it, she understood.

Determined not to let that happen, she concentrated on disarming him using the only weapon she had, her mind. She lifted her pelvis toward him as if his kneading had turned her on and moaned. Rio's ears swung forward even more.

"Hot damn. Hot damn." He demonstrated his delight by sliding both hands between her legs and forcing them apart. Despite her revulsion, she didn't protest. Calling on her admittedly limited acting skills, she panted and gave him what would have to pass for a look of appreciation and anticipation.

"Holy shit." On that note, he tugged his pants down a few more inches. "Here's daddy. Got what you been waiting for."

He'd lifted her leg closest to him in preparation for getting in position when she heard a sharp, commanding voice.

"Rio, guard!"

Mitch had barely begun to react when a snarling Rio slammed into him, knocking him away from her and onto his back. Scrambling onto her knees, she watched. Rio, her mild-mannered dog and companion, had turned into a fierce creature she barely recognized. In the past he'd taken aggressive stances in response to her commands, but he'd never attacked before, never buried his fangs in flesh. His eyes seemed to burn.

Screaming, Mitch threw up his arms in an attempt to protect his face. As a result, his hands and forearms took most of the punishment. At the same time he was trying to scoot out from under a still-growling Rio who straddled him much as Mitch had been about to straddle her. Each time Mitch jerked away, Rio followed, paws on his chest or belly or the ground next to him, fangs delivering unrelenting punishment. Blood flowed from numerous punctures. Despite the punishment, Mitch managed to protect his throat.

"Stop him! Stop him!"

Convinced that Mitch no longer represented a threat to anyone and alarmed by Rio's wild aggression, she tried to order him to stop, but her sounds were muffled and incomprehensible. As the attack continued, she finally gathered her senses enough to look at where the command had come from.

Despite his bonds, Lonato was sitting up. Blood trickled down the side of his head, and he seemed to be having trouble remaining upright. Despite that, his harsh glare left no doubt of what he was thinking.

He'd become as much of an animal as Rio.

"No, no," she managed. Unable to articulate more, she wildly shook her head from side to side. Lonato turned his attention from the attack to her. Still, she wasn't sure he recognized her, didn't believe enough of the civilized man clung to him to care that a man was being ripped apart.

No! Make it stop! she said with her eyes.

"Rio." Lonato bit out the word. "Down."

Although it seemed to her that it took a long time for the command to reach Rio's brain, at length the Doberman lowered himself to the ground. He'd positioned himself so the now blubbering Mitch remained within easy reach. Eyes telegraphing his terror, Mitch cradled his wounded arms against his chest. Otherwise he didn't move.

"I'm sorry," Lonato said. "Damn it, so sorry."

Because she believed Rio wouldn't attack again unless Mitch did something stupid, she shifted her full attention to Lonato. He stared back at her, lips pressed together, head tilted slightly to one side as if trying to distance himself from his wound. His nostrils were flared. His muscles strained against his restraints. And his eyes continued to be those of a wild creature.

Despite her fear of him, her concern was even stronger. Knowing what she needed to do, she stood on shaky legs and walked over to Lonato. As she came closer, he studied her unblinkingly. In her mind they'd become animals drawn together for nothing more than survival.

When she dropped to her knees beside him and slid around so her hands were near him, he rolled over onto his belly. It took awhile and a near prone position on her part but finally her searching fingers found his bound wrists. After fumbling some more, she located the knots and started tugging at them. She broke a nail but no more than two minutes after she'd started, she'd freed him.

"Good, good," he said. His voice sounded slurred, and he was slow to sit up and pull the rope out of her mouth.

She didn't speak while he freed her hands and did the same to his ankles. They now sat inches apart, she naked, him maybe not fully conscious.

"I thought you were dead," she finally told him. Tears were so close.

Not responding, he struggled to a standing position. He started to reach down to help her up, but when she saw him sway, she stood on her own. She wanted to put her arm around him and help support him, but the thought of being touched by any man repulsed her. Unable to mentally separate him from her near rapist, she backed away.

He nodded and kept his gaze on her face as if refusing to acknowledge that she had a body.

"How are you?" she asked.

"Alive." He closed his eyes for several seconds. When he opened them, she no longer saw pain in their depths. Some of the savage he'd been remained, making it impossible to determine whether he was clearheaded. He stared at her, maybe seeing things she couldn't comprehend. "I need to make sure he doesn't get away," he finally said.

Because she wanted to make sure Lonato didn't pass out, she waited until he'd gathered the weapons and tied Mitch's legs before looking for her clothes. She could barely force herself to touch what Mitch had taken off her, but knowing Rio had made it impossible for the blubbering man to use his hands helped. She was a civilized woman. Treating Mitch's wounds should matter to her. But at this moment she didn't care.

She just wanted to be left alone, untouched until she'd learned whether she'd ever feel clean again.

* * * * *

Lonato waited until Carlin had finished dressing before pulling out his cell phone. As he'd hoped, the relatively flat area around the lake made reception possible. He wanted her to hear everything he had to say so stood within earshot but hopefully not so close that she felt threatened by his presence, his male presence.

He made his call to the man who'd signed his name to the retainer he'd received after agreeing to take on this assignment, but the chairman put him on speakerphone so he could explain everything to the entire board. News of Dowells' death shocked them, but once they'd expressed their horror, they started interrupting each other in their haste to try to decide how to tell investors and the public. After letting them debate what to put into a press release, he interrupted.

"I need two float planes up here before dark," he insisted. "One to carry Dowells' body and the other man. The second will be for me and a woman and her tracking dog. I'm not having her travel in the same plane as those two. Call me when they're ready to take off, and I'll start a fire so the pilots can locate this place."

As he'd anticipated, the members demanded to know what woman he was talking about. He'd explain everything in his report, he replied. And yes, he trusted her not to let anything leak to the press.

"Can you do this?" he asked her after hanging up. "It'll be a couple of hours before the planes get here."

Her nod lacked the conviction he'd hoped to see, but what did he expect? She'd nearly been raped, seen a man killed and another attacked by her dog. As for her reaction to his wounding...

When she said nothing, he told her he wanted to collect their packs so everything would be ready to go. And he wanted her to accompany him. "If you don't feel up to it yet we can wait," he said.

"No. Let's do it now, if you're strong enough."

In truth his head throbbed, and he felt nauseated. His vision, although improving, was still blurred. Because this wasn't the first time he'd been wounded, he knew the glancing blow his skull had received wasn't serious. Thank god. If he'd been killed — thoughts of her fate made him shudder.

He'd been trying to decide how to make sure Mitch wouldn't try to get away when Carlin pointed out that she could command Rio to guard him. When she directed the Doberman to stand over the wounded man, Mitch whimpered and tried to crawl away.

"I wouldn't do that," she told him. "Movement excites him."

"Is that true?" Lonato asked once they'd begun backtracking. "Along with his other talents, Rio's a guard dog?"

"No, but Mitch doesn't know that." Because there weren't any trees where they were walking, they were side by side which meant he could see her brief smile. The gesture gave him hope that she was coming out of shock. But how long would her journey take, and was his presence making it worse?

I'm sorry. I'd have given anything to prevent you having to go through what you did.

The words filled him, but he held back from giving them life. Maybe not talking about what had happened was what she needed. Maybe the best thing he could do was wait until she felt ready to talk, if she ever did.

"I don't understand," she said after a short silence. "If a float plane can land in the lake, why didn't Dowells do that instead of hiking the way he did?"

"My guess, he didn't want to take a chance on anyone seeing a plane. He didn't dare have his pilot drop him off and risk the pilot blabbing."

"Oh." She stared at him. "And you had to come on foot so you could surprise him? You had no choice but to hire me and Rio?"

"I didn't believe I did," he told her. "I didn't know where the cabin was because he'd never brought any board members here. They knew he had a hideaway somewhere in these mountains, but there was no way I could know for sure that that's where he'd decided to hide out. I took a chance. It worked out."

When she nodded, he fought the urge to embrace her and tell her how sorry he was. Much as he wanted to, her body language continued to give out the message that she didn't want to be touched. Maybe she'd never want that from him.

* * * * *

Mitch was where they'd left him when they returned from gathering their belongings. Because getting the man to tell the board members everything he knew was essential, Lonato made tending to his wounds the next order of business. After freeing his legs, he helped him to his feet and started herding him toward the cabin.

"Do you want to join us?" he asked Carlin who was on her knees embracing Rio. "This is going to take awhile."

"I'm not sure. The idea of being inside…"

Because he couldn't begin to reach her demons, he left her with her dog, but even as he took in the compact but expensive-looking place, his mind remained outside with her.

Mitch shook but obeyed when he ordered him to sit at the kitchen table and hold out his arms. After drawing water from the well-fed faucet, he selected some antiseptic from his backpack and began cleaning the wounds. Mitch whimpered.

"Shut up," he warned. "You got what you deserved."

"What's going to happen to me? Am I going to jail?"

"I don't know, and I don't give a damn. It's up to the men who hired me to make that decision."

"I knew I should have never agreed to Dowells' fucking plan. The man was crazy, thinking he could get away with—"

"It doesn't matter, does it? He's dead. And because of what you tried to do to the lady out there, I should do the same to you."

That shut Mitch up. For the rest of the time his bites were being treated, he slumped defeated in his chair. Finally he stared at his bandaged arms and started crying. "Shut up," Lonato ordered. "Feeling sorry for yourself's the last thing I want to hear from you."

"I'm sorry, man, sorry I did anything to your broad. Least I didn't hurt her."

Lonato clamped a hand over Mitch's jaw and forced him to look at him. "She isn't *mine*, got that? And she's a lady, not a broad."

"You're right," Carlin said from where she stood in the doorway. "I don't belong to any man."

Chapter Seven

∽

Long shadows had reached the clearing by the time the small float plane settled onto the lake's surface. Carlin had walked out onto the dock with Lonato but didn't say anything when the pilot introduced himself as the man who'd always brought Dowells here.

"I could tell you things about who and when comes to this place," the twenty-something man said. "Talk about a good old boys' club! I don't know what the hookers earned, but they looked expensive if you know what I mean."

"Tell that to the board," Lonato said shortly. "I asked for two planes."

"Not going to happen, sorry. I'm the only one who can get in here without getting snagged on the trees. Gonna have to make two trips."

"But you can't fly at night, can you?" Carlin made herself ask. The chill she felt had nothing to do with the rapidly cooling air.

"You got that right. But I'll be back as soon as I can in the morning. There's plenty of booze and food in there."

For just Lonato and me.

Lonato glanced at her before leading the way to Mitch and Dowells' body. If the pilot was horrified by the thought of having to transport a dead man, he gave no inclination. Instead, his manner was that of someone who'd come to expect anything in his job. His main concern was making sure Mitch wouldn't cause him any trouble.

She deliberately didn't look as Lonato and the pilot deposited Dowells' body in the plane's storage area but

293

watched them secure Mitch in one of the seats. Not until they were done did it register that there was room for four passengers. She and Lonato could have left tonight.

No, I can't! Can't be closed in with the memories of what happened and nearly happened.

"Are you hungry?" Lonato asked after the plane had taken off and they and Rio had gone back inside the cabin. "Maybe you'd like a drink first."

"A drink, yes."

As she fed Rio from the rations in her backpack, Lonato poured them each a healthy shot of whiskey. Then while she curled up on the couch, he stoked the woodstove. He sat in the leather chair opposite her. Sipping, she concentrated on the distance between them. Rio settled in front of the stove.

"I don't think you'll have to testify," Lonato said. "My guess is the board is going to explain Dowells' death in a way that will keep everything quiet."

"The police won't get involved?"

"I'd be surprised if they are."

"Good." She savored the burning liquor on her throat. "Good. What about the first dead man and Mitch?"

"Without Rio's help, that body will probably never be found," he told her. He'd turned on a generator-charged lamp, the soft light not reaching the room's recesses or enough of his features for her to read his mood. She hoped the same was true of her. "And I'm willing to bet that Mitch just wants to disappear, unless you decide to charge him."

"With attempted rape." She had to force the words. "No. I'm not going through that."

"Are you sure?"

"He got what he deserved," she said, thinking of the numerous punctures Rio had inflicted. "Do you think there was nerve or muscle damage?"

"Do you care?"

"Not now, maybe later," she admitted. "Right now I just want to forget."

"It isn't going to be possible."

Don't play shrink with me! You have no idea what's going on inside me.

"Carlin?"

He expected a response. Damn it, he wasn't getting one! "Don't go there," she warned.

"Sometime you're going to have to talk about what happened."

"Nothing did!" she shot back. If this was booze talking, she was grateful. "I didn't get raped."

"Just about."

He knew because he'd seen everything, watched her humiliation. No wonder he'd left the room in near darkness. Having to look at her would only remind him of what she'd been reduced to, reinforce in his mind why he didn't want to touch a woman who'd been mauled by another man.

Angry and upset, she downed the last of her drink and got up to pour herself some more. He waited until she'd replenished her glass and then did the same.

"You must be feeling all right," she said. "Otherwise I'd think the booze would upset your system."

"I'll live."

Of course you will. You're macho man.

"What happens now?" she asked. "What are you going to do when we get back?"

"Make my report to the board and then Recovery."

Recovery. The group or whatever it was he worked for. "And after that?" she pressed. "On to another assignment? Maybe you'll take a vacation."

"I haven't decided."

Unable to absorb the emotion in his voice, she listened to burning wood snap and Rio snore.

"What about you?" he asked. "What are you going to do?"

"Cash the check you'll be giving me for Rio's services and use it to buy new tires for the vehicle I haul my dogs with."

"That's not what I'm talking about!"

"I know it isn't!" she snapped. With her outburst, the numbness that had settled around her fell away. She felt so damn vulnerable, naked, helpless. Trapped in memories, she stood and paced the confining space. She would have fled for the outdoors if she hadn't removed her boots. Barely aware of what she was doing, she started opening kitchen cupboards. "What do you want to eat? It looks as if there's canned everything."

"Anything. I don't care."

Irritated because he wasn't being any help, she finally settled on canned clam chowder and green beans. She supposed she should be impressed by how complete and modern the cabin was given its isolation, but the only thing that mattered was that Robert Jacob Dowells' money had been responsible.

Someday she'd have to learn more about the man and his business or businesses, but right now she felt overwhelmed by the question of how she was going to make it until morning. From what she could tell, there were two bedrooms downstairs and a loft. She didn't care where she slept as long as it was alone.

Alone?

Just this morning her body would have sprung to life just thinking about spending the night with Lonato, having sex in a real bed, hours and hours of fucking. But although she deliberately focused on that part of her anatomy, she felt dead there. No, not so much dead but as if what made her a woman had gone into hiding. Given the way she'd been manipulated and humiliated, she shouldn't be surprised. Maybe she would need counseling in order to come to terms with what she considered her dehumanization, but if she sought help, she'd be expected to reveal details she couldn't possibly voice.

Reduced her to a sexual object. That's what they'd done by stripping off her clothes, tying her, forcing her body to respond to their cruel probing.

And Lonato had seen.

Sick, she turned toward him. She expected him to be staring at her, his eyes saying he knew what she was thinking about, maybe reliving what had turned Dowells and Mitch on. Instead, he'd placed his drink on the small table beside him. His head had fallen back so it rested on his chair. His eyes were closed, his body limp and vulnerable. At least he was breathing, thank god.

"Lonato?" she managed. "What's the matter?"

Slow, too slow, he straightened a little. "Aftereffects. Guess it's caught up with me."

I know what you mean. "Can I do something?"

"No. That's all right." He again let the chair back support his head, and his eyes closed to slits. About to chalk his response up to stupid macho pride, another thought struck her. This man had been alone for so long. His parents' murder-suicide had robbed him of a normal childhood. Maybe that had been stripped away even before he'd lost them.

Given his innate sexuality, she had no doubt that many women had shared their beds with him, and maybe he'd even opened his bedroom door to some of them. But once hungers had been satisfied, he closed those doors and slept alone. Because she'd lost her mother at a tender age, she understood some of his emotions and experiences, but she'd had a support network that had been denied him.

Alone. Alone because tonight I too am wounded and neither of us knows how to get past that.

* * * * *

Once the aspirin she'd given him had taken effect, Lonato had joined her in a light dinner. He'd made a phone call to someone he referred to as Chief and given him a thumbnail sketch of what had happened. Then, in response to a question she didn't hear, he said he didn't know when he'd be in. She assumed he was speaking to a fellow member of Recovery, maybe his superior if he had one.

Feeling trapped by her own body, she'd tried to distract herself by going through the reading material and CD collection, but the magazines were all porn. She didn't want to hear what music porn-reading men listened to.

"What's going to happen to this place?" she asked.

"I don't know."

I don't care, she translated. *I've closed that chapter in my life.*

Finally she found a men's adventure magazine and struggled to concentrate on what she suspected was a fictional article about the author's confrontation with a grizzly. Sitting had the desired effect. She could barely keep her eyes open.

"Where are you going to sleep?" she asked.

He looked at her, but she couldn't read his thoughts. "I don't care. You're going to be able to sleep? Do you think you might have nightmares?"

"If they come, I'll deal with them. All right. I'll put my sleeping bag on the bed in there." She pointed. It went without saying that she was repulsed by the thought of crawling between those sheets.

His gaze followed her while she untied her sleeping bag from her backpack. "What?" she demanded.

"You aren't all right. You're so uptight I can feel it."

"Do you blame me? The things that were done to me today—tell me something. What took you so damn long to show yourself? What was it? You got off seeing me being handled like a piece of meat?"

He stood, showing no sign of weakness, and quickly closed the distance between them. "No. Damn it, no!"

"That's what it looks like to me."

He reached for her, but she sidestepped and held up her hands, warding him off. "I was hoping they'd stand side by side so I could get a drop on both of them," he said. "And I wanted them so focused on you that they'd let down their guard."

She couldn't decide whether that made sense, couldn't force herself to replay the sequence of events right before he'd barked his order. "But they weren't together."

"You screamed. I wasn't thinking. I…"

Unable to breathe, she waited for him to finish. Instead, he turned and headed for his own pack. "I can't think tonight," he said with his back to her. "And I don't believe you're in a position to listen even if what I said made sense. Maybe in the morning—"

"In the morning we're going home."

"Yeah."

✼ ✼ ✼ ✼ ✼

Filthy hands reaching for her. Trying to scream but unable to make a sound. Scared. So scared. And so angry the emotion almost consumed her.

She tried to fight the unrelenting presence, but something had hold of her arms. Caught in a world of heavy, dark shadows and the taste of fear in her mouth.

Naked. Exposed.

Gasping for breath, Carlin fought her way free of the nightmare. As consciousness returned, she struggled to remember where she was. No light reached her, but at least her sleeping bag felt and smelled familiar.

"Carlin. Carlin, it's me."

Acting more out of instinct than conscious effort, she turned toward the voice.

"I'm here," Lonato went on. He sounded closer than he had a moment ago. "I heard you cry out. A nightmare?"

"Yes," she admitted because she felt too raw for anything else.

She sensed more forward movement on his part so was ready when he sat on the side of her bed. Darkness felt right. Unable to see him, she could concentrate on her emotions — and his impact on them.

"I've seen people in the aftermath of a trauma before," he went on. He found her and brushed hair off her face. His fingers lingered at the side of her neck. "Nightmares can be a healthy way of dealing with what someone can't talk about. They can serve as a release valve. Don't be afraid of them."

"You weren't the one having it."

When he chuckled, the sound seeped inside her. "Good point. Earlier you said you didn't want to talk about what happened. I respected your wishes, but I'm not sure that was the right thing to do."

He'd become a disembodied voice, an unseen presence that all but took up her world. Needing to put substance to sensation, she began by covering his hand with her own. When she ran her fingers up his arm, she discovered that he was naked at least from the waist up. "It's cold. You should have something on." *Like he needs mothering.*

"It's all right. Do you want me turn on a light?"

"No."

"Do you want to talk?"

"I'm not sure."

Again he laughed. "We're making progress. Carlin, I've been lying there in my bag mentally talking to you for the past hour. I'd like you to know what I've been thinking. And I'd like to hold you while I'm doing it, but I'm not sure you're ready for that."

"Even though I took a shower, I still feel dirty."

"No. Never."

"You saw—"

"I saw someone I care deeply about being manhandled by a couple of monsters." He gripped her hand in both of his. "You did everything right. You didn't panic and you didn't try to fight what would have been useless to fight."

She heard *care deeply*. The rest registered only slightly. The long T-shirt she wore at night had become tangled around her waist and made her feel trapped, but she didn't want to extricate her hand from his.

"I couldn't make sense of what was happening," she admitted. "I've never felt so helpless. When my mother died, I was overwhelmed, but I was still living in my safe and secure world. This time...this time I'd been wrenched away from everything that made sense. Dropped into..."

"A nightmare?"

"Yes." The word was so complex and multilayered and more than she could or wanted to put her mind to tonight.

"It felt the same way to me."

"You? But you've been in situations like this before."

"No, I haven't."

She started to sit up, and he helped her finish. Although she could have balanced herself without help, when he offered his chest for her to rest against, she didn't resist. In part she wanted their warmth to blend. As for the rest of the reason she needed to feel his beating heart—

"You didn't let them know I was there," he said. "I kept thinking you'd give that away, cry out for me. I wouldn't have blamed you. Instead, you took them on all by yourself. Why?"

"I-I'm not sure."

"I think you do."

Because he needed the truth from her and because she needed it herself, she forced herself to relive the unthinkable. "I knew that if I said anything, it would rob you of the element of surprise. You were my only way out of what was happening. I had to trust, had to give you the opportunity to act."

"You trusted me?" He kissed the top of her head.

"Believing in you kept me sane."

He placed his mouth near her temple. "And fear for you made me insane."

Layers upon layers of complexity lay behind his simple words, but she couldn't put her mind to sorting through them. "You? Insane?"

"It's never happened to me before. I pride myself on my ability to think in a crisis. It's what has kept me alive. But when Mitch tried to—"

"Don't say it."

"At least he didn't finish what he started," Lonato said. "At least I stopped him from doing that." He sighed. "But I got shot because I panicked. Because your life became more important than my own."

"You mean that?"

He squeezed her tight and strong. After a moment he relaxed his grip, one hand stroking her arm as if trying to assure himself of her presence.

"Yes," he whispered. "I do. That's what I couldn't tell you earlier. I needed time to come to grips with my emotions."

The things they'd revealed to each other had exhausted her. At least her mind felt wrung out. In contrast, with each passing second, her body was becoming more and more aware of him. She could tell that he was wearing briefs and the flesh on his thighs was becoming chilled. But if he was aware of it, he gave no indication. Neither did he act like a man who was feeling the aftereffects of a head wound.

He could have been killed! If the bullet had come any closer, she'd be alone tonight. Alone and swamped by what she felt for him.

"I need you," she told him.

"You mean it? Earlier —"

"I know what I said earlier, that I wasn't sure I ever wanted to be touched by a man again. But I'm alive. We both are."

He cupped his hands over her cheeks and lifted her head. Lips parted, she waited. The first contact was slightly off-center, but they corrected, and the resulting kiss quickly resonated throughout her. She let him know by arching her back and pushing her breasts against his chest. The kiss seemed endless, like a fire steadily being fed. Sensation surrounded her. It was most focused in and around her cunt but left no nerve endings untouched. When, finally, he drew back she first tried to keep him with her but then lifted her arms so he could pull off her shirt. He just as quickly dispensed with his shorts before easing her onto her back. Once he'd unzipped her sleeping bag and pulled it open, she raised her hips so he could remove her panties.

The undressing had taken so little time, a wordless but mutual agreement that the time for sex had come.

She opened her legs and gripped his shoulders so she could direct him to her. Instead of heeding her message to hurry the coupling, he lay down beside her. His fingers stroking her thigh nearly drove her crazy. She felt her core heat and dampen in preparation. One hand went to his head so she could run her fingers through his hair. With the other she began caressing her own breast. Her breathing became ragged, and she kept trying to turn onto her side to bring herself closer to him.

"I need you," he muttered. "Need you so damn much. But first..."

When he lifted and bent the leg he'd been stroking, she sensed what he had in mind. Tiny shivers became more pronounced. She increased her grip on his hair, not to stop him but because she could barely contain herself.

She felt the bed shift as he positioned his head between her legs. His warm breath chased over labia and clit. Gasping, she reared back, breasts seemingly reaching for the ceiling. She lifted her hips off the bed as far as she could. Before the strain could become more than she could handle, he slid a hand under her buttocks, exposing her sex fully.

"I did this to you before," he muttered.

"I know."

"You're ready for it again?"

"Yes. Yes."

He kissed her there, his tongue working hot flesh until she thought she'd lose her mind. Gentle, so gentle, he licked her lips and bathed her unbelievably sensitive clit. She sobbed as she spread herself as wide as she could. Her thigh and buttocks muscles felt as if they were clenching. A climax danced just out of reach, forcing her to move her hips from side to side as she sought it. Instead of granting her wish, he briefly abandoned her there to nibble at the inside of her thighs. Then, with her gasps perhaps commanding him, he returned. This time he concentrated his attention on the space between her vagina and anus. He licked, mixed her fluids with his own, licked some more.

She felt herself gather and boldly embraced her climax. Tiny spasms caused her to live fully in the experience. She heard herself sob and gasp as the climax continued. Then, sensitive beyond belief, she tried to free herself, but he wouldn't have it. Despite her thrashing, he again found her clit, blessing and torturing it at the same time.

"I can't— Stop. No more. Please, no more!"

Finally, when she thought she might lose her mind, he let her go. She dimly sensed him sliding up beside her and snuggled into his embrace. Her body continued to throb in the aftermath of the most intense climax she'd ever felt.

"Do you understand?" he asked.

Unable to speak, she nodded.

"My gift to you. My way of letting you think of yourself as a fully sexual woman again."

"Thank you. Thank you," she muttered. "Oh god, thank you."

* * * * *

Not that it mattered, but Carlin believed she'd briefly fallen asleep after Lonato had brought her to climax and put her back in touch with her body. She woke to find him stretched beside her with an arm resting on her breasts, his breath on the top of her head, and his naked flesh warming hers. Instead of trying to go back to sleep, she kissed his shoulder.

"I'm here," he muttered.

"I kind of figured that. Something just occurred to me."

"Did it?"

"Yes. You took me over the top, but I haven't returned the favor. Not really."

"You feel like it?"

Are you ready to put the nightmare behind you? she heard. "Oh, I feel all right. The question is, do you?"

"You have to ask?" He thrust his pelvis at her.

"No," she told him because his rod left no doubt of his arousal. "I could insist on climbing on top of you and play the dominant role, but it isn't necessary. In fact, I want to be on the bottom."

"Whatever you want."

"For tonight?" Sudden fear of a future without him rendered her nearly speechless.

"No, not just tonight." Even as he spoke, he rose to a kneeling position and leaned over her. "I'm not walking away from you, Carlin. I don't want to, and I don't believe you do either."

She ran her nails down his hard chest. "I think...I think that the possibility of losing you, of you being dead, scared me nearly as much as what we both went through. I'm changed because of you." Taking a deep breath, she went on. "In the short time we've been together, you've touched me in ways I didn't know was possible."

Instead of speaking, he dipped his head and flicked his tongue over first one breast and then the other. Moaning, she clamped her hands around his waist and guided him between her legs. When he stretched out over her with his arms bracing his upper body, she bent her knees and lifted her pelvis, offering herself to him. He lowered himself, the head of his cock immediately finding her opening.

"I belong here." Awe tinted his words. "Inside you." Thrusting forward, he slid home.

She took him full and deep, pussy muscles closing around him not because she feared he might withdraw but because she wanted him to understand that her body was her gift to him. "This feels right, so right."

Over and over again she alternated between lowering and lifting her buttocks in a series of short, jerky movements. She would have lost him if he hadn't followed her lead. In a few moments she felt the strain in her thighs and back but continued because she sensed him coming closer and closer to release. She'd focused so on giving pleasure that her own took her by surprise. They worked as one, bodies in unison, riding together. Although she couldn't see him, she kept her eyes open as she imagined his expressions, the intensity of a man on the brink of climax, the look of a man in love.

Love! The word carried her over the edge.

It was still there in the morning when she woke to find him sitting beside her with the same emotion deep and strong in his eyes.

"Welcome to tomorrow," he whispered. "Our tomorrow."

Also by Vonna Harper

൧

Brothel Night

Captive Warrior

Dangerous Ride

Dark Touch

Equinox (*anthology*)

Equinox II (*anthology*)

Forced

Hard Bodies

Her Passionate Need

Jungle Cries

More Than Skin Deep (*anthology*)

Night of the Cougar

Refuge

Scarlet Cavern

Scarred Hearts

Spoils of War

Storm Warnings (*anthology*)

Thunder

Virgin Afternoon

About the Author

৪৩

Under her "real" name, Vonna Harper has published more fiction than she can keep track of. These include category romances for the major players as well as the juicy stuff. She also penned a series of well-received Native American historicals. One earned her finalist status in both the Women Writing the West Willa award and Pacific Northwest Booksellers Association. Before discovering romances, both erotic and otherwise, Vonna "confessed" all kinds of nonsense for the confession magazines.

When asked about erotica research, she insists, Of course I've time-traveled to the ancient Everglades, infiltrated bondage strongholds, done wilderness search and rescue, and spent a night trapped in a workout gym with Mr. Universe. How can I possibly write about something I haven't experienced?"

As for day jobs, I've been a commercial pilot, brain surgeon, worked as a white-water river guide, bee keeper, snake charmer, and garbage collector.

And if you buy all that, she'd like you to check out the bridge she has listed on eBay.

Vonna welcomes comments from readers. You can find her website and email address on her author bio page at www.ellorascave.com.

Why an electronic book?

We live in the Information Age—an exciting time in the history of human civilization, in which technology rules supreme and continues to progress in leaps and bounds every minute of every day. For a multitude of reasons, more and more avid literary fans are opting to purchase e-books instead of paper books. The question from those not yet initiated into the world of electronic reading is simply: *Why?*

1. *Price.* An electronic title at Ellora's Cave Publishing and Cerridwen Press runs anywhere from 40% to 75% less than the cover price of the exact same title in paperback format. Why? Basic mathematics and cost. It is less expensive to publish an e-book (no paper and printing, no warehousing and shipping) than it is to publish a paperback, so the savings are passed along to the consumer.

2. *Space.* Running out of room in your house for your books? That is one worry you will never have with electronic books. For a low one-time cost, you can purchase a handheld device specifically designed for e-reading. Many e-readers have large, convenient screens for viewing. Better yet, hundreds of titles can be stored within your new library—on a single microchip. There are a variety of e-readers from different manufacturers. You can also read e-books on your PC or laptop computer. (Please note that Ellora's Cave does not endorse any specific brands.

You can check our websites at www.ellorascave.com or www.cerridwenpress.com for information we make available to new consumers.)

3. *Mobility*. Because your new e-library consists of only a microchip within a small, easily transportable e-reader, your entire cache of books can be taken with you wherever you go.

4. *Personal Viewing Preferences.* Are the words you are currently reading too small? Too large? Too… ANNOYING? Paperback books cannot be modified according to personal preferences, but e-books can.

5. *Instant Gratification.* Is it the middle of the night and all the bookstores near you are closed? Are you tired of waiting days, sometimes weeks, for bookstores to ship the novels you bought? Ellora's Cave Publishing sells instantaneous downloads twenty-four hours a day, seven days a week, every day of the year. Our webstore is never closed. Our e-book delivery system is 100% automated, meaning your order is filled as soon as you pay for it.

Those are a few of the top reasons why electronic books are replacing paperbacks for many avid readers.

As always, Ellora's Cave and Cerridwen Press welcome your questions and comments. We invite you to email us at Comments@ellorascave.com or write to us directly at Ellora's Cave Publishing Inc., 1056 Home Avenue, Akron, OH 44310-3502.

MAKE EACH DAY MORE *EXCITING* WITH OUR

ELLORA'S
CAVEMEN
CALENDAR

☥ WWW.ELLORASCAVE.COM ☥

erridwen, the Celtic Goddess of wisdom, was the muse who brought inspiration to story-tellers and those in the creative arts. Cerridwen Press encompasses the best and most innovative stories in all genres of today's fiction. Visit our site and discover the newest titles by talented authors who still get inspired - much like the ancient storytellers did, once upon a time.

Cerridwen Press

www.cerridwenpress.com